Whatever the poison was, it wasn't quick

As Trader slipped helplessly down the wall to the floor, his heart felt squashed in his chest, crushed into a space so small it could hardly beat against the surrounding pressure. He labored against the pain and the terror for an eternity, then both seemed to miraculously lift.

Trader realized he was looking down on his own body from a vantage point along the ceiling. He watched his own legs jerk and kick, and his head bang the floor, leaving a broad smear of blood.

It didn't matter; the pain was no longer part of him.

It belonged to the body, the dying physical form to which he felt not the slightest kinship.

COLLECTOR'S EDITION

JAMES AXLER

DEATH LANDS®

Encounter

A GOLD EAGLE BOOK FROM

WORLDWIDE®

TORONTO • NEW YORK • LONDON
AMSTERDAM • PARIS • SYDNEY • HAMBURG
STOCKHOLM • ATHENS • TOKYO • MILAN
MADRID • WARSAW • BUDAPEST • AUCKLAND

First edition February 1999

ISBN 0-373-81197-7

ENCOUNTER

Printed in U.S.A.

CONTENTS

THE DEATHLANDS SAGA

This world is their legacy, a world born in the violent nuclear spasm of 2001 that was the bitter outcome of a struggle for global dominance.

There is no real escape from this shockscape where life always hangs in the balance, vulnerable to newly demonic nature, barbarism, lawlessness.

But they are the warrior survivalists, and they endure—in the way of the lion, the hawk and the tiger, true to nature's heart despite its ruination.

Ryan Cawdor: The privileged son of an East Coast baron. Acquainted with betrayal from a tender age, he is a master of the hard realities.

Krysty Wroth: Harmony ville's own Titian-haired beauty, a woman with the strength of tempered steel. Her premonitions and Gaia powers have been fostered by her Mother Sonja.

J. B. Dix, the Armorer: Weapons master and Ryan's close ally, he, too, honed his skills traversing the Deathlands with the legendary Trader.

Doctor Theophilus Tanner: Torn from his family and a gentler life in 1896, Doc has been thrown into a future he couldn't have imagined.

Dr. Mildred Wyeth: Her father was killed by the Ku Klux Klan, but her fate is not much lighter. Restored from predark cryogenic suspension, she brings twentieth-century healing skills to a nightmare.

Jak Lauren: A true child of the wastelands, reared on adversity, loss and danger, the albino teenager is a fierce fighter and loyal friend.

Dean Cawdor: Ryan's young son by Sharona accepts the only world he knows, and yet he is the seedling bearing the promise of tomorrow.

In a world where all was lost, they are humanity's last hope....

Prologue

The travelers' campfire raged against the oppressive blackness of the surrounding deep woods. The one-lane, dirt-track road that had brought them all to this lonely place was no longer visible beyond the bubble of light created by leaping flames and sheets of sparks flying into the overcast sky. These wayfarers, their faces starkly lit, crouched as closely as possible to the blaze, both for warmth and safety.

Night in Deathlands was a scary time.

Night was when the beasts hunted, creatures whose size and appetites had been magnified by the radiation effects of the global nuclear holocaust of generations past. Night was also the time when packs of mutants—known variously as stickies, scabbies, scalies—roamed the countryside in search of living victims. Of Deathlands's many terrible predators, these monsters were arguably the most dangerous—cunning, ruthless and capable of unthinkable violence.

Accordingly, when Deathlands folk were caught at night in the open, it was safer to dispense with sleep altogether, to light a big bonfire and feed it until dawn, with a loaded blaster held cocked in one's hand. Along with their readied weapons, the travelers each gripped a jar filled with a colorless, homemade, distilled hard spirit. Before sundown, these folks had been strangers on the road. Justifiably wary and suspicious, they had been prepared to defend themselves from one another, to fight to the death if necessary to keep their meager goods and their lives. Now that they had supped together, and washed down the meal of char-roasted jackrabbit with plenty of white lightning, they were passing around hand-twisted black cheroots, and laughing and telling stories like old friends.

Sooner or later in such an amiable gathering, when tongues had been loosened, when guards had been lowered, when the heat of the fire mingled inextricably with the heat of the liquor in the belly and brain, the subject turned to a man whose exploits, both heroic and commercial, were the stuff of legend. He was known simply as Trader.

While more than a few men and women made their daily bread by running Deathlands's dangerous and unreliable roads, by swapping quantities of this for quantities of that, only one of their number merited the name Trader with a capital *T*. Over the years, he had earned a reputation for hard dealing and uncanny luck, a genius for finding the secret stockpiles of goods hidden by the United States government prior to doomsday. Trader and his crew plied the ruined highways and backroads in heavily armored convoys, dispensing looted blasters, bullets, fuel, medicine and canned food to whoever had the necessary jack, or its equivalent in barter goods. He specialized in moving predark weapons, which were as vital as food and water in Deathlands, a place where no law, no social order offered protection from hunting packs of muties and the radiation-altered beasts of the field, or from bands of "norm" human marauders that preyed on the unwary and the foolish.

Of all the Trader stories that circulated around the nightly campfires of the hellscape, and around the crowded gaming tables at the gaudy houses in the villes, the one most often told was, not surprisingly, the most disturbing. It spoke of a private revenge so vicious that it inspired shock and loathing in a thick-skinned people accustomed to accounts of savagery. And because the vengeance it described was so complete, it inspired wonder, as well, wonder at the impenetrable darkness of one man's soul.

On this pitch-black night, in this place surrounded by thick woods, along this scrap of a road two days' walk from the nearest ville, beside this roaring fire, a man with a long, weather-seamed face and a pale, wispy beard began the familiar tale on a personal note, as did almost everyone who ever recounted it.

In a loud, clear voice, he said, "I know a man who knows a man, who come on the place known as Virtue Lake the morning after Trader did the dirty deed."

Heads nodded appreciatively around the fire. Sometimes the witness's name was Bob, sometimes Tom or Jim, but he was always "a friend of a friend." The gathered men and women carefully set their blasters between their boots and, cupping hands around half-full jars, leaned closer in order to better hear, hoping to pick up a new fact or a fresh twist.

"This man, name of Bob," the storyteller went on, "was three hours' walk from Virtue Lake when he started smelling smoke. Of course, Virtue Lake always had a peculiar downwind stank to it, which come from the refinery's tall stacks, but right off Bob knew this was different. It had a sharpish, burned-wood tang, more like a forest fire. As he topped the rise that overlooked the ville, off in the distance, through the smoke haze squatting on the dry lake bed, he saw the dust from Trader's convoy, heading west.

"Below him, everything built by the hand of man was charred to cinders. The whole ville was flattened to the ground like a giant's foot had stomped it. All them triple-swell gaudies you heard so much about were gone. Baron's big house was gone. Squatters' huts down by the lakeshore were gone. Warn't no sign of the big old predark oil refinery, neither. Up until that very day, hundred years after skydark, it'd still put out a passable grade of gas, though some folks claimed it was cut fifty-fifty with goat piss.

"Bob started down the hill to have himself a better looksee at all this nukin' strangeness. Where the refinery used to be, there was nothing but a great big hole in the ground. And it was on fire. Bob thought he heard someone screaming down at the bottom of the hole, but he couldn't get close, what with the pillars of flame and oily black smoke shooting up from the pit.''

The storyteller let his audience ponder this image of damnation while he paused to wet his whistle with a swig of sixty-proof hooch. Refreshed, he resumed the tale.

''The stank in the ville was like nothing Bob had ever smelled before. He had to cover his face with a rag or puke his breakfast jerky out his nose. Stank of death it was, rank, foul, nasty ripe. It was plain to Bob where it was coming from. Everywhere there was bodies laying about. Close to the refinery pit, the corpses were all blown to pieces. Arms, legs, heads scattered in with the piles of smoking trash. Farther off, where the gaudies used to be, the dead folk were whole and their bellies was already swelling up in the heat of the sun. Some looked like they'd been poisoned to death, their faces had gone all black, tongues black, too, and sticking out, dried green froth on their tight-stretched lips. See, Trader hadn't just done in the ville's sec men. Everybody was dead. Hundreds of people. Too many for Bob to count. Women, children, little bitty babies. The sheep and goats in the livestock pens were chilled, too. All the corpses left unburied as a warning by Trader....''

The man sitting next to him piped up, ''Don't do me no wrong, unless you want some of the same.''

The storyteller nodded in agreement; that indeed was the grisly message Trader had set adrift in his wake.

The baron of the ville, he was a crazy, sick fuck, and the people who lived there were by reputation all liars and sluts, chillers and thieves. Or they were slaves working the refinery until they dropped in their chains. The kind of place where, even if he was careful, a man could wake up dead for no good reason. Now Trader, he was never one to turn down a profitable deal no matter who it was with. Point of pride to him. Brung his goods up the pike and expected a fair return for the effort, even from Satan himself.

"I'm not gonna lie to you. No one knows for sure what happened at Virtue Lake because there were no survivors left to tell the tale. But it's a safe bet that the ville done Trader a biggish wrong, and in return Trader made them pay, biggish."

"A hard man," someone on the other side of the campfire said.

"Don't come no harder," the storyteller agreed.

In Deathlands, hardness was the personal quality that counted above all else. It made the difference between living and dying. And between just dying, and dying well. In that regard, Trader's legend shone like a hammered steel icon, an icon that was polished nightly by folks he'd never laid eyes on.

"Huzzah to Trader!" one of the women exclaimed. And with a ragged chorus of "huzzahs!" they all drank a toast to his name.

Afterward, a man on the far side of the fire said, "I heard even the flies on the dog shit was dead."

"Yeah," another woman added, "and I heard even the buzzards wouldn't touch all them swoll-up bodies. Circled and circled high overhead, then just flew off with empty bellies."

On cue, the storyteller delivered the anecdote's customary final line. "Some people say all the bones are still there, right where they fell, right where Trader left them."

Satisfied that the tale had been told right, the travelers leaned back, settling into their own private reveries as they lifted jars to thirsty lips. To chill a man or two, or even a woman or two, over some soured business deal was one thing, but to lay waste to a whole damned ville was another. Beside the fire's roaring heat, with white lightning filling their veins with courage, each of the travelers took a moment to ponder the question of whether, under similar circumstances, he or she would have had the solid-brass balls to do what Trader had.

To chill them all.

Around the bright circle, no one smiled. No one spoke. Some closed their eyes and pretended to doze. In their secret heart of hearts, as well as they knew their own names, they all knew they could never hope to measure up to Trader's terrible revenge.

Of course, as was often the case with myths told around campfires, the truth about what really happened at Virtue Lake was an altogether different story....

Chapter One

The recon wag's wheelman let out a groan as, an instant too late, he caught sight of the tank trap on the road just ahead. A single glance told Giles that the crude slot hacked across the roadway was wide enough and deep enough to bury the wag's front end past the axles. He slammed on his brakes, but it didn't do any good. The wag was going way too fast. It skidded on the rotten tarmac and abruptly nosed over into the ditch. The crunching impact slammed Giles headfirst into the driver's ob slit. As the starflash of concussion inside his skull faded, he opened his eyes. The world around him started to spin violently and his vision began to tunnel in. Gritting his teeth, Giles fought back the wave of dizziness and nausea. To black out now meant capture, and capture meant death.

Shifting the wag into reverse, he floored the accelerator. The wag's rear drive wheels dug in, and it jerked back a foot or two out of the ditch, then something on the under-carriage hung up and the engine stalled. The wag crashed back down.

Giles punched the starter button and pumped the pedal, relieved when the engine instantly roared to life.

''Come on!'' shouted the long-haired man sitting in the front passenger's seat beside him. ''Move it!''

Blood bathed half of Jonathan's face as he reloaded a fresh 30-round clip into his folding-stock Ruger Mini-14. Before he could poke the muzzle back out the gun port, before Giles could get the transmission in reverse, a flurry of bullets rattled both sides of the wag. The wheelman and his front passenger ducked as a hail of armor-piercing slugs cut through the wag's half-inch external steel sheathing like so much tissue paper. Hard points of light pierced the relative darkness of the wag's interior, which, after a couple minutes of intense combat, was starting to look like the inside of a cheese grater.

"Shit, they nailed Billy!" Hammerman cried from the back seat. "Aw, he's fucked up, big time."

Giles still thought they had a chance. Grinding the gears, he jammed the wag in reverse, then came another burst of autofire and both back tires blew out. He tromped the gas anyway, sending bare hubs spinning, flat tires flapping, shredding apart, but the wag didn't move at all. Through the ob slit, Giles saw two tall figures step in front of the ditch. They had M-60 machine guns; the belts of linked 7.62 mm ammo were dragging on the ground. As they took aim from the hip, he threw himself below the level of the dash.

The wag shuddered violently as a torrent of AP rounds thudded into its still howling engine. There was a horrible grinding noise, then a loud clank and the engine went suddenly dead. The machine gunners stopped firing. As the dust cleared, through his ob slit the wheelman could see more figures moving in. A glance through the rearview periscope told him there was nothing behind them but empty road.

"Where's Shabazz?" he asked. "He was supposed to cover our asses!"

"Bastard double-crossed us," Hammerman snarled.

A steel rifle butt clanged on the wag's roof. "Out!" someone shouted at them.

When they made no move to exit, the voice said, "Get out of the wag right now, or we'll set it on fire."

Giles, Jonathan and Hammerman looked at one another. They knew it wasn't an idle threat.

"We're fucked," Jonathan moaned. "Stone fucked."

"I don't wanna burn to death in here," Giles said. He

cracked open his door and, putting out his empty hands first, said, "Don't shoot. I'm coming out. I got no blaster."

As he exited the wag, he raised his arms high in the air.

Giles realized with a start that the odds against them had been much worse than he'd been led to believe. The bastards popped out from behind the boulders on either side of the road. There were forty or fifty of them, all ages, from stooped whitebeards to skinny kids no more than ten or twelve. As he looked from face to face, he noticed a striking similarity in their features: the squinty set of the eyes, the pattern baldness of the males over twenty. He also noticed that all of them, even the kids, were armed with a heavy-duty autoblaster. And there were five of the armor-chewing M-60 machine guns, carried by the biggest of the men. They wore homemade clothes, sewn from pieces of olive drab canvas, repaired many times with patches. Most of them had ratty canvas boots. Some of the younger kids were barefoot.

Giles figured there wasn't much point in telling them that the recon wag meant no harm. His crew had been the ones to open fire first. He looked back over his shoulder, down the road, to the entrance to the pass below. Three of the inbred bastards lay there, sprawled facedown in the dirt. And Trader Shabazz was still nowhere in sight.

Jonathan and Hammerman got out of the destroyed wag, then, on the shouted order of one of the whitebeards, ducked back in and pulled Billy's limp body from the rear seat and dumped it on the ground. Half his head had been shot away. After the corpse had been moved, the same geezer waved for them to step over and stand beside Giles.

"You come here to rob us," the whitebeard told them, "and rape our women and girls."

Giles couldn't tell how old he was, but he looked like he still had plenty of muscle to him. His yellow-tinged, straggly white hair hung to his shoulders, and he was as bald as an egg on top. A plastic-sheathed badge hung on a leather thong around his neck. There was a color picture on it, too small to make out.

The wheelman looked over the clan's prized clutch of stocky, waistless females. There was a sameness to them, not just in body shape but in features, as well. They looked like droolies: cross-eyed and slack mouthed. Most of them were pregnant, even the twelve-year-olds. Giles shuddered to think how young those cherries had been picked. As he looked over the men, he wondered which were the fathers, brothers, grandfathers.

Giles waved his hands. "No, you got us all wrong," he protested. "We aren't robbers or rapers. We're just trying to find a way over the mountains. Thought the road here would get us to the other side." He gestured over his shoulder with his thumb. "The chilling down below was a mistake, and we're real sorry about it. But I figure we're even, since you killed our poor Billy there."

"Don't work that way," the whitebeard said, spitting out a fibrous white gob he'd been chewing.

For the first time, Giles noticed that almost all of them, women included, were grinding their jaws, working away at big old cuds of their own.

"This here's holy ground," the whitebeard went on. "Been that way since skydark. And ever since, we Palmers been on watch in this gorge, doing our duty, guarding the Spirit in the Mist with our lives. When you come up the road in that wag, you violated a sacred place."

The leader stepped a little closer, and Giles got a better look at the badge around his neck. The laminated plastic was badly discolored. It had to be pre-Apocalypse. At the top, big red letters said TOTCON, for Totality Concept, but which meant nothing to Giles. Under that was a name, Captain Paul Palmer. Giles squinted at the two-by-two-inch photo. The young man's grim, narrow-eyed visage resembled to a remarkable degree the living, angry faces that surrounded him.

Giles realized he didn't know shit about who these people were. And up until a few minutes ago, he wouldn't have given a rusty fuck to find out. He'd believed the assessment of Levi Shabazz, that they were just a bunch of triple-dim savages who thought they could control a road the trader wanted unlimited access to. Shabazz had discounted the rumors down in Virtue Lake that the Palmer clan was very bad news. "Scumbags with no wags," he'd said. "We'll roll over them, just like we always do."

Not quite, as it turned out.

"We guard and nourish the Spirit," the whitebeard told Giles. "Spirit's got to be watered with warm blood of trespassers."

Giles didn't like the sound of that, one bit. "Mebbe there's something else the Spirit needs?" he asked. "Or something that you people need? We got access to blasters, gas, ammo. Looks like you could all use some new boots. Mebbe we can make a trade in return for your letting us go."

Of course Giles was bargaining through his hat; as a simple wheelman, he had no authority to make deals with anybody. And knowing Shabazz, he figured the trader would rather keep the blasters and boots, and find new men to replace those he was about to lose.

"Spirit in the Mist gives us what we need," the whitebeard said. "From the beginning, it has provided everything."

Giles glanced sidelong at Jonathan and Hammerman and hoped to hell he didn't look as scared as they did. It was time to get tough.

"Mess with us," he growled at the clan leader, "and you got Trader Shabazz to deal with."

The whitebeard seemed unimpressed.

"He's a triple-mean coldheart," Giles went on, with all the conviction he could muster. "And he'll come back here in full force. Men, wags, blasters. He'll skin you alive and leave the meat for the wild dogs. If you want to keep on doing whatever the fuck it is you're doing here, you'd better think twice before you do us any more harm.''

"Your backup wag turned tail the minute we opened fire," the whitebeard stated as he took a fresh chunk of white root from his trouser pocket, packed it into his cheek and began to chew it to pulp. ''The crew's watching us from just over there.''

Giles followed the leader's pointing finger to the forested ridgeline opposite.

"If there was a halfway good shot among them," the whitebeard said, "I'd be killed dead by now. Don't seem interested in saving you from the Spirit, nor in venging you, neither.''

When the wheelman caught the flash of sunlight on a lens, his heart sank. ''Shabazz, you dirty, lying fucker,'' he muttered.

"Bring along the dead one," the whitebeard told two of the younger clansmen. ''His blood's still warm. He, too, will serve to fill the belly of the Spirit.''

The two men grabbed Billy by the heels and started to haul him up the road at a speedy clip. At blasterpoint, Giles, Jonathan and Hammerman were forced to follow the flopping, dead arms and ruined head as it bounced over the rutted pavement.

The narrow roadcut had been dynamited through granite bedrock. High above the sheer-sided channel were densely forested slopes, and above that, a blue sky streaked with thin white clouds. Those same clouds hid the mountain's peak from view. With fifty blasters massed at their backs, there was no way to escape, nowhere to run.

Giles and the others marched uphill, walking into the gusts of frigid wind swirling down from the summit. After they'd climbed about a half mile, they saw a number of foot-wide quartzite rocks lined across the road ahead. They were neatly spaced, a border of some kind, laid out carefully by

hand. A short distance beyond it, the road appeared to come
to a dead end in a wall of granite. Behind them, the clan of
savages had spread out from one side of the road to the
other, their blasters at the ready.

The wheelman scanned the way ahead and saw no sign
of any spirit. No mist to speak of, either. But he knew that
didn't mean much. Inbred for better than a century, probably
born addicted to some kind of rad-blasted loco weed, these
Palmers no doubt had their own peculiar way of seeing
things. Perhaps the Spirit in the Mist was just a figment of
their imaginations.

As they got closer to the line of rocks, Giles searched the
pavement between that border and the spot where the road
ended in the cliff face. There was nothing out of the ordinary: no pools of blood dried on the tarmac, no bone fragments scattered about. Of course, that didn't necessarily
mean anything, either. In a place as wild as this, there had
to be scavengers that could easily carry off a man's head or
hindquarter.

The clanspeople herded them right up to the line of rocks
before their leader signaled for a halt.

The whitebeard stepped over the barrier, raised his arms
over his head and said in a booming voice, "Spirit of the
Mist, awake!"

When Giles saw the first tendrils of fog appear out of
nowhere, he thought it was some kind of trick, a hidden
smoke bomb like he'd seen in a couple of traveling carny
shows. A bomb with some kind of a voice-activated trigger.
But this stuff didn't act like any smoke he'd ever seen. It
didn't rise straight up in the air, as it should have; instead,
it spread out sideways, then flowed down, billowing over
the road like a mattress of liquid cotton.

"Palmer the Guardian," the whitebeard went on, "offers
up a sacrifice to you."

At a signal from their leader, the two young clansmen
picked up Billy's body by wrists and feet and, with a mighty

heave-ho, chucked it over the row of rocks and onto the road.

By this time, the fog had spread until it filled the roadway from shoulder to shoulder in a layer about three feet thick. Then, out of the central mass, a single, cautious feeler appeared. Like a python made of mist, the appendage extended itself, growing in length as it crept inch by inch over the road's surface toward the still body. Giles took an involuntary step backward as, without warning, the cloud suddenly quadrupled in volume, surging in all directions, blocking out the dead end, the forested slope above it, even the sky.

It was close now, and it didn't feel like fog. It wasn't cool and wet inside the nostrils. It burned, like weak acid vapor, and it smelled of ozone. It didn't look like fog, either. The interior of the cloud seemed to glow, pulsing with a dull yellowish light.

Then it began to snow.

Huge wet flakes materialized out of the front of the fog bank. It was crazy. Over Giles's shoulder, the sky was piercingly blue, and the sun blazing hot on his back. The snowflakes melted as they lightly brushed his face and drifted onto the road. Something crackled and snapped deep in the fog's belly. Electricity. It made the hairs on his arms prickle and stand up. And the ozone smell got even stronger.

Giles sensed movement behind him and as he turned, he saw the guardians had pulled well back. They still blocked the road, and their blasters were now raised and aimed. He was sure they were going to open fire.

He was wrong.

The fog tendril wrapped around Billy's legs, then retracted. As it did so, it moved the corpse, scraping it across the pavement a good two feet. Giles watched in astonishment as in similar increments, his dead comrade was drawn inexorably into the cloud.

"Sweet meat," Jonathan gasped.

For his own part, Giles felt like he was about to piss himself.

Then he saw the fog reach out for Hammerman. Before he could cry out a warning, an arm made of mist snaked out and brushed the man's unprotected chest. When it touched him, there was a loud crack and a blue flash. Hammerman screamed as he went flying through the air. He landed with a thud, facedown on the tarmac. Then a wave of mist rushed out from under the edge of the main cloud, boiling over the roadway, boiling over Hammerman where he lay. As he, too, vanished, there was a louder crack and a brighter flash, and something warm and wet spattered Giles's cheek. Automatically he reached up to wipe it away with his hand. When he looked down, his fingers were red and slick with blood.

Beside him, Jonathan spun to face the assembled blasters. All of the savages took aim at him, ready to thwart a panicked dash with bullets.

For a second, Giles thought Jonathan was going to run at them anyway. Before the man could move, the fog took him from behind. As it slithered around the front of his throat, Jonathan's eyes went wild with fear and his mouth dropped open. It jerked him off his feet, snatching him into itself. From deep in the core of the fog bank, there came another crackling blue flash.

Giles turned on the clan leader and shouted, "Isn't that enough?" One look at the man's face and he knew it wasn't. In that instant, he made up his mind. It was far better to die by bullets, by something you could understand, than to be eaten alive by some hellish freak of nature. Giles lowered his head and charged the line of savages.

Autofire rattled. Slugs sparked off the asphalt all around him, and Giles realized he was falling. He didn't feel the pain until after he hit the ground. Then he felt it. He'd been shot in both shins; the long bones were shattered, his legs useless.

"You fucking bastards!" he howled, too racked by agony to do anything but curl up in a ball. "Why didn't you just chill me?"

"Spirit prefers its meat still breathing," the whitebeard said matter-of-factly.

The clammy mist swirled around Giles, and his world quickly faded to white. He couldn't even see the asphalt right under his nose. He gasped, tasting acid in his throat and feeling its burn deep in his lungs. He was blind, alone and suffocating. The sensation of being slowly smothered touched some primal fear in him, and despite his injuries, galvanized him to move. Shattered legs and all, Giles clawed at the tarmac, dragging himself forward, hand over hand.

Right behind his head something sizzled angrily, like a big hunk of flesh dropped into a red-hot frying pan. Then the fog seized him in its powerful grip and began to pull on his wrists, ankles, head. It stretched his prostrate body in every direction at once, until the shoulder, neck and hip joints cracked, until the sinews snapped their tethers with bone and the flesh itself started to rip away.

Giles died an instant before the flash, with a screaming curse on his lips.

A curse for Levi Shabazz.

As THE PIERCING SCREECH echoed down the mountain pass, Trader Shabazz watched the fog retreat in front of the cliff. The cottony mass got smaller and smaller, as if it were slipping down a mouse hole, and then it simply vanished. He lowered his telescope's field of view and carefully scanned the roadway between the line of white rocks and the sheer granite wall. The mist had taken three of his men, apparently swallowing them whole; there wasn't so much as a scrap of hide or hair left behind. He took the telescope from his eye. Except for the loss of the recon wag, which had been a regrettable but necessary sacrifice, Shabazz was pleased with the turn of events.

Up his nose, he had the scent of something big.

Something bigger than big.

Like the many other looters searching Deathlands for pre-dark spoils, Shabazz and his crew made their living by ferreting out and then pillaging the secret stockpiles the long-dead government had laid down in anticipation of a nuclear holocaust. After a century of this kind of scavenging, most of the easy pickings were gone. The stockpiles whose access tunnels had been uncovered by the initial blast effects, and by subsequent earthquakes, chem rain and erosion, had already been hit hard. There was nothing left inside the concrete-walled storage areas but a litter of MRE wrappers and the remains of ancient campfires.

Though Shabazz had stumbled onto some fine hauls in the past—crates of unfired M-16s, bulk 5.56 mm ammo and grens, brand-new fatigue uniforms—he usually dealt in overpriced low-quality goods. More often than not, the blasters he sold were black-powder firearms, and the military clothing he stocked was secondhand and well-worn. Unless you were a triple stupe, before you put down your hard-earned jack for one of Shabazz's blasters, you field-stripped and test fired it. Likewise, you not only tried on the clothing, but you checked it for bullet holes and creepy-crawlies.

When the going got thin, as it invariably did from time to time in Shabazz's business, he wasn't above liberating the inventories of his fellow traders, or of marauding isolated villes, looting them like they were nothing more than stockpiles. Which, of course, they were, in a manner of speaking, except that the folks living in them rarely agreed to give up what they had without a fight. That didn't bother Shabazz one bit. In Deathlands, humans were commodities, too. There was always a good market for slaves, if they were strong or pretty.

In the ten years that Shabazz had been running the roads with his band of chillers, holding his operation together with a mixture of bullshit and brutality, he'd been looking for a way out of the hand-to-mouth existence, for the big score. Again, he wasn't alone in this goal, which was shared by every other scrounger with a pickax and an empty belly.

In a place like Deathlands, where small, impoverished communities were isolated by hundreds of miles of desolate waste, wild rumors abounded. There were stories about rad-blasted monster bugs that crawled up your butt while you slept and ate you from the inside out. About plagues loose in the land that turned your eyes to goo and made blood spurt out your ears. And, of course, about incredible wealth, always tantalizingly out of reach. If you believed the latter tales, every mountain range had its own dazzling treasure of predark goods, socked away by the government. From personal experience searching for such troves, Shabazz figured ninety-nine percent of the talk was pure crap. It was the other one percent that interested him.

One of the oft-repeated stories concerned a glorious stockpile of stockpiles. Every ditchwater ville had its own version of the tale, embellished to fit its location, but the important details were always the same. Whether concealed in miles of limestone caves under a wide plain, or carved out of the belly of some tall mountain, this ultimate stockpile was a storage area as vast as a pre-Apocalypse megacity. It had everything imaginable, from wags to blasters, from ammo to fuel, from canned food to warm clothing in amounts that boggled the mind. Powered by its own nuke reactor, its computerized control system could use the array of automated machine shops to re-create in mass quantities any manufactured item of the late twentieth century. From its similarly controlled cloning laboratories and hydroponic gardens, it could produce enough fresh food, both animal and vegetable, to feed a million people a day.

According to every version of the story, this biggest of

stockpiles had been built by the government for one purpose: to jump-start the postholocaust rebuilding of America. For that reason, it had been named Spearpoint.

Levi Shabazz thought he'd finally found it.

Everything he'd seen so far supported Doc Tanner's story about a ghost city hidden under the mountain, a story the old man had given up only after several days of torture. The unnatural and deadly fog was exactly as Tanner had described it. He'd called it "the Hound of Hell," or some such crap, and claimed it had "claws and teeth." As Tanner had said, the road that had been laboriously blasted through the mountainside led nowhere. Both of these elements fit the key details about Spearpoint that Shabazz had collected over the years. The old man had been right about the band of droolies guarding the road, too. The only thing the old fool didn't describe was their defensive capabilities.

And now Shabazz had seen that for himself.

He was impressed.

The guardians had turned the uphill stretch of roadway into one long, grinding killzone. Because of the distance involved and the direction of the prevailing winds, Shabazz realized that the extremely nasty manner of chilling that he'd had in mind for them wouldn't work.

Without major military wags, the kind with extrawide wheelbases, long undercarriages, high ground clearance, two-inch-thick, hardened-steel armor plate, maybe even tank tracks fore and aft, Shabazz knew there was no way he and his crew could penetrate past the vehicle traps or survive the onslaught of heavy-caliber machine-gun fire. In all of Deathlands, there was only one such land armada, and it belonged to a man he had locked horns with several times over matters of business. Each time, Shabazz had come out a big loser.

He shrugged off the rush of unpleasant memories, of burning wags and lost cargoes. Things had been different then, he told himself. Those violent encounters had come about by chance, and every time he had been surprised and outgunned. Never again. This time he had the weapons to do the job right, and his crew would be backed by reinforcements. This time he would do all the surprising and all the chilling.

Not a bad deal, he thought as he sucked at his teeth. Get rich and settle with Trader, all on the same fucking day.

Chapter Two

Trader craned his head up into the access tube of one of the rooftop machine-gun blisters he was having installed on his mobile command post, also known as War Wag One. "Get your butt down out of there, J.B.," he growled around the unlit stub of a black cheroot he clenched in a corner of his mouth. "Let me have a look-see at what you've done."

Reluctantly John Barrymore Dix, Trader's chief weapon smith, stepped down the metal ladder that connected the newly welded turret to the main deck. J.B. pushed his steel-rimmed glasses back up the bridge of his nose, leaving a glistening smear of black grease on its tip. "Not ready to test fire," he said.

"All the same, I want to see how it's coming," Trader said. He smoothed back his hair, then climbed into the blister's access tube. The short, cylindrical passage was a tight fit for a man as powerfully built as he was. However, once he got his head and shoulders inside the blister, it was much roomier.

The ongoing design problem, and the subject of much discussion, if not debate, between Trader and his armorer had been how to give the twin MG posts maximum fields of fire and still protect the gunners from incoming bullets. Per Trader's instructions, J.B. had lengthened the arc of the six-inch-high firing slit until it now exposed close to three hundred degrees of potential killzone. He had fashioned the blister's exterior hull out of double-thickness, tempered armor plate, which would withstand standard armor-piercing slugs, gren blasts, light cannon shells—everything but rounds jacketed with spent uranium, which Trader knew were about as rare in Deathlands as a virgin bride.

The blister's armament was a 75-round, drum-fed RPK light machine gun. J.B. had cut down its bipod legs and ball-bearing-mounted them on a well-greased track that ran around the inside of the blister's shell.

On paper, the RPK's maximum rate of automatic fire was 660 rounds per minute. But in the real world, the MG couldn't be operated for any length of time at more than eighty shots a minute because of the heat buildup. There was no way to change a superheated barrel under combat conditions and thereby counter the cook-off effect, which caused chambered rounds to ignite and made the weapon fire full-auto even when the trigger wasn't pressed.

In the blister application that Trader had in mind, the low sustainable rate of fire was actually a good thing. Because the turret was ninety-five percent enclosed, ventilation inside it was dicey, at best. With a higher cyclic rate, the gunner would need an oxygen mask to keep from suffocating on the accumulated gun smoke. And because of the smoke, half the time he wouldn't be able to see what the hell he was shooting at.

Trader snuggled into the RPK's buttstock and swept the point of aim from extreme right to extreme left, and back. He was pleased with the way the addition of ball bearings had smoothed out the tracking. His fire zone went from directly in front of the MCP, all along one flank, to the rear. On the other side of the wag, this turret's twin did the same thing, only in mirror image. Coupled with the assault-rifle firing slots along the port and starboard hulls, the 20 mm cannons stationed up front and the rocket pods to the rear, War Wag One could produce a rolling, 360-degree circle of death.

He edged up on his toes and, untucking the RPK's butt plate from his shoulder, raised its pistol grip, tipping the weapon's barrel as far down as the setup would permit it to

go. When the buttstock grazed the blister's rooftop ventilation holes, he swept the light MG through its arc of fire.

J.B. stuck his head up from below. When he saw what
Trader was doing, he frowned and said, "That's one of the
bugs I'm still working on."

"The way you've got this set up," Trader said, "the gunner can't hit anything closer than twenty-five feet from the
side of the wag. That won't do. Needs to be at least fifteen
feet, but ten would be even better."

"I'm going to move the bipod joint back toward the magazine some more," the Armorer told him. "That way I can
shift the MG forward and get the barrel farther out of the
firing slit. Another three or four inches should change the
down angle enough to do the job."

Trader grunted in agreement, then followed J.B. down the
ladder, back to the main deck. As he used a rag to wipe the
gun grease from his hands, he said, "How's the self-destruct
system coming?"

"Got the whole convoy mined, just like you wanted,"
J.B. told him. "There are C-4 blow packs inside the ammo
magazines of the war wags and wrapped around the fuel
tanks of the transports. On the war wags, I rigged an external cutoff switch. It's concealed under a casing on the chas-
sis in the front of the retractable cat tracks. On the transports, the external switch is hidden alongside the
undercarriage skid plates. The cutoff switch disarms the
booby traps and gives us safe access to the wags' door locks.

"Inside all the wags, we have two separate detonation
systems. One that arms the boobies for explosion five
minutes after the triggers are tripped, which lets intruders
get inside and make themselves at home. The second self-
destruct system operates on a preset time cycle. The switch
inside the wag has to be manually reset before the time runs
out. That way, if the wag is unmanned for longer than, say,
four hours, or if the switch isn't reset, ka-boom!"

"Good work," Trader said. He had designed the whole

self-destruct system in his head, then explained it to J.B., whose job it was to make it so. Trader had to do things by word of mouth, as he'd never bothered to learn how to read and write.

Of all the improvements to his convoy of assault and transport vehicles, it might seem that the mining of the vehicles would be the most difficult for his wag crews to swallow. It was one thing to be sitting on a war wag's ammo magazines or in a transport loaded with cans of .308 Military Ball; it was another to be riding on armed booby traps, day in and day out for months. But if there had been any grumbling among the troops, it had been done in private, out of Trader's earshot. While they sometimes found it hard to take his obsession with security and countermeasures, the crew couldn't deny that attention to detail was one of the things that made him the very best at what he did. Trader rarely bothered to explain the reasons for the specific changes he ordered. If you ran with Trader, you trusted him with your life; if you didn't trust him, you packed up your belongings and beat feet.

In the case of the boobies, the crew didn't need an explanation. Their purpose was obvious: to dissuade potential ambushers. Trader's long-term goal was to make his wags virtually untouchable; the self-destruct systems were a step in that direction. Even if road pirates or double-crossing barons chilled every person in his convoy, a feat that would cost the opposing side dearly in lives, the boobies would make sure they'd get no profit from a hijacking; their only reward would be more death. Trader knew that when word of his mining the fleet of wags got out, it wouldn't stop all comers—some of the mutated crazies loose in his world didn't care a rad-blast about dying—but it would stop a goodly number of the smartest ones. Plus, there was always the satisfaction of getting some payback for a chilled wag crew.

Trader started up the long, narrow corridor that led to the

driver's compartment. The MCP had been changed a lot since he and Marsh Folsom had first found it so long ago. He could still recall the shock and wonder when they stumbled onto the collapsed cavern. They had been on the run, looking for a place to hide from a big pack of cannies who were out for their blood. Marsh, who had a nose for such things, had seen the telltale cleft in the slumped-out forest slope. A bit of rapid digging on their part had uncovered the entrance to a concrete-lined tunnel, and beyond it, stretching back into the hillside was a vast blast- and radiation-proof cavern packed with all types of vehicles.

At that glorious moment, Marsh had cried "Golconda!" And he was right. In a world of pedestrians and pack animals, this indeed was a treasure mine. The first treasure they looked upon was the MCP. Engineered to control complex field operations for battalions of light armor and infantry, it had been a huge mother.

But it was even bigger now.

Trader had been refining his land flagship from day one. Much of the original onboard equipment was useless because of missing technical documentation; without it, comp-systems taken for granted a hundred years before were unfathomable mysteries. Trader had ripped out all the comps to make room for more vital gear.

War Wag One had also come equipped with electrically fired, Gatling-type multibarrel cannons fore and aft. They sucked huge amounts of dry-cell power, their batteries and drive units took up valuable space and their complicated electrical systems were vulnerable to breakdown. Experience had taught Trader that simpler was better.

So he'd had the Gatlings pulled. In the front of the wag, he'd dropped in a pair of EX-29 cannons, which could be mechanically fired at a rate of 250 to 550 rounds per minute and accepted either API or HEI ammo. Another plus, the EX-29s could be repaired on the road, in the small, mobile machine shop that J.B. had put together. The twin 20 mm cannons were mounted on either side of the MCP's bow, in fixed, nonswiveling positions, and were fired from a single button on the driver console. That eliminated the need to haul around another 180 pounds of gunner and meant War Wag One could carry that much more weight in ammo instead.

There was no sophisticated optical targeting system for the driver. He had a TLAR—That Looks About Right—sight etched into the ob slit in front of him. The barrels were laid so as to cross-fire at seventy-five yards. The driver simply steered the pneumatically shock-mounted cannons on target and punched the red button on the dash. Trader had never intended them to be precise weapons; they were often fired when the MCP was rolling and under attack. And in that situation, the idea was to spread confusion and terror among the attackers, or to blast a path through a hijacker barricade. The high-ex or antipersonnel rounds always scattered enemies in a hurry. If the driver wanted to nail another wag, all he or she had to do was stop and crank the TLAR on the target.

Though the EX-29s had proved themselves many times, Trader was always on the look-out for something better. It was his habit to change things every so often, trying this or that, discarding ideas when the results didn't satisfy him. Over the years, he had worked hard to make sure no other wag in Deathlands was the MCP's equal in size, speed, mobility and firepower.

As Trader approached the half-open bulkhead door, he heard sounds of a loud argument in progress. The shouting stopped the second he stepped over the threshold into the driver's compartment. Two of the three men inside were standing practically nose to nose; both bore the long-healed marks of near-mortal combat.

The tall, muscular, dark-haired young man had only one eye, the right one, and it was startlingly blue. His left eyebrow, which was partially concealed by a black patch that masked the empty socket, was split by a wicked blade scar that trailed off down his cheek like a waxy teardrop. Though Ryan had ridden with Trader for more than a year now, how he had come to lose his eye still remained a mystery. Unless pasts interfered with on-the-job performance, they meant nothing to Trader; he was more interested in the here and now, in what a man or woman could do for him today. Ryan was quite simply the most skilled hand-to-hand fighter Trader had ever seen: impetuous, daring, capable of blinding speed, both of hand and foot, and battlewise way beyond his twenty-odd years.

The man who faced Ryan in the driver's compartment was only an inch or two shorter, but he was ten years older, his grizzled, prematurely gray hair shaved to a stubble, his bulging, bare biceps encircled with matching tattoos: twisted bands of thorns dripping drops of bright blood. He called himself Poet, and it was by that name that Trader had known him for the past five years. As far as Trader could tell, the man wrote no verse, read no verse and never had; his name referred to his ability on the battlefield: precise, ingenious, artfully devastating. Trader had been present when Poet had received his disfiguring wound. During a prolonged alter-cation over the price of a shipment of canned goods, a heavy-caliber longblaster slug had clipped him in the left forearm, leaving behind a large, angry lump of scar near the elbow, and an arm that he couldn't completely straighten.

Poet was Trader's strategic expert, a war captain seasoned in many campaigns and skirmishes. He had the kind of an-alytical mind that could see all the options and present them for Trader to pick from. Ryan had a similar ability, but was much less conservative in his suggestions and much more impatient with indirect methods. Poet had learned the hard way, by losing comrades in battle, that skirting a fight could sometimes be the best option. Ryan never wanted to back down. Both men were arrogant and competitive. The friction between them had been ongoing since the day Ryan arrived, and it had gotten much worse as the one-eyed man had quickly risen to the rank of war lieutenant. Normally Trader liked to encourage competition between crew members because he figured he got more out of them that way. In this case, however, he could see that things were close to getting out of control.

Trader's strict no-fist, no-knife fight policy was all that had kept Ryan and Poet from coming to blows. To disobey that order meant you were out on your butt, no explanations. Trader had laid down the rule because good people were hard to find and sometimes impossible to replace. He knew a fight between his top two advisers would probably end with the loss of them both. Ryan was almost impossible to turn off, once he got his blood up.

Abe, the thin mustached guy standing beside the two much larger men, seemed uncustomarily frazzled and glum.

"What's going on here?" Trader asked.

"Minor disagreement," Poet said.

"Major disagreement over something minor," Ryan corrected him.

Trader glanced at Abe, who just shook his head. "Well, the disagreement is over," he told the two men. "Ryan, go check on the loading of the ammo crates."

"Gladly," he said, turning immediately for the bulkhead door.

"Poet, give J.B. a hand in the starboard turret."

The older man hesitated a second, giving his adversary time to make a clean exit.

After they had both left the compartment, Trader said, "Abe, what the fuck's going on?"

"Trouble," the gunner replied. "Some of the crew don't want no part of Virtue Lake. Want to give the place a wide berth. Others want to close the deal way outside of town, someplace secure."

"And?"

The man drew himself up to his full height and looked

Trader in the eye. "Since you're asking, nobody's happy about your trading top-quality predark military blasters and ammo to a stinking pile of nukeshit like Baron Zeal. Figure someday we'll end up looking down the wrong ends of all them shiny-new bores."

"What do you figure?"

"It's a possibility."

"You want to stay behind, Abe?"

"Didn't say that," he protested.

Trader didn't ask the gunner for names; he didn't want to know who was doing the grousing. He could guess that Poet was against driving straight into Virtue Lake. He could guess Ryan was for it in a big way. Poet wasn't a coward, by any means. But because he had seen so many comrades take the last train west, he was cautious. Prudent. He knew that nobody, no matter how skilled in combat, had a charmed life. Because he had ridden for years with many current members of the crew, Poet was concerned for their safety.

Ryan, on the other hand, was relatively new, hadn't formed any deep friendships, and his only responsibility was to himself. In regard to danger, the younger man went one-eighty to Poet, feeling that everybody in the crew ought to be willing to take the same all-out, crazy-ass risk that he was.

"Pass the word," Trader said. "Get everybody together outside. I need to tell them all something."

Abe nodded. "Give me a couple of minutes," he said, then hurried out the door.

A short time later, Trader climbed up on the roof of the MCP and looked over the troops assembled in the cavern, all of whom stared up at him expectantly. Abe, Poet and Ryan were right in front. Of the seventy or so people present, forty-six had been handpicked by Trader to man the convoy. Drivers. Gunners. Mechanics. This convoy was going to be one of the biggest he'd organized to date. He was taking seven transport wags, each with crews of three, and four war wags, each with crews of five, plus the MCP, which carried ten people.

The rest of the men and women standing around were mostly mechanics and laborers. Their job was to cobble together working wags from the buried predark fleet. Because the vehicles had been stored for more than a century, their drive systems had to be completely disassembled, cleaned, regreased and reassembled before they could be started up. Spare parts and replacement wags for his convoys had never been a problem.

Fuel—that was the problem.

Before the nukecaust, the cavern had had its own gasoline reservoir, meant to supply the entire fleet for decades. But the earthquake that had partially collapsed its roof had also breached the fuel bladder. Most of it had leaked away into the subsoil beneath the cavern long before he and Marsh had discovered the place. As a result, Trader was always looking for new, untapped sources of gasoline, but he hadn't found any close to the cavern site. He usually ended up dealing with a middleman, like Baron Lundquist Zeal.

Trader raised his arms for quiet, then said, "Anybody that's got cold feet about this run can stay here. Won't think the worst of you, and you got my word on that. Of course, if anybody backs out, they'll miss their share of the profits for the whole circuit."

There was stone silence.

Abe's eyes widened, and his jaw dropped.

Trader had been setting up this trip for more than six months, taking orders from villes along the proposed route, and he'd be moving goods looted from stockpiles and goods traded from villes all through the East. He expected to come back after three months with a tidy profit, which was always divided, by shares, among those who took the risk and went along. Anybody staying behind was going to pay a big-time penalty.

"Anybody got any questions," Trader said, "now's the time to ask them."

A few people gave him hard looks; most didn't look at him at all. They looked at one another, or at the ground.

If there was extra tension in his crew, Trader knew it was largely his fault. He'd been pushing them extrahard to get the convoy prepared for the delivery at Virtue Lake. *Prepared*, in the case of the madman Lundquist Zeal, meant adding the booby traps and other tricks. The ville was notorious as a den of chillers and thieves. Yet Trader was still willing to do business there because Zeal had agreed to pay top price for the load of new blasters in pure gold, which he had collected in exchange for his gasoline. Gold was good because it was easily portable and everybody wanted it. Many villes had their own local jack, but gold was still a standard. In the case of Virtue Lake and its baron, big risk equaled big profit. The risk was why he was taking all four of his operational war wags to defend the convoy.

Trader broke the heavy silence. "Anybody who's supposed to go that wants out," he said, "step over by the far wall right now." While he waited for the first person to move, he gnawed on the soggy stub end of his cheroot.

Nobody moved.

Nobody backed out.

"Well, if that's it," he said, "then break time's over. Let's get crackin'. I want to be rollin' in eighteen hours."

Chapter Three

Baron Lundquist Zeal thrust his bare foot under Doc Tanner's nose. The old man stared at the appendage, which in the past two months had countless times booted him around the perimeter of that very room. Staring at the symbol and the instrument of his oppression, Doc felt suddenly giddy. He also felt a powerful urge to open his mouth and apply his strong, white, even teeth to said foot, to bite off one of the toes that had made his life such a torment and misery. He could almost feel the bone breaking between his incisors.

Dry and crisp.

"What are you waiting for?" Zeal demanded. "Kiss it, you worthless old bastard!"

Doc didn't look up into the baron's face. To do such a thing was to commit an act of insubordination. Insubordination was punishable by a prolonged and agonizing kickfest played upon his backside and rib cage. Nor did Doc bite the foot that subjugated him; that was something that would've gotten him instantly killed. Instead, the Oxford University–educated doctor of philosophy puckered up his lips and planted a single kiss on the proffered toes. As he drew back, he stifled the urge to gag at the pervasive odor, which wasn't unlike an overripe Stilton cheese. Gagging was another crime against the baron's person. In the presence of Zeal's exposed foot, anything but total adoration was punishable by a sound and prolonged beating.

"I think the geezer is getting to like it," Levi Shabazz commented. "Pretty soon, he'll be licking your feet like a squirmy bitch dog."

As far as the humbly kneeling Theophilus Tanner was concerned, Zeal and Shabazz represented the twin poles, the positive and negative, the yin and yang of evil. Shabazz was big and brutish, a bullying braggart. He had a great sprouting black beard and dense black hair, which was coiled in a thick braid at the back of his head. He was a ham-fisted animal with a single remarkable gift: he had a surprisingly inventive mind for torture.

Baron Zeal, on the other hand, was tall and slightly built, with an overlarge head, narrow shoulders and long, spindly legs. His naturally skeletal appearance was made even more horrifying by his reliance on eye shadow and rouge, which he used in liberal quantities. The baron's power came not from physical strength, which he largely lacked. He relied instead on his cunning, absolutely ruthless brain and a genius for manipulation and unlawful acquisition. He used greedy thugs like Shabazz to accomplish his ends, playing them like hand puppets.

"Is he right, Tanner?" the baron asked, wriggling his toes under the old man's nose. "Are you having fun yet?"

Doc mumbled something into the floor.

"Speak up!"

"Forgive me, noble sir," Doc croaked, "but I am overjoyed to the point of speechlessness."

Which made Zeal and Shabazz explode with laughter.

Doc suffered their taunts with a lowered head. He was caught in a nightmare from which he couldn't wake. Or perhaps more precisely, caught in an unending series of different nightmares. Like boxes within boxes, when he escaped one horror, he found himself trapped in an even more unpleasant circumstance. Of late, he had endured an unbroken string of keepers, inquisitors, torturers. Some had appeared in the guise of science, a discipline in which the university had well grounded him. Others were more like Levi Shabazz, with no guise at all, something to which his matching, splinted little fingers could attest.

Though Doc didn't look physically older than seventy, chronologically he was more than two hundred years old, having been born on Valentine's Day of 1860. The nightmare had begun when he had been forcibly kidnapped, ripped bodily from the bosom of his family, and, without so much as a by-your-leave, pulled forward in time to the year 1998.

Doc arrived in the future with his keen mind intact, retained his understanding of the philosophy of science, which he discovered hadn't changed substantially since the time of Newton and Descartes. Science as philosophy involved the asking of carefully worded questions. Doc's habit of answering his captors' questions with questions of his own proved most annoying to them. Their supposedly objective scientific interrogations often took the form of violent arguments and ended with Doc locked up in solitary confinement.

Doc was familiar with the type of investigator Operation Chronos recruited. Similar persons—arrogant, insensitive, cruel, convinced of the righteousness of their cause—had existed in his own time. Such a mind-set, it seemed, was an affliction of the well-educated, as well as the ignorant. In the end, the whitecoats tired of his truculence and, to be rid of him, with as much care and consideration as they had shown when they had plucked him from the bosom of his family, they hurled him further forward in time, to the post-holocaust future and the hell on earth called Deathlands.

How could a life packed with such promise, such joy, devolve so suddenly into an existence as cursed as this? he asked himself. How could God—or Fate—be so cruel? To show a man the bliss of happy children, of a generous woman's love, of satisfying work only to snatch it all away in an eye blink? Dr. Theophilus Algernon Tanner knew he should have died two centuries earlier. Died with his dear wife by his side, and long before his precious children. Instead, he was here, on his knees.

A sudden blow from Zeal's heel to the top of Doc's head snapped him from his reverie of grief.

"Let's hear it!" the baron shouted at him.

It was time for the jester to earn his keep.

"In a universe of wretched feet," Doc intoned, apparently from the heart, "of abject, unworthy, bunion-bound dogs that stumble from here to there, misshapen, spavined, graceless, I find no counterpart to the exquisite sculptures now before me. Hewn by some now nameless Grecian master. No doubt inspired by a holy vision to construct from perfect alabaster the feet of Apollo. Heavenly baron," he concluded tearfully, "would that with my humble tongue your Gemini deities bathe."

Shabazz guffawed. "Where does he come up with all that shit?" he said in delight.

"Enough!" Zeal said, jerking his foot from under Doc's nose before the old man could apply the promised tongue. "I think you're right, Shabazz," he said. "I think the old triple stupe's gone and fallen in love with my foot."

The baron put his shoe back on. Like its mate, it was a red satin pump with a four-inch heel. The man's taste in footwear had struck Doc as strange when he'd first arrived at Virtue Lake, but he had quickly grown used to seeing the baron clunk about his big house in predark women's high-fashion shoes.

"He'll be trying to hump it next," Shabazz said. "Now, that would be comical."

"Now, old man, let's have the song about Spearpoint," Zeal demanded.

It was the one entertainment that the baron never tired of. Perhaps because it was less a ballad than an inventory of projected spoils.

Doc rose slowly and took a deep, gathering breath. When he had first fallen into the hands of these twin demons, he had been in a terribly confused state. Unsure of whom or what he was talking to, he knew only that he was in pain, and he had made certain unfortunate admissions about where he had come from and how he had traveled from there to Virtue Lake. The admissions had prompted Zeal and Shabazz to spend the next week or so torturing him to get the full truth. So many times had he been forced to recite the same series of facts that as a survival mechanism his brain had formed them into a kind of mnemonic sequence. He could recall the details without thinking about them, even in his sleep, or when otherwise thoroughly confused.

Doc closed his eyes and began. "Those who brought on Armageddon planted a seed a century ago, in the months before their science turned God's glorious green earth into a ball of dust. Perhaps they had had a premonition of what was to come, a middle-of-the-night awakening, drenched in cold sweat? Perhaps it was a decision based on mathematical probabilities. Perhaps it was nothing more than a make-work, social-welfare project. Whatever the cause, the men and women in power took this precious seed and pressed it deep in the largest cave they could find. Where it still awaits the nourishing light of day. On this secret, sleeping spindle, the future enemies of freedom were to be skewered. Friends, I give you Spearpoint, the locus of the rebirth of the United States of America...."

Doc took another deep breath before starting on the stockpile's inventory. Zeal didn't like pauses in that part of the recitation. "A thousand transport wags, with spare parts. A thousand armored wags with Cat tracks, cannons and electrically fired machine guns. An ocean of fuel and lubricating oil. Enough 5.56 mm automatic rifles and 9 mm pistols and ammunition to equip an army of fifty thousand and keep it in the field for a decade. Food, water and emergency medical supplies for the troops. Automated manufacturing plants and agricultural stations, which combined can feed, clothe and house up to a million people. A fully self-contained and nuclear-powered biosphere with EM blast-shielded electronics and computer systems, all staged and ready to link with any and all artificial satellites still in orbit. And if none are available, the capacity to launch its own surveillance satellites at the touch of a button. This same system can target and launch stored intercontinental ballistic missiles with multiple thermonuclear warheads.''

At the end of the speech, there was silence. Doc steeled himself and prepared to do the whole thing over again, from the top. Then Zeal and Shabazz applauded.

''Very nice, I must say,'' the baron told Doc. ''You put some real feeling into it this time. Especially the part about the arsenal. Shabazz, just think what we could do with all those war wags and blasters. We could roll over this place like a plague of locusts, taking whatever we want and burning the rest to the ground.''

''Yeah. Rebuild America, my ass.''

''And I've always wanted to nuke the shit out of something,'' Zeal confided to the bearlike trader.

Chapter Four

Ryan stopped the one-man scout buggy on the side of the road, picked up his spotter scope and got out. From the top of the high, rounded hill, he looked down on the settlement of Virtue Lake, which was about four miles away. Between him and the ville was a yellowish brown dust bowl; all that was left of a lake were a few scattered ponds, stagnant and rainbowed with crude oil. Dominating the far landscape, jutting out on what had once been a peninsula, was Baron Zeal's oil refinery. Its three tallest smokestacks poured forth black smoke, adding to the haze that overhung the valley. Tall blue flames flickered and danced from a series of shorter stacks, as the refinery by-products were burned off. Even at that distance, Ryan could hear the sound of the plant, a sawing, low-pitched hum.

According to local lore, the industrial complex predated the nukecaust by twenty years; it had survived the disaster with tumbled smokestacks, but remained otherwise intact. A handful of townsfolk, descendants of the original workers, it was said, continued to run the petroleum-cracking plant on a very small scale, selling gas by the jug out of their shanties. That was before Zeal took over the entire operation by force. He had brought in his own slave labor, and used it to push the refinery to predark half capacity. The source of the crude oil that fed the cracking plant lay under the existing lake. Zeal had had the body of water drained to make it easier to drill his wells.

The draining of Virtue Lake had created a hideous sunken plain, dotted by makeshift oil rigs along the far shore, and transected by lines of pipe leading to storage tanks up on the former peninsula.

Even though an inferior-grade gasoline was hard to come by in Deathlands, the enterprise was a great success, and that success encouraged a boomtown atmosphere. Gas was more precious than gold to would-be industrialists, fuel traders and road pirates, and they lined up to trade the yellow metal for it. The promise of food and shelter and easy jack drew desperate people from the far-flung corners of Deathlands, people who came willingly to work and ended up as slaves to the company store. Because of the influx, the ville's population had soared to nearly one thousand. To service the needs of the refinery workers, and recoup most of the wages he paid out, Zeal had set up the gaudy houses that lined either side of the main street, and put a handful of his cronies in charge. In return, he got a huge percent of the gross from the moonshine, green beer and gaudy sluts.

Beyond the wells and the refinery, stretching along the former shoreline, was the ville. Ryan could see the sprawl of shanties that surrounded the gaudy houses on all sides. A haze of bluish oil smoke overhung the buildings and the lakeshore. Stair-stepping up the bluff, at the far end of the lake bed, the houses were better built, and the topmost and largest structure sat on a shelf cut into the side of the cliff. Baron Zeal's big house overlooked the ville, the refinery and the wells, and its compound was protected by a perimeter wall made of stockaded logs.

Pointing the scope back to his side of the lake, Ryan saw there was still only the one way into town for Trader's convoy: a narrow dirt road that ran around the edge of the dried-up shore. As the road bent around the far side, before it reached the edge of the ville, it was cut by a barricade of oil drums and heaped steel automotive scrap. Baron Zeal's sec men manned the barricade from barracks that stood on either side of the road, and Ryan knew they would most likely be demanding a heavy toll for passage in or out.

Then he heard the low rumble of vehicles coming up behind him.

He turned to see War Wag One lumbering over the ridge top in a cloud of dust. Behind it came the daisy chain of the convoy. The MCP stopped atop the rise, and Trader, J.B. and Hunaker jumped out of the starboard-side door and stepped over to the viewpoint.

Trader scanned the ville in the distance through a pair of binoculars. "Looks meaner than the last time I saw it," he said. "Baron has added to his sec force. Only used to be one barracks next to the barrier."

Poet climbed from one of the smaller war wags and immediately took up his usual position at Trader's elbow. He always made sure he had the ear of the boss, and it was a habit that never failed to piss Ryan off.

After one look at the approach to the ville, Poet said, "If we take the convoy through the gate down there, we're going to have a hell of a time getting out. They've staggered the barricades so there's no room to turn around. If we're caught under fire inside the fence, K-turning all these wags is going to be a bitch. And then we'll have to blast our way back through the barricade. Trader, we're bound to lose transport wags and people."

Ryan smiled. Once again, the man had revealed his broad yellow stripe.

"Only if Zeal plays us wrong," Trader replied.

"Expect the worst," Poet said, "and you're never disappointed."

As Trader considered this, Ryan stepped up and put in his own two cents' worth. "Why should we give a damn how many sec men Zeal's got?" he said, glaring straight at Poet. "If he tries to pull something on us, there's more than enough firepower in War Wag One to flatten the place."

"Mebbe so," Trader agreed, "but I'd hate to lose any wags or cargo this early in the circuit just to prove you're right. We've got a whole lot of miles to cover before we head back home again. Knowing how Zeal operates, I want to make rad-blasted sure he's got something worth trading before we move our goods any closer.''

Ryan opened his mouth to say something more, then thought better of it. He knew his words would have been wasted. Not because Poet was necessarily right. In situations like this one, where large amounts of weapons and ammo were to be transferred, and where the other party had a long history of bad business, Trader always followed the same procedure: keep the cargo at a safe distance, count the gold or whatever and only then make the exchange.

It was Poet's turn to smile.

Ryan felt a sudden rush of heat under the skin of his face and an insensate fury building inside his chest. Once again, it was all coming to a head. Expectation and reality dovetailing. He wasn't disappointed. This time, he knew the outcome would be much different. As he stared back at Poet, he thought that soon he would find a way to chill the war captain before he chilled him.

At Trader's direction, the wag drivers circled their vehicles in a defensive position on the hilltop, with the transports clustered in the middle and the war wags on the outside. When they were parked in that formation, on triple-red alert, no attacking force could touch them. Once the staging was complete, Trader waved Ryan over.

"Get a couple of the miniwags unhooked from the tow bars and ready to roll," he said. "We'll take a small scout party down to meet Zeal and scope out things.

"Abe, you're in charge until I get back. If there's trouble, you know what to do."

"Roger that, Trader," the gunner said. "We rocket the shit out of them from up here."

It was no idle threat. The MCP's clusters of 2.75-inch HEAP rockets could turn the refinery into a blazing inferno in seconds.

Ryan hurried to uncouple the miniwags. They were bigger

than the scout car he had been driving, big enough to hold three people each, with a driver in the front seat and a pair of passengers behind. The camouflage-painted, all-terrain vehicles had huge, knobby tires and a ground clearance of a yard to the skid plates of their undercarriages. The M-60 machine gun mounted on the roof was accessed by the back-seat passengers through an armored sunroof.

Poet, J.B. and Trader got into one of the minis. Ryan, Hunaker and Samantha the Panther climbed into the other.

With Trader in the lead, Ryan steered the miniwag down the winding, rutted road. Zeal didn't run any gas-tanker wags of his own on this track. He made his customers, who were desperate for fuel, come to him. That meant that transport and security were their problems, not his.

The squalor Ryan had seen from a distance became even more of a horror story as they approached the outskirts of Virtue Lake and the trash heap of shanties where the slaves lived. The air was thick with the smell of sulfur, wood fires and human excrement, and it seemed to vibrate with the grinding roar of the petroleum-cracking plant that ran non-stop.

On both sides of the road were abandoned, bullet-riddled vehicles. Ryan hadn't seen them from the hilltop because they had been pushed nose-first into the drainage ditches. Most of them faced away from the barricade, windshields shot out front and rear. Glass glittered everywhere on the road's shoulder.

"Some of the baron's satisifed customers?" Samantha the Panther said as Ryan braked to a stop behind Trader, who had come up against the barricade's closed hurricane-fence gate.

"Not customers," Ryan said to the mutie black woman. Sam's "special equipment," exceptional nightsight and hearing, was well-hidden in a lean and muscular but otherwise norm woman's body. "These wags never made it into the ville. Check out the barriers on the other side of the gate." He pointed at the staggered concrete-block obstacles that forced an approaching driver to make a series of tight, alternating turns in order to reach the ville's exit. It was an obstacle course that gave the sec men plenty of time to aim and fire.

"Those folks stopped on this side of the barrier," Ryan said, "then turned and tried to beat it back up the road. They were running away from the barricade when the sec men blasted them from behind."

"Fuckers," Hun growled.

The baron's security men stepped out from behind the cover of the barriers with their autoblasters leveled at the two miniwags. The blasters were a variety of beat-up-looking predark Beretta KG-99s, a couple of short-barreled 9mm Heckler & Koch machine pistols with 30-round clips. The dozen sec men wore a uniform of sorts, a long-billed, dark blue cloth cap, a bulletproof vest, khaki BDU pants and combat boots.

The beady-eyed guy in charge, who was so fat he couldn't close the Velcro tapes on his armor vest, waved his machine pistol at them through the wire of the gate. "Get out of them wags," he ordered. "And keep your hands in the air and away from those MGs."

Trader climbed out of the lead miniwag, hands raised. Ryan and the others did the same.

"Now," the fat sec man said, "real careful, I want you to put your blasters on the ground and then take three steps back."

Trader put down his Armalite, then nodded to his people. Ryan unholstered and laid down his .357 Magnum Ruger Blackhawk.

Once they were disarmed, the fat sec man waved for the gate to be opened. Right away, he waddled over to Hun and Samantha and sized them up appreciatively.

"Bringing in a couple of fresh whores, are you?" he

asked Trader. "We could sure use them. Tired of banging the same sour-faced slags."

The other sec men grunted in agreement.

"You got it wrong, bud," Trader said.

"Think we'd better give them a tryout first," the fat guy said, ignoring Trader's words. "Yeah, you two come on in the barracks with me. I got some friends in there who want to meet you, too. Gonna give you a welcome party."

When the threat didn't seem to faze either of the women, the fat guy leered viciously and added, "We'll crack your bones real good. Get you nice and loose for the lineup on Saturday night."

Still no reaction.

Sensing big fun, the other sec men crowded in for a closer view.

"Though I'm partial to the dark meat," the head sec man went on, "the one with green hair is mighty interesting. Makes a guy curious, you know, to see if it's the same color down there. Mebbe I'll take me a bit of a look-see right now...." He reached out and grabbed Hun by the left wrist, then snatched hold of the front waistband of her BDU pants.

Ryan saw Hun's free hand dip into her back pocket. With the speed and precision that came from much practice, she unclipped her knife's black Zytel handle from the cloth, then thumb-wheeled open a wickedly serrated blade four and a quarter inches long.

A blast of pure adrenaline slammed Ryan's brain.

Joy!

That jagged, G-2 stainless-steel edge could slice through a standing length of one-inch manila rope in a single swipe. It went through muscle and tendon even easier. Maybe Hun couldn't cut off the arm with one slice, but she could part the meat down to the bone, rendering both the arm and the groping hand useless deadwood for the rest of the sec man's miserable life. Assuming, of course, that the slob didn't bleed to death on the spot.

Ryan made no grab for his leg-sheathed panga. The two-to-one odds against them weren't as bad as they seemed at first, what with the sec men standing so tightly packed. Ryan guessed that they would hesitate to shoot one another, which was exactly what they were going to have to do if they wanted to chill all of Trader's crew. Like Hun, he was confident in his own speed with the edged weapon. In the seconds that remained before all hell broke loose, he measured the distances and picked his angles. The panga, with its massive blade and eighteen-inch overall length, could sever a man's arm at the wrist. Or, in a pinch, even cleave a head free from a stoutly muscled neck.

In this instance, its edge wasn't put to the test.

Trader let out a growl and intervened, shoving the fat man back with a solid straight arm to the chest.

"Unless you want more trouble than you can handle," he said, "you'd better back off and tell Baron Zeal that Trader's here."

"Trader?" the fat sec man said. "If you're Trader, where's your fucking convoy?"

"That's between me and Zeal. Go tell him I'm here, and I want a face-to-face right now."

"If you got no convoy," the sec man said, "you and your friends are dead meat. All except the pretty, pretty whores. They're *live* meat." He smacked his lips nastily.

Ryan watched as the fat man slowly walked back through the open gate and laboriously climbed into a dented wag. As he sat behind the wheel, the vehicle groaned mightily on its springs and sagged on the driver's side. After slamming the door, he gunned the engine and headed toward the center of the ville.

"Dumb fuck didn't have a clue how close he came to singing soprano," Hun said as, behind her back, she broke the top-lock and folded up her predark SOG one-hander.

"Both of you better watch yourselves extracareful," Trader told the two women.

Then to everyone, he said, "And don't chill anybody unless they give you no choice. We're way outnumbered here."

As they waited by the side of the road for the fat man to return, the other sec men whistled and made catcalls to Hun and Sam like a pack of lovesick mutts. After seeing how Trader had backed down their leader, they kept their distance, though.

Meanwhile, Poet surveyed the peninsula, or what he could see of it from the road. Without seeming to, he was looking for weak points. Ryan had to admit that the older guy was damned good at seeing the big picture. He'd had lots of practice. Poet would say if they did this and this, then they could break out, or break in. And for at least as long as Ryan had been riding with Trader, Poet hadn't been wrong yet.

The one-eyed man didn't care. He had hated the man on first sight, hated Poet's gimp arm, which so reminded him of his older brother Harvey's gimp leg. He hated the way Poet always hovered around Trader, offering advice, and hated the way the man always listened to it. It made him recall how his brother Harvey had hovered around their father, filling his head with lies, maneuvering, setting him up for the big fall.

Harvey, sick with the lust for power, and stuck in the middle of the order of rightful succession, had arranged for the murder of Morgan, the eldest of the three sons. When he'd discovered this unspeakable treachery, Ryan had done his best to explain it to his father, but he couldn't make the man see who Harvey really was. Baron Titus had always believed Harvey; he was blind to the evil beneath his son's twisted exterior. In the end, Harvey had robbed Ryan of everything—family, friends, estate, fortune, even his eye. And he had cast out his own younger brother, alone and half-blinded, into the wilds of Deathlands.

A universe so quickly turned on its head, perverse, and

unrepentantly so, had taught Ryan the hardest of lessons: that a man had to be prepared at all times for betrayal. From a brother, by an overt act of cruelty; from a father, by an act of omission. This was the template of Ryan's reality, and the wellspring of his terrible anger.

Others in the crew, including Trader, saw the conflict between the two advisers as a simple matter, stemming from the fact that Ryan coveted Poet's job. Jealousy really had very little to do with the animus. After all, Ryan could appreciate the skills and accomplishments of the other members of the crew without feeling somehow less important, or physically threatened. But not when it came to Poet. Never with Poet.

From day one, he had been on his guard, hand on his weapon, determined this time to strike first.

After fifteen minutes had passed, the fat sec man returned. He stopped on the ville side of the gate, leaned his head out the wag's driver's-side window and shouted, "Trader, you ride with me up to the big house. The others have to stay down here in the ville."

"Not acceptable," Trader replied as he stepped closer to the wag. "We travel together."

"Then the deal's off," the sec man said. "Baron Zeal says only you can enter his stockade. He give me these tokens for your crew to use in the gaudies." He showed Trader a small cloth bag tied at the top with a thong. "So they can amuse themselves while you and he discuss business. Tokens are good for brews and screws."

The fat guy tossed the bag to Trader.

"What about their blasters?" Trader asked.

"Yeah, yeah," the sec man said. "They can keep them. So can you. We don't take people's blasters unless they mess up. And then we take them off their dead bodies after we shoot them all to hell."

Trader nodded to his crew, who immediately bent and picked up their blasters. As Ryan reholstered his Blackhawk, he saw Hun check the chambers in her 10-gauge, double-barreled, side-by-side riot gun.

"Mighty big piece for a pretty little lady to carry," the head sec man commented through the driver's window.

"I like a big blaster," she said, snapping the barrels shut with a flick of her wrist.

"Then you sure come to the right place," fat guy said, grinning as he pointed down at himself.

Hun smiled back. "And you've come to the wrong one."

"Going in alone might not be so smart," Poet said to Trader.

It was one of the rare times that Ryan openly agreed with the war captain. "Zeal might try and take you hostage," he said.

"It'll be okay," Trader assured him as he handed over the bag of tokens. "The baron knows he's got nothing if he chills me. The convoy will just move on to the next ville on the list and off-load the new blasters there. He doesn't want that to happen. Just keep together and stay on your toes. After the meet with Zeal, I'll find you."

WHEN TRADER GOT in the front passenger's seat of the sec man's wag, his weight only partially righted the driver's-side tilt of the vehicle. Cranking the steering wheel hard over, and puffing from the effort it cost him, the fat guy turned the wag and accelerated for the center of the ville.

They drove past row after row of shanties, some made of scrap sheet metal, some made out of tree limbs and plastic sheeting, all of it spilling down the grade to the shoreline of the dry lake like the slope of a garbage dump. An inhabited garbage dump.

In the middle of the dirt road, standing in a spreading mud puddle, was a big tanker wag. Since the lake had been drained, water had to be trucked into the ville. Sec men were doling it out to townspeople who were lined up with plastic jugs or buckets. Trader watched as the sec men put a mark on each of their forearms with an indelible ink marker. It meant they'd had their share. Water was rationed, as was everything else in Virtue Lake. If you didn't work, you didn't drink. There were few women in the line, and even fewer children. All of them were dirty looking, with sores and scabs.

They gave the fat sec man and his passenger looks as he drove by.

Looks that could kill.

The ville was divided into three parts, which Trader recalled from his last visit here. First came the garbage dump–slave quarter, which Zeal's sec men didn't waste their time patrolling. In this area, people built their shacks wherever they could find room, with whatever materials they could find or steal.

The second part of Virtue Lake consisted of the predark company town that had supported the refinery before skydark. At the heart of the ville were two facing rows of mini-strip malls that had once housed the supermarket, the optician, the pizza takeout restaurant, the video store, the doughnut shop, the dry cleaner, the coin laundry and the auto-parts store. Now they housed the ville's single-story gaudies.

Zeal hadn't bothered to change the facades to suit the buildings' new tenants. He'd left the signs and marquees as they were. After all, the refinery workers weren't picky; they just wanted a warm place out of the chem rain to rut and get blind drunk. Though it was midday, men in various stages of drunkenness spilled out of the open doorways onto the minimall parking lots. Loud music blared from open doorways. On the other sides of greasy plate-glass windows, naked women danced on tables, enticing the wandering crowds to enter. Trader noticed that sec men drove through this area in armored wags.

Per capita, there were more gaudies and saloons here than anyplace Trader had ever seen. Workers earned not only water, but moonshine and slut time, which they paid for with the baron's tokens. The refinery ran twenty-four hours a day, in three shifts. So did the gaudies.

As they drove past the Quick-Way Market, four sec men hurled a pair of drunks out the front door. They landed on their bellies on the asphalt a good distance away and didn't move.

Past the end of the main street, the road started to wind up the bluff. There was a clear border here, from the falling-down slum to the predark tract houses that the engineers and workers of the oil company used to live in—houses that were now occupied by the gaudy operators and refinery bosses. More armed sec men on the prowl patrolled this area, assigned to keep out the riffraff.

The fat sec man slowed as he approached a wall made of ax-sharpened logs, two stories high. The logs were bound together with coarse rope, and they marked the limits of the baron's compound. On each of the facing corners of the wall, little log huts peeked up above the level of the spikes; they were the machine-gun posts that controlled the road leading to the gate. Trader could see sec men moving behind the blaster ports. Recognizing the wag, they didn't bother tracking it in their sights.

The log gates opened at once, the massive doors swinging inward.

The sec man drove onto the packed-dirt courtyard and stopped. Trader saw that a walkway below the top of the spike logs connected the MG posts. It also offered 270-degrees' worth of firing positions, down onto the ville, the dry lake and the road. The other side of the compound abutted the front of the bluff, and was protected by it. To the left of the main gate was a sec-man duty shack; taking up about half of the space inside the wall was Zeal's private residence. Also built of logs, it had a sheet-metal roof and a wide porch that faced the wall's gate.

The fat sec man jerked a thumb at the bug-splattered

windshield. "Up the steps to the big house," he said. "Make it snappy, Trader. The baron don't like to be kept waiting."

Trader got out and started across the compound. Immediately he drew an escort of armed sec men, one of whom relieved him of his Armalite. They led him through the door and into the baron's mansion.

The front room had high ceilings with exposed rough beams; the floors were made of polished wood. Dominating the room was a massive stone fireplace and mantel. Above the mantel, up the front of the fireplace, was a collection of mounted heads—some animal, some human. The humans, which were all male, appeared to be screaming, glass eyes bulging, jaws agape, tongues extended. The skin of their faces had an unnatural, burnished red color.

"Admiring my little trophies, Trader?" asked a husky voice behind him.

Trader turned and faced the self-appointed ruler of Virtue Lake. Lundquist Zeal was dressed in a floor-length robe made of dense brown fur that might have been mink. As the tall man teetered toward him, Trader caught a flash of bare white, spindly leg and thigh, marked by a tracery of blue veins.

The baron was naked under the long coat.

The idea made Trader wince; he winced again as he took in Zeal's unusual choice of footwear. Where in rad blazes, he asked himself, had the bastard found a pair of red stiletto heels in size eleven?

On either side of the baron, more sec men stood with their handblasters drawn.

"You chilled all those guys by yourself?" Trader asked, gesturing at the wall of heads.

"No, but I did the taxidermy myself," Zeal replied. "Lifelike, aren't they? I designed the display as a tromp l'oeil. It's like they're sticking their heads through a hole in the wall."

If that was the case, Trader thought, then something really, really terrible was happening to them on the other side. "Amazing," he said.

"One does what one can to alleviate the monotony."

Zeal cultivated the reputation of being as crazy as a shithouse rat. If Trader hadn't known better, he'd have thought the bastard was even further gone than that. He might have figured the baron had caught himself a case of the oozies and that the disease's little spermoid-wormoids were happily eating thousands of tunnels in his brain. But Trader was no triple stupe.

Though Zeal sported the gaudy slut makeup and the high heels, he wasn't effeminate. He lumped around in those high-heeled women's shoes like a drunken spider. He dressed that way for the shock effect, in order to become even more a figure of hatred and fear. The idea being, with a guy who looked as rad-blasted queer as he did, you never knew what the fuck he'd do, or when. It no doubt helped the baron control both his slaves and sec men.

"Do you want something to drink?" Zeal asked Trader. "I have everything from champagne to rye whiskey."

"I'll drink with you after we finish our business."

"Fair enough. Where are my blasters and ammo?"

"They're safe. They're close by."

The baron scowled at him. "I sense an element of mistrust. That makes me very unhappy."

"Well, don't take it personal," Trader said with a laugh. "In case you haven't heard, I don't trust anybody. That's how I stay in business. Before we make the switch, I'd like to see the color of your gold."

"And if I refuse?"

"We move on."

"And what if I won't let you?" Zeal asked, raising a crookedly penciled eyebrow.

"We level the place, and then move on."

The baron searched Trader's face for a hint of weakness.

He found nothing in the eyes, in the line of the mouth. Nothing that could be used to gain advantage. "Very well. Follow me."

With the sec men bringing up the rear, the baron led him through the big house, toward the end of the building facing the bluff. The mansion had been furnished to suit Zeal's taste, which ran to everything gaudy. Garish, violent paintings clashed with upholstered sofas that clashed with rugs. The rooms were obstacle courses, thanks to his collection of perfectly godawful crap.

Zeal stopped in front of a diorama made up of objects that had been traded for fuel. Trader couldn't read the nameplates, but he recognized one of the life-sized statues. Marsh Folsom had once shown him a picture of a red-haired clown known in predark times as Ronald. Made of hollow plastic, it was positioned in a conversational setting with three female fashion mannequins dressed in black garter belts, thong panties and stiletto heels, and to one side, as if conspiring, a pair of short hairy men wearing fur togas. To Trader, these last two looked like swampies.

Zeal didn't explain the purpose of the odd tableau. At a signal from the baron, his henchmen moved the big clown out of the way, opening up the access to the far wall. Zeal slid his hand along the paneling until he found a hidden catch. The panel slid to one side, exposing a door.

"Turn your head," he told Trader. "I have to disable the boobies before we can proceed."

Trader put his back to the baron. The two swampies had definitely seen better days. Chunks of plaster were missing from their elbows and cheeks. Their fur wraps were motheaten. Why anyone would want to make a statue out of a swampie was a mystery to Trader. Of course, if he could have read the nameplate, he would have realized they were a pair of Neanderthal replicas looted from a natural-history museum in Chicago.

"All right, come ahead," Zeal said.

The door opened onto a hall hacked into the limestone bedrock. The ceiling and walls were buttressed by peeled logs. The baron took a torch from a stanchion and set it ablaze. Then he and Trader followed the corridor, which wound back into the bowels of the hillside, before it finally ended in another door. This one was steel with massive hinges. Again the baron directed Trader to turn his back.

After a moment, Trader heard the metal door creak open behind him.

"All right, come on."

Zeal's treasure room was a chamber roughly ten by ten, lined, floor, walls and ceiling, with rough-sawed boards. In the flickering torchlight, Trader could see a row of strongboxes along the foot of the far wall.

"The shipment we arranged was ten crates of predark autoblasters," Zeal said, making no move to open the chests. "Unfired blasters. Ten to a crate. Still in factory packaging. And the ammo was to be two hundred rounds per blaster, which makes it twenty thousand rounds of government-issue, caliber-compatible, full-metal jacket."

"You got it," Trader said. "One hundred blasters, with ammo, in exchange for fifty pounds of gold."

Zeal leaned down and opened one of the chests. Heaped gold flashed in the torchlight.

Trader stepped closer and took a look. What he saw was a collection of old wedding rings, earrings, cufflinks, fountain pens and wristwatches. But most of the volume was made up of predark dental gold no doubt sourced by grave robbers: crowns, chunks of filling, bridgework. The precious metal was no longer used in dentistry in Deathlands, where bad teeth were simply pulled.

"May I?" Trader asked, gesturing at the contents.

"Of course."

Trader dipped his hand in and picked out some samples. After examining them, he dumped the lot back in the box. It wasn't what he'd expected. "Our deal was for pure gold," he said. "Half this shit still has teeth in it. Or it's just ten-karat plating. Our arrangement was that I'd be paid in ingots of pure gold. Is this all you've got?"

"Gold is gold."

"Not if it's like this. What else have you got to trade?"

Zeal dipped a hand into the pocket of his fur coat and pulled out a slender glass vial filled with an amber liquid. He unstoppered it and handed it to Trader, who held it up to the torch.

"Not too close to the flame," the baron warned him.

Trader took a sniff. It was gasoline, all right. He put the test tube to his lips and took a sip. He swished it around in his mouth for a second, then spit it onto the floor. "Not more than seventy-five octane," he pronounced. "If I put that sheep piss in my wags, it's going to make them knock like rad blazes. Nukin' hell, it's no better than your so-called gold."

"You don't have to use it yourself," Zeal told him. "You can trade it somewhere on down the line. Other villes will be happy to get it."

He was right, of course. Beggars couldn't be choosers.

"I'll give you three drums of gas for every blaster," the baron said.

"We're talking fifty-five gallons?"

"Of course."

"Make it six drums, and I'm only delivering ten blasters with a hundred rounds each."

"I'll pay you six drums per blaster for the original one hundred."

"No way. I can't haul that much extra fuel. Won't be any room in my transport wags for anything else."

Zeal frowned, but then completely surprised Trader by conceding the game without further argument.

At 330 gallons of gas per blaster, even with the hundred rounds thrown in, the baron was getting reamed, big time. And he had to know it. When presented with such a thorough no-kiss screwing, a hard-nosed businessman like Zeal should have gone ballistic and threatened to chill Trader and his entire crew.

Instead, ever so amiably, the baron said, "Now that the deal is set, let's go back into the big house and get ourselves some refreshments."

A shiver passed up Trader's spine, like someone had just walked over his grave.

Chapter Five

As Ryan and the others walked through the shantytown on their way to the gaudy strip, they drew a small crowd of children. Half-naked and caked with filth, the young of Virtue Lake pressed in around them. The expressions on their tear-streaked faces were heartrending. Each held one hand open and outstretched, and with the other pointed desperately at his or her open mouth.

Ryan caught one kid trying to steal his panga, but not before the light-fingered little crook had it pulled halfway out of its leg sheath. "Wait a minute!" he said, catching the boy by the wrist and giving it a firm squeeze. "You don't want to be touching that unless I say so."

"Gimme food," the boy demanded, making the dirty fingers-to-mouth gesture. The look in his eyes was as hard as flint. He was no more than ten or eleven.

"Got no food," Ryan told him.

"Gimme token, then."

J.B. laughed out loud. "What can a snot-nose squirt like you do with a gaudy token?" he said.

"Same as you, Goggle Eyes. Brew and screw."

The companions exchanged dark looks.

"Catch us on the way out of the ville," Ryan told the boy. "We'll have some food for you and your friends."

The child studied his face. "You're just tryin' to get rid of us so you can go get shit-faced."

"Yeah, that's right, but I'm not kidding about the food. I wouldn't joke about something like that."

After a brief conference, the pack of children parted and let them pass.

"For a coldheart mean son of a bitch," Hun said as they walked on, "you got a hell of a soft streak, Ryan."

"He's a regular Santy Claus," Sam said with a giggle.

As they neared the double row of gaudies, Ryan tossed the bag of tokens in the air and caught it with the same hand. "We might as well start at this end of the line and work our way to the other," he said. Then he looked at Trader's war captain and added, "That is, unless Poet's worked up a safer strategy for tackling the sluts of Virtue Lake."

The older man was used to Ryan riding him hard at every opportunity, so he didn't stiffen at the gibe, but his eyes flashed a warning. As Poet opened his mouth to reply in kind, a flurry of blasterfire broke out from the mall to their left. Two heavy-caliber shots rang out, followed by four lighter-sounding cracks. The crowd milling in front of the strip mall immediately took to its heels, spreading out over the parking lot.

Ryan saw two guys facing each other on their knees under the facade's long portico. Their blasters hung limply in their fingers. Both, it seemed, had been mortally wounded in the close-range exchange. After a few seconds of hard breathing, and hard bleeding, they slumped over onto their sides on the concrete. Someone cheered, then the crowd swarmed in, stripping the still-kicking corpses of their few valuables.

"Stick together," Poet reminded the others as they crossed to the other side of the street. "And watch each other's backs."

Under the circumstances, Ryan considered the warning unnecessary and annoying.

Four RVs were parked in front of the row of gaudies, all of them painted bright pink, all of them without tires and wheels, sitting on the asphalt on their bare axles. They were unmobile mobile whorehouses. Through the uncurtained side windows, Ryan could see a few naked sluts parading back and forth, offering the same delights as the permanent establishments, but at cut-rate prices.

One of the women turned her bare backside to him, pressed it to the inside of the windowpane and bent over.

"Would you look at that!" Hun said as she paused to take in the goods on display. "Hey, Sam, I think I'm in love."

"You don't want to go in there, pilgrims," said a sallow-faced hawker standing twenty feet away, in front of the open door to the Very Best Dry Cleaners. He was dressed in a long khaki duster and holed sneakers.

"And why's that?" Hun asked him.

"For one thing, them cheapish sluts'll rob you blind. For another, they'll put an itch on you that won't never go away. But the real reason to give them a miss is they got no floor show."

Raucous live music blared from the open entryway, which was blocked, as were the windows, by heavy black fabric curtains. Peals of coarse male laughter erupted from inside.

"Come on in, pilgrims. There's no cover charge and no minimum. You'll have the time of your lives, I guar-an-tee it!"

Just then a customer of the gaudy came stumbling out from between the velvet curtains. Gasping for breath, eyes as big as saucers, a frozen grin on face, he was clearly stoned on jolt. He lurched for the nearest concrete pillar, then wrapped his arms around it like it was a life preserver.

"See what I mean?" the hawker said. "Nothing but fun, fun, fun."

"Got to admit," J.B. said to Ryan, "I'm curious about the entertainment."

So was Ryan. He brushed the curtain aside and entered. He was struck at once by the acrid smell of spilled liquor and old cigar butts. The clusters of tables and chairs were deserted, except for a dozen or so bored-looking sluts dressed in tattered and grease-stained negligees. All of the paying customers were packed in close to the stage at the far end of the room.

The band consisted of a snare drum and trumpet, played by bare-breasted female musicians. They kept repeating the same syncopated two-bar riff while on the stage, a grossly fat woman danced naked in the light of gas lanterns suspended from the ceiling. She had a gargantuan belly, huge, pendulous breasts and enormous buttocks and thighs. Her body was covered, head to foot, with a fine white powder that looked like bread flour. She wore the long coils of her thick brown hair piled up on top of her head, but a few stray wisps had fallen loose. As she stomped and shimmied along the front edge of the stage, her mounds of flesh shuddered, and the white powder drifted onto the mirrored floor beneath her feet.

"Dark night!" J.B. breathed.

"Whole lot of woman there," Hun said.

"Enough to make three, mebbe four normal-sized girls," Samantha agreed.

The drunken, all-male crowd cheered and catcalled as the dancer did a hip-rolling 360-degree turn that showed off everything she had.

"Come on, Big Dumpling," one of the men shouted, "you know what we want."

"Yeah," someone else called out, "give it up, Big Dumpling."

There were more cheers and whistles.

Holding her arms out wide, her elbows draped with sagging masses of fat, the entertainer threw back her head and let loose with a strong, throaty tenor. "I'm so light and fluffy," she sang to the snare drum's beat, "so tender, tasty sweet, that you'll praise the Lord Bejesus, there's lots of me to eat...."

Facing front again, she gripped her doughy right breast

and lifted it to her mouth. Sweat was starting to wash away
the dusting of flour in places. From under her raised breast,
rivulets ran down over the vastness of her belly. As she
continued to dance, she began to kiss and lick her own nip-
ple. Which, as the flour disappeared under the lashing of
her tongue, appeared as an enormous, carmine red bull's-
eye.

The crowd went wild.

"Talented lady," was Hun's dead serious comment.
"Wonder what else she can do?"

"I think we're about to find out," Sam said.

The entertainer stepped down from the stage and started
wending her way through the whooping, hollering audience.
The spectators soon had their hands and faces dusted with
white as, one by one, the dancer gripped their ears and
pulled their heads into her bosom and thighs. The men
emerged from the brief embrace gasping for breath and
blinking flour.

"These guys are either deprived, depraved or delirious,"
Poet stated.

"I've seen enough," Ryan said. "I need a drink. Let's
sit down."

They took a table against the wall. A pair of sluts trooped
over at once, and began throwing out their best lewd poses
in the hopes of drumming up some business.

"Just bring us three jugs of your best 'shine," J.B. told
them.

"And a gallon of suds for chasers," Hun added.

"That'll be fourteen zealies," the taller of the two sluts
said. "Up front."

Ryan spilled the metal tokens onto the tabletop. The bar
girls snatched them up, then scuttled over to the service
window set in the wall. They passed the tokens through the
window's barred grate and waited there for the barman to
fill the order.

Meanwhile, the crowd was getting wilder and wilder,

chanting "Dump-ling! Dump-ling!" to the insistent beat of snare and trumpet. A bunch of the drunks hoisted the huge woman into the air and started passing her around the room over their heads while she squealed and kicked.

When the bar girls returned with their refreshments, Sam asked the tall one, "Do they ever drop her?"

"Yeah, sometimes they do," the gaudy said. "But she usually falls on top of them. Customers the only ones get hurt."

Then the bar girl looked at each of the men in turn, one hand resting on a cocked hip, the fingers of the other one dipping so far down into the front of her G-string that it looked like she was trying to scratch the small of her back. "Get you boys anything else?" she asked.

Poet shook his head emphatically.

"Forget it," J.B. said.

"Then how about the girls?"

"Mebbe later," Hun said, shooing her out of the way.

Big Dumpling was trapped in the grasp of a group of ten men, obviously a crew from the practiced way they worked together. The men held Big Dumpling up over their heads, but they didn't pass her on. They were led by a tall coldheart with a shaved skull. He had a coiled snake, a cobra with its hood spread, branded into back of his head. The red, raised, permanent welt was a popular method of tattooing in Deathlands.

"Let's splat the hog bitch," the tall one said. "Come on! One, two, three!"

With a tremendous grunt, all ten of them tossed her up in the air, trying to hit the ceiling with her.

The huge, doughy body flew up, and with a resounding thud smacked the sprayed-on predark ceiling, then dropped back. The men caught her, staggering under the falling weight.

"Stop! Stop!" Big Dumpling moaned.

When a few customers who were standing close to the

action tried to make the men do just that, a pair of the crew stepped out and made motions as if to draw their handblasters. The customers backed up in a hurry, their own hands raised, apologizing.

"Again, harder!" the tattooed man said. "Mebbe we can make her stick up there. Like a big white loogee."

"No, please!" Big Dumpling cried as the men prepared to launch her.

"One, two, three!"

Big Dumpling smashed into the ceiling. The impact shook the whole room, and there was blood on her face, her knees, her elbows, as she dropped into their waiting arms.

"Where's a fucking sec man when you need one?" Sam complained.

"Probably sleepin' in some parked wag," Hun said.

"What's the big deal?" J.B. asked.

"If they keep that up, they're going to chill her," Hun said.

"So what's your point?" J.B. followed a swig of white lightning with a long swallow of room-temperature beer from a plastic jug.

"So, I liked her singing," Hun said, "and I ain't going to let her die for nothing."

Before Ryan could stop her, the green-haired woman rose from her seat, swept up her 10-gauge double-barreled shotgun from against the wall and fired once from the hip. A tongue of flame a yard long roared from the muzzle. Double-aught buckshot ripped a jagged, two-foot-wide hole in the wall opposite. The blast's concussion made bits of ceiling rain to the floor.

At the warning shot, everything stopped—the music, the yelling, the fat-woman-tossing.

Big Dumpling slipped out of the grasp of the crew and landed on the floor with a soft thud.

There was nothing left to do but back Hun's play. Ryan's Blackhawk cleared hip leather in a blur, and as it did, he thumbed back the single-action hammer. Likewise, J.B.'s Browning Hi-Power Mark 2 came up, as did Poet's CAR-15 and Sam's 9 mm H & K P-7.

The branded man was irate at the interruption, practically spitting mad. "Are you bastards triple crazy? All we was doin' was just havin' a l'il fun...." When his eyes locked on to Ryan's face, they widened in recognition.

Ryan had crossed paths with this man before, before the shaved head, before the snake tattoo. Ryan knew him as a crew leader for Levi Shabazz, a trader of deservedly poor reputation.

"I really like your new snake brand, Vernel," Ryan said. "But you should have put it on the front side of your head. It would've improved your looks."

A smile spread over the cobra man's lips. "No call for you to haul out all them blasters," he said to Ryan, showing off his empty hands. He wore a blue-steel autoblaster in a cross-draw rig on his left hip. The hammer was locked back in ready-to-fire position.

The others in his crew raised their hands, as well.

"We don't want no trouble," Vernel said. "No real harm been done here. Just funnin' with the lady. All part of the show, and the show's over. No need to do any more shootin'."

Ryan didn't like the look in the man's eyes. A laughing look. As he sized Vernel up, he saw similar branding marks on both his arms, matching snake bodies wriggling down from his elbows, hooded heads fanned out on the backs of his hands. Ryan had the bastard dead to rights. He knew he'd be doing the world a favor by pumping a Magnum slug into Vernel's guts, then pulling up a chair to watch him die. But Trader had said to play it close to the vest. No chilling unless lives were at stake. And Trader was the boss. Ryan dropped the Ruger's hammer to half-cock.

"If you don't want trouble, you and your crew better leave now," Cawdor said.

"That's fine with me," Vernel said with a shrug. "We're going."

Ryan and the others tracked the men with their blasters until they'd all slipped out through the curtained doorway.

Over by the stage, Big Dumpling required assistance from members of the audience to regain her feet. The blasterfire and subsequent standoff had cast a pall over the gaudy's festivities. The drummer and trumpet player started up the music again, but their enthusiasm was gone. Instead of resuming her act, Big Dumpling limped over to the table where Ryan and the others stood. She didn't bother to conceal her nakedness.

"I 'preciate what you just did for me," she said. Trickles of blood from a lip cut dripped over her numerous chins. "Those men of Shabazz's are triple mean, and they don't like being whupped in public. I'm afraid you all put yourselves in a world of danger on account of me. If there's anything I can ever do to repay you," she said, looking meaningfully at Ryan with huge doe eyes, "anything at all…"

"Thanks for the offer," he replied, "but we've got to be on our way."

J.B., Sam and Hun picked up the 'shine bottles and the beer jug.

"Y'all come back," Big Dumpling said to their backs. "Come back real soon, now."

"What's wrong?" the hawker asked as they filed out through the doorway, blasters at the ready. He stood well to one side of the entrance, out of the potential line of fire.

"Floor show got a little heavy for us," J.B. said.

"Didn't you like Big Dumpling? Everybody likes Big Dumpling."

"You mean, everybody licks Big Dumpling," Hun said.

"She's very generous with her person," the hawker agreed.

"Uh, Poet, Ryan…" J.B. said.

"I see them," Ryan answered.

The tattooed man and his pals were loitering around the front of the next gaudy. A couple of them already had their blasters out, holding them half-hidden along the outside of their thighs. The crew leader looked over and gave Ryan that nasty smirk again.

"Too late to cross the street," Poet said.

"Not unless we want to get shot up the backside," Ryan stated.

"They've regrouped out here," the war captain said. "You can bet they have a plan by now. Going to try and chill us for sure."

"We got to face them down, or blow them down," Hun said, the centers of her cheeks starting to flush with excitement. She cracked the breech of shotgun, pried out the empty hull with her thumbnail and inserted another high-brass-buckshot load. As she snapped the action shut, she added, "Me, I vote for blow them down."

Which was no surprise to anybody. Hunaker always voted that way. Sometimes Ryan thought the chilling got her off.

Poet turned to Ryan, but he didn't speak. The look on his weather-seamed face said it all. It said, "You're faster, you're stronger. This one's yours to call." Ryan cracked a big smile and nodded.

"Then, let's fucking well do it," he said.

As they advanced, the refinery workers standing under the portico sensed the impending butting of heads and scooted out of the way. Those turned to statuary by drink and jolt were helped to one side by friends who could still move.

Ryan stopped about ten feet from Vernel. "You're in my way," he said.

"Yeah, I suppose I am."

"Move your ass, or lose it."

The tattooed man shifted his weight to the balls of his feet. His right hand didn't move for the pistol butt, but his fingertips lightly brushed together, as he anticipated the grab.

"Don't think I like your tone of voice," Vernel said. "Seems kind of unfriendly."

"Then I guess you aren't near as triple dim as you look."

J.B., Poet, Sam and Hun fanned out on either side of Ryan, giving themselves clear firing lanes.

"Mebbe you can't count, One-Eye," Vernel taunted. "We got ten blasters to your five."

Ryan scanned the other man's crew. Because they thought they had the odds on their side, they were all itching for a fight. The one-eyed man laughed out loud, an unpleasant, grating sound. "Take a closer look," he told the tattooed man. "Half your people don't figure in. They're pissing themselves already. They know they're going to die hard. They're thinking about turning tail."

When Vernel took a half step closer, Ryan saw the wrinkles etched deeply in his forehead. Wrinkles that hadn't been there a second ago. And he knew he had gotten to the bastard. The muscles of the human face were the ultimate tell, the true indicator of an opponent's state of mind and heart. And like Trader always said, "The man with a frown can be taken down."

"I'll bet that smart mouth of yours is what cost you your eyeball," Vernel wisecracked. "You must be a triple stupe, Ryan, because it didn't teach you nothing at all. How's about I take that other peeper of yours for a prize? Leave you alive, stumbling around with a tin cup the rest of your days."

The rest of Shabazz's crew smiled and nodded. The two men with blasters already drawn seemed to relax. Their shoulders slumped ever so slightly. They weren't fooling anybody. Ryan knew they were going to open fire as soon as their leader took another step closer. Another step would bring Vernel well within arm's reach and allow him to block or deflect Ryan's draw.

The one-eyed man didn't wait for that to happen. As he sidestepped the tattooed guy, the Blackhawk was already coming up in his hand. Its long barrel was slow on the swing, or he wouldn't have had to move to make his play.

At the same instant the Blackhawk's hammer locked back, Ryan heard the hard whack of a 9mm round and felt the bullet whiz past his ear. Then he acquired the target, and the big Ruger boomed and bucked in his grip. The .357 Magnum slug hit the shooter in the left leg well above the knee, shattering four inches of thighbone. It exited the other side and passed through the fleshy part of his right thigh, as well. The crewman dropped his blaster and spun to the ground, eyes bulging, mouth gaping in a silent, breathless scream.

Ryan grabbed Vernel by the shoulder and turned him, locking a forearm across the front of his throat. Flesh sizzled as he jammed the blazing-hot muzzle of the Blackhawk against the man's temple and recocked the hammer.

Vernel's crew went for their blasters as Poet, Sam, Hun and J.B. swung up their weapons. It was a standoff.

"Tell your boys to back down," Ryan ordered the tattooed man, "or I'm going to turn your skull into a soup bowl."

Vernel opened his mouth, but before he could speak there was a screech of brakes as a familiar-looking wag skidded into the parking lot, further scattering the crowd of spectators. The fat sec man pulled himself out of the driver's seat. Three more sec men exited the wag and, with their hand-blasters drawn, took up firing positions behind the wag's fenders and hood.

"You with the eye patch," the fat sec man said over the wag's roof, his KG-99 braced in both hands, "let Vernel go, or we'll chill you dead."

"Looks like I'm rescued, Ryan," the tattooed man said over his shoulder, "and your ass is nuked."

A lesser man might have tried to explain the circumstances to the rightful authorities, might have claimed that the other group had drawn and fired first, that the shooting had been in self-defense. Ryan was no whiner. When someone pushed him, he pushed back, harder.

"It figures that you sec men would side with these scumsuckers," Ryan growled as he swung around the Blackhawk's muzzle and took careful aim at the fat man's forehead. "If you think that sheet metal is going to stop a steel-jacketed .357 Mag, you got a big surprise coming."

"I'm not going to tell you again," the fat man warned him. "Put down your blasters and step back."

"No," Ryan said. "You put down yours."

Over the sights of the Ruger, he could see the sweat popping out on the sides of the sec man's face, rolling like raindrops down his steeply sloping cheeks. "I'm going to count to five," Ryan said in a voice without emotion, "then I'm going to open fire." He paused for a beat, then said, "One…"

Actually Ryan intended to start shooting on the count of two. His finger was already tightening on the trigger, taking up the scant bit of slack to the break point. He knew his companions were doing the same thing. It was a trick Poet had come up with for head-to-head situations just like this. Nobody expected the blasting to start on two.

Maybe on three or four, but never on two.

"Hold it!" a familiar gruff voice shouted.

Trader burst through the edge of the crowd, the pistol grip of his Armalite in his right fist, its barrel leveled at waist height. "Everybody, hold your fire!" he told the sec men. "You know goddamned well me and my crew's got business here. Important business with the baron."

Out of fear, or stubbornness, or some of both, the fat man held his position behind the wag.

Trader shouted at the back of his head. "If you want to cost Zeal some biggish profits, go ahead and start shooting. Otherwise, put away the blasters."

The sec men glanced at one another, then at their chief. Finally the fat man relented. "Vernel, call off your rad-blasted dogs," he said as he lowered his weapon. "I mean right now. If Trader decides to call off the deal on account of this, Zeal will nail my head to his chimney. He'll do the same for you, too."

Over Vernel's shoulder, Ryan could see the look on Trader's face as he stared down the tattooed man. Reading the murderous intent in his boss's eyes, and not wanting to get tagged by a through-and-through 5.56 mm tumbler, Ryan abruptly shoved Vernel away from him.

But as much as he seemed to want to, Trader didn't open fire. There was still a profit to be made.

Vernel straightened and in a slightly shaken voice told the others, "The fun's over, put away your blasters."

Trader pointed at the wounded man on the ground with his Armalite. "Best get tourniquets on those legs or he's going to bleed out on you."

"Yeah, see to it," Vernel said to his men.

Then to Ryan, he added, "Some other time, One-Eye..."

"Sooner the better."

Vernel snorted, then pushed past his crew and vanished into the milling crowd.

Trader and the others didn't stick around.

As they backed away from the scene, J.B. said, "We cut that pretty fine."

"Too damned fine," Poet grumbled.

"Man!" Hun exclaimed, her eyes wide with excitement, nostrils dilated, full-blown roses in her cheeks. "Was I ever pumped to cut loose on those thieving, dickless bastards! Kaaaa-boom! Kaaaa-boom! Check this out...." She held up her trigger hand for them all to see. It was trembling violently.

"Better start breathing through your nose," Trader advised her. He nodded for J.B. to pass her the 'shine. They stopped while she took a long pull on the jug.

Ryan angled his body so Poet couldn't hear what he had to say to Trader. "Levi Shabazz must be somewhere close by," he said. "He never travels without his crew. Not a good sign for us."

"Definitely not a good sign," Trader agreed. "I didn't catch sight of Shabazz up at Zeal's compound." The tiniest flicker of a smile crossed his battle-hardened face. "But then again, I wasn't turning over any rocks."

Chapter Six

As Trader accelerated up the dirt road, he checked the mini-wag's side mirrors to make sure Zeal's sec men hadn't jumped in their own vehicles and followed them out of the ville. Behind him, there was nothing but his own swirl of dust on the winding track that rimmed the dry lake. He didn't really expect to see a bunch of wags in hot pursuit. The baron knew better than to try something like that. He had to figure that a man as savvy as Trader would set up an ambush to cover his retreat from Virtue Lake.

"I never guessed old Zeal would roll over so far on a deal," Trader said to Ryan and Poet, who sat grim faced and shoulder to shoulder in the narrow back seat. "Know damned well it goes against his grain not to be the one coming out on top. Can't see why he'd be so anxious for the blasters and ammo that he'd take the screwing I gave him. And what's he think he's going to do with ten new blasters and a thousand rounds of government, anyway?"

"Not much," Ryan replied.

"Very suspicious, if you ask me," Trader said.

"We could always just move on," Poet offered.

Ryan let out a snort of disgust.

The older man ignored him and went on, "We can always off-load the autoblasters somewhere else down the line. Sell them one by one, if we have to. Plenty of barons be glad to pay top dollar for goods like that, even if they couldn't afford to take them all."

"That's not an option," Trader said.

"Why not?" Poet asked.

"Because I'm not running from Levi Shabazz."

"You really think he's in the ville?"

"Oh, he's there, all right. He's the tail that wags the dog named Vernel. Question is, how is he hooked up with Lundquist Zeal? And what kind of ugly plan have they got hatched?"

"The answer there's easy," Ryan said. "They plan on taking us down, ripping us off for the whole cargo. Wags, too."

"Mebbe," Trader said. "But then again, mebbe not."

"As I see it," Poet stated, leaning forward in his seat, "we've got two options. We either uncircle the wags and leave right now, or we sit tight and see it out. If we stay, we got to go on triple red, shift our wags and mass their firepower to defend the road. We put the trade goods meant for Zeal outside our defensive perimeter, mebbe even mine them for a little extra protection. That way, if we had to, we could always just let them have the fucking blasters. No way could Zeal and Shabazz take the rest of the cargo from us."

"What do you say to that, Ryan?" Trader asked.

A glance in the rearview mirror told him what the younger man thought of the plan. There was a thoroughly disgusted look on his face.

"We've been butting heads with Shabazz for as long as I've been part of this crew," Ryan said. "He's not much of a trader. Doesn't have half the brains for the job. He's always made his real living by robbing and chilling. I don't know about you, but I'm tired of smelling that bastard's stink every time I turn upwind. I'm tired of looking over my shoulder for his blaster barrels every time we nail down a big score. And I'm tired of hearing about how he's fucked over another dirt-poor ville for everything but the shit in the latrines."

Trader knew what Ryan was talking about. He had heard the rumors, too. Road scuttlebutt had it that Shabazz had recently taken up extortion in a major way. As the story went, the trader claimed to have a stockpile of nerve gas he'd looted from some government cache. Given the few secret sites the man had actually found in his career, this sounded like nothing more than a bluff to Trader. Shabazz was mostly bluff, when it came right down to it. At any rate, he supposedly had threatened to gas an entire ville unless they gave up gold and slaves. The latter was another reason why Trader had a hard-on against the bastard. Shabazz not only thieved and murdered, but he also routinely did business in the skin trade. He supplied slave sluts, slave whores, and slave field hands for East Coast barons. And no doubt he helped keep Zeal's refinery labor force fully manned.

"Fucker gives the profession a bad name," Trader said around the stub of his cheroot.

"So, let's do something about it," Ryan argued. "Instead of squatting up on top of the hill like a bunch of toothless old hags, with our treasure under our skirts, let's take out the bastard. We've got enough firepower in War Wag One to split those barricades wide open and send the baron's sec men running for the Darks. We can use the miniwags to drive Shabazz from cover, then we personally put him on the last train west. If he and Zeal have got a plan worked out to do us harm, you know Zeal won't go it alone. If we get rid of Shabazz, we can trade the blasters to the baron, take our profit and move on."

"Well, Poet?" Trader asked.

"If we knew for sure that Shabazz was after our cargo, I'd agree. But, we don't. He could be here for some other reason that has nothing to do with us. Trying to take him out presents a major risk to the convoy down the line. We could lose war wags and crew in the attempt. And it's not a sure thing that we'd get him in the end, either. Our best option is to stand pat and defend the convoy with massed blasters, do our business with Zeal and hopefully roll away without firing a shot.''

"You think Shabazz is just going to let us drive off?'' Ryan shouted at the man beside him. "Are you high on jolt or something?''

"Shabazz isn't going to try and take us if he knows we're ready for him," Poet said. "He's way smarter than that.''

Ryan started to yell something more personal and inflammatory, but Trader shut him up with an abrupt wave of his hand. From their first meeting, Trader had recognized much of his own younger self in Ryan—a meeting in which the one-eyed man held him at blasterpoint while they discussed the terms of his employment. Like the young Trader, Ryan was arrogant, headstrong, quick-tempered, unbending in battle. Excellent attributes, to be sure, but Trader also knew that the only reason he had lived long enough to see his first gray hairs was that he had learned to step back from the intoxicating brink of combat and listen to reason. As far as he was concerned, it was high time Ryan started listening, too.

"Like it or not, Poet's right," Trader said. "You got the heat up, Ryan, and you're not seeing the picture clearly. If we go in there with blasters blazing, rockets roaring, we could touch off the baron's gasoline stockpile, or mebbe even the whole rad-blasted refinery. Ain't so many places around here making even half-assed fuel that we can afford to let one go up in smoke. Be a cold day in hell before these folks build themselves another refinery.''

Ryan said nothing. His blue eye stared unblinking at Trader's reflection in the rearview.

"And even though Zeal's gas is the staggering shits," Trader went on, "we got villes along our route that are desperate for it. No matter how much it makes their wags knock and ping, they want it, and they'll trade their best goods for it. And there's another thing. These military blasters we're trading Zeal for fuel, only a real special buyer like him is going to have the extra jack to spend on them. They're what you might call a luxury item. Like sweet-smelling soap, or toothpaste, or one of those predark sex magazines. Gas is another story. Everybody needs it—if not for wags, then generators. And it can be resold in small quantities by middlemen. You can't split a longblaster up into half pints. It either shoots or it ain't nothing but spare parts. What I'm saying is, we can make a real sweet profit here if the deal goes through.''

"I think you're overestimating Shabazz's smarts,'' Ryan said, ''and way underestimating his greed. Not to mention the fact that he's got Baron Zeal pulling his chain.''

Trader shrugged. He knew that his war wags could handle anything that Zeal and Shabazz could throw at them. He had the biggest blasters, the most powerful armored vehicles in all of Deathlands and the most skilled and deadly battle crews.

"If that sorry son of a bitch comes after us,'' Trader said with confidence, ''it'll be the last thing he ever does.''

Chapter Seven

The mutated scorpion was two and a half feet long, its body amber and black. In the heat of the day, it moved incredibly fast: legs a blur, wicked front pincer claws raised and curved stinger, which was longer than Hun's SOG blade, held high over its back, poised to strike.

Unlike its prenukecaust ancestors, this creature was an aggressive daytime hunter, and its preferred food wasn't other, smaller insects, but mammal meat—size no object. That was thanks to an adapted venom, which was a thousand times more potent than that of its forbears, enabling it to kill in a matter of seconds literally anything that walked the hellscape that was Deathlands. It feared nothing, and it never retreated.

"Shit! Damn!" Hun cried, trying to line up the scuttling, scrambling thing with the bead sight of her scattergun.

"I got it!" Poet said, shouldering his CAR-15.

"No!" Ryan barked. The edge of command in his voice was so powerful that it made both of his companions hold their fire.

Ryan already had his panga drawn, and he held it by the tip of the blade, paused, then made a lightning-fast throw. It was hard enough for a man with two functioning eyes to hit a fast-moving target, but for a man with only one, it was a real feat. Ryan had spent a lot of time adjusting to his terrible injury, learning how to compensate for the loss of stereoscopic vision, and for the resulting changes in his depth perception. He developed an uncanny ability to anticipate in a millisecond what an opponent was going to do, where it wanted to be, how it intended to get there.

The massive blade gleamed as it turned over in the air, its track coinciding perfectly with the movement of the huge insect. With a crunch, the point skewered the creature's back, the blade slid through to the hilt, pinning it to the ground.

"Yow!" Hun exclaimed as she lowered her 10-gauge.

"No need to waste a round" was Ryan's terse, after-the-fact explanation.

The big scorpion was still alive.

Legs scrabbling on the rocks, it humped up against the panga's cross guard, trying to break free of the ground. Creamy yellow gore oozed out around the blade, and the curved ebony point of its stinger struck the panga's pommel over and over. Click. Click. Click.

Ryan stepped up, and, without ceremony, stomped the scorpion's palm-sized head flat with his boot heel. After a few more reflexive stings, it shuddered and died.

"Not a very big one," he said as he reached down and jerked his panga free. He wiped the blade and handle clean with handfuls of dirt before brushing it off on his pants and sliding it back into its leg sheath.

"Hey, have a look at this," Hun said, waving Ryan and Poet over to where she stood. She pointed down at a dark hole in a pile of rocks.

The hole was filled with small scorpions, roughly six inches long. There were about fifty of them, squirming over one another, waving their claws and stingers.

"The big one was hunting food for them," Poet said.

"No food coming now," Hun stated. She lowered the muzzle of the 10-gauge to the edge of the hole and, smiling, touched off the left barrel.

The shotgun boomed and belched flame. Double-aught buckshot and high-brass concussion shredded the packed mass of baby scorpions into a fine mist. White gun smoke poured out of the much widened opening in the earth.

"Lots more where they came from," Poet said, apparently struck by the futility of the act.

"So what?" Hun snapped back as she ejected the spent hull and reloaded.

"So, nothing," he replied.

After a pause, she said, "Hey, Poet, why don't you have a look-see over that far rise?"

"A look-see at what exactly?"

"At whatever the fuck is over there. Just leave me and Ryan alone for a few minutes."

The gray-haired man glanced at her bright eyes and burning cheeks, then at Ryan, whose face was as cold and impassive as steel. He shrugged. "Yeah, why don't I scout on ahead, then," he said, laying his CAR-15 along the top of his shoulder and heading away from them across the boulder field.

Ryan knew if there'd been any real strategic point to the long recce, Poet would never have agreed to break up the threesome. Ryan and Poet had been sent out in the hottest part of the day to hoof it five miles over some rad-blasted ground because the Trader was tired of hearing them battle over the defensive strategy. It was his way of saying to his two war advisers, "Go out there and don't come back until you've worked it out." Ryan took satisfaction in the knowledge that as far as he could see, Poet had no more interest in "working it out" than he did.

Hun, too, was making the others in the crew nervous. She was still way amped from the gaudy set-to—talking wild, acting wilder. Homicidus interruptus.

Of course, Ryan knew what was coming as soon as Poet nipped out of sight. But it pleased him to act like he didn't have a clue. He stood on the edge of the hill, surveying the far shore of Virtue Lake with his telescope, doing his job.

To his back, Hun said, "Sure is hellish warm out here."

Ryan didn't turn. He didn't have to. Out of the corner of his one good eye, he could see her carefully set her shotgun against a rock and kick out of her well-worn boots. Then she unfastened the waistband of her BDUs and started rolling them down over her hips. Underwear was one of those predark "luxuries" Trader was always going on about.

"You got something I want, Ryan."

"Lucky me," he said through a half smile, still not turning. He pretended to concentrate on the view downrange.

Hun moved up against him from behind. She had taken off her sleeveless gray T-shirt, as well. He could feel her bare breasts, which were small and very firm, push into the middle of his back, and over his shoulder he caught the cinnamon smell of her hot skin. She reached around his waist for his belt and unbuckled it.

"You're damned right you're lucky," she told him. "I could always get it from Poet."

"Why don't you, then?" he said flatly.

Hun exploded with laughter. "It was his turn last night. I think it nearly chilled him. Besides, you know I like a change of pace."

With a practiced jerk, she dropped his fatigue pants down around his boot tops.

Foreplay with Hun was virtually nonexistent; she liked nothing better than to get right down to it. Though they'd had an off-and-on thing going for many months, she and Ryan had never kissed, and they had never touched each other except in a purely sexual way. There was no real tenderness between them, only intense desire.

Fury.

And fulfillment.

Ryan laid her on her back on a big flat rock and plunged into her, without further preamble. The sun blazed against his back, and her interior was just as meltingly hot; sweat poured down his spine as he thrust, parried, thrust.

Beneath him, Hun made none of the typical woman

sounds, none of the shrill whimpers, the soft moans. She gasped hoarsely for breath, grunting from the effort as she rose to meet him. And when she opened her eyes inches from his face, they were crazy. Not seeing him. Or anything.

Once Hun got the heat all the way up, the way she had it up now, she was hard to cool down.

Given his young years, Ryan had already been with more than his share of women, some prettier than others. Hun wasn't all that much to look at, but there was something about her. Something magical, electric. A buzzing excitement that she could pass on with a look, a touch. When it came to sex, Hunaker had the power to raise the dead.

She raised Ryan three times in short order, using her skin, her tongue, her teeth, her fingertips. Then it was his turn on his back on the blisteringly hot rock while she rode him, hard, their bodies lathered and slippery.

With drops of her falling sweat spattering his face and chest, Ryan stared up into the endless blue sky. For an instant, he caught a glimpse of the edge of infinity; in that same instant, he glimpsed his own death. Then, arching violently up from the stone, he drove into her.

POET KNELT OUT of sight on the far side of the boulder field, watching the two of them go at it. Though the distance was better than forty yards, he could still clearly hear their panting and the wet slap of their colliding flesh.

He had no proprietary feelings when it came to Hunaker. Only a fool could. After all, Hun's appetite for both men and women, singly and in various combinations, was legendary among Trader's crew. Nor did he covet Ryan's youth or his awesome staying power. It was like he'd happened on a pair of lions mating in some clearing in the jungle bush. He had to stop and stare.

He was called Poet because of the way he saw things, not because he could write verse, or even write his own name, which of course he couldn't.

Because he was who he was, he didn't view Ryan's taking over his war captaincy as a defeat. He saw it as inevitable. Like death. He harbored no ill will toward the man. Even so, he was determined to fight to keep his position as long as he could; he had earned it through hard work and his own spilled blood. For him, it was a matter of personal honor.

Over the years, Poet had faced many men with murder in their eyes. There was a different kind of fire burning in Ryan, a fire of pure hate, rather than one of ambition or lust for power. And it seemed to flare up most violently whenever Trader took Poet's advice over his, or whenever Trader pulled Poet aside for a private confab. It wasn't simple jealousy, though Poet had thought as much in the beginning. Jealousy would have been something understandable. Even natural. Expected. This seemed more like outrage at some ultimate unfairness, at some awful betrayal. At times the anger appeared as much directed at Trader as at him. As if the sight of the two of them together forced Ryan to replay some horrible events from his past.

No one had ever asked Ryan about it. Certainly not Poet. In the company of road warriors such questions were best left alone.

In his entire life, Poet had come across only a few others so afflicted, so conflicted, so full of rage. Each one had lost everything of value in his life. Possessions gone. Families horribly chilled. All they had left was the desire for self-destruction. To push, and push, and push the limits, until death finally found and released them from their torment. Unlike the others, whom he'd watched flare briefly and then burn out, Ryan's bottomless, barely controlled anger was coupled with an array of incredible physical skills—speed, strength, agility. Poet had realized many months ago that Ryan was the most dangerous man he had ever met.

Given that fact, and Ryan's feelings toward him, Poet had little doubt that someday the final question between them would be decided with knives or blasters. He knew that Deathlands offered much worse ways for an old warrior to check out. A clean chill from a skilled hand in combat was a merciful and comforting thought.

Poet frowned. Watching other people rut, no matter how enthusiastically, had a limited fascination for him. His mind was wandering.

He pulled back silently, leaving Ryan and Hun to it.

He followed a gully to the saddle of the next overlook, then used the back of his hand to shield the sun from his eyes as he scanned the road. The breeze had picked up. Squadrons of dust devils danced toward Virtue Lake.

Poet knew the long-range recce wasn't necessary under the circumstances. The convoy's present position dominated the terrain, and it had overwhelming firepower at its command. The recon was more of Trader's way of getting Ryan, Hun and him out of the way, while the crews moved the vehicles and prepared for the exchange of goods.

The trade was supposed to take place before sundown. Raising his binoculars from their neck strap, he could see Zeal's transport wags lined up along one flank of the refinery. Six wags were being loaded with metal drums. They would haul the gas up the road to the meet site. After the swap, Trader planned to hunker down overnight on triple red, then pull his wags out at first light.

The rumble of a powerful engine drew Poet's attention to the barricade. He refocused his binoculars. A single wag drove past the barrier and started up the road. From the high ground clearance and huge knobby tires, he figured it for an off-roader. He could see four people inside, but at the distance he couldn't tell if they were men or women. The driver shifted gears and started to accelerate around the lakeshore. Poet watched the wag as it followed the snaking road, then it disappeared around a deep curve.

He waited, but it didn't reappear around the bend.

Poet lowered the binoculars and listened. He could still hear the engine howling, but it was growing fainter.

It had to have cut off cross-country, he thought. He didn't really consider it a potential threat. It wasn't anywhere near Trader's encampment.

Maybe ten minutes later, something caught his eye as he looked over toward the convoy. On the back slope of the hill, beyond the circled wags, a flock of birds suddenly took flight. Flushed from cover, they wheeled away, screaming, white bellies and underwings flashing in the sun.

Poet grunted like he'd been booted hard in the guts. He saw the panic of the birds and he instantly knew where the people in the off-road wag had disappeared to. Spitting a torrent of curses, he turned and ran to fetch Ryan and Hun.

Chapter Eight

From the rooftop of the MCP, Trader surveyed the deployment of his force. The knoll of the hill fairly bristled with armored wags and weapons, in a display of cannon and rocket, of machine gun and autoblaster that made his lips curl around the soggy stump of his cheroot in a fierce grin. In the center of the defensive circle, the cargo bays of a pair of his largest transport wags stood open; ten of his crew were just finished up the shifting of contents between them in order to make room for all the drums of Virtue Lake gasoline.

"Look okay?" J.B. shouted up to him from the ground.

Trader stepped to the edge of the roof. "Did you mine the blaster crates yet?"

By way of answer, the Armorer tossed up a small black plastic device. Trader caught it between his hands. It was a remote detonator. "What's the range on this?" he asked.

"In the terrain around here," J.B. replied, "I'd say you've got about four miles to make up your mind, one way or another."

"I like it," Trader said. "Let Zeal get all the way back to the ville with his goods and then boom! No more Zeal. Be well worth the price of ten unfired longblasters."

"Folks down in Virtue Lake would probably put up a statue in your honor," J.B. commented.

Samantha, who was standing by War Wag One's starboard door, added, "They'd probably name their squinty-eyed brats after you, too."

"Now, there's a fucking scary thought," Trader muttered

as he slipped the detonator into the side pocket of his desert-camouflage BDU pants.

Shielding his eyes from the sun, and the bits of dust driven by the hot afternoon breeze, he looked downslope, to the area where he'd sent Hun, Ryan and Poet. He'd avoided pairing the two men on a recce of late because the friction between them had escalated. Today's decision had been a hard one; he knew he could lose both men if they couldn't straighten things out, head to head. But he trusted Poet's instincts. He trusted him to look into the younger man and find a way to get past their troubles.

What he really wanted was for Ryan to start listening to and learning from the senior crewman. Poet had much to teach, much of real value to Ryan, and it was different stuff than what he had managed to teach himself. A man with Ryan's grade of reflexes didn't have to rely on his smarts; he ran on autopilot. Acting. Reacting. Which was fine for a second officer, but not a first. What Trader hoped to end up with, somewhere a year or two down the line, was a war captain with Poet's vision and Ryan's strength. An unbeatable combination. But there was only one way for that to happen: both men had to survive and come to an understanding.

Was it worth taking the risk of throwing them together? And chucking a hell-raiser like Hunaker into the mix for good measure, just to stir up the pot a bit more?

Rad-blast if Trader knew.

But things had to change, or sooner or later the conflict between them would infect the rest of the crew. Not that the two of them would start choosing up sides, calling on this one or that one to back them up, but in the end it would be the same as if they had. It was the natural course of things. And once that happened, the smoothly functioning team Trader had worked so hard to assemble would be destroyed.

He had only heard the one shot so far, a scattergun blast,

which had to be from Hun, as Poet was carrying his trusty CAR-15 and Ryan had a scoped Remington bolt gun in .308 caliber.

Trader took this for a positive sign.

Off in the distance, he caught the whine of an overrevving wag engine. The road below was clear. Whoever it was, was going the other way.

CRISSCROSSING BELTS across his bearlike chest strapped Levi Shabazz into the rampaging wag's driver's seat. He drove overland, up a fifteen-foot-wide streambed, all four huge knobby tires spinning as he worked his way through the soft spots, throwing up towering plumes of dirt. He used the stream-side bushes for traction, trammeling them and half climbing up the banks when he thought it would give him some advantage.

As there was no front windshield in the off-road vehicle, he wore goggles to protect his eyes. Except where he'd drawn a clean spot with the ball of his thumb, the lenses of his goggles were caked with powder-fine, ochre-colored dust; the wag's interior—dashboard, seats, floor—was adrift in it. He carried three passengers with him—three of his very best gren chuckers. The objects they were about to chuck lay in a pair of low wooden crates between their boots: dark green canisters with yellow writing, stainless-steel safety rings on the fuse pins, fluorescent yellow bio-hazard symbols spray-painted on sides, top and bottom. The two crates represented about twenty percent of Shabazz's cache of predark nerve agent.

The other men in the wag hung on to roof straps and roll cage with both hands. Like Shabazz, their goggles were caked over. Like Shabazz, their beards and hair were well dusted. They kept their mouths shut behind the strips of rag they had tied over their mouths and noses.

Shabazz disdained such niceties, showing his great, horse-like teeth as he drove, occasionally hawking a gob of spit that was near mud out his side window. He was thinking only about one thing: what the nerve gas was going to do to Trader and his crew. He hadn't actually used it on humans yet. He hadn't had a reason to. Shabazz remembered all those sheep and pigs in the Byrum ville pens, dropping like they'd been brained with three feet of lead pipe. Maybe it was too quick a death for a bastard like Trader, he thought, too merciful.

Nah.

He had looked into the eyes of those dying beasts. He knew they had felt not only terrible pain, but wild panic at their sudden and complete helplessness. He wanted to see that desperate, on-the-verge-of-death look on Trader's face. To see him crapping himself while his arms thrashed and his legs kicked and he fought to keep from eating his own tongue.

The buggy took an unanticipated five-foot drop that, despite the safety belts, slammed the top of Shabazz's head against the metal roof. The impact made him see stars, but he recovered in a fraction of a second. Laughing, he looked over at the man sitting in the bucket seat next to his. And then he laughed some more. The guy had his mouth rag pulled aside and was spitting bright blood into the palm of his hand.

Shabazz followed the streambed around the back side of the ridge, then broke away from the channel, climbing the slope at a shallow angle. He couldn't drive in a straight line; it was too risky. He had to swerve to miss the big rocks or they would tip over the wag and send it rolling down the hill. When he'd circled around behind the hilltop that Trader's convoy sat upon, he stopped the wag and shut off the engine.

"Everybody out!" he ordered.

Three very dusty men lugged the gren crates out of the wag and set them on the ground.

"We going to use all of them?" the man with the split lip asked.

Shabazz looked over his supply. "Better take the lot with us. That way if we need more grens, we got them. Pack them real careful. Make sure you're rattle proof."

The chuckers loaded down their pockets and knapsacks with the dark green cans. Shabazz didn't carry anything except his side arm, a matte finish .44 Magnum Desert Eagle that was holstered under his left armpit, and a long black commando dagger in a forearm sheath.

Shabazz took the lead and started to work his way up to the summit. A hot wind from the plains behind him was blowing across the slope. He wasn't concerned about being seen by the sentries on the back side of the hill. For one thing, four men on foot wouldn't be considered a threat to the convoy. For another, they weren't even carrying any longblasters. They looked more like a bunch of locals out scavenging, maybe for snake meat or cactus fruit. If Trader was worried about anything, he would be worried about the road, about a fleet of wags and sec men coming up it.

Shabazz caught a glimpse of a man standing on a big smooth boulder above. He had an autoblaster slung over his left shoulder, and he raised his hands to his face. He was looking down at them through binoculars.

Shabazz waved.

After a pause, the sentry waved back.

Shabazz got a kick out of that. "See that dim-fuck up there," he said to his men, "he's asking himself, what are those fools doing wandering around down there in this heat?"

"We going to have to chill him?" one of the crew said. "Could be a problem if we do. Others up there might see it."

The trader knew his men were feeling vulnerable, and they had every right to be antsy. They were approaching a vastly superior force from downhill, with scant cover and no long-range weapons.

"No problem. Wave at him. Everybody! Ha! See, there, he waves back."

They advanced up the slope until they were close enough to make out the sentry's clothing: a leather vest, no shirt under it, baggy olive-drab pants, a web belt with extra mags around his hips. As the man lowered his binoculars, they could see the twisted rag headband that kept his shoulder-length brown hair out of his eyes.

Shabazz bent and pretended to examine something on the ground, turning over some small rocks.

"Just do what I do," he told his men, "and keep your heads down."

Thus occupied, the four worked their way to just below the sentry's position. As they approached, he unslung his longblaster and held it at the ready. After a few minutes of watching them grub around in the dirt, he took a seat on the boulder.

Shabazz moved to the foot of the big rock and mopped his forehead with the back of his hand.

"What're you hunting for?" the sentry asked. His long-blaster lay across his lap; his finger no longer rested on the trigger guard.

"After these little white bug eggs," Shabazz told him. "Taste real sugary sweet."

"Eat bug eggs, huh?"

Shabazz reached up and caught hold of the man's ankle, and before he could make a sound, jerked him down over the smooth boulder face. As the sentry came down, Shabazz's right fist came up. In it was clenched the ten-inch-long killing dagger. The man's own weight drove the tri-angular point up through his stomach and into the middle of his heart.

Shabazz left the dagger in him and let the twitching body slump to the ground.

"Quick now!" he said to the other three.

They scrambled the last twenty yards to the hilltop and peered over the edge. In a ring on the barren summit were all of Trader's beautiful wags. A few men and women were walking around inside the perimeter.

The chuckers quickly set out their grens on the slope, then picked one up in either hand.

"Watch the wind," Shabazz warned them. "Throw the grens way upwind, and let the gas drift down over the convoy."

The men did exactly as he ordered, pulling the safeties with their teeth, cocking their arms and tossing the bombs in unison. Nobody from the convoy even noticed when the first three cans hit the ground, or when the second three landed. Only when all six exploded in a string of dull whumps and the gray smoke boiled out of them did Trader's astonished crew realize they were under attack.

Way too late.

Those caught standing outside the wags were swept up in the deadly mist. They staggered a step or two, then pitched onto the ground, clutching at their throats. The gas was so potent they didn't even get out a scream. There were many more crew inside the vehicles, Shabazz knew.

"Give them another round!" he said. "Drop them closer to the wags this time."

The chuckers adjusted their aim. Seconds later, six more green cans exploded, this time at the heart of the encampment. The resulting clouds of gray death partially obscured the vehicles for a moment, then the steady breeze pushed the roiling mass downslope, thinning it rapidly, first into wisps of sparkling vapor, then into nothingness.

Chapter Nine

"I got three haunch of deer meat," Loz told Trader as he read over the list he'd written on a much folded scrap of paper. He scratched his hairy earlobe with an inch-and-a-half-long stub of Number Two pencil. "Not big 'uns, though. Enough for five, mebbe six days if we stretch it real thin with taters and roots and such like."

Trader stood with his back to the wall of the cramped galley, arms folded over his chest. Loz, the cook for War Wag One, was also the food supply master for the whole convoy and, as such, he always knew how much fresh trail meat they had left in stores. It was hard to keep raw meat for long inside the wags. There was no refrigeration, and the air-conditioning systems didn't work often, or well. After a week, the vehicles started to smell like slaughterhouses; a few days more and it got really bad.

"Then we'll be sucking the bones on the last night?" Trader asked.

Loz nodded. "Course we got MREs up the bummocks."

"I hate to break into the quick heats so soon," Trader told him. "It's bad for morale. Crew always expects new meat, and plenty of it, at the start of a circuit."

"Well, there sure ain't no sign of big game around here," Loz said. "Not enough feed on these hillsides to hold them. But come evening, there should be plenty of small stuff for the pot. Rabbit. Bird. Groundhog. I do a real nice jugged groundhog. Leave the head, feet and claws on, for extra flavor. Man, you'll be sopping up the brown juice with your hardtack."

"Long as you take the hair off, I'll eat it," Trader said as he turned to leave.

"Shit, boss," Loz said through a broad grin, "hair's the best part."

Trader exited the galley and headed up the narrow, windowless companionway toward the port-side door. He intended to track down each of his drivers and let them know that he wanted one member of each wag crew to do some hunting for the pot come sundown.

Despite the wind outside, it was hotter than hell inside the MCP. The hilltop was a treeless knob of dirt and rock, so there was no shade to park beneath. Using War Wag One's battery-powered fans was a luxury under any conditions. And in the present situation, Trader knew he didn't want to draw down the level of stored current. If things went sour during the exchange with Zeal, he figured he would need all his available battery power for floodlights and the like. A prolonged firefight could run well into the night.

Always nice to see who you're chilling, he thought.

He was halfway down the corridor when he heard muffled explosions outside, a cluster of them, like a short string of firecrackers popping off under a wet blanket. He didn't know what they were; he knew only what they weren't. They weren't frag grens, blastershots or incoming HE rounds. He spit out the stub of his cheroot and ran for the closest exit. As he did so, he was thinking two things. If it was an attack from Zeal's sec men, he had to contain and repulse it. If it wasn't an attack, he had to keep his crackerjack blaster crews from raining all of hell's fury down on Virtue Lake. The second cluster of explosions, which burst virtually on top of the MCP, convinced him that the convoy was, in fact, under assault.

"J.B.! J.B.!" he shouted.

The Armorer appeared ahead of him, at the far end of the corridor. Right off, Trader could see something was very wrong. J.B. was moving strangely, staggering off balance, like the wag was rocking from side to side. Before Trader could reach him, the man slumped to his knees on the deck, his face going purple, greenish foam ringing his lips.

At the same instant, something tickled deep in Trader's lungs. He tasted battery acid, and his heart began to flutter wildly. Suddenly everything became clear to him. Horribly, horribly clear. Trader turned and rushed back the way he had come, the strength draining from his legs with every step. Gasping, he reached up to the interior wall and slapped the power switch to the wag-to-wag intercom system.

"Hit the fans!" he shouted into the microphone. "It's nerve gas! Hit your fucking fans!"

Whatever the poison was, it wasn't quick.

And it wasn't painless.

As Trader slipped helplessly down the wall to the floor, his whole skin was on fire and his heart felt squashed in his chest, crushed into a space so terribly small that it could barely beat against the surrounding pressure. Likewise, each agonized breath took all his effort; he couldn't even manage to whimper. He labored against the pain and the terror for what seemed like an eternity, then both seemed to miraculously lift.

Trader realized he was looking down on his own body from a vantage point along the ceiling of the corridor. He watched his own legs kick and jerk, and his head bang against the floor, leaving a broad smear of blood.

It didn't matter.

The pain was no longer part of him.

It belonged to the body, the sad, dying physical form to which he felt not the slightest kinship.

When Trader looked up, instead of seeing the MCP's ceiling, he was confronted by a widening, brightly lit aperture, like the canal of birth. Or resurrection.

RYAN, HUN AND POET arrived at the viewpoint as the second volley of gas grens burst amid Trader's circled wags.

Each of them knew instantly what was going on, that the smoke released wasn't CS or CN, announcing an attack on a superior force with a barrage of nonlethal gas would have been nothing short of suicidal. Each of them knew that the wild rumors about Shabazz's stockpile were true. They were too far away from the hilltop to do anything but watch in horror as the nerve agent settled down over the convoy.

"The fuckers!" Hun sputtered in frustration and outrage. "The dirty fuckers!"

Ryan and Poet stared in silence at the swirling gray mass that now hid the circled wags from view.

After a minute or two, the steady breeze had whipped the clouds of gas away from the convoy and dispersed them. Ryan raised his spotting scope to his eye. He could see the bodies on the ground, sprawled, in the center of the circle. So could Poet, who looked through his own binoculars.

"Is anybody alive?" Hun demanded. "Could anybody still be alive?"

Before either of the men could answer, there came a series of three tightly spaced blastershots.

"Signal," Ryan said at once.

"Yeah," Poet agreed, turning his gaze back down the road to the ville. "The all-clear."

Out from the barricade came a line of sec wags. They roared up the road toward the hilltop, and as they did, they honked their horns.

Ryan caught movement around the convoy, four figures quickly advancing from the far side of the knoll.

"It's Shabazz," Ryan said, lowering the scope.

"Let me see," Hun insisted, taking it from him. "Son of a bitch! The bastards are turning over the bodies on the ground, making sure they're chilled."

Actually it was worse than that.

Shabazz and his crew were dragging the fresh corpses to the very center of the ring, then lining them up side by side, like trophies of the hunt.

"They're smiling and laughing," Poet said.

Ryan grabbed his scope back from Hun in time to see the bearded road pirate, Shabazz, wave his men over to War Wag One. They cracked the port-side door, climbed in and started to pull the bodies out. They threw them out the doorway in a heap, like bags of cement.

Ryan saw them throw Trader out. His body was limp when it hit the ground. It didn't move.

Under the circumstances, this was something Ryan expected. But surprise or not, the sight of his dead leader treated like so much garbage was more than he could handle. His anger exploded, and it exploded close to hand.

"You got him chilled!" Ryan snarled at Poet, hurling down the spotting scope. "You gutless sack of shit!"

Poet growled a curse under his breath.

What happened next occurred in the space of a heartbeat. It occurred because the two men involved were both in their prime, both skilled in the deadly arts and hard-focused on chilling. Their handblasters cleared holsters and came up simultaneously. Ryan's thumb locked back the Blackhawk's hammer as Poet dropped the safety on his own side arm.

They were standing close, virtually toe-to-toe. There was no room for either of them to maneuver. No time for one to try to block the other's draw or deflect the aim.

The muzzle of Poet's Colt Government Model came up hard against Ryan's mouth. And as it did so, Ryan jammed the barrel of the Blackhawk under the older man's chin. The one-eyed man smiled, letting the muzzle of the Colt push between his lips and grate against his front teeth.

Point.

Counterpoint.

Two coldhearts locked together—three eyes, unblinking.

Both warriors had drawn their triggers hard up to the break. All that separated either one from oblivion was an ounce or two of pressure on the other man's index finger.

Ryan smelled the familiar sweetness of blaster solvent,

and he tasted its poisonous bitterness. Somewhere, miles away, Hun was yelling something at him. Ryan couldn't make it out. He thought she might have been slugging him in the back, too. Hard to tell. He was that tightly focused and caught up in the moment. What he had in his right fist was what he had wanted all along. An ending. No fear.

Just fury.

And fulfillment.

In Poet's eyes, Ryan saw a landscape of resignation, as flat and smooth as his forehead. The older man was ready to die. Maybe he even wanted it a little bit. Then Poet opened his mouth a crack, and words came out of his throat in a hoarse rush. "As sure as this blaster's in my hand, I will send you to hell, Ryan, but I am not your demon."

Ryan gave the Ruger a savage twist, making the front blade sight cut into the skin of the older man's throat. "What the fuck do you know about *my* demon?" he demanded.

"Only what I said, that it isn't me. It's somebody else."

"Never said it was you," Ryan hissed.

"No, but you let yourself think it. And you acted like it was me from the moment we crossed paths. A man calls things by their true name. Always by their true name."

Ryan blinked. Despite himself, he blinked.

The true name of his demon was Harvey. His own brother Harvey, who, out of greed and envy, had murdered their brother, Morgan, who had cunningly turned their father against Ryan. Harvey, who had slashed out Ryan's left eye and had driven him from family, friends and ancestral home.

Hun moved in closer beside them. She had a deft touch. Her quick, light fingers slipped between hammers and firing pins and locked down, preventing them from firing, for an instant at least. "Enough of this!" she exclaimed. "Stand down, the both of you. We got enough trouble without your blowing each other's brains out for no good reason."

Neither man moved. They stood on a tightrope, face-to-face over the abyss.

"I got no grudge against you, Ryan," Poet said in a voice without a trace of emotion. "Even after this thing here, I got no grudge." He still held the Colt Government Model pressed hard between the younger man's lips. After a pause, he added, "And I will prove it to you."

With that, he slowly drew his arm back and lowered the blaster to his side.

Ryan stared at him, stone faced, with that one icy blue eye. The Ruger was still angled under Poet's chin so as to take off the better part of the back of his head. Ryan didn't move a muscle.

"If you're going to do the deed, for nuke's sake get the fuck on with it," Poet told him after a full minute had passed. "I'm getting tired of standing here, waiting."

Ryan let him wait another fifteen seconds before he dropped the hammer to half cock. As he lowered the weapon, he said, "You were on the last train west, War Captain."

"So were you, Ryan. Window seat."

Hun gave them both hard pushes on the shoulder to get their attention. "Question is, what are we going to do now?"

"I know what I'm going to do," Ryan said, unslinging the bolt-action Remington from his shoulder. He flipped up the lens caps and raised the stock to his cheek. "I'm going to get me some payback."

Before he could acquire a target on the opposite hilltop, Poet reached out and grabbed the heavy barrel six inches from the muzzle crown. He twisted it aside and down.

"All that's going to do is put them onto us in a hurry," he told Ryan. "If any of the others are still alive, we can't help them if we're running to save our own skins."

"And if they're all dead?" Hun asked.

"Then we can't exact the maximum revenge."

Ryan reslung the Remington .308. Like it or not, he could see the man had a point.

That made two.

Chapter Ten

Trader came to, gasping, as he was hit in the face by a bucket of water. Not only did he have the worst headache of his life, but it also felt like someone had been trying to stove in all his ribs.

And someone still was.

"Guess who?" Shabazz said as he reared back a leg and booted him another good one in the side.

Groaning, Trader struggled up on one elbow. He shook the dizziness from his head and forced his eyes into focus. His heart sank at what he saw. It looked like everyone in the crew but him was dead. Bodies still lay all over the inside of the convoy circle. Zeal's uniformed sec men and Shabazz's crew of road pirates were busily going through their pockets, stripping them of valuables.

The fat sec man hunkered over Sam had another idea in mind. He had pulled her T-shirt up over her collarbone and was mauling her bare breasts with one hand while with the other he tried to get the waistband of her fatigue pants undone. He was so preoccupied with his own animal satisfaction, he didn't seem to care who was watching, and Trader could tell that the tub of guts wasn't going to stop until he got everything he wanted.

"Ain't all of them dead," Shabazz said, noticing where Trader was looking. "At least not yet, anyway."

The fat sec man had to have been squeezing Sam really hard, because she woke up with a start. And she came out of unconsciousness fighting and kicking. The sudden violence caught her molester by surprise. Like the other females in Trader's battle crew, the Panther was no frail sister. If she wasn't stronger than most men, she was a hell of a lot faster. And she knew instinctively, without mulling the pros and cons over in her mind, exactly what needed to be done. First she lashed out with a vicious flat-footed left leg kick to the fat man's groin that paralyzed him, gape mouthed, in his squatting position. Then, before he could stagger back out of range, she followed up with the knockout: a solid snapkick with her stronger leg to the point of the chin.

Her boot made a funny sound as it connected with that flab-shrouded jut of bone. It sounded just like a dry tree limb breaking underfoot.

The fat man's chin snapped up, pointing at the sky; his thunder thighs caved, splitting wide apart as his flabby butt dropped. He hit the ground flat on his back, and as he did, his legs slowly straightened in short, twitching movements; his arms remained limp and still. He lay there with his mouth hanging open. There was some blood, leaking from his lips, but not much. He wasn't breathing as far as Trader could see. His bugged-out eyes stared up at the sun.

It was all over so fast, it left the baron's sec men and Shabazz's crew just standing there, gawking.

Sam was already up on her feet, jerking down her T-shirt to cover herself. Then she had her hands up, her feet moving, eager to kick some more ass if she got the opportunity.

"Grab that crazy bitch!" Shabazz shouted.

In a rush from all sides at once, the sec men overwhelmed the black woman. They held her arms pinned behind her back and fastened manacles to her ankles and a wide metal collar around her throat, all three joined by short lengths of chain. Trader had seen that type of restraint before. They were used to transport slaves to market and to lead the condemned to the gallows. Sam was then forced to her knees with blaster muzzles against her head. She grimaced in pain.

Trader watched Shabazz walk over to where the fat man lay like a beached whale. It was plenty hard to stay alive with a busted neck. Especially a break right up around the jawbone. Trader squinted hard at the body and decided that he still had a little bit of life left, after all. The blood-flecked lips moved, opening and closing. No sound came out.

Shabazz drew his Desert Eagle, aimed at the man's up-turned face and, without a word, fired once. There was a tremendous boom and flash; the head flew apart, and chunks of skull and brains pelted the shins of the assembled pirates. There was little if anything left of the fat man from the shoulders up, just a smoking crater in the earth.

"Now, get this stinking pile of nukeshit out of the road," Shabazz snarled at the baron's sec men.

"Nice stroke, Sam!" Trader shouted over to the woman, who despite her predicament and her discomfort, immediately brightened.

Shabazz pressed the Desert Eagle's muzzle to the top of Trader's head. "Won't have no more of that hoo-ha, now," he warned. "Any of your people act up from now on, and I'll start chilling. Won't be no fooling around. Just chilling. You understand?"

Trader nodded.

Shabazz and two of his crew jerked Trader to his feet. He couldn't have stood without their help. Before he completely regained his senses, they had clapped an iron collar around his neck and manacles around his ankles. As with Sam, all three iron bands were connected by lengths of stout chain. The chain sections were made short on purpose, so a captive couldn't fully straighten or run far without falling on his or her face.

"Well, well," Shabazz said, stepping back to admire his handiwork. "The mighty Trader ain't so rad-blasted mighty now, is he?"

Trader said nothing. He was looking over the bodies of his crew and was grateful to see most of them were stirring now, either on their own, or thanks to kicks or punches from the enemy.

Most, but not all.

There were a dozen or so stretched out to one side who weren't moving, and nobody was bothering to kick them awake. To Trader, it looked like the corpses were already going stiff. There was green foam around their open mouths, and their tongues were all swollen and sticking out black.

Because Trader always handpicked his crews, he knew all their names, knew if they liked to joke or if they were cold fish, knew if they had families waiting for them back at the cavern. At that instant, his sense of failure was personal and complete. This disaster was, ultimately, his responsibility. No sooner had the feeling of defeat surfaced than he shut it down, slammed the door on it. It was of no help to those who were still living. He had to keep his mind open, alert for the opportunity to make things right.

While he looked on, the baron's sec men clapped the chains on every surviving member of his crew, then they forced everyone into a line. J.B. got shoved in behind him. Ahead of him was Samantha. The sec men linked up all the neck collars, running a long, single length of heavy chain through the iron rings welded at their fronts.

When this was done, and the sec men had moved away, J.B. said softly to Trader's back, "We lost eleven."

"Mebbe they're the lucky ones," Sam said.

Trader ignored the remark. Shabazz's crew was splitting up and piling into the doors of his wags, which in the confusion and suddenness of the gas attack hadn't been sealed. Nor had their external mines been armed. One by one, the pirates started up their engines. What pissed him off most of all was the sight of Levi Shabazz's hairy head sticking out of War Wag One's driver's compartment vent hatch. The bastard was in control of everything he valued.

Under a heavy hand, the MCP's engines roared to life. The exuberant Shabazz revved the wag hard and long, holding it at redline until Trader was sure it was going to throw a piston. It didn't, though. Shabazz shifted it into low and drove it alongside the line of prisoners. When he reached the head of the line, he braked and shouted to his crew, "Hook them up!"

Two of the road pirates grabbed the first man in the line and connected his neck collar to the rear bumper of the MCP. Counting Trader, there were thirty-three captives in tow.

The sec men shot their blasters in the air as War Wag One started to lumber down the road. The chain jerked tight, making Trader and the others stumble forward, forcing them into lockstep behind.

Over his shoulder, Trader could hear J.B. cursing. He let loose with an unbroken string of expletives as they staggered in the cloud of dust and exhaust thrown up by the MCP.

He stole a quick glance behind. All the other commandeered wags were following.

"J.B.!" he growled. "J.B.!"

The swearing stopped. "Yeah, Trader."

"Still got your watch?"

"Yeah."

"How long until the internal boobies blow?"

Sam, hearing this, looked over her shoulder with wide eyes.

"We got a little more than three hours before they kick off."

"Be plenty dark by then," Sam said.

"No way, Panther," J.B. said. "When those charges of mine go off, it's going to look like dawn."

"What about the externals?" Trader asked him. This to confirm his own belief.

"They aren't set, far as I know."

"Then we've got to figure out a way to arm at least a couple of them."

"Going to be tough," Sam interjected, "the way things stand now."

"Pass the word," Trader told both of them. "Send it up and down the line. Anybody who gets the chance should try to trip one of the switches, if they can do it without being seen."

It took the better part of an hour for the column of prisoners and booty to creep down to the outskirts of Virtue Lake, an hour with no water, amid choking dust, under an afternoon sun that was ragingly hot. The line of wags approached the barricade with a mad honking of horns.

Because he was being towed in the middle of the chain gang, the only time Trader could see ahead was when the MCP angled around a bend in the road, and then only if the breeze blew the dirt cloud to one side. When this happened, he could make out a large gathering of people at the entrance to the ville, people waiting for them to arrive.

The assembled crowd sent up a rousing cheer as the MCP crept through the gate, then started to zigzag through the obstacle course.

The pelting of captives began almost at once. Yelling and hooting, the mob started to throw rocks and garbage. As Trader covered his head with his arms to keep from being coldcocked, something cold, brown and nasty splattered against his leg. From the stink of it, it was fresh pig shit. He saw the celebrants had plastic buckets of the stuff lined up at intervals along the parade route, and they were reaching in bare-handed for gobs to throw.

"Chill them! Chill them!" someone shouted.

Trader could see that not all of the townspeople were participating in the abuse. In fact very few of the assembled folk were actually throwing stuff. Most stood silently behind the active ones, watching in silence. The active ones also appeared to be the best dressed and the best fed.

Trader figured that they were the ones destined to share in the spoils of the robbery, the family members of the sec men and other Virtue Lake bigwigs. As for the mute, ragged mob standing behind them, he could only guess that they had been made to turn out at blasterpoint, or that it gave them some small comfort to see others in a worse plight than they were.

It was a miracle that no one in his crew was felled by one of the flying stones. Rocks whizzed past Trader's head and hurtled into the crowd of tormentors on the other side of the road, which made them duck and so spoiled their aim.

When War Wag One reached the minimalls with its human chain, it pulled into the left-hand parking lot, drove all the way to the end and stopped. The wags immediately behind followed it in and pulled up close before stopping, as well. Because there were so many vehicles, some were left out on the road, idling.

Shabazz jumped onto the roof of the MCP and shouted to the drivers directly behind him, "You park here."

Then through cupped hands, he called to the wags still standing in the road, "Park in the other lot!" He waved them in that direction.

While those drivers turned their wags into the mall opposite, the ones who had pulled in behind the MCP shut off their engines. Then they exited the vehicles and slammed the doors shut.

Trader figured it was probably now or never when it came to arming the booby traps. Stuck in the middle of the line, there was no way he or J.B. or Sam could reach the nearest wags. They would have had to drag thirty other people along with them. The only person who really had a chance was the guy at the back end of the file. Because of his position, he had some freedom to move wide to the right or the left.

His name was Betters. He was a sawed-off little guy who talked in a funny high voice, real squeaky and hoarse, like someone had his balls torqued down in a bench vise. Triple-mean bastard, though, because he had taken so much shit all his life about the way he talked. Betters didn't hesitate when he saw his opportunity. He hopped to the right and dived under the nearest war wag, chain and all.

"Get that stupe out from under there!" Shabazz bellowed.

It took a minute or two for his crew to accomplish this because Betters had himself a good hold on the wag's undercarriage, and because the crew members chained up next to him did everything they could to slow down the process. In the end, they had to pull him out by his heels.

Betters stood up to his full height and looked over at Trader, not smiling with his mouth, which was a grim little slit, but smiling with his eyes. The booby was armed.

The blastershot came out of nowhere. It came so unexpectedly it even made Trader flinch. It took poor Betters in the middle of the chest. A big puff of dust rose from his shirtfront, and a fist-sized gob of purple shit blew out the middle of his back. The man dropped dead on the spot.

"Cut him loose from the others," Shabazz said, lowering the lever action Marlin carbine.

He turned to Trader and said, "I told you no more acting up, otherwise there'd be chilling."

Trader watched the sec men as they uncoupled Betters's corpse from the line. Mean little shit. Hard as granite rock, right down to his core. Not a man to grieve or shed tears for. A man to be proud of, though. One of Shabazz's crew had squatted, halfheartedly looking under the wag, where Betters had crawled.

The pirate straightened almost immediately. Like his boss, he probably figured the dead guy didn't have time to do any damage to the vehicle. Hell, he didn't have anything but his bare hands to work with.

"Keep a close watch on the wags," Shabazz told his drivers. "Keep the gaudy-house drunks from crawling on them or in them."

With that, he climbed back in the MCP's driver's compartment and pulled the monster wag out of the lot and back on the road. The line of humans, less one, followed like a living tail.

About a quarter mile farther on, Shabazz pulled up next to a hut made of corrugated sheet metal, stuck his head out the driver's vent and started to holler at the four men sitting on inverted five-gallon buckets in the strip of shade. They got up, but were in no hurry to do his bidding.

"Is that it?" Sam said, pointing at the rows of barred grates set into the ground. "Is that the jail?"

The jail facilities of Virtue Lake consisted of nothing more than a series of rectangular pits, six by six, hacked into the bedrock. There were about fifteen of them, all roofed over with iron bars. Inside there was no shelter from the sun, except early in the morning or late afternoon, no shelter from the chem rain, if it decided to pour.

One by one, the four jailers unlocked and opened the doors to half the cells, then hauled out the prisoners and let them go.

Dazed and weak-kneed, the freed men wandered off in the direction of the shantytown. There were no women in the pits, Trader noticed. He guessed female offenders were forced to serve out their sentences elsewhere, unless they were too old to attract even the blind drunks.

The jailers then unhooked Trader and his crew from the MCP and started pulling the heavy chain through their collars. As the crew members were released, the jailers used the butts of their shotguns to push them into the pits. The drop was no more than six feet. Trader could just stand up inside. The shorter J.B., who stood beside him, had plenty of headroom. In one corner of their cell was an overflowing shit bucket.

Shabazz sneered down at Trader through the open door. "Now, don't go and make yourself too comfortable," he said. "You won't have these fine accommodations for long." Then he booted the cell door hard over, and the bars clanged shut.

After Shabazz turned away, J.B. did a quick survey of the walls and floor.

"Well?" Trader said as the Armorer straightened.

"Good news is the rock isn't that hard. Bad news is, we can't use the plastique I got tucked into my bootsole."

"Why's that?"

"If I blow the bars above, the side walls will cave in on us. They'll bury us alive. Not to mention the fact that a chunk of C-4 big enough to do the door will probably take our heads off, too. There's no place to hide from the blast in here."

Trader glared at the bars just over his head and then at the narrow walls. None of his crew was stupid enough to try it. Not while they still thought they had a chance to survive. "All the cells looked the same to me," he said.

J.B. nodded. "Me, too."

"Then nobody's going to be able to blow the doors."

"Not and live to tell the tale."

"How long do we have on the internal charges?"

J.B. looked at his watch. "We got one hour and forty-nine minutes until all the wags blow."

Chapter Eleven

Baron Lundquist Zeal was soundly napping when the wags blew. The thunderous boom sat him bolt upright in his huge, sheet-tangled bed. Heart thudding, he pushed aside the naked women who had been dozing with him, and who were now also startled wide awake. His first thought was for the refinery, that an enormous blowout of some kind had occurred.

He raced barefoot across the floor of his master bedroom, pausing only to snatch up his spikes and fur robe. As he ran through the big house, he cinched the waist tight with its matching fur belt. By the time he reached the front porch, his sec men already had the stockade gates open and his wag waiting there, idling for him.

"What was it?" Zeal demanded as he hurtled down the steps. "Was it the refinery?"

"Nah, something blew over by the gaudies," said the man holding open the rear passenger's door of the wag.

Zeal knew the only thing with explosive potential over by the gaudies was Trader's captured convoy. "Let's go!" he shouted at the driver as he piled into the back seat.

The baron's personal transportation was a passionate pink 1997 Lincoln Towncar, with side and rear window glass replaced with one-inch tempered steel plate. The front windshield was likewise protected, except for the driver's ob slit. Armored skirts covered all the wheel wells, defending the tires from everything but rocket attack and cannon fire. What with all the added weight it carried, the Towncar was a sluggish performer on the uphill climb to the big house.

But this trip was all in the other direction. The Lincoln fairly roared down into the heart of Virtue Lake.

When Zeal jumped from the wag, he was immediately surrounded by a phalanx of sec men with their weapons drawn. He roughly shoved them to one side and stepped forward so he could view the damage. He saw at once that one of the small war wags had exploded, taking with it the transport parked alongside. The combined blast effect was devastating.

Ground zero had been the middle of the minimall parking lot, which was now marked by a huge, smoking crater. Ninety feet away, two of the storefronts were completely demolished, turned into nothing more than heaps of smoldering debris. All the other facades were scorched and windowless. There were human bodies and body parts strewed far and wide.

"What the hell happened here?" Zeal demanded.

No one dared answer.

Then Levi Shabazz stepped up beside him. "Trader must've mined his fucking wags. One of my drivers probably touched this off by accident."

Zeal looked at the captured vehicles that surrounded them, and his eyes suddenly went wide.

"You mean they're all mined?"

"Most likely."

"Can't we deactivate them?"

"Mebbe," Shabazz said. "Mebbe not. Trader's no triple stupe. He's got to have five backups for every detonator we find. And it only takes one to make things go boom."

Zeal turned to his sec men. "I want everyone cleared out of this area at once. Everyone! I want an armed perimeter set up around the gaudies. Rope off the whole area. No one is to enter without my permission. If anyone tries, chill them. No warning shots. Aim to kill. Do you understand?"

Heads nodded.

Before Shabazz could slip away with the others, Zeal

grabbed hold of his shirtfront and pulled him up until they were almost chest to chest. "This doesn't make me happy," he said.

The baron's mascara had badly smeared, blurring on his eyelids, turning the sockets into black pits. The lipstick on his mouth had likewise spread far and wide, and the makeup on his cheeks and chin had dried out and begun to flake. In other words, he was a perfect fright to behold.

"This doesn't make me happy, at all," he repeated. "Why the hell did you bring Trader's wags into my ville if you thought they might be boobied?"

"I didn't think that," Shabazz said. "Who would? I mean, he's riding in the goddamn things himself. Got to be out of his mind to run a booby-trapped convoy on these roads."

"I'd say Trader knew exactly what he was doing," Zeal replied. "Now that we have his wags, we can't move them a foot, let alone use them to reach our objective. If they all blow, it could level the whole town. The way things stand now, my gaudies are out of business. No telling what it took to set off the first blast. Mebbe a goddamn sneeze. I can't have drunks and jolt-heads wandering around a fleet of live bombs. I'm going to have some real trouble if the gaudies don't come on-line in short order. That's how I keep my work force happy."

"You could always set them up someplace else, till we get this straightened out."

"Line the mattresses up in the street? Serve the white lightning from the curb? Somehow it doesn't seem quite the same to me. The only thing we can do is make Trader disarm the mines."

"You don't make a man like Trader do anything," Shabazz said. "He's going to want something in return. Something big."

"Like?"

"Like his freedom. Mebbe all his wags back. He's the

one down in the shit-hole, and the fucker still has us by the short hairs.''

Beneath the peeling makeup, Zeal's face darkened. ''Mebbe not. Mebbe he doesn't know what he really wants until we show it to him. Come on, let's take a ride.''

The two got into the Lincoln and, at the baron's direction, headed for the jail with three sec wags in close pursuit. The entourage stopped alongside the Trader's cell. Zeal and Shabazz got out and looked into the barred pit.

A grinning face stared back up at them, striped with shadows.

''Somehow I figured you two would be around right sharpish,'' Trader said. ''You ready to deal?''

''Get him out of there!'' Zeal told the jailers.

The cage was promptly opened, and Trader was unceremoniously pulled from the cell.

''Well, what's it going to be, gentlemen?'' he said. ''Your money or your lives?''

''I'm not talking serious business out here in the open,'' Zeal replied. ''Get in the back of my wag.''

They headed for the open door of the rear compartment. As Trader started to get in, Zeal stopped him with a hand on the shoulder. ''Take off those boots of yours first,'' he said. ''I don't want what they got on them stinking up my wag.''

Trader looked at what was caught up in the tread of his boot sole. ''Oops,'' he said. ''Wonder who that belonged to?''

''Just ditch the boots.''

Trader obliged and climbed in the wag in his bare feet.

After Shabazz had shut the door behind them, Zeal said, ''We've got a proposition for you.''

''And that is?''

''We know you've got your wags mined. We can't move them. And we need them for a big job.''

Shabazz was an echo. ''Yeah, a real big job.''

"So that's the reason you had me swing by Virtue Lake?" Trader said. "You don't want my cargo. You want my wags."

"You've heard of Spearpoint, of course," the baron stated.

Trader's eyes narrowed. "Everybody's heard of it."

"Well, we've found it."

This put the great Trader at a momentary loss for words. When he recovered, he said, "You mean, you *think* you've found it?"

"I'm sure enough to bet everything I've got on it," the baron said. "Everything you've got, too."

"Where is it?" Trader asked. "Is it close?"

"Close enough. How'd you like to be in for a full tenth share of the proceeds?"

"In return for which," Trader said, "you want me to turn my crews and wags over to you?"

"All we need are skeleton crews," Shabazz told him. "My people will do the rest."

"We need guarantees that the wags won't blow up on us," Zeal said.

Trader lifted his right foot, hooking the heel over the top of his left thigh and started to look at the horny hunk of callus on his big toe. "Must be some near-nuclear shit to cut through between here and Spearpoint," he said, "otherwise you could do the job with your own wags. But you don't have anywhere near the firepower, do you?"

"What's your answer?" Zeal asked.

"I'm going to need more than a tenth share," Trader said, using the edge of his fingernail to scrape some of the dead skin away. He blew it off onto the Lincoln's rug.

Shabazz glowered at Zeal.

"How much, then?" the baron asked.

"My wags, my score" was his terse answer. "I'll give you two a total of twenty percent off the top. No more. Rest is mine."

Shabazz went ballistic. "I'm going to take this piece of shit outside and gut him!" he snarled. "And after I pull out his innards, I'm going to loop them around his neck and strangle him to death!"

Zeal tried to calm the man. "Easy, easy," he soothed, "we need to do some negotiating here."

"What are you talking about?"

"If we explain things to Trader in a way he can understand, mebbe he will change his mind."

"Face it, Zeal," Trader said, "you can barely negotiate your way out of a latrine."

"How about this for a negotiation?" the baron snapped back. "I pull the rest of your crew out of the cells. I take them and you over to the refinery, where I have some special motivational equipment already set up. All I need is an hour or so and I'll adjust your fucking attitude."

"It's already adjusted," Trader told him. "I'll make it thirty percent. That's my final offer."

"You don't know when to quit, do you?" Shabazz said.

"No, I never quit."

"We'll see about that," the baron promised. "I'm going to give you my special tour. A real eye-opener."

Chapter Twelve

The sun had already begun to drop low in the sky as Ryan, Poet and Hunaker descended the far side of the hill, out of sight of the ville, with the goal of infiltrating Virtue Lake and freeing wags and captives. The choice of route had been Poet's, and though Ryan had problems with it, he hadn't been able to come up with a safer, faster alternative.

Because they were on foot, and because the only road terminated in a barricade and what amounted to a firing squad of sec men, they couldn't go in that way. To circle behind the ville would have taken them the better part of the night. The best way in, as Poet had explained, was over the dry lake bed. And they didn't dare wait until dark to make a start because of the hazards of traveling over an unfamiliar landscape full of sink holes, tar pits and the devil knew what else. They had to take advantage of the last of the daylight, both for safe movement and for cover. Poet had then pointed out something that Ryan had already considered—if they headed toward Virtue Lake from the west, the setting sun would help hide them from anyone who happened to be looking in that direction.

One by one, they shinnied down a steep gully that emptied onto the lake's silty floor.

Ryan moved into the lead, without hesitation. The two men had agreed on the division of responsibility, based on experience and skill. Discussion of the matter had been unnecessary. The man with the best eyes, or in this case the best eye, always took point. Ryan set off across the flatland, quickly crossing the stretches of open ground, slowing when he came to some cover.

There wasn't much growing in the lake bed, mostly needle grass, in scattered clumps, which he took great pains to avoid. The nests of fine spikes were as tough as tempered steel, and if stepped on by a careless traveler, could easily pass through the sole of a boot and into the foot. A deep-tissue infection was almost guaranteed. Such an infection meant amputation or death, and more often than not, the former merely preceded the latter by a matter of days. There were other weeds, as well, also widely spaced. Some were noxious smelling, meaty like unwashed humanity or an abattoir; others smelled so strongly of licorice that it made the breath catch in the throat. None of the wild plants were taller than waist high.

As far as Ryan could see, there were no trees of any kind in the lake bed. Probably because the crude oil that had leaked from the pumping wells had poisoned the soil for large vegetation. There were ponds of black, tarry liquid everywhere he looked. The wells and their toolsheds made up the only real cover to be had, and they, too, were widely separated.

Ryan estimated the distance to the edge of the ville at two miles as the crow flew, which was how he led the way. He knew a zigzag course would increase their chances of being seen. It was better to come straight on, as much as possible. A straight-on target was much harder to pick out against the steady glare of sunset. He lined up his course well to the right of the refinery's tallest smokestacks. Flames gushing from a shorter rooftop pipe glowed orange against a landscape backdrop now tinted with rose.

As he entered another stand of waist-high weeds, he heard sudden, violent scuffling sounds ahead, a shrill squeak, then silence.

The three companions froze in midstep. Ryan pointed in the direction of the last sound, then reached down to his leg and unsheathed his panga. Whoever, whatever it was, there would be no blasterfire because it would give them away.

Stealthily the trio advanced, and when they were very close, Ryan signaled for them to fan out. Then he crouched low and parted the weeds with the point of his panga.

In a tiny clearing in the middle of the weed patch, a figure hunkered over a freshly killed rabbit. The man was nearly naked, his body covered with dirt, his hair matted against his head, his long beard a tangle of grease and burrs. Great weals, lash marks, festered along his shoulders and buttocks. Ryan watched as he slashed at the carcass with a sharp piece of broken glass, splitting the hide around the neck, stripping it down around the back feet. He then began to eat like a wild animal. Taking the raw flesh between his teeth, he hacked it free with the edge of the glass, and bolted it down without chewing. He made soft, whimpering sounds as he attacked the meat.

Ryan waited until the others were in position before he stood and stepped forward, his panga at the ready. The man blinked at him in astonishment, lowering the carcass, his mouth, chin and beard smeared with blood, then he turned to run. He ran right into Hun and Poet. Dropping the rabbit at once, he raised the piece of glass to defend himself.

"No yelling," Ryan said in a soft, calm voice. "No yelling, and we'll let you live."

"Then you're not some of Zeal's sec men?" the man croaked.

"Not likely," Hun replied with a snort. "Who the fuck are you?"

The wild man tucked his glass knife into the side of his greasy loincloth, leaving the rag-bound handle sticking out. "I'm called Paste," he said. And to further explain who and what he was, he lifted the stiff mass of hair that was his beard, showing them the iron collar still welded shut around his neck. "Baron had me for a slave in his refinery. Meant to work me to death, like all the others. I seen that part coming.''

Paste looked hungrily at the dead rabbit on the ground and made another whimpering noise.

"Go ahead," Ryan said.

The ex-slave fell on the carcass. He gave the meat, which had fallen in the sand, a perfunctory dust-off before he went at it, tooth and nail. In two minutes he had the thing stripped of flesh down to the coiled bowels. Ryan was pretty sure he planned on eating the guts, too. The smell in the clearing was already ripe; it didn't need the added aroma of rabbit shit. He stopped Paste before he could rip into the intestines and said, "So you escaped from the refinery?"

The man let a coil of greenish gray bowel slip from between his teeth and burped resonantly.

"Got away two weeks ago, by my best reckoning," he said. "Been hiding out here in the lake bed ever since. Hoping to stow away on some wags hauling gas out of here. When I saw that big convoy pull in earlier, figured I had my big chance. Then the baron went and captured it.''

"Our convoy," Poet said.

"Took your people away, too," Paste stated. "Took them for slaves. I seen that."

"Where might he have taken them?" Hun asked.

"Well, there's the jails for a start. Over past the gaudies. Bunch of holes dug in the ground with bars over them. If some of your crew is female, and under forty, most likely they'll spend some time in the gaudies, on their backs or bellies, but sooner or later all of them will end up in the refinery, which means they'll be dead in their chains in mebbe a week, depending on the work detail they draw. Some chill off even faster than that.''

"How did they get you?" Ryan asked.

Paste scratched his chin, then shook his head in disgust. "Truth of it is, I come here willingly. I was tired of scraping the rad-blasted dirt to grow my own food and half starving for all my sweat. I believed what I was told about easy work, full plates and good wages. Walked right into a death camp, smiling from ear to ear.''

''Did they send sec men out here after you?'' Poet asked.

''If they did, I never saw them. You know, I don't think they even noticed I was gone. Things are kind of loose in the refinery. Hundreds of workers inside. Nobody in charge knows their names. It's always 'Hey, you!' Why bother learning a crew's names if they're going to be dead so quick? There's lots of noise and confusion, too. All the time, men and women keeling over from the heat, or getting burned, or crushed, or legs cut off, and the bosses just make the other workers shovel them to one side to die. Let them bleed out over the sewer grates because it don't make such a mess that way. Some people lose their will to live, right off. Eyes go dim. Stop eating. Won't talk. Others think they can survive if they take advantage of their fellow slaves, make them do the hardest work while they slack off, steal their bread and water when they're too tired to eat. Can't blame them, though. Guys like that are just trying to make the best of a bad situation. Trying to come out on top. Me, I seen it right off that there was no way to win. I told myself that the refinery would grind me up and spit me out, dead. Only thing to do was escape, even if I got chilled trying.''

''How'd you get away?'' Ryan asked.

''Me and this other guy named Harris were chained side by side by the ankles, working on some leaky steam pipes at the lake end of the refinery. They always pair you up like that when the job is real dangerous. They put the neck collar and ankle chains on and hook you to someone else so it's harder to run. And if one person tries to make a break, both get whipped half to death.

''Anyway, like I said, Harris and me were seeing to these cracked steam pipes. Everything in the place is falling apart. It was real hot work, and with the steam pouring out it was hard to see what we were doing. We were trying not to get too badly scalded, had rags wrapped over our hands. Then I don't know, something just blew up. I think Harris touched something he shouldn't have. I know I didn't. The both of us got blown right off our feet, and we landed ten feet away from the pipes on our backs.

"I looked over at Harris and there was this hole in his chest. I mean big." Paste showed them the full span of his hand. "He must've got nailed by a three-inch iron plug from one of the steam pipes. Blood poured out of him in a river, and his legs were kicking. Something came over me as I watched him dying. Right quick I lay on top of him and smeared his blood all over my shirt. I put it on my face, too. Then I lay back beside him and pretended to be dead. The bosses came by, took one look at us and told some other workers to drag the bodies off. They didn't even bother to check to make sure we were both hurt. They unhooked the ankle chains. They always unhook the chains before they move the bodies. It's easier that way. They took me by the wrists and ankles and slung me over in a corner on a pile of oily rags. They threw Harris on top of me. I waited until no one was around, then I lit out the big old hangar doorway as fast as I could, ran down to the lake bed and hid myself. I've been keeping low during the day, coming out at dusk to hunt for food. You're the first folks I've seen up close in two weeks."

Ryan slid the panga back into its sheath. "We're going into the ville to rescue our wags and our crew."

"And deliver some biggish payback for the ones Zeal had chilled up on the hilltop," Hun added.

"If you come along with us and show us the way to our friends," Poet told the wild man, "you'll get your ride out of here—my word on it. You'll ride in style."

Paste's face took on a tortured expression as he weighed the pros and cons, then he shook his head. "Nope. Won't do it. I don't never want to see the inside of that place again. I don't care if I die out here on this dry lake. Starve. Die of thirst. Snakebite. Anything's better than the tank. And if they catch me as a runaway, that's where they'd put me, straight off.''

"What's the tank?" Hun asked.

Paste seemed to draw into himself, head lowered, shoulders huddled, back slumped. He refused to explain.

"We've got to be going," Poet said after a moment, "before we lose all the light. You take your rabbit and go, too. And you keep an eye on the road. When you see us rolling out of the ville in our wags, you come running. You done us a favor, Paste. You'll get your ride out of here. You just tell them Poet said so."

Without a word, the wild man scooped up the remains of the carcass and vanished through the weeds.

"Sad bastard," Hun said. "Eating raw meat and guts like that. Think he's crazy from what he's been through?"

"Hard to say," Poet said. "As to the raw rabbit, he don't dare risk a fire out here, even if he had the wherewithal to start one."

"Yeah, I guess that's right. But still, there was something in his eyes that made me think he wasn't all there. Like he'd stripped the gears inside his head."

"Sun's going," Ryan said, putting an end to the discussion. He took the lead again.

A quarter mile from Virtue Lake, the light started to turn purple and soft. The dancing orange fires in the shantytown and the fires from the refinery were reflected, along with the last of the sunset, off the glass windows of the bosses' houses on the hill, and off the tall, dominating marquee of the Quick-Way Market. The crosswind had stopped, and Ryan could smell the ville, its petro stink, its human stink. The baritone rumble of the plant was a constant droning in his ears.

They moved on a dead run the last three hundred yards. The slave shanties drifted all the way down to the edge of the dry lake, onto a dusty beach. They were a shambling mess of dwellings, most sharing walls, if not roofs. There was no thoroughfare between them, just a narrow, winding footpath, down the middle of which a sewage ditch had been hacked. It was really nothing more than a shallow latrine as there was no extra water to push the excreta into the lake bed. As Ryan led his companions up the path, he saw open rubbish fires here and there. A few laborers were huddled around them, even though the evening was very warm and still. They looked over as Ryan, Poet and Hun passed. They didn't look for long, though. The sight of the holstered blasters and shoulder-slung longblasters made the slaves avert their eyes. Blasters always meant trouble. Maybe they thought they were a trio of sec men or three coldheart robbers.

At any rate, no one shouted a challenge.

Perhaps, Ryan thought as he moved quickly on, life started to mean too damned much when you could feel it leaking out of your body day by day. You could see yourself getting weaker and weaker. See the muscle shrinking, see the skeleton showing around the eyes and cheeks. Death crawling up on you like a chill wind. Maybe the slaves needed a warming fire of burning plastic and old greasy rags because the fire in their bellies had gone out.

At that moment, Ryan's own inner fires were raging. If he felt no personal loss for the dead members of the crew, he felt a sense of violation at the other crimes: the theft of the wags and the imprisonment of the surviving crew. And above all, taking Trader hostage.

He no longer blamed Poet for the disaster on the hilltop. Or himself, either. After all, even Trader, who knew practically shit-all about everything, hadn't seen the gas attack coming. The only way to have avoided it would have been for them to pack up and roll the convoy out, turn tail and run. And that was something Ryan had refused to consider then, just as he refused to consider it now.

He was fairly certain that Shabazz couldn't have used up

all of his nerve gas in the assault; he had counted only six grens popping off. Damned things came in crates of twenty, which meant the pirate trader had to have the rest of his supply close at hand, probably hidden somewhere in Virtue Lake. There was no defense against the gas, no antidote to the neurotoxin. Ryan figured the strong wind blowing at the time of the attack was the only reason everyone in the crew hadn't been chilled. It pushed the gas away from the convoy before lethal doses of it could seep into the wags.

Trader had come across caches of the stuff before in hardened bunkers. Ryan knew because he'd been with him when the gas grens were found. Trader always made sure the bunkers were covered back up, real carefully. Handling predark nerve grens was a risky business. After sitting around for a century, the canisters sometimes leaked, and the chemicals inside often became unstable. If there was a leak or a blowout, you could be dead before you knew it.

Even so, Trader could have found plenty of buyers for the weapons. But he said there was some merchandise that should never see the light of day. He said there weren't enough people in Deathlands as it was. And those that were here, were only just now crawling up out of the muck and ruin of post-skydark. Trader reckoned that chemical weapons could drive their heads back under again, maybe forever.

Ryan never thought about things like "forever." The present always seemed to put more than enough on his plate.

On either side of him were walls made of tattered, clear plastic sheeting. He looked into dirt-floored private chambers so small that a man had to curl up in a ball in order to lie down. There was more than one man curled up in them, too. Piles of workers, in fact, sleeping the sleep of the nearly dead until the blast of the refinery horn roused them to make their next shift.

What kept them all here? he wondered. Not the fence across the road. Shit, they could bypass it and light out over

the lake as Paste had. Not the blasters of the sec men.
Though the baron's thugs were well armed, there weren't
enough of them to hold back a mob this size. It wasn't the
chains, either, because most of the workers weren't hobbled
with manacles. It wasn't even the rad-blasted desert landscape that surrounded the ville. Four days' walk would put
an escapee well out of the badlands and another day would
put him in sight of the nearest ville. If it wasn't any of those
things, then what was it? What made the slaves give up their
lives so meekly?

Ryan was thinking about this dilemma with one small part
of his mind. With the rest, he was searching the jumble of
rooflines, the sagging walls, the doorless doorways for potential threats. Even so, he didn't see the small, quick figure
step out into the lane behind him.

"Hey, you!" came a high-pitched shout at his back.

Ryan turned and looked down at someone he recognized.
It was the young, would-be panga thief.

"You lying bastard," the boy said. Then he quoted Ryan,
throwing his own promise back in his face. "'I'll give you
some food on the way out. My word on it.'"

"It couldn't be helped," Ryan told him. "I got no food
with me now, either."

The boy glared up at him. "My stomach's growling so
loud, One-Eye, that I can't even sleep. Got any zealies
left?"

"No."

"What are you three doing down here anyway?" The boy
sized up Hun and Poet suspiciously. "Looking to get yourselves chilled? Don't nobody come down here unless they
have no choice."

"Got a proposition for you," Ryan said. "What's your
name, son?"

The boy stiffened and took a step back. "I don't never
do that kind of thing," he said angrily. "You want sex, go
to a rad-blasted gaudy."

"You got it all wrong," Ryan assured him. "I'm talking about a scouting job."

"You got nothing to pay me with."

Ryan reached down to his leg and half raised his panga from its sheath, showing him the wide blade and its bright, razor-sharp edge. "You help us out and you get this."

The boy's eyes widened. "The blade?"

Ryan nodded. "Your name?"

"They call me Guy-ito."

"Spanish sounding," Poet said.

The boy shrugged. "What sort of scouting you need done?" he asked. "Must be something biggish or you wouldn't part with your stabber."

"We need to find our crew that Zeal took away, and our wags."

"What you gonna do when you find them?"

"That's our business."

"Finding them ain't gonna be hard," Guy-ito said. "Not being seen by the sec men—now, that's gonna be hard. I got to say, you don't look like the folks living around here. You look more like road pirates, or coldheart mercies." The boy stood up straight and puffed out his scrawny little chest. "But you come to the right scout. Far as the big stabber goes, you got to pay me off when I show you what you want to see. I can't be hanging around while you do your business or the sec men will chill me for sure."

"Fair enough."

Ryan could see that heads were starting to poke out of doorways, the corners of sheets of plastic being pulled back so furtive eyes could stare out at them. The stink as he stood over the sewage ditch was gut-wrenching. "Lead the way," he said.

"Stick close, now," Guy-ito told them. "The path winds some, and it's hard to find if you lose it. No sec men ever come this way."

The kid immediately took off at right angles to the lane

they'd been following. The track he took was no wider than a deer trail, and there were obstacles that were hard to see in the failing light. Almost at once, they came upon a broad heap of overturned fifty-five gallon oil drums that had been thrown out as scrap from the refinery. They were without tops or bottoms, and people were sleeping in them. Sometimes two or three.

A little farther on, right in the middle of the trail, lay a dead man. He'd been stripped to the skin, his teeth were bared, eyes nothing but whites as they stared blindly up at the first stars of evening. There were muddy boot marks on his pale chest and stomach where other pedestrians had carelessly trod. The boy vaulted the stiff corpse, as quick as a spider. Ryan trotted around, then had to double-time to catch up.

It was hard for the one-eyed man to maintain his bearings, what with all the cutbacks and roundabouts the boy was taking. Inside the middle of the shantytown, the press of haphazard structures was so tight that he couldn't see so much as a foot beyond the shacks that surrounded him on all sides. Only the stars overhead told him that they were progressing, if slowly because of the elaborate route, in the right general direction.

The narrow, twisting path opened suddenly on a wider patch, sort of a clearing that was maybe ten by ten, in middle of which was an oil drum with a rubbish fire burning in it. A half-dozen men stood around the drum. They were taking turns cooking big rats skewered, ass to mouth, on thick metal wires. They hadn't bothered skinning their supper. Once the meal was cooked, they drew back to eat the hissing, smoking meat.

Ryan sensed their fear as they first caught sight of him, then their hate. They lowered their food. Their hands dropped to the shadows where cudgels had been leaned. The one-eyed man reacted automatically. Smooth and fast, the Blackhawk cleared hip leather, and as it came up, his thumb prying back on the hammer spur made the hefty weapon go click. Ryan wasn't worried about touching off a few rounds now. A bit of blasterfire in the middle of the shanties wouldn't attract much attention. And even if it did, no sec man in his right mind would venture in to find out what was going on.

"No!" Guy-ito yelled at Ryan as he darted between the warrior and the cluster of workers.

Then to the men, he said, "We're just passing through. Nothing to get twitchy about. These folks mean us no harm."

"Mebbe we mean them some harm," one of the men said, smacking the head of his club into the palm of his hand. "Got no entertainment tonight. Gaudies all shut down."

"They all got blasters," Guy-ito said.

"We can see that. Mebbe we'll take them. And them good boots."

There was a murmur of approval around the blazing oil drum.

Ryan took one step, wide to the left, giving Poet and Hun, who stood behind him, a clear zone of fire.

"They're gonna stick it to old Zeal," Guy-ito said.

After a moment of stony silence, the man doing most of the talking barked a laugh. "Better get on with it, then," he said. "And good luck to you."

"Yeah," the man standing next to him added. "Pipe a lead pill up his butt for me."

The workers watched with amusement as Ryan, Poet and Hun carefully circled them and moved on.

Ryan was starting to see how and why the people of Virtue Lake had earned their reputation as chillers and thieves. The baron had turned them into little more than animals, making them grub through the refuse for rats to eat, forcing them to live in their own stink and filth, working them to death in his refinery. No wonder they chilled and robbed whenever the opportunity came their way.

Their docile acceptance of Zeal's authority and subjugation still puzzled him. He had been around slaves, and near slaves, before. In his experience, they were usually broken in spirit, if not in body. How had Zeal broken so many? Not with his outlandish clothes and makeup. Not with the terrible nature of the work. Or the sec men. Then, how? The unanswered question gnawed on the surface of his brain; it itched as he jogged after Guy-ito.

Ahead, above the shacks, he could see the roofline of one of the strip malls. They approached the structure from the back side. Guy-ito's path skirted the edge of the shanties until he came to a narrow gap in the dwellings. He stopped and waved Ryan forward for a look.

What the one-eyed man saw didn't please him. He looked end on at the mall. It was completely roped off with yellow plastic tape. Inside the barrier were half of the convoy's wags. Outside the barrier was a line of armed sec men. He was amazed to see the damage the blast had done. One of the wags was entirely gone; there was a pit in the ground where it had been parked. Beside it, half-canted into the hole, were the remains of a transport. All that was left of it were the frame rails and axles, and the far-side front door. The rest had been sheared away.

The row of gaudies had likewise been hammered by the explosion. They were dark and deserted. Nothing moved inside the tape barrier.

As far as the workers were concerned, the novelty of the blast had worn off. They no longer stood around staring blankly at the devastation. Instead, they wandered, drinkless, slutless, along the ville's main road.

Although Ryan was confident that the sec men wouldn't risk a volley of blasterfire into the parking lot for fear of setting off another explosion, he knew that freeing the wags was going to be tough duty.

Then he felt the slightest of tugs at his leg. His right hand swept down and caught the scout trying to lift the panga again.

"Hey! We had a deal," the boy said, only letting go of the handle reluctantly.

"We still do, Guy-ito," Ryan said. "But we're only half-way there."

Chapter Thirteen

Trader was helpless, chained by the neck to the base of the refinery's interior wall. It was all he could do to tear his gaze from the slowly rotating tank and the long line of leaping blue flames. He forced himself to look elsewhere, to look for a way to save those in his crew who still had a hope in hell of surviving. It was hard for him to concentrate, surrounded by awesome noise and head-spinning stink.

In his wide travels, Trader had toured the insides of a few of Deathlands's functioning refineries, but none of them had operated on anywhere near this scale. Zeal, it seemed, was trying to make up for the lack of quality with quantity. The refinery's main structure was three stories tall; the ceiling high overhead was mostly obscured by the sides of towering steel processing and holding tanks, by the series of metal catwalks that stair-stepped them and by the blue exhaust haze that hung below the rafters. Above the steady, grinding roar of pumps and blowers was the shrill, chittering whistle of steam safety valves pushed to their limits. The once polished concrete floor was crazed and chipped, and stained by caustic chemicals.

Everywhere Trader looked, the machinery and the pipework was held together with duct tape, rags and baling wire. Zeal's refinery was falling to pieces in a million places, all at once. In a place this large, there were many hundreds of thousands of parts that could fail, and when they eventually did, if they couldn't be replaced, they had to be repaired with whatever was at hand. Accordingly, separated pipe joins and cracked valve casings were turned into great lumpy gnarls of rust that constantly hissed or dripped, or did both.

Though the plant had been originally designed to be comp automated, Trader knew that skydark's global electromagnetic surge had to have cooked all of its printed circuits, the same way it had cooked every other circuit that wasn't safely tucked away in a deeply buried, blast-hardened bunker. In order to make the place functional again, Virtue Lake's nukecaust survivors had had to disconnect all the useless comp controls and jury-rig manual operation. Sometime thereafter, Trader decided, the refinery's network of conveyor belts had to have fallen apart. There was simply nothing available that was strong enough to replace them, though there was still some evidence that attempts had been made. Tanned animal skins just couldn't withstand the weight of fuel drums. With the conveyor system permanently out of commission, the heaviest items in the place, the fully loaded fifty-five gallon barrels of gasoline, were moved by human power. Slave power.

Trader watched as laborers struggled to lift their impossible burdens. Some of them were laughing uncontrollably, their minds numbed and befuddled by the overwhelming sulfurous stench of cooking crude oil. Some laughed even as they were flogged to their knees by their pinstripe-overalled overseers.

The look-see was fruitless. Trader saw no opportunities for escape. He did have a strong sense of the refinery's impending total collapse. Roof. Walls. Everything finally vibrating apart and ending up in a heap and cloud of dust.

Not that he figured to live long enough to see it.

Like the rest of his crew, he sat with his back against the refinery's interior wall, with his butt on the cold concrete. The baron had separated him from the others, and chained him by the neck to a heavy steel I beam. The crew members were connected to one another by a long chain that passed through their ankle restraints. In front of them was a stain-

less-steel tank ten feet high and fifteen feet long. Its entire
surface, except for the ends, was blackened with soot. The
tank had been turned so it rested horizontally, and the large
pins at either end were attached to a series of gears, which
were driven by a gas engine, and allowed the huge tank to
be rotated.

It was rotating now at slow speed, one revolution every
thirty seconds or so.

And as it revolved, something inside thumped.

And screamed.

It screamed loudly enough to be heard over the deafening
roar of the cracking plant.

The ''something'' went by the name of Wisehart. He was
a balding, bearded man who'd ridden with Trader for three
years, working as a mechanic, driver, gunner, a jack-of-all-
trades. Rumor had it that Wisehart had three or four wives
spread out over the breadth of Deathlands, and a passel of
kids who were going to inherit his stocky frame, wide nose
and evil sense of humor. Short of a miracle, it looked like
Wisehart had sired his last.

Under the belly of the elevated tank and running its full
length was a row of gas burners, and from the row of burners a wall of blue flame leaped up a good four feet.

Trader could hear the thunk-thunk-thunk of Wisehart's
bare feet hitting the inside of the wall of the tank as he
jogged to keep from coming in direct contact with the red-
hot steel.

Baron Zeal teetered over to where Trader sat and said,
''Normally I would gradually decrease the tank's rotational
speed, and increase the height of the flame. To keep his feet
hard to it. In this case, however, I don't have the time to
waste. Stop the tank and drop the flame!'' he directed two
of the bosses.

The tank stopped turning, and the fifteen-foot row of gas
flame winked out.

The baron stepped over to the porthole-type door at one

end of the tank and pounded on it with his fist. "Where are the wags boobied?" he shouted at the steel. "How do we disarm them? Tell me now and I'll let you out."

A gabble of sounds came from within the cylinder, high-pitched, unintelligible.

"I think we've finally cracked your precious code," Zeal taunted Trader.

Then to Shabazz, he said, "Get the damned door open, so we can hear what he's got to say."

The rogue trader undogged the door and swung it back.

Smoke and steam rushed out, as did the sweet, unmistakable smell of roasted flesh, which cut through the refinery's petrochemical fog like a knife blade.

Zeal reached in the doorway and snatched hold of the man inside. He took him by the root hairs of his beard and pulled his head out of the circular opening. Wisehart's face was a crimson color, the fringe of hair above his ears drenched in sweat. "Well?" the baron demanded. "What are you saying? Let's hear it!"

"I said, 'Fuck you, sir,'" Wisehart croaked from his parched throat. "Fuck you very much, and can I go around again?"

Trader's men and women broke out in a chorus of hooting laughter, stamped their feet and rattled their chains.

With a brutal shove, the baron forced Wisehart's head back inside the tank, then slammed the door shut himself. "Turn on the heat," he told the bosses. "Turn it up to half."

As the line of flame licked along the underside of the tank, Zeal again approached the grim-faced Trader. "Like I said," he went on, "I usually stretch the whole process out, varying the speed of rotation and the temperature. I find that I get the best results over a three- to four-day period."

From inside the tank, there came a terrible cry, then a violent thumping as Wisehart tried to jump away from the heat.

"You've already seen some of my finest work."

Trader glared at Zeal. No way was he going to ask what the bastard was prattling on about.

"On my chimney," the baron explained. "Oh, I stumbled onto it, really. Just playing around here in the refinery. I learned that after a certain number of hours of intermittent slow roasting, the muscles of the human face lock up permanently. The end product makes a most unusual and striking decoration, don't you think?"

Trader's eyes glittered as he recalled the double row of tortured heads. Inside the tank, Wisehart's screams were becoming more and more frantic.

"I don't think he's going to talk, after all," Zeal said with a heavy sigh.

The baron nodded at the bosses, who cranked the flame up to the maximum. The resulting heat was so intense that the crew cringed against the wall, raising their arms to shield their faces. Within the smooth-walled tank, there was nowhere to shrink to.

Trader stifled the urge to cover his ears and block out the terrible shrill screams, something Zeal would have taken pleasure in seeing. Wisehart knew he was going to die the moment he was selected by the baron. He knew that the code of silence was part of what Trader demanded of his crews. No matter what was done to you, you could never, ever give anything up.

It took several more interminable minutes before the thumping and screaming finally stopped. Over the roar of the flames and the hiss of the gas jets, Trader could hear the sizzle of flesh as it cooked furiously.

After another minute or two, Zeal ordered the fire dropped and the tank reopened. This time, dense clouds of rank smoke poured out the doorway. Smoke from burned hair, clothing, skin, all mixed together.

The bosses reached into the opening with pairs of long-handled iron tongs and with considerable effort pulled out the smoking body and dumped it unceremoniously on the concrete floor. The eyeballs were cooked dead white, like a poached trout's. Half the face had been scorched off, right down to the red skull bone.

Not entirely a success, from an artistic standpoint.

But every member of Trader's crew rose to his or her feet and began to cheer and clap hands, applause for the dead man's courage. He had kept to the creed.

The display of respect and defiance hit Zeal hard. Trader noted anger, even outrage on his hideously painted face. This was the very last thing he had expected to see.

"You!" the baron yelled at Samantha, jabbing a finger in her face. "You're next."

J.B. scrambled to his feet. "No, take me!" he shouted.

"No, over here," said someone at the other end of the chain. "I'm up for it!"

Then, as if on cue, all thirty-one of them, Trader included, were yelling the same thing, rattling their chains at him, mocking him.

"Take me! Take me!"

It warmed the cockles of Trader's flintlike heart.

"Zeal!" Abe hollered out. "You're just jealous 'cause she's got a better ass than you do!"

"Hers has probably been rode less, too!" J.B. bellowed through his cupped hands.

Trader thought the baron was going to have a stroke. His face purpled, and he staggered on his four-inch heels as he waved his arms wildly about. "I'll cook you all!" he shouted at them. "I'll melt you down to tallow and make candles out of you! I'll burn every one of you insolent bastards twice!"

Shabazz put a hand on Zeal's shoulder, then leaned close and whispered something in his ear. The baron stiffened. He stopped waving his arms, and he closed his open mouth. Shabazz whispered some more. From the ugly look on his face, it was something mean.

After a moment of one-sided discussion, Zeal seemed to get himself under control. When he turned and stared at Shabazz, the pirate trader nodded, a sly smile spreading over his hairy mug.

"All right, Trader," Zeal said, "you've made your point. None of your crew will talk, even if I roast every one of them for a week. If there's no way to disable the mines, then we can't use your wags. Bottom line is, we need your wags. Shabazz and me are ready to do business with you."

Trader's crew didn't cheer the victory, even though their necks had just been saved. They knew better than to make a ruckus when their boss was closing a deal.

Trader took the measure of Zeal's face. What had made him change his mind about chilling them all? What could Shabazz have told him? Under the smeared blue-and-purple war paint, the clotted black mascara, there was an evil luster to the man's eyes.

Whatever it was, it was nothing but trouble; Trader was sure.

From the frying pan into the fire—that kind of trouble.

Chapter Fourteen

It soon became clear to Ryan why Guy-ito wanted to take his payment early and slip quietly away. Finding the wags was the easy part of the job. From the cover of the shantytown, they had had a safe observation post. Not so with the jails. To reach them, they had to travel along the ville's main streets, keeping to the shadows. As they got closer to the residential area where the bosses all lived, the number of other pedestrians dwindled, even as the number of slowly patrolling sec wags increased.

Guy-ito started to lead them across the main avenue to the other side of the street, but suddenly changed his mind, turning and pushing Ryan back into the darkness.

"Down!" the boy whispered urgently.

The headlights of a crawling sec wag appeared around the bend ahead. As it advanced, the driver turned on the rooftop spotlight and moved it slowly over the opposite side of the street. It stopped moving when it illuminated a man leaning up against a no longer functional lamppost, in the act of relieving himself. The light pinned the drunk like a startled deer, and like a deer he froze, swaying to keep his balance.

The sec wag roared up to him, screeched to a stop and its doors flew open. Three sec men jumped out with truncheons in hand. They didn't ask any questions; they just started pounding on the man. They beat him to the pavement, then beat him senseless. And when he was totally rag limp, one of the sec men stepped back and popped open the wag's trunk. The other two pitched him in and slammed the lid shut. Then the wag zoomed away.

"Seen the last of that one," Guy-ito said with certainty. "He's rat food."

"Pretty harsh sentence for pissing in public," was Hun's comment.

"It's not for that," the boy said. "He was in the wrong place at the wrong time. And he was too shit-faced to run when the sec men caught him with the spotlight. We're getting near where the bosses live. They don't like to see his kind wandering around at night. Even when it's just one at a time, it makes them real nervous in their beds."

When the boy moved on, Ryan and the others followed. There was no clear demarcation line between the commercial and residential zones of Virtue Lake. An area of warehouses, some of which had collapsed in on themselves, was intermixed with small groups of predark dwellings. As the street climbed the hill, the dwellings got more and more elaborate.

Guy-ito didn't take them in the uphill direction, though. He headed through the warehouse district, toward the lakeshore. The boy hopped over a low concrete-block wall that formed the streetside border of a cluster of six small bungalows: three facing three, separated by a badly cracked and heaved-up concrete walkway. He crept along the inside of the wall with Ryan on his heels. When he reached the break in the wall where, in happier times, a wrought-iron gate had once stood, and where now only the spalling hinges remained, he stopped.

"The jails are just over there," he told Ryan, hooking a thumb toward the opposite side of the street.

Ryan rose up and had a look. The only light was from a gas lantern hanging from the roof of a little shack. Under the lamp, four men sat on plastic buckets and ate their suppers, which smelled like MREs to Ryan. One of the men was passing around a glass jug. Next to them was a stretch of open land, steeped in darkness.

"Don't see any cells," Ryan hissed at the boy.

"They're set in the ground," Guy-ito replied, popping up to point them out to him.

"Yeah, I got them," Ryan said. He dropped back behind the wall and unslung his longblaster. "Going to go over and see what's what," he told Poet as he carefully laid down the Remington.

"Too risky, Ryan," Poet said. "Don't do it."

"We have to know if our crew is in there, don't we? Can't tell that from here."

With that, the one-eyed man was up and running, his .357 Magnum Ruger in his fist. He passed through the break in the wall and angled across the street, right at the jailers. All had their backs turned to him. They were laughing, slapping their thighs, stuffing their faces, pouring white lightning down their throats. They didn't hear the sound of his footfalls.

He made it standing up to the first row of cells, then dropped into a low crouch. He worked quickly, moving between the pits. A bunch of them were empty. Those that held prisoners, didn't hold any of Trader's crew. Ryan had just completed his search when he heard the rumble of a sec wag's engine. It was growing louder in a hurry, coming down the street in his direction. There was no place on that side for him to hide. As he had no choice, he abandoned the jail and beat feet back over the road.

He was nearly all the way across when he was hit by the brilliant glare of headlights from his right. Pressing on, he vaulted the low wall and dropped down behind it, beside his companions.

Almost at once, the white glare of a spotlight swept over their position.

"They saw you!" Poet said.

"We've got to pull back before they get any closer,"

Ryan growled, snatching up his longblaster as he waved for the others to retreat down the concrete walk between the little houses.

Retreat they did.

Each of the bungalows had a small concrete porch, accessed by a short flight of concrete steps. Poet grabbed Guy-ito by the collar and pulled him into the shadows behind the stairs. As it was the only cover, Ryan and Hun jumped in after them.

No sooner had they ducked down than a spotlight from the street pinned the porch.

"You, in there!" a sec man shouted through a megaphone. "Come on out! Don't make us come in and get you!"

Above them, the door to the bungalow opened inward, then the screen door, what little was left of it, swung out. The head that appeared in the gap had long, wavy brown hair. Beneath it was a mountainous body wrapped in a vast pink chenille bathrobe.

"What's going on out there?" cried a familiar musical voice.

"Seen some prowlers around," the sec man barked back.

Big Dumpling stepped out on the little porch. She looked down at Ryan, Hun, Poet and Guy-ito, crouched together in the shadows of her stairs. She didn't hesitate a beat. She turned back to the sec wag and said, "Well, there's nobody here now. You boys must've scared them good. They've already run off. Thanks for your help." Then she waved a cheery goodbye to them.

The wag didn't move on until Big Dumpling had reentered her house and shut the front door. As soon as the vehicle was gone, the door opened again and the gaudy songstress whispered out at them, "Come on! Get inside! Quick before someone sees you."

With Guy-ito hanging back and bringing up the rear, the four of them scrambled up the steps and into the tiny dwelling. The low-ceilinged living room was lit by a series of candelabra, each filled with scented candles; it reeked of sandalwood and patchouli. The room was barely big enough to contain a threadbare sofa and duct-tape-patched armchair. The sofa had a big sag in the middle, and the armchair's arms were splayed out wide. The doorways leading to bedroom and kitchen no longer had doors, but they still had hinges and pins. Doors opening and closing would have restricted the interior space even more.

"Thanks for hiding us," Hun told the large woman.

"Wouldn't have done it for anyone else," Big Dumpling said, "but you saved me from some serious hurt earlier, and I figured I owed you a return of the favor."

Then to Ryan she said, "What're you doing hanging around here after dark, anyway? Don't you know any better?"

"Zeal kidnapped the rest of our crew and took our convoy's wags," Poet explained. "We thought we could spring them from jail tonight. But they aren't there."

"Then those were your friends I saw getting dragged out of the cells about an hour ago," the singer said. "Zeal himself took them away in a bunch of transports, and that's never a good sign. Hope this don't sound too harsh, but if they aren't back by now, they may never be back."

"We can't go unless we know for certain," Poet said.

"I understand that."

"Mind if we wait here awhile until we're sure?" the war captain asked. "We can keep a safe watch on the jail from that window."

"No, of course not. Stay as long as you want. I'd say make yourselves comfortable, but that's near impossible in this dollhouse."

"Who's she?" Hun said, nodding at a torn, fly-specked color poster tacked to the wall. It showed a generously built woman dressed in a black fringe leather jacket, half-unzipped to show off her considerable cleavage, skintight black pants and black spike heels. She had long, flaming red hair, deadwhite makeup, big painted lips and held a microphone in one hand, into which she was singing. The position of her legs gave the impression that she was dancing up a storm while she sang. On the stage behind her were grinning male musicians in broad-brimmed hats and string ties.

"I don't know who she is," Big Dumpling said. "Her name was ripped off at the bottom of the thing when I got it. But she must've been a great big singing star before the nukecaust. I think there's a resemblance between me and her." Big Dumpling opened the lapels of her bathrobe a bit and struck a pose. "Do you see it?"

"Yeah, I think I do," Hun said. "You could have been sisters."

"Say, if you don't mind my asking," Ryan said, "how'd you end up in a place like this?"

"A sad story," she replied. "At one time, I had my own traveling show. I sang and danced, and I had a five-piece orchestra backing me up. Even had some comedy acts in the show—a bat-eared boy, and a pinhead who ate live chickens. We worked the southern baronies for years until the show fell on hard times. I ended up signing on with Gert Wolfram as a featured entertainer in his Deathlands Carnival and Freak Show. Rode with him for a couple of months before he made the mistake of pulling in here. Zeal held old Wolfram and his whole carny hostage, wouldn't let it leave without the payment of ransom. In return for safe passage out of town, Wolfram handed his best acts over to the baron, so he could use them in his gaudies. Of course, one of them was me." She sighed heavily. "Now, I'm just a bird in a poorly gilded cage."

Big Dumpling's eyes suddenly widened. For the first time, she seemed to notice the boy, who was taking pains to keep his back to the far wall and his face hidden behind Poet's back.

"You keep that nasty little beast away from me," she said, pointing an accusing finger at him. "He's always sneaking around the gaudies. Won't leave the working girls alone. Dirty pawing hands. Always trying to insinuate them where they don't belong, if you know what I mean. Like the brat actually knew what he was doing."

Guy-ito took this as a challenge. He stuck out his chin and said, "Mebbe you wanna try me, Dumpling?"

Hun cuffed him hard behind the ear. "Watch your mouth, you little shit-ball. Didn't your folks ever teach you to be polite?"

"Got no folks no more," the boy snapped back. "Both of them got themselves chilled last year. Pop got his in the refinery. Something fell on him, they said. Never saw his body. Mama got hers in the gaudy. One of the bosses high on jolt cut her up good. I saw her after. My mama died plenty hard."

Guy-ito's eyes darted to the sheathed panga.

"What're you thinking, boy?" Ryan demanded.

Guy-ito grinned fiercely back at him, showing the broken edges of his front teeth.

Ryan took that look for an answer, and he didn't like it. Not one bit. "You're thinking the wrong thing, then," he said. "You don't have the size for something like that yet."

"So now you're not gonna pay me?" the boy cried. "On account of what? You don't know what's in my head. Shouldn't matter none to you, anyhow. I scouted for you, didn't I? I brought you here safe, just like I said I would. Not my fault that your friends got took."

"He's right," Hun said. "Not his fault."

"I'll give you the blade, because that's what I promised," Ryan told him. "But you take good care where you stick it, understand?"

Guy-ito nodded.

Ryan unsheathed the panga and passed it over to the boy, handle first.

Guy-ito took it in both hands, made a slashing cut through the air, then turned and ran out the door. The screen banged shut after him.

"You shouldn't have given it to him," Poet said, shaking his head. "He ain't gonna live out the night."

"This is a rad-blasted rough ville," Big Dumpling agreed.

"Why do you stay here, then?" Ryan asked her.

"Because it's way better than what I had with Wolfram," she confessed. "I didn't just get to sing and dance. He used to make me do things with some of his other attractions, and he'd make folks pay to watch us through peepholes in the side wall of the tent. He had a couple of swampies that would take turns...." Big Dumpling paused, eyes shut tight, shuddering at the memory. When she opened her eyes again, she said, "It was no life for an artiste."

The room fell to silence.

It was all starting to make a little more sense to Ryan. Strange as it seemed, there was safety of a sort inside the barricade of Virtue Lake. You sure didn't have to worry about rad-mutated beasts dragging you out of a sound sleep and feasting on your heart and liver. Maybe the workers hadn't all figured out that they were never going to leave here alive. Maybe they didn't care. Maybe they were just looking for a moment of calm in the eye of the chem storm. At least life was under *somebody's* control in Virtue Lake, even if it was a madman like Lundquist Zeal. And if there was endless brutal work, there was a steady supply of booze and sluts, unlike farming or trapping or mining in Death-lands, in which there was no reward for one's daily toil except the sight of another sunrise, and nothing to look forward to but more of the same until you dropped stone dead. Which you were going to do sooner or later anyway.

The sound of approaching wag engines derailed Ryan's train of thought. He followed Poet and Hun to the window. As they watched, a line of transport wags pulled in beside the jail and stopped. A hot pink Lincoln brought up the rear of the file.

"Looks like your friends made it back, after all," Big Dumpling said as she peered over Hun's shoulder.

Sec men opened the rear doors of one of the wags, and men and women in chains were forced out at blasterpoint. None of them had boots. Ryan saw J.B. and Sam among the first wag load. The jailers held open the cell doors while the sec men kicked the prisoners into the pits. One by one, the transports were emptied. When the last crewman was dragged out, Poet said, "Trader's not there."

"He could be in that long pink wag," Ryan said. "Can't see inside it because of the armor plate over the windows."

"That's Zeal's personal transportation," Big Dumpling stated. "It's blasterproof."

"If Trader's inside," Ryan said, "you can bet he's working some kind of angle on Zeal."

"Trader could also be dead," Poet countered.

"Whether he is or isn't changes nothing. We've still got to get the crew out of those cells and free the wags before we can stick it to Zeal. I say we do it in just that order. Break the crew out of jail, round up some weapons, then take the convoy back."

"Won't work," Poet said flatly.

That news didn't sit at all well with Ryan, whose blood was up. "Why not?"

"The jailers are done with their supper, and now they've got their duties to attend to, lots of prisoners to abuse. We're not going to get close to the cells without their seeing us and starting a firefight. A firefight will bring all of the baron's sec men down on us. Probably before we can free everybody. Certainly before we can gather up enough blasters to fight back."

"What do you suggest, then?" Ryan asked. For once, he was willing to hear the older man out.

"We've got to face facts. As things stand, we can't rescue

the crew. And without the crew, we can't free the wags. So, we've got to forget about both of them for the time being and take another tack. What we need is a bargaining chip. One so big that Zeal will have to surrender to us or lose everything he's got."

A grim smile lit up Ryan's face. He knew what the intended target was at once. "It can't be a bluff, though," he said. "We've got to be prepared to follow through, all the way."

"I agree," Poet replied. "If he calls us on it, we'll have to blow up the refinery."

A coarse laugh burst from Hun's throat. "Serve the twisted son of a bitch right!"

"Oh, my!" Big Dumpling exclaimed as she hurriedly stepped away from them. "You folks are really scaring me now. I don't think I want to hear any more of this. No, I'm sure I don't want to hear any more of this. I'm going in the bedroom for a bit of a lie-down. Just close the door after you when you leave."

"Thanks for your hospitality," Ryan said to her pink-chenilled back.

The hefty songstress didn't turn, didn't speak; as she disappeared through the doorway, she just waved bye-bye over her shoulder.

Chapter Fifteen

Levi Shabazz leaned over the baron's stove, lifted the lid on the bubbling pot and sniffed deeply at the fragrant steam. "Now, that's some chiller gravy," he said.

"Sauce," the baron's cook stated. "It's a sauce."

The bearded trader dipped a grimy finger into the simmering liquid and hooked it into his mouth. "Mmm," he said, smacking his lips. "Don't care what the fuck you call it, that shit is triple tasty."

The cook started to say something, then thought better of it and kept his trap shut. Some people just couldn't be educated. And trying to play teacher could get a person's neck broken. The cook turned and hobbled toward the other end of the long stainless-steel counter, his manacle chains rasping over the wood floor.

The swing doors to the kitchen opened, and Baron Zeal walked in, his hairy ankles wobbling as he struggled to maintain his balance on the towering, red high heels. Under his right arm was a small, apparently extremely heavy metal box. On top of the box was a pair of thick gauntlets.

Shabazz leaned back against the edge of the stove and scratched his throat. He was very pleased with himself. Every once in a while, he had what seemed like a moment of pure genius, an insight so clear and wonderful that it surprised even him. To Shabazz, it sometimes seemed like the really great ideas were just floating around out there, like motes of dust in the sunlight, and occasionally he would open his mind and suck one in. That his ideas always had to do with torture and pain seemed only natural.

So what was it that he had whispered to the baron in the refinery? What inspired, magic words had turned the trick, convincing Zeal to forego his immediate pleasure in exchange for something even better? Shabazz had put them in the form of a question, actually.

And the question he whispered was, "Ever seen a guy die of rad poisoning?"

Zeal had ceased his sputtering and fuming at once. Realizing that he had captured the baron's full attention, Shabazz had then described the whole abysmal sequence in gory detail. He had waxed poetic over the way radiation caused the entire bowel lining to slough off and slide out the backside like a misplaced afterbirth, over the way the butt hole poured forth a river of bright blood, over the incredible burning pain in the guts, and the massive, rapid sepsis leading to brain-melting fever and a terrible, tortured death.

Zeal hadn't answered an audible "No" to the question, but the answer was there in his eyes. He hadn't ever seen it. Alongside the "No" had been a "But I would like to, very much."

And that wistful hope was very close to coming true.

The baron deposited the metal box and gloves on the kitchen counter. "It still bothers me," he said, "that we had to leave Trader alone in his wags for so long. No telling what he was doing inside."

"Yeah," Shabazz countered, "but if all the wags were set to blow up like he said, and we were standing too close, looking over his shoulder, we could've gotten blown up with them if something had gone wrong."

"If, if, if," Zeal fumed. "Don't you see what's going on here? We're taking Trader's word for things at every step. He's making us jump through hoops!"

"One of the wags blew. We know that."

The baron snorted. "We don't even know if any of the other wags were mined. But you can bet they're all mined now. He had plenty of time to do it when he was inside, all by himself. Seems like no matter what we do, the bastard is always ahead of us. Like he's got the whole thing mapped out and we don't have a clue where he's going. Let me tell you, it pisses me off, biggish.''

Shabazz nodded at the metal box on the counter. "He ain't gonna be one step ahead for long. His butt's gonna be dragging real soon.''

"That's what you said before,'' Zeal reminded him, "about the nerve gas. It was supposed to chill them all, as I remember. Seems to me that your precious deadly grens didn't work for shit.''

Shabazz didn't like being called on the carpet for something that wasn't his fault. The wind had screwed up his delivery system. "Nothing wrong with the grens,'' he said. "If you want another demonstration, I got plenty more where they came from.''

Zeal eyed him archly. "I warned you before and now I'm telling you, flat out. If I find you've stashed that nerve gas somewhere in my ville without my consent, I will personally shove every single gren up your backside.''

Shabazz made a mental note to relocate the crates of weapons, which were currently hidden in the refinery warehouse, among the many tiers of full fuel drums awaiting buyers.

"Don't worry about Trader,'' he said, quickly changing the subject. "I figure a day or two will be all he'll last, which should give us plenty of time to capture Spearpoint with his wags. That's all we need him for.''

The baron scowled, which only magnified the effect of his fright mask of a face.

Shabazz knew Zeal as well as anybody could. He was a man who loved nothing but himself. And his goal in life, it seemed, was to sweep all things into his talons. Was the man insane? Yes. Did he always seem to make a profit? Yes. Did the two balance out in Shabazz's eyes? Yes again.

Zeal pushed up the sleeves of his fur robe and donned

the heavy gauntlets he had brought, then unlatched the lid of the metal box. When he opened it, Shabazz could see that the box's walls were six inches thick, and that the narrow cleft that remained held a single, gleaming silver cylinder the size of a man's index finger. On the inner surface of the lid was a purple-and-yellow Caution Radiation Hazard warning.

The baron carefully removed the cylinder from its resting place and unscrewed the top in slow, even turns like it contained high-ex. "Doesn't look like much," he said of the fine, shiny black powder inside.

"Deadliest shit since nukeday," Shabazz pronounced. "Plutonium dust. Not only does it chill you dead, it chills you ugly dead."

"Never thought I'd have a use for it," Zeal said. "I took it in trade for fuel, along with a bunch of other nuke stuff, a few years back."

"I think Trader's grub could use a touch more seasoning," Shabazz said as he removed the lid on the saucepan.

At the other end of the kitchen, the cook glanced over, shrugged and looked away.

Zeal sprinkled some of the dust into the sauce, holding it close to the surface so as to keep it all in the pot. As Shabazz stirred it in, the baron moved on to the soup course. The cook had prepared homemade oxtail soup. Zeal shook a good amount of plutonium into it, and it sank immediately to the bottom.

Likewise, he doctored the accompanying jug of strong ale.

"Don't forget the dessert," Shabazz reminded him.

Dessert sat on the sideboard. The pie shell had been precooked and filled with plump purple berries and a thick, sugary liquid. The unbaked pie top sat to one side, awaiting the cook's final touch. Zeal emptied the last of the vial into the pie filling.

After replacing the container in the box, locking it shut

and removing the long gloves, the baron ordered his cook front and center. "Get that pie in the oven," he said. "I want Trader's dinner on the table, right sharpish."

The cook immediately started to apply the strips of unbaked crust into the latticework that would form the top of the pie. "Be fifteen minutes more," he said.

"One more thing," Zeal told him, leaning so close to the cook that he couldn't help but flinch. The man knew better than to draw away. "And I want you to listen to me very carefully. You must throw away all the pots and pans you've used to cook this meal. Toss out the utensils, as well as every plate, cup and saucer you use to serve him. Don't wash them. If I see them in this kitchen again, I will hang you from the gates of the stockade by your balls. Do you understand me?"

"Throw everything out," the cook repeated, a pained expression on his face.

TRADER SAT IN THE BARON'S living room, smoking his hand-twisted cheroot, scattering the ashes on the sofa and rug. He was thinking about his wags and the autodestructs. He hadn't actually shut down the system, of course. As he'd moved from wag to wag, he'd reset the time to detonation, pushing it forward twenty-four hours. He figured if his crew wasn't back in charge by then, they'd never be.

Because none of the external mines were set, he didn't have to do anything to get at the door locks. Once he'd done his work inside, though, he'd tripped all the outside switches. His crew always checked the switches before they tried to enter the wags. Anybody else looking to hop a ride was going to get a big surprise.

Trader didn't think it was very likely that Zeal and Shabazz had located Spearpoint; he had always figured the stockpile of stockpiles was a tall tale. And even if they had found it, he never expected to see any part of the fifty-fifty split he had worked out with them. He knew the two snakes would dispose of him as soon as they could. Right now, he had them off balance, and he planned on hanging on and digging in his spurs a bit more. Poet, Ryan and Hunaker were still out there somewhere, and he couldn't have picked three better crew members for the job of freeing the convoy. He wasn't worried that they hadn't tried anything yet. He knew there would be better opportunities for ambush and rescue outside the ville.

A servant approached from the other side of the room. He stepped up and said, "Your dinner is ready. If you'll follow me, it's this way...."

Trader wasn't expecting dinner. Out of gratitude to his cross-dressing captor, he stubbed the cheroot on the arm of the sofa, leaving a nice black hole in the floral-print upholstery. Then he dropped the hot butt in his shirt pocket and followed the servant through a doorway and down a corridor.

"Not serving smoked human head tonight, are we?" Trader asked.

"Of course not," the servant answered, taken aback by the question.

"Good, because that's what I had last night and the night before that. Getting kind of tired of it. Especially the ears..."

The servant blinked at him.

"Chewy," Trader said without expression.

The servant visibly blanched. "I've already laid out your meal, sir," he said stiffly. "It's right through there."

Trader entered a spacious dining room. Evidently he was the only guest. The servant walked past the table heaped with food and passed through a pair of swing doors, into what Trader figured had to be the kitchen.

Scraping back a chair, he sat and started digging in. First thing he pulled the berry pie in front of him. One sniff and his mouth began to water. He couldn't remember the last time he'd had blueberry pie. He shoved aside the silverware that had been set out for him to use and drew his own knife. The SOG Pentagon model dagger was double edged, and one edge was serrated, for cutting tree limbs, thighbones or piecrust. He slashed the dessert into four huge wedges, then wiped the purple-stained blade on the linen tablecloth.

Using his fingers, Trader proceeded to wolf down the entire pie. He had started out with every intention of going slowly, so as to get the maximum enjoyment out of it, but the damned thing tasted so good he just couldn't stop himself.

"Hell of a cook!" he bellowed toward the kitchen when he was done. "Goddamned chef, that's what you are! If you ever feel the need to put some miles under your boots, you always got a ride with me!"

Then he let out a sonorous belch.

He noticed a kind of funny grit in his mouth. He thought it was from the berry seeds or the wheat flour in the crust. Disdaining the crystal beer mug set out before him, he picked up the flagon and drank straight from the spout. The beer was heavy and had just the right balance of bitterness and sweetness. It sure wasn't the thin, green donkey piss they served in the Virtue Lake gaudies. He emptied the jug down his throat in a single pour, slammed the empty vessel on the table and shouted, "Going to need some more of this ale!"

The servant hurried out and took the flagon away. By the time he returned with another foaming jug, Trader was well into the main course. He held the china plate tipped to his mouth and, using the tip of his dagger, shoveled in the fricassee of game birds—quail, prairie chicken and chukar. He paused only for breath, and to groan with pleasure. Each of the birds had been boned and cooked separately, to preserve its unique flavor and texture. They were only stirred into the sauce at the very end. The effect was marvelous.

Trader used a hunk of fresh bread to mop the last of the

sauce from the plate, then returned to the ale to refresh his palate.

He took on the oxtail soup last, spearing out the hunks of tender meat with the tip of his knife; then when he'd cleared the field, he picked up the soup bowl and drank it down to the last drop.

"Can I bring you anything else?" the servant asked as he cleared away the empty plates.

Trader laced his fingers behind his head and propped his feet up on the edge of the table. "No. That was perfect."

As the servant turned away, he whipped out a fresh cheroot and lit it up. Stomach well packed, brain warm and slightly buzzed from two quarts of strong ale, Trader blew smoke rings at the ceiling. If it turned out that this was his last meal, he thought, it was a damned fine one.

After a bit, the servant came back with a carafe of brandy and a cut-crystal glass. "In case you'd enjoy a drink with your cigar, sir."

"Zeal's not trying to get me drunk, is he?"

"I wouldn't know that, sir. But please, help yourself."

"Well, he can try all he likes," Trader said, filling the tumbler to the brim. He downed the brandy in a single gulp and promptly refilled the glass. "I can put any man under the table."

"I don't doubt that, sir," the servant said as he left the room.

Trader blew more smoke rings, guzzled more of the baron's fine brandy and generally felt on top of the world.

This while, inside his overstuffed belly, a time bomb ticked.

Chapter Sixteen

It took twenty minutes for Ryan, Poet and Hun to retrace their steps back to the minimall because they had to keep diving for cover from the sec patrols. They reentered the shantytown and, from the cover of a lean-to wall surveyed the milling armed guards, the yellow-tape barrier and the rows of parked wags beyond. They got an almost immediate and very welcome surprise.

Hun nudged Ryan with an elbow.

"Yeah, I see him," Ryan hissed back.

In the glare of headlights, they watched Trader, cigar firmly clamped in one corner of his mouth, duck under the plastic tape and walk over to the pink long wag. Ryan recognized the man who stood outside the rear door, holding it open for him. It was Levi Shabazz. Trader climbed in the back of the wag; Shabazz entered after him and closed the door. Then the hot pink Lincoln rumbled away in the direction of the big house.

"What was all that about?" Hun said.

"Got to be the internal autodestructs," Poet said. "We've been out of the wags for more than four hours. By now, all the mines should have blown. Trader must've told Zeal and Shabazz about them. That he had to disarm them or the whole convoy was going to go up."

"I can't believe those two pirates let him inside the wags all by himself," Ryan said. "How the hell did he pull that off?"

"A smooth-talking son of a bitch, that's Trader," Hun said.

"More like he gets you in an armlock, then puts on the pressure until something goes snap," Ryan said.

"It ain't exactly fair, is it?" Poet stated. "Almost makes you feel sort of feel sorry for the thieving, chilling bastards."

"Wouldn't go that far," Ryan said.

"I said 'almost.'"

"Which wag has got the cases of C-4?" Hun asked.

Ryan pointed to one of the smaller transports parked in the lot closest to them, the lot that hadn't been cratered. "It's in that one," he said. "I know because I watched J.B. pack it in himself. He's real particular about how his high-ex rides."

"Figure there's enough to do the job we got in mind?" Hun queried.

Ryan shrugged. "J.B. would know that better than me. I guess there must be at least fifty pounds of the stuff in the wag, and plenty of rigging wire, blasting caps and predark detonators. We aren't going to leave any explosive behind. Take it all, use it all. You've seen the fuel plant. It's huge. If it takes more than that to bring it crashing down, I suppose we're shit out of luck."

"Got to add in the gas that's already stored there," Poet reminded him. "Plenty more explosive potential there. I figure we can make a mighty big boom with what we've got. Especially if we're crafty about where we place the charges inside the refinery."

"Major fireball," Ryan agreed.

"What about the folks in the ville?" Hun asked.

"What about them?" Ryan said.

"Big blast could do them some bad damage, too. Especially if you're planning on making the gasoline catch fire and explode. Whole ville could burn down."

"We're not planning on touching off the C-4," Poet assured her. "It's a last resort. Just in case we can't come to an agreement with Zeal. And I'm thinking mebbe the baron might want a look-see at our mining job, just to make sure we're not trying to skin him with nothing but hot air. If it comes to that, he's got to find a real threat to his refinery or we're goners, and so is Trader and the rest of the crew.''

''I see what you mean,'' she said.

Ryan wasn't paying much attention to their discussion. He was watching the sec men along the tape barrier, trying to figure out a way to get past them to the transport wag without being seen. The trouble was, the barrier was set up a good way from the parking lots, which left a stretch of open ground they would have to cross even after they reached the tape, allowing the sec men plenty of time to aim and fire. On the upside, there wasn't much available light, only the shifting glow given off by trash fires the guards had lit in fifty-five-gallon drums. The fires were few and far between, and the area they lit up wasn't large.

''If we're seen going in,'' he said to the others, ''and the sec men raise an alarm, I figure they won't shoot at us for fear of hitting the wags and setting off another big blast. But if they see us going in, they'll be waiting for us to come out, and their blasters will be massed. In which case, we're chilled. We've got to find the weak spot, or make one.''

Poet smiled like he thought something had finally sunk in.

A day before, that same grin would've made Ryan want to lay hands on the man. Funny thing, though, now it didn't seem so insufferable. Now it seemed like the war captain was actually proud of his progress.

''Go on,'' Poet prompted.

''We can't raise a ruckus, either. We don't want anybody to know we've been in there until after we get the charges set.''

''Hard set of problems, there,'' Poet said. ''One piled on top of the next. How do you figure to solve them?''

''Way I see it,'' Ryan said, ''the first thing we do is this....''

"CRYING SHAME about the gaudies," the skinny sec man said to the guard standing next to him, this for perhaps the tenth time. He was talking just to keep from falling asleep on his feet. The perimeter they were supposed to be guarding was so big—it encompassed four square blocks of Virtue Lake's commercial district—that the sentries were strung out pretty thin. The nearest other sec men were more than 150 feet away, and they had an oil drum, the lucky bastards. A fire was something that kept the mind occupied. And the body, too. A fire you could tend. You could feed. You could poke. You could watch the flames shoot up.

The skinny sec man could no longer even pretend to watch the edge of the shantytown for possible trouble. Nobody was coming his way. After what had happened earlier in the afternoon, who would want to break into the convoy area, anyway? Be like walking into a rad-blasted minefield. Hours earlier all the gawkers and the drunks had drifted off. There wasn't even anybody to warn to stay back anymore. He had hoped to be able to fire a few warning shots over somebody's head, or into somebody's head if the opportunity arose, but that hadn't happened, either.

"Yeah, a shame," said the sour-faced sec man standing next to him. Eyes glazed over with boredom, he was picking at the huge gaps between his teeth with a sharp splinter of wood.

"Pizza Man was my favorite," the skinny one went on. He lowered his machine pistol and let it hang down by its shoulder sling. Then he pushed it out of the way behind his hip so he had room to talk with his hands. "That gaudy had the best beer in the whole damned ville. At Pizza Man you'd never find something nasty in the bottom of your glass. Nothing with legs, anyway."

"Yeah, good beer."

"There was some friendly women there, too. Not much to look at. Seen trash-can lids with more sex appeal. But real friendly, even if you didn't have a zealie to spend on them.''

"Yeah, friendly."

"You know I seen the bodies carried out, and then had me a look-see at the place before we got the order to pull back. Man, there was nothing left inside the walls. Just heaps of crushed concrete block and broken glass. Do you think all the sluts got chilled? Man, that would be a shame. Kind of chokes me up, to tell the truth.''

"Yeah, me, too."

After a long pause, the first sec man added, "But it was quick, you got to figure it was quick. There's a mercy in that.''

When his companion didn't parrot a reply, the sec man started to turn. As he did, he heard a strange rasping sound. What he saw beside him was a woman with short green hair and a fierce expression, her teeth bared like an animal, stepping out from behind the other guard.

Then he saw that his companion was crumpling to the road, and that his armor vest was sheeting blood from a throat cut ear to ear. The green-haired woman snatched the bill cap off the dying man's head and slammed it down on her own. A serrated blade gleamed wetly in her fist.

The skinny sec man lunged for his weapon. Something moved, close to his right. He craned his head around and found himself staring into a single blue eye.

Ryan caught hold of the machine pistol's strap with his left hand, holding the weapon pinned to the sec man's side. His right hand clamped over the man's open mouth. Hun was already moving around the sentry, who could see her coming, his eyes was big as doorknobs.

Expertly she reached in above the collar of the armor vest and made one lightning-quick slash at the side of his neck with the first two inches of blade. In passing, she ripped the bill cap off his head.

Ryan held the skinny man until he lost consciousness,

which took ten seconds with the blood flow to the brain cut off. Blood was flowing everywhere else, though. Ryan let the guy slip to the ground, then stripped open the Velcro tapes on his armor vest, jerked it off and tossed it aside.

Meanwhile Poet and Hun moved shoulder to shoulder, blocking the view of the sec men over by the burn barrel. Due to their captured bill caps and the poor light, nothing seemed amiss.

The distance to the nearest garbage container was roughly one hundred feet. Ryan caught one of the men by the heels and dragged him over to it. Then he propped the body up and tipped it in. He did the same with the other corpse.

No alarms were raised.

No one noticed.

Just as he'd figured, the sentries were lost in their own thoughts. The weak point was their boredom, after hours of doing nothing but staring into the darkness.

Ryan crossed into the taped-off area, keeping to the deep shadows. When he reached the small transport, he moved to the back side. He crawled in under it and found the cover plate for the external mines. He tripped the switch, then crawled out again.

After tapping in the lock-release code, he opened the well-greased starboard side and slipped inside. Because the blasterports along the corridor were unblocked, he couldn't risk a light. He fumbled his way down the narrow hallway toward the cargo hold. His fingers grazed the bulkhead door. Before he opened it, he felt along the adjoining wall for the crowbar that was mounted on a clip bracket.

Inside the cargo bay, it was darker than hell. So dark, that Ryan had a moment of complete disorientation. Reaching out to grip the doorjamb, he forced himself to remember the layout of the hold. Only when he had it clearly in his mind did he proceed. He felt his way down a narrow aisle, passing his hands over stacks of crates and drums as he moved toward the middle of the cargo area, where he'd seen J.B.

working. He remembered that there had been drums lined up on either side. His fingers found drum lids, then a gap, then more drums.

He retraced his steps.

Leaning over the rims of the barrels, he touched the tops of two wooden crates, laid side by side. Because of the surrounding heavy drums, they were well-braced in place.

Using the tip of the pry bar, Ryan popped open the nearest crate and slid his hand inside. After brushing aside the excelsior packing material, he felt rows of solid blocks, individually packaged in oiled paper.

C-4.

Ryan silently thanked J.B. as he tore the lid away.

Chapter Seventeen

Doc Tanner sat huddled on the floor in the far corner of his cell, with his forehead resting on his knees and both arms wrapped around his shins. The light from a guttering candle on the barred windowsill cast bizarre shapes around the bleak prison chamber, dancing spirit forms. Doc's mind, because it was a rational organ, and because it belonged to a man well-trained in making sense of nothing, took those fleeting, erratic movements and made them into things familiar. While tears rolled down his cheeks.

He saw children skipping, heard them laughing.

A horse and carriage, clattering as it rushed past.

A ballroom crowded with stately dancers. Stringed instruments tuning up somewhere behind the milling throng.

Only when the candle finally burned out did he regain his sense of surroundings. He was plunged back into the dank and musty cell, oppressed by the weight of the iron collar and chain that bound him to the ring set in the wall above his head.

If this was reality, he told himself, then life had no meaning. Its myriad cruelties were senseless. And largely redundant. Theophilus Algernon Tanner, a man of faith, was coming to the end of his tether.

He tipped up his face to the blackness that hid the ceiling and cried, "I need no more instruction!"

His words echoed, and then the echoes faded away.

Doc could weep no more; he'd emptied himself of grief. In the center of his mind, the terrible curse was already formed and enunciated. On the tip of his tongue, an oath against God, the Creator.

Was to think it the same as uttering it?

Did God hear thoughts?

If the Lord heard prayers, Doc decided, He could hear thoughts.

"I have prayed to you hourly to bring about the moment of my death," he said aloud, his voice cracked and strained with bitterness. "That I might be delivered from the hands of these malefactors. And you answer me not.

"Tomorrow," he said to the darkness, "I will most likely die. When the doors of Spearpoint part at my command, Zeal and Shabazz will surely have me killed. Then I will see at last. I will see whether there is an intelligence behind all this torment, this unspeakable evil, or whether it is merely an engine, a machine running without an operator, the grim embodiment of Descartes's mathematical universe.

"Deep in my heart, I now believe that I will find only oblivion on the other side of the eternal gate. No welcoming arms of Emily, no Rachel, no Jolyon. After all this, after all I have suffered, all that I have lost, I tell you now, God who never answers, oblivion will do very nicely."

With that, Doc Tanner closed his mouth and closed his eyes. In his endlessly long life, this was his darkest hour. The terrible weight of it seemed to suck the energy from his body. Exhausted, he slipped into a heavy, dreamless sleep.

IN ANOTHER PART of Baron Zeal's big house, in a much more genteel cell, Trader was starting to feel poorly. His abdomen had become severely bloated. So bloated that it was painful for him to move about.

Had he drunk too much ale? he thought. Or perhaps it was the brandy? Trader was a man used to hard drinking, and it had never made him feel like this before. Perhaps it was the rich food? Or the speed with which he had devoured it?

With an effort, Trader pushed up from the bed and propped himself up on an elbow. He was decidedly woozy, not to mention weak in the legs, flushed in the face, sweating like a pig, stomach churning and distended, like it was filled with air.

He let himself slump back to the bed and stared at the ceiling of his room. Could it have been the food? he asked himself. Had some of it been bad? What he was experiencing felt like a case of food poisoning. But when he went over the menu in his mind, there was nothing that he could recall tasting the least bit off. On the contrary, it seemed like only the freshest and highest-quality ingredients had been used.

Because Trader was accustomed to the byzantine, dealing as he did on a regular basis with Deathlands's most ruthless barons and backstabbers, and because Zeal and Shabazz had already tried to chill his entire crew with nerve gas, the idea that he might have been poisoned did occur to him. But no matter how he turned it around in his mind, it made no sense to him. If he died in the night, Zeal and Shabazz could forget about using his wags for their pillaging. Trader's crews would never cooperate with them. From the recent demonstration, tankside, they had to know that.

Could they be trying to weaken him so he'd be easier to deal with come morning? A helplessly ill man would present much less of a danger to them. That was a possibility, he knew, although it seemed like a terrible risk for them to take. If they had slipped him too much of whatever it was by mistake, he could die. And if he died, no convoy.

There was another possibility, as well. One that didn't require a poisoner's hand. During the few hours that he'd been in the ville, he'd passed in and around the pestilent shantytown, and come in contact with slaves and sec men. It was possible that he had been infected with some kind of naturally occurring disease, something particularly virulent that had been born and flourished in the unsanitary conditions of the slave quarter.

All of these ideas churned in his head, his mind spinning from one possibility to the next. Then he felt a violent surge of pressure in his bowels. Lurching to his feet, groaning mightily, he staggered for the chamber's commode. Though he felt desperately ill and had ingested a large quantity of "plutonium dust," the fates had smiled on Trader that day. The substance Zeal had acquired years earlier possessed only a speck of radioactive material.

Chapter Eighteen

Hun stepped away from the curb into the middle of the street and into the oncoming lights of the sec wag. She waved her arms over her head for the vehicle to stop.

The driver of the wag must have been fooled by the uniform cap she was wearing and the bloody Kevlar vest, because he hit the brakes. The vehicle's front end dipped low to the road as it screeched to a halt.

Hunaker gave the driver and his passenger the thumbs-up sign. "Perfect!" she said as she started to walk toward them.

From either side of the street, at almost the same instant, two blastershots rang out. The wag's windshield quivered as if sledgehammered, caving in as the pair of heavy slugs passed through it. Inside the wag, the sec-man driver and his sec-man passenger were slammed back against their seats, both of them head shot. They bounced forward onto the dash and steering wheel, respectively.

The wag's horn blared as the dead driver collapsed over it. His foot had to have slipped off the brake pedal because the vehicle started to creep slowly forward.

Hun hurried around to the driver's door, opened it and, grabbing the corpse by the arm, hauled it off the seat and out into the street. She reached in and took the engine out of gear. On the other side of the wag, Poet was evacuating the other dead guy. While the two of them stripped the sec men of all identifying clothing and gear, Ryan lugged the three, fifteen-pound gunnysacks of C-4 and J.B.'s detonator bag over to the wag's trunk. He popped the trunk lid and put the plastic explosive inside; the detonator bag he kept.

Poet and Hun tossed the sec men's clothing onto the floor in the back of the wag. To the right of the vehicle, the two corpses lay where they'd been dragged, facedown in the gutter. A pair of bodies left naked by the roadside, both with grievous blaster wounds to the head, wouldn't draw attention from anybody in Virtue Lake, except maybe the street-cleaning crew.

"Don't smell too good up here in front," Hunaker commented as she slipped behind the wheel of the still-idling wag. The headliner was a bloody mess, and the inside of the passenger compartment was peppered with bits of flesh and bone, and twinkling fragments of safety glass.

"Smells worse back here," Poet said from the rear seat.

"Then let's air the place out," Ryan said. He sat in the front passenger's seat. He lifted his boots above the dash and, with three brutal kicks, crashed the crazed windshield onto the hood.

"That's better," Hun said as she pinned the accelerator and cut a savage U-turn. The rapid maneuver sent the window glass sliding off the hood and into the street.

She roared off in the direction of the refinery.

Neither Ryan nor Poet suggested that she slow down. Both knew it wouldn't have done any good. Hunaker was in kill mode.

As she approached the looming structure, Hun cut the headlights and took her foot off the gas. The wag coasted to a stop next to the curb two blocks away from the plant, which was lit up bright as day, inside and out. Through the open hangar doors, they could see workers moving about, lugging oil drums, lengths of pipe. Some were in chains; some weren't.

There was a sec-man presence outside the refinery. Three guards manned a little hut at the entrance to the grounds, and two men were at the giant doorway, checking the workers as they entered and left. More guards stood inside the structure, and they traveled in squads of five and six, enforcing the order of the men in pin-striped overalls, the crew bosses, with clubs and bull whips.

"Getting in isn't going to be so easy," Hun said.

"Getting out, either," Ryan added.

Poet leaned forward between the seats and started to say something. His words were drowned out by the mind-rattling screech of the factory whistle. The single piercing note stretched on and on until they thought the thing had stuck. Then silence. Then another awesome blast.

Shortly after the second shriek ended, refinery workers started to file out the hangar doors. Only those without chains, it seemed. The sec men stationed there looked over ankles and necks for collars and manacles. Those with chains didn't leave the plant.

"Must be the shift change," Poet commented.

"Replacement workers will be coming in soon," Ryan said. "That'll be our chance to get inside."

While they waited for the graveyard shift to appear, Hun took off her sec-man bill cap, thumb-wheeled open her SOG one-hander and started to saw off the brim. In a few seconds, she had turned it into a skull cap, which mostly hid her alarmingly green hair.

While she was thus occupied, Poet was rummaging through J.B.'s detonator gear in the back seat. "J.B.'s got some real sophisticated stuff in here," he said. He held up a handful of devices for Ryan to look at. "Check the hazard symbol on the back. These babies are nuke powered. Range on the signal has got to be a couple of miles or more."

"Yeah," Ryan said. "Those are all motion-vibration sensing detonators, with mercury switches. J.B. didn't make them. He traded for them. Those are predark, state-of-the-art."

"Got a bunch of standard contact detonators in here,

too," Poet said as he rummaged through the bag. "How do you want to play this?"

Ryan looked over the seat at the older man. "You're the war captain," he said, "you tell me."

"I want to hear how you'd do it."

The one-eyed man didn't have to think about it. He already knew. "Be nice to use those motion sensors. That way, we don't have to be around to trigger the big boom."

"Might not even be alive to do it," Hun said.

"The way I see it," Ryan went on, "we need a small, conventional, remote-detonated charge, and we need to set it someplace on the edge of the refinery. We use it to prove to Zeal that we mean business, that we've been inside his plant, and we've laid our mines. After we blow up the sample charge, we tell him to evacuate the plant. And after he does that, we remote-arm the motion sensors. We show him one we haven't rigged with C-4 to let him know what he's up against, that if anybody sets foot inside, the whole place will blow. Then we sit down and make a deal for Trader and all our wags. And we don't disarm the mines until we're over the top of the farthest rise."

"Boy, is that gonna piss the bastard off," Hun said. "Zeal's gonna be tap dancing in those high heels of his."

"And assuming your plan works," Poet said, "assuming that we get the crew and the wags back, what then? Do we just roll off into the sunset like none of this ever happened?"

"That's up to Trader," Ryan said. "He's the boss. And he's the one who's been put through the mill by Zeal. If it was up to me, I think you know what I'd do."

"Stop on the way out of town and lob one 2.75-inch rocket into the plant?" Poet said.

"You got it."

As the first graveyard-shift workers started to shuffle past the sec wag, Poet and Ryan began to sort the detonators for rigging. Hun exited the vehicle and moved around to the trunk. She opened the lid halfway, carefully shifted to one side the scoped Remington, the CAR-15 and her 10-gauge, and pulled out the gunnysacks loaded with C-4. Because of the sec men posted at the plant's entrance, they couldn't take their longblasters inside with them, only their handblasters. Her own current side arm of choice, a compact 9 mm Beretta 92-SB-C, rode in a ballistic nylon clip rig concealed under her T-shirt at the small of her back. Of course, if they got stopped with the three gunnysacks on the way in, the shit was going to hit the fan anyway.

With the bags of explosives clutched in her hands, she rounded the side of the wag. She slid the gunnysacks into the back with Poet. "Looks like the biggest bunch of workers is coming up the street toward us now," she said. "They're about six blocks away, and they don't seem to be in any hurry. Better get ready to move in four or five minutes, though."

Poet dumped out the contents of one of the sacks. Working as fast as he could, he cut down the big blocks of plastic explosive with his dagger and passed the resulting one-pound chunks over the front seat to Ryan, who fitted the detonators and then slipped the finished bombs back into the sack. Not a Dix-quality job, for sure, but good enough for demolition work.

When they finished the last charge, Hun opened the door and pulled the loaded bags out into the street. A mob of workers was passing on either side of the wag.

"I'd better take the biggest gunny," Ryan said as he exited the wag. "It'll give me something to hide behind. I tend to stand out even in a crowd." He grabbed the heaviest sack and slung it over his left shoulder. By holding the burden close to the side of his head, he figured he could conceal his eye patch and scar.

The three companions melded in with the silent, grim-faced flow of humanity. Like zombies, the workers shuffled along, eyes bleary, arms barely swinging. Ahead of them was the guard hut.

The sec men seemed much less interested in the people going in than they had been in those going out a few minutes before. It was understandable. These weren't potential chain-gang escapees. These poor bastards were meekly arriving, ready to accept whatever fate dealt them. The sec men had their backs to the crowd, discussing something of importance, as Ryan, Poet and Hun moved by.

Ryan could see he was going to have a problem at the hangar door. The guards there were actually doing their job, looking over the incoming workers with what passed for professional interest. On top of that, Ryan was the only person he could see who was carrying anything with him. Why would a worker bring something into the plant? If anybody was going to get hassled, it was going to be him.

He swung the gunnysack from his shoulder and carried it in one hand by his leg.

At his side, Poet saw what he'd done and nodded his approval. Then he looked at Ryan's face and frowned.

There was, of course, still the matter of the eye patch, which could also draw unwanted attention. It was possible that the sec men might recognize Ryan from the earlier encounter at the gaudy.

Ryan stripped the thing off and wadded it up in his hand. Head lowered humbly, after the fashion of his fellow laborers, he passed not ten feet from the guards at the hangar door.

"Would you look at that one!" one of the sec men said, pointing at Ryan's ruined face.

"Man, is he ever fucked up!" the other guard exclaimed.

"Hey, Scar-face!" the first sec man shouted at him. "Come on over here, and we'll fix the other side for you!"

"Yeah, we'll fix it so it matches."

Ryan kept on walking. The sec men catcalled to his back.

They were too busy looking at his face and mocking him to notice that he was carrying something.

Once he was inside the refinery, Ryan immediately replaced his eye patch. He had worn it so long that he felt naked without it. Beneath its cover, his healed-over wound was truly horrendous—the missing eye, shrunken lids and socket, and the jagged white scar that divided brow and cheek like a lightning bolt contrasted shockingly with his brutally handsome undamaged side. A wound to his soul that all could see.

Ahead of them, a group of men in pin-striped overalls had climbed up on gantries on either side of the main thoroughfare. As the mass of workers filed past this reviewing platform, they shouted and pointed at individual laborers.

Ryan didn't understand what was going on at first. He saw the group of sec men standing beneath the gantry push into the crowd and yank those the bosses had indicated out of line.

"Slow down, Ryan," Poet hissed a warning behind him. "They're pulling people to replace the dead ones from the previous shift. You don't want to be up at the head of the line when they've still got places to fill."

Ryan could see that he was right. After they'd dragged the workers to one side, the sec men were clapping leg irons on them. And he remembered what the runaway slave Paste had said about how they always chained the workers in pairs if the job was extradangerous. The sec men were doing just that, linking the workers, ankle to ankle.

The bosses had to have filled their quota because they stopped yelling and pointing and just stood there on the platforms, looking very pleased with themselves.

With Poet in the lead, the companions moved out of the flow of foot traffic. They angled around and between the bases of the rows of two-story-tall holding tanks, and were soon out of sight of the plant's main concourse.

Ryan put his bag on the concrete, opened it and took out

one of the charges. "This one with the green wire," he said, showing the others the bomb, "is the demonstration mine. We'll set that last, on our way out." He took a small black oblong box from his trouser pocket. "This is the detonator. I'll stash the both of them here, behind the tank support, just in case...."

He didn't have to finish the sentence. Poet and Hun knew what he meant. With all the sec men wandering about, there was no guarantee that any one of them would make it back to the rendezvous point.

They split up without saying goodbye. Goodbyes were bad luck. They each carried a sack of prerigged charges. Ryan headed for the north end of the plant, figuring that if the idea was to totally destroy the refinery, then the best place to start was the storage area for full gas drums.

Ryan made his way down the concourse and entered the long, adjoining shed without being challenged. Though he passed bosses and sec men, no one seemed to notice him in the chaos and noise. Inside the metal-walled-and-roofed shed, the fuel drums were on pallets stacked three high. Because the barrels were so heavy, the workers used a ceiling crane and pulley system to do the stacking. Ryan moved around behind the tiers of drums, then reached in and stuck one of the charges between two barrels at floor level.

He worked his way down the length of the shed, leaving behind five more of the deadly little packages. He spaced them and placed them so the explosions would begin at the wall that connected the shed to the plant, and so that the subsequent blasts from the igniting gas drums would sweep toward the dry lake, taking out the entire north side of the refinery.

When he was finished, he returned to the factory proper, looking for other demolition sites. He mined the sides of the crude-oil holding tanks and stuck his C-4 charges on the I beams that held up the three-story walls.

After the fact, as he waited in the shadows for Hun and

Poet to return to the rendezvous point, it seemed like they were using a whole lot of high-ex for the job. Because he wasn't an expert like J.B. he didn't really know what it would do. He'd never worked with so much plastique before.

Poet appeared around the side of the tank; Hun returned a moment later. She went straight to the place where Ryan had hidden the conventional charge and reached in for it.

"Can't set that yet, Hun," Poet said.

She rose up, empty-handed.

"We can't leave here until the next shift change," Poet explained to her. "Not without getting hassled, mebbe snatched up by the sec men."

"How long until the change?" Hun asked.

"Four hours."

"Man…" Hun groaned.

"I don't know about you two," Ryan said, stretching his arms, "but I could use a few winks." He started to scoot his legs in under the massive holding tank, in the gap between its bottom and the floor. "Figure the shift-change whistle ought to wake me up," he told them. "Damned thing's loud enough to wake the living dead."

Chapter Nineteen

Shabazz nudged Zeal as Trader emerged from his quarters a full five minutes after a servant's knock had awakened him. The man looked pounded. His face was deathly pale. There were pain lines deeply etched around his eyes. And he walked with an agonized, almost bowlegged gait.

"Rough night?" Zeal asked as his guest struggled up.

"I've had worse," Trader replied.

"Yeah," Shabazz said, "look on the bright side."

Trader stared out the window and saw that it was still dark. "Up kind of early, aren't we?"

"We've got some things to do before we get on the road," Zeal told him. "Do you want something to eat before we go?"

It seemed to Trader that there was a taunt in the man's voice. He glared at Zeal for a long moment, wishing he had a blade or blaster close to hand, then he grimaced and licked his dry lips. "No, thanks," he said, shaking his head, "I think I'll pass on breakfast, if it's all the same."

Outside the big house, the armored pink Lincoln awaited them in the courtyard, as did a fleet of sec wags and crews. Trader climbed into the back of the Lincoln with Zeal and Shabazz, then the whole entourage started to roll down the hill.

Looking at the expressions of his fellow passengers, Trader had the feeling that they both were on the verge of breaking into laughter. Their private joke wasn't a secret, of course. It was still burning like a red-hot poker deep in Trader's guts.

The pink Lincoln stopped at the bottom of the hill. Outside, wag doors slammed shut. Trader couldn't see out the side or rear windows because they were completely blocked by armor plate, and the driver's ob slit was too narrow and too far away.

"Don't get your butt all in a twist," Shabazz said to him. "We're picking up a transport wag to carry your crew to the convoy."

"Now, that's thoughtful," Trader said.

The Lincoln started to move again. At slow speed, they drove another half mile or so before they stopped again. When Shabazz cracked the rear door and got out, Trader could see they'd arrived at Virtue Lake's subterranean prison.

"You let the jailers know which crew members you need," Zeal told him. "I want only one or two to a wag. You just point them out, and the jailers will free them from the cells. Then tell your people to get into the transport. Tell them if they make trouble, they'll get chilled."

Trader slid across the seat and stiffly exited the pink wag. The jail cells were lit up by the glare of the surrounding sec wags' headlights. He started walking toward the rows of cells. His backside felt like it had been augered. Repeatedly. It was the worst case of Montezuma's he'd ever had.

What he had been ordered to do right now was even scarier. And certainly as painful. Zeal was making him choose the ones who were probably going to live—at least they were going to have a chance. By default, he was also choosing the ones who were going to die. It wasn't the first time he'd had to do it, of course. A commander operating in a free-fire zone like Deathlands had to make those kinds of regrettable decisions too often, decisions forced on him by circumstances, by a strategic situation outside his control. It was just that he'd never faced the prospect of sending so many of his people to their deaths all at once.

As Trader walked along the cells, he saw faces he knew

well; some of them he'd ridden with for many years. Faces hopeful, prayerful, even, of an impending release. Trader continued on without stopping. There was crushing disappointment, shock, maybe even an accusation of ultimate betrayal in their eyes.

"Hey, Trader! I'm down here!" a familiar voice said.

He looked down at Abe, who was staring at him through the bars, and shook his head. Trader walked on.

"Hey!" Abe shouted.

Trader didn't stop. Walking on was a hard thing for him to do, hard to see the surprise and hurt on his old friend's face.

Though all the members of the convoy were good at what they did, or they wouldn't have come along, Trader could only take the very best for the job as he saw it. That meant leaving some of the regular drivers behind so he could take the men and women who were the better fighters in close quarters, with everything on the line. That meant taking the young ones.

He freed J.B. and Sam from their cell first. Two of the jailers reached down and hauled them up from the stinking pit.

"Tell your jailers to get these fucking shackles off them!" Trader shouted over at Zeal. The effort cost him mightily; for a second he thought he was going to pass out. But the wave of dizziness passed.

After their ankle chains had been removed, and Trader had waved off the jailer, J.B. took a good look at his face and exclaimed, "Man, what'd they do to you?"

"Tried to poison me last night," Trader said matter-of-factly. "Guess I was too tough for them. Won't give them another chance, though. I'm on a no-food diet until we put these bastards behind us."

"Sure you're all right?"

"My legs are still kind of shaky, but don't worry about me, I'll hold up just fine."

Trader moved on down the line, calling for this one or that one. When he was done, more than half of his crew members remained in their cells. The freed ones stood close to him, awaiting their orders.

"We're going to make a little unscheduled side trip with the baron and Shabazz," he told them. "Seems he's got a looting he needs some help with. Wants to use our war wags and transports to facilitate things."

"What's in it for us?" Sam asked.

"We help him," Trader said, "and he lets us roll out of here. Our wags will have sec men and Shabazz's crew inside. They'll be the ones manning the weapons systems. From what I gather, the people in control of Zeal's target aren't too friendly. We can expect some serious blasterplay sometime today. Stay alert."

Trader didn't have to say more to them. And there was really nothing more he could say, under the circumstances. He couldn't predict what was going to happen in the next few hours, so he couldn't give them hard and fast orders. The situation was fluid, and likely to remain so for a while. The crew members knew to look for their main chance, and he trusted them to recognize it when the time came.

After he directed his people toward the transport, Trader got back in the pink wag.

Zeal's wide grin showed off the lipstick on his front teeth. "Bet they were glad to see you," he said. "At least the ones you let out of jail."

Trader said nothing.

Miffed that he didn't get a rise from his captive, the baron leaned over the back of the driver's seat and smacked his wheelman on the side the head. "Let's roll, you numskull!" he said.

It took another four minutes to reach the minimalls where the convoy was parked. The baron's entourage paused while the tape barriers were removed, then the line of sec wags and the transport advanced down the main street and stopped across from the parking lots.

"It's up to you which of your crew rides where," Zeal told him as the other trader pushed the door open. "But I want you to ride in the big wag with Shabazz."

Trader joined his people beside the transport, made his assignments and the crews filtered off to their respective wags. The first thing they did was to clear the external mines. They did it quickly and surreptitiously, flipping the detonator switches as they pretended to check drive shafts and Cat-track turnbuckles.

Once they had all the wags idling, Zeal leaned out of the rear of the Lincoln and waved for Trader to join him. When he stepped up, the baron said, "We need to make one stop before we leave the ville. Have your wag crews follow in line behind us."

After Trader had arranged that, he got back in the Lincoln. Zeal's driver led the motorcade around the block, and if Trader's sense of direction was correct, in the direction of the dry lake. They didn't travel far before stopping again. Shabazz exited the vehicle and gestured for Trader to get out, too.

When he did, he saw that they were in the ville's warehouse area. A big group of workers was standing in front of the open bay doors of a long, windowless, concrete-block building.

"What's all this?" Trader asked.

Zeal answered from the Lincoln's back seat. "We need to make room for our new cargo," he said. "Have your people open the doors of your wags' cargo holds. My workers will unload it all for you."

Trader shouldn't have been stunned, but he was. At his sides, his hands clenched into fists. He was being ripped off, royally, and there was absolutely nothing he could do about it. His heart thudding in his throat, he walked down the line of idling wags, telling his people what had to be done.

Some gave him incredulous looks. Others looked angry, and they had a perfect right to be. After all, the assembled cargo was the result of months of their collective effort, and here they were giving it up without a fight.

Seeing the early-warning signs of protest in his drivers' eyes, Trader held up his hand for silence. Now wasn't the time.

Because the wags were so carefully and fully packed, and because the baron's underfed, underpaid workers were in no particular hurry to get the job done, it took better than two hours for them to completely unload all the wags. For two hours, a stream of crates, boxes and drums flowed from the open doors of the convoy into Zeal's warehouse. By the time the job was finished, the inside of the once empty building was choked, wall to wall, with liberated goods.

The sight of it all sitting there, all taken from him, and with nothing whatsoever to show for it, made Trader's stomach clench hard. A stab of white-hot agony pierced his bowels, and he had to put out a hand to the side of the Lincoln or drop to his knees.

Whatever they'd done to him, one thing was sure—he wasn't completely over it yet.

Shabazz was watching him intently and, from the smirk on his face, enjoying what he was seeing.

"If that's the lot," Zeal said as he exited the back of the Lincoln, "it's time to go."

"Come on, Trader," Shabazz said. "You and me are riding together. If you're real good, mebbe I'll even let you drive."

As Trader and Shabazz started for the MCP, Zeal headed for one of the smaller war wags. The baron waved impatiently at the sec car parked alongside. The back door of the wag popped open, and a tall, skinny figure was thrust out, into the waiting arms of a pair of sec men. The sec men then pushed the old man in the strangely cut coat and tall leather boots toward the war wag ahead of Zeal, who gave him a series of cuffs to speed him up.

Trader only had that fleeting, ultimately forgettable glimpse of the old man before he was shoved headlong through the doorway of War Wag One by Levi Shabazz. In the corridor inside, J.B. and Sam were waiting for him. They both looked highly agitated.

"For nuke's sake, just keep it together," he said as he limped past them. "Don't do anything crazy. Don't do anything at all."

"But these bastards robbed us!" Sam said as she fell in behind him.

"We can replace the barter goods," Trader told her. "We gotta bide our time if we want to turn this thing around."

"What are you jabbering about?" Shabazz said as he climbed into the corridor. "Get up forward, the lot of you."

J.B. and Sam followed Trader up the narrow hall. He couldn't help but check out each open doorway. It pissed him off to see Shabazz's crew at every turn, nosing around in the bunk rooms, turning the galley upside down. Anything not nailed down was going to be stolen or eaten—that was for sure. What fried Trader the most, though, was seeing the road pirates monkeying around with the MCP's various weapons—fingering the rockets, pawing the machine guns in their blisters, even toying with the rear-firing cannons. He identified deeply with this machine, and with its firepower, which was, after all, a product of his own imagination and sweat.

To Trader, it felt like they were playing with his privates.

There was plenty of room in the MCP's driver's compartment for all of them. They could stand or they could sit in the jump seats along the rear wall. The first thing Shabazz did was to shoo his crewman out of the driver's seat.

"Stand over there by the door," he ordered the man as he plopped down in the worn contour chair behind the steering yoke. "And keep your blaster pointed at these three."

The crewman drew his wheelgun from its shoulder holster, aimed the double-action .38 Colt at belt height and held it steady.

"You can fill me in on the forward-facing fire controls as we go," Shabazz told Trader over his shoulder. With that, he gunned the big engines, and with a lurch, they set off at the head of the file.

The driver's compartment window hatches were undogged and tipped up to let in the breeze. Trader watched the MCP's headlight beams sweep over the ville. When they rumbled past the jails again, Shabazz honked the air horn at the jailers, who waved and whistled back at them. The sun was just breaking over the tops of the distant hills when they reached the barricade. Shabazz had to slow down considerably to wind his way through the obstacle course of offset concrete bulwarks.

The violent lurching from side to side started Trader feeling weak again. He thought for a second he was going to have to make a mad rush for the head. Then he belched, and lava came up in the back of his throat. It left an evil taste in his mouth—metallic, rancid. He gritted his teeth and swallowed hard.

"What does this red button do?" Shabazz asked, holding his thumb over the cannon trigger.

Trader didn't feel up to explaining. "J.B.," he said, "you tell him. Tell him anything he wants to know."

"That's right, J.B., you tell ole Shabazz all about it."

Trader was only half listening as the Armorer detailed the sighting and fire control for the fixed cannons. It was only the beginning of a long interrogatory. Shabazz wanted to know about the rocket pods, about the Cat tracks, about the maximum ramming speed.

"Sounds like you've got big plans for War Wag One," J.B. commented.

"Sure do."

Sensing an opportunity, Trader pulled himself together.

"Yeah, so how about your finally letting us in on them? After all, we're all in this together now."

Shabazz reflected on this for a few seconds, then said, "Sure. Why not. Place we're headed is a pass. It's mebbe twenty-five klicks from here. Guarded by a band of inbred maggots."

"These inbreds, they're what's keeping you from what you're after?" Trader asked.

"Yeah, they're blocking the way to Spearpoint."

Sam and J.B. glanced at Trader. The question on both of their faces was the same: was this shit for real? He shrugged.

Hell if he knew.

Hell if he cared.

"Must be some triple-tough maggots if you need something like the MCP to get through them," Trader said to Shabazz.

"They got the place well defended. There are steep rock walls on either side of the road, makes it like driving in a ditch. These inbreds have cut deep trenches across the road to trap any wags trying to use it. They got heavy-caliber machine guns, and the droolie bastards know how to use them. It's like a shooting gallery."

"A setup like that would make it pretty tough going for Zeal's regular sec wags," J.B. said.

"Make it suicide," Shabazz agreed. "I know because we already tried that, of course."

"Of course," Trader said. "So, that means these inbreds are probably not going to be surprised to see you again."

"Mebbe not, but when they see what we brought with us this time, it should make them squirt shit."

Trader thought about Ryan, Poet and Hun, about how maybe they were already chilled. About even if they weren't, how slim the chances were of their being able to stop and defeat an entire convoy. If there was no rescue attempt forthcoming, Trader and the others were going to have to try to overpower Shabazz and his crew without a diversion from the outside.

The bearlike trader had to have been reading his mind.

Over his shoulder, Shabazz called out to his crewman, "Better put some leg irons on these three. And make triple sure the black bitch is cuffed good and tight. Hate to see our passengers get themselves into trouble."

Chapter Twenty

Ryan was awakened not by the sound of the shift whistle but by a chorus of wag horns rolling past outside. Familiar-sounding horns, it seemed to him. He pushed out from under the tank at once, and found Hun and Poet standing in the shadows with grim expressions on their faces.

"What's going on?" Ryan asked them as he straightened.

"The whole damned convoy just drove by," Poet said. "Looks like they're on their way out of the ville."

"I stuck my head out the door when no one was watching and got a real good look at some of them," Hun said. "It was our wags, all right. And they were all running light, too. Way up high on their suspensions, like their cargoes had been unloaded."

"Fireblast!" Ryan swore.

"We're in a world of hurt now," Poet said, shaking his head. "We can't hostage the refinery for the wags if they're gone who knows where."

"Zeal might be selling them off," Hun suggested. "There're lots of barons who'd pay large for something like the MCP. Baron could already have his buyers lined up."

"We've got to go after them," Ryan said.

"Yeah!" Hun said. "Chase and chill."

Poet frowned. "We've got to figure they're gonna have a good lead on us. The shift doesn't change for a while yet."

"Don't worry," Ryan told him, "whatever time we lose, we'll damned well make it up on the road."

The next half hour was one of the hardest in Ryan's life.

Like his companions, he had to just sit there, waiting for the time to wind down so he could get out of the plant. This, while every fiber in his body screamed for him to haul out the Blackhawk, blast his way free and catch the convoy before it left Virtue Lake. The reason he didn't was simple. He could see the value of having the refinery secretly mined. Even if they couldn't use the explosives the way they'd planned, and there was still a chance that they might, he could foresee a time when the mines could be useful. For payback, if nothing else. Ryan knew he couldn't shoot his way clear because that would've given away the fact that they had been inside, messing around.

It was harder still for Ryan to hang back and let a good third of the workers file out before he and the others slipped into the largest part of the exiting mob.

"I'm driving," Ryan said as he trotted up behind the commandeered sec wag.

Hun was already at the trunk, popping the lid and pulling out the longblasters. Tossing her 10-gauge side-by-side into the back seat, she quickly passed the other two weapons through the front passenger's window to Poet. Laying his CAR-15 across his lap, he leaned the scoped Remington muzzle up between the front seats. Ryan started the engine with a roar.

Before Hun got the rear door shut, Ryan stomped the gas pedal and the wag peeled away from the curb.

"Where're you going?" Hun said.

"We've got to get the crew out of jail," Ryan said, steering out of a wild sideways skid. "We might not be back this way."

"You're right," Poet told him. "We've got to try to free them now. We're not going to get a better chance."

Finally able to take some aggressive action, Ryan ripped a page out of Hun's driving manual, pushing the wag to the limit, smoking the tires around corners; on the straightaways, he highballed it, engine howling for mercy.

As the prison came into view over the low rise ahead, Ryan could see the jailers scattered around the site. Two of them were taking turns jabbing long sticks down into the second row of cells—long sticks with sharp metal points. Two other jailers were leaning against the hut; it looked like they were resting. The fifth was nowhere in sight.

Without hesitation, and without slowing, Ryan veered the wag toward the pair doing the poking. It crashed over the curb, went airborne and came down hard on the unfenced border of the prison grounds, thirty feet away.

The two jailers looked up from their fun, astonished to see the sec wag leave the road and roar straight for them.

When Ryan drove over the first row of cells, the wag was traveling better than sixty miles per hour. Tires juddered on the bars for no more than an instant before they were on top of the second row. Ryan aimed for the jailer on the left. The guy was too panicked to even try to run. The wag caught him dead amidships. With a crack, the poking pole snapped off against the bumper; with an almost simultaneous thud, the jailer hit the grille, then bounced sprawling over the hood. His head rammed through the glassless windshield, his face contorted in agony.

For a second, the guy's nose was practically in Poet's lap.

Then the war captain reared back with one foot and, before the man could even start to bleed, booted him onto the hood.

As he did so, Ryan raised his Ruger.

"Oh, fuck!" Hun cried from the back seat, clamping her hands over her ears.

The .357 roared like a howitzer. Three feet from the muzzle, the jailer's head exploded in a puff of pink, and the violent impact literally blew him off the wag's right fender.

"Get that other torturing bastard!" Ryan snarled. After he bounced over the last row of cells, he hit his brakes and spun the wheel hard over, positioning the wag for another pass.

The second poker-man wanted no part of that. He threw down the tool of his trade and ran for his life.

Poet brought the adjustable butt of his CAR-15 to his shoulder and touched off a long, full-auto burst through the front window frame.

It was loud. Really, really loud.

In the back seat, Hun had her hands over her ears and she was yelling to equalize the pressure in her head.

As a cascade of smoking hulls clattered against the passenger's door, downrange the 5.56 mm tumblers whacked the dirt, sparked off the cell bars and chopped down the fleeing jailer in his tracks. Hit a half dozen times, the man stumbled and fell, sliding face-first over the bars of a cell.

Swerving to the left, Ryan fought to bring the wag in line with the little jailers' hut. The wag hesitated, still sliding sideways on the smooth ground between the rows of cells. Gunfire erupted from around the hut, and 9 mm slugs drilled into the vehicle broadside. Then Hun's 10-gauge boomed out the rear passenger's window.

Ryan had a glimpse of a man flying off his feet, arms outstretched as if crucified, crashing against the wall of the hut.

The fourth jailer knelt beside the hut, which was the only cover he had, and continued to fire at them with his machine pistol. There was a shaky hand on the trigger. Bullets sprayed around the onrushing wag, but not into it. Both Ryan and Poet opened fire over the hood. Ryan drove with his left hand, and fired the big blaster with his right.

The hail of high-powered slugs jerked the man up to his feet, then hammered him into the earth.

Ryan skidded to a stop beside the hut and jumped out with the Blackhawk cocked.

"This guy's gone," Poet said, after giving the bad shot a sound kick in the head.

"Gotta be one more," Hun said, slipping over beside the hut. "Yoo-hoo!" she called. "Anybody in there?"

By way of answer, autofire ripped through the corrugated-metal walls. Nine millimeter slugs whizzed high and wild, making Ryan and Poet duck behind the wag.

But Hun was ready. Standing her ground, she cut loose with both barrels at once. Though she was well braced, the recoil of the 10-gauge knocked her back a full step. The double dose of double-aught buck cut a ragged two-foot gash in the side of the shack at about knee height. The impact against the wall of the structure raised a big cloud of dust.

Hun shifted the shotgun to her left hand and drew her Beretta from the small of her back. She ducked her head low around the corner of the shack's doorway and stole a look inside, then ducked back.

Whatever she saw in there, it had to still have been alive.

She rounded the doorway with the Beretta out front. Ryan was sure he heard her say something to the wounded man inside. He couldn't make out the words; she didn't repeat them. They were punctuated by three shots from the 9 mm pistol.

"Get the keys!" Ryan said as he stepped around the wag's grille.

Poet was just straightening from one of the dead jailers. "Got them."

They hurried to the nearest cell, and Poet knelt and unlocked the door.

Loz, the cook for War Wag One, stared up at them; the relief on his face was almost comical. "Never thought I'd ever see your ugly mugs again," he said. Then he held up his arms so the two men could pull him out.

The second man out was Abe. "Zeal and Shabazz took about a dozen of the crew away," he said excitedly. "Must've been forty minutes ago. Took Trader, too. I didn't get a look, but it sounded like they had the whole convoy up and running."

While Poet and Hun moved down the line of cells, freeing

their comrades, Ryan handed Abe one of the jailers' machine pistols. "We're going after the convoy and Trader," he said as the little man dropped the SMG's magazine, checked the round count, then snapped it back in place. "But we only got the one wag. We need mebbe four more to carry everybody."

"Well, here come two right now," Abe said as he gave the charging handle a quick flip.

A pair of sec wags zoomed over the crest of the street. They were really flying, dropping by to check out all the blasterfire, no doubt.

Ryan didn't have to warn anybody about avoiding the tires, engine compartments and fuel tanks.

Five or six blasters cut loose on the sec wags. The hands holding these blasters weren't shaking. They were rock steady. The windshield of the lead wag shattered, then the vehicle slewed in a long, out-of-control skid. The second wag swerved to avoid a collision and took dozens of rounds at side window and door height. Over the sights of the Blackhawk, Ryan saw the torsos inside kicked around by the volley of lead.

Both wags slammed sideways to a stop against the curb; one of them half hopped it before coming to a halt.

Right away, Ryan knew the two wags were all they were going to get. There had been too much blasterfire. If they waited around, they'd have the baron's entire sec force on top of them. And then they'd never make it out of the ville.

"Come on!" he shouted as the last pair of captives was freed. "We've got to roll!"

Then, like the pack of pinhead clowns in Gert Wolfram's carnival, the crew hurriedly crammed themselves into the three commandeered sec wags. Only in Wolfram's carny show, dirty-faced savages didn't hang out the windows waving submachine guns.

After wedging himself back in the driver's seat, and slamming the door with difficulty, Ryan dropped his wag into gear and beelined for the street. The wag picked up speed very slowly, and the steering had gone all soft. When he drove over the curb, the weight of all the people riding with him made the frame scrape on the concrete.

Ryan wasn't worried about the quality of their transportation. Even as loaded down as the wags were, they could make much better time than the convoy, assuming of course that the springs didn't bottom out on a deep pothole in the road and make them break an axle.

He was worried about the barricade, and the sec men that he knew would be waiting there, ready for them.

Chapter Twenty-One

Palmer the Guardian knelt on the cliff edge, on the very rim of his world, and stared southwest across the desolate plain. He could see the spiraling dust cloud from the war caravan, like a tornado whipping over the desert. Palmer knew that the Spirit in the Mist had called these things to it, and he was unafraid. There would be much blood, and the Mist would be greatly satisfied. In the months to come, there would be good hunting, seasonable weather and many male babies.

The clan had been preparing for this day for months; they had been awaiting it for better than ten decades. It had been foretold in the diaries of First Palmer, a collection of lengthy handwritten documents that had been handed down from guardian to guardian since the Apocalypse. Much of the clan's life-style and belief system was based on these diaries. First Palmer had found several women and multiplied with them. He also multiplied with the female offspring of those unions, in effect setting the standard for the group's conjugal philosophy.

The diaries had laid out detailed plans for the defense of the road, which subsequent Palmers had followed to the letter. First Palmer had seen this approaching juggernaut, perhaps in a vision brought on by the devil's club plant. Perhaps the Spirit had showed him. Most emphatically the diaries said, "First the few, then the many. First the few, then the many. First the small, then the big."

Working from the diagrams, the Palmers had carefully expanded and deepened their antitank trenches. Now they were much higher than a man's head, and longer than five men laid head to foot. And they were hidden. The clansmen had buttressed and reinforced with timber and rock the fixed machine-gun positions above the cliff face on either side of the road. And they had positioned, only after much grueling labor, a series of enormous rockfalls along the cliff edges. These man-made avalanches were designed to crush anything attempting to climb the road below. Or failing that, to at least block in an attacking wag, fore and aft, so it couldn't maneuver its blasters and it couldn't escape the mountain men.

In the diary, First Palmer had made diagrams of many different types of battle wag. These pictures showed clearly where all the air-intake vents were. It showed how to seal them off with tarry rags and baling wire. It also showed how to connect the engine exhaust pipes to the vents with lengths of hose. First Palmer wrote that if you could stop a war wag in its tracks, you could turn it into a coffin for its crew, by either cutting off their air and sealing them in, or forcing them to abandon it and come under your blasters.

Palmer the Guardian was hoping that there might be some fresh women among the coming caravan, suitable for breeding purposes. Whenever the clan happened upon such females, they were made available to all the males for seeding, as was the case with the women and the girl children born to the group. Much of the time of the females of all ages was spent in collecting, cleaning and preparing the root of the devil's club for consumption.

According to the legend passed down since skydark, *Oplopanax horridum,* a member of the ginseng family, had been the Spirit in the Mist's gift to First Palmer. It flourished on the slopes of the mountain, and was easy to spot with its broad green leaves and above-ground canes that were covered with thousands of yellow, needlelike thorns. The plant's creeper, the rootlike sucker vine that grew just under the soil, contained the magic elixir. One only had to peel the bark away and chew the pithy inner stem. It vanquished pain and gave a man the strength of three.

The leader of the Palmer clan had been chewing devil's club for most of his life. He even chewed it in his sleep. He awakened automatically when all that was left was the dry, fibrous cud. He spit the gob across the floor of his cave, reached into the bowl beside his sleeping mat, selected another chunk and packed it in. So ingrained was the grinding motion of his jaws that he could do it while unconscious. Because of his virtual twenty-four-hour-a-day intake, the level of psychotropic drug in his bloodstream had been more or less constant for the past forty-nine years. He got no distinguishable "high" from it, but he was completely addicted to it, as were all of the other adults, male and female, and many of the children. It gave them a sense of well-being. Of wholeness. Of connection to the larger universe.

Though their parents were addicted, the children weren't born in a similar condition. The root seemed to have no effect on the development of the clan's fetuses. None that could be sorted out, anyway. A much bigger problem was the limited nature of the Palmer gene pool. More of a puddle, really.

The cud in Palmer's mouth had begun to dry out. It scratched the inside of the cheeks and gums. He patted his pockets for more and, finding none, was loath to spit out what he could still manage to chew. He looked around for a woman, and seeing one standing at the machine-gun post farther along the cliff edge, waved for her to come in a hurry.

While he waited, he watched the nearing dust cloud. His clan was embarked on more than just the defense of all that they held sacred. This was the fulfillment of First Palmer's great prophecy. And as such, the vindication of all that they believed. It was a time for joy. For dancing. For congress. For fertilization. What luck, he thought, to have been born, to have been present when it all came to pass. He knew that

for hundreds of years after this day, Palmers yet unborn
would hear the stories and wish they could have been alive
to see it.

For as long as seven decades, there had been no room in
the group for doubters or dissent. Those who speculated
aloud that the Spirit wasn't in fact the physical embodiment
of God, or who dared to glance sidelong during the equinox
ceremonies, were summarily cast over the white stones to
meet their Maker.

This interpretation of the Mist as God wasn't part of the
original canon. First Palmer had referred to the Mist meta-
phorically as a beast of flesh and blood. Or he had used
terminology that was beyond the understanding of his prog-
eny. What did they know of molecular computers, of trans-
substantial intelligence, of vaporous membranes? Even
though they could read the words, after a fashion, they had
no clue as to their meaning. So it was far easier for them
to deal with this thing that was always hungry, that could
never be chilled, if they thought of it as God.

And to them it seemed that their monstrous fog bank of
a God provided everything. If only because they made it
responsible for all the good and bad that happened in their
lives. Poor hunting. Rainy summers. Bat-eared babies. Like
most other members of their species, the Palmers were desperate to make sense of the chaos and pain that surrounded
them. And afraid to leave the pain that they knew for the
pain of the unknown. The world beyond the mouth of the
canyon was filled with dangers they could not imagine or
understand.

The woman approached Palmer the Guardian, bearing on
her head a large basket woven of pine needles. She was
indistinguishable from nine-tenths of her fellow clans-
women: cross-eyed, slack mouthed, waistless, stocky and
pregnant. She lowered the basket to her hip, tipped it down
and offered its bounteous contents to him.

It was heaped with chunks of freshly peeled devil's club.

Palmer picked over the top of the pile, selecting a handful of the best. Spitting out his cud, he popped a fresh chunk in his mouth and began to chew. His molar teeth were worn down flat like a cow's or an elk's, from so many years of grinding the stringy root to extract the psychoactive juice.

After he had worked up a good saliva, he made the woman sit next to him on the rocks. She remained placid, almost catatonic, as he absentmindedly stroked her stringy hair, then her shoulders and, reaching through the armholes of her loose shift, her bare breasts. Her pregnancy was far enough advanced to show in her breasts, and her belly had begun to swell. When he fondled her, she stared off into the middle distance, not seeing the oncoming war party, or if seeing it, not caring in the least, the tiniest of smiles on her face as she, too, chewed.

Palmer the Guardian felt himself getting powerfully aroused, which angered him, and he roughly pushed her away.

There was no time for that.

Women had no sense of propriety or proportion, he thought. They were good for gathering the root, for making food and for making babies. They couldn't conceive of complex and important problems, or weren't interested in trying. Palmer found this highly irritating. Though he had to admit, some of the females could fistfight passably well and some could even hunt small game with throw-sticks. Most of them were more like this one—eager to please in certain areas. In areas of their own limited self-interest. And in all other areas, impossibly dense and stubborn.

The woman looked disappointed for a second, then with a gleam in her eye, she started to lift the hem of her shift over her dirt-smeared thighs.

Palmer the Guardian waved her off with an impatient gesture. Chewing his cud furiously, he pulled back from the lookout to check on his fighters and make sure they hadn't succumbed to temptation.

Chapter Twenty-Two

Ryan peered around the sheet-tin outer wall of a roadside shanty. The first of the series of concrete berms designed to keep insiders in the ville—and outsiders out—lay across the dirt track ahead. It was four feet high and triangular in shape, with the widest and heaviest part flat on the ground, which made it virtually impossible for even the biggest wag to ram it aside. The configuration of berms formed an offset pattern, like a herringbone tweed, so incoming or exiting wags had to make a series of hard alternating turns to get around them. All vehicular traffic slowed to a crawl, and was forced to move broadside to the sec men's massed blasters.

Ryan's biggest concern was the safety of the wags they'd stolen. Any hope the crew had depended on them. Even if he and his people managed to get past the barricade's defenders and out the ville's gate, if the wags didn't make it all in one piece, too, they were never going to catch up with the convoy and Trader. And worse, being then stranded on foot, it would just be a matter of time before the baron's sec men chased them down in off-road wags and ran them out of ammunition.

At Ryan's side, Poet was thinking the same thing. "Got to leave the wags well back," he said. "Can't risk getting them all shot up. Try and take the barricades on foot."

Ryan looked behind them, where, around a bend in the road and hidden from view of the berms, the three captured wags sat idling. "Poet," he said, "better collect the crew and have them move up with me. Leave three behind to drive the wags.''

Ryan knew that Poet would assign the driving jobs to crew members he knew were steady. The same ones Ryan would have picked.

As Poet hurried off without hesitation or complaint, as if he were the lieutenant and Ryan the captain, the one-eyed man felt no rush of satisfaction. Which surprised him a little when he realized what had just happened. The balance of authority between them had subtly shifted without his even noticing it. The ground rules of their relationship had changed. Competition had given way to cooperation, at least for the time being. A function of their desperate straits, perhaps, and perhaps because of the absence of Trader.

Perhaps even because of a new mutual respect.

Ryan craned his head around the wall once more. He scanned the top of the barricade and what little of the bunkhouse he could see. There was no sign of movement, anywhere. Which he took to mean that the sec men were already all in position, forewarned by the clatter of blasterfire from the heart of the ville. Their object was clear: to keep the would-be escapees pinned inside the ville long enough for the rest of the sec men to arrive in force at the rear. Then it would just be a matter of mop-up, single bullets behind the ears of those still breathing.

Ryan had left the Remington back in the wag. He figured it would be nothing but a hindrance in the coming fight. It was too long, too slow to come on point and too slow to reload. He thumbed open the Ruger's loading gate and spun the cylinder, making sure that every chamber was loaded with an unfired cartridge. He had no idea how many of the opposition were hiding in among the berms, but based on the sec men he had seen on the way into the ville, and the size of the bunkhouse, it figured to be an even fight.

The crew members hurried up along the edge of the road with Poet in the lead. When they arrived, Ryan waved over those who were unarmed. "You follow us over the obstacles," he told them. "Pick up the blasters from the dead sec men, then move ahead."

To Poet, he said, "We can't wait until we reach the gate to start moving the wags forward."

"Yeah, that's what I thought, too. So I told the drivers to head into the barricades as soon as we gain some ground. That way, we can defend the wags using the berms for cover if more sec men come at us from behind."

"We go at them straight on until I give the signal," Ryan told the assembled crew. "Then we split wide, right and left. The idea is to flank them, make them bunch up in the middle of the barriers. When you've cleared out an area, wave the wags forward. We've got to move fast. This can't turn into a pitched battle, or we're all going to get chilled. It's got to be hit-and-git."

With that, Ryan sucked in a deep breath, waved his Blackhawk in the air and broke from cover. He sprinted into the center of the road, running right into the muzzles of the blasters along the berm. The others followed him, also on a dead run.

The blastershots started almost at once. Slugs zipped past Ryan's body and struck the ground on either side of him. He didn't think about them, about how close or how far away they landed. All he thought about was getting to the break-off point as quickly as he could.

When he was close enough to see the faces of the men shooting at him, he cut right, his long legs pumping.

One of the sec men abruptly rose from behind the concrete cover, thinking he had a clear shot at the dark-haired escapee in front.

From behind Ryan, a short burst of autofire ripped the air, the first fired by his crew. The standing sec man toppled over backward, his weapon flying out of his hands. For a few seconds, all firing stopped as the baron's sec men took in the sight of one of their own, suddenly dead.

As the crew members following Ryan peeled off, left and right, Poet and Abe knelt in the middle of the road and sent bursts of skimming fire along the tops of the concrete barriers. The sec men kept their heads down long enough for Ryan to reach the far end of the first berm.

He vaulted it, slapping his left hand on the top, kicking his legs around over it. As he cleared the top, he saw three sec men crouching, spread out to his left along the inside of the wall. The Ruger boomed in his fist as he fired across his own body without looking down the sights. The closest man clutched at his chest and slumped to the road. Landing on the balls of his feet, Ryan thumb-cocked his blaster and charged the other two.

Maybe it was the confusion of the all-out attack, the noise of the big Magnum blaster, the threat of sudden death, because although they fired full-auto, neither of the sec men managed to hit the onrushing Ryan. He, on the other hand, nailed them both with successive shots to the center chest. He wasn't fussy about where he hit them, just as long as they stayed down for the count.

Ryan turned away from the writhing bodies and vaulted the next barrier. Behind him, he could hear the others, the tramping of their boots, the grunts of effort as they cleared the berms.

Autofire rattled in his ears.

Bullets blistered at him, sparking off the top of the next berm, clipping free chips of concrete. Shielding his good eye with his hand, he dropped down to cover.

So far, the sec men were either dying or pulling back. As anticipated, they were playing the stall game. To Ryan, it looked like there were another four or five of the staggered walls between him and the gate. From the rear, he could hear the wags begin to advance through the maze, engines growling as they crept around the berms.

He quickly reloaded the Ruger with cartridges from his shirt pocket, then snapped the cylinder gate shut. Turning, he motioned for the crew members spread out behind him to stay where they were and wait for him to make his move. He then ran along the front of the wall toward the opening that allowed traffic to pass.

Ryan rounded the corner with the Blackhawk up and blazing in his fist. Like a giant's finger, it flicked the bodies of the sec men clustered there, sending them twisting down, screaming, or dropping them stone dead in their tracks. Those who survived closed ranks and tried to return fire, but Ryan was already across the open roadway to the safety of the berm on the other side.

Straight ahead of him, he could see Poet and Abe hurdling over the barrier, and when he looked back the way he had come, he could see the rest of the crew jumping the berm there, as well. Just as he'd planned, the frontal assault had allowed the crew to get into chilling position on the flanks of the main sec-man force.

Autofire raged back and forth as Ryan moved out from cover. In the confusion of blastershots, he could pick out the sound of Poet's CAR-15: it made an almost chimelike tone as it spewed death. And there was no mistaking the rocking boom of Hun's 10-gauge.

As he ran down the narrow traffic lane, Ryan scooped up one of the dead sec men's weapons. It was a KG-99 auto-blaster that had been converted to select fire. He advanced along the ends of the openings in the berms, shooting the machine pistol in short, controlled bursts, driving the remaining sec men ahead of him. They were in full retreat, now, no longer even attempting to put up a fight.

At the edge of the last berm, he stopped and again took cover. Beyond it, the surviving sec men had their backs up against the mesh of the wire gate. One of them was fumbling with the gate's bolt, trying to get it open.

"Put the blasters down!" Ryan shouted. "If you lay them down, you can walk away."

Whether it was from their blind panic, or whether they

were used to dealing with people who didn't keep their word, the sec men instead opened fire.

It was a big mistake.

There was no gunfight. It was more like an execution. The sec men were held standing, quivering against the wire by the hail of lead Ryan and the rest of the crew poured into them.

"Enough!" Poet shouted over the din.

And the blasterfire faltered, then ceased.

Ryan tossed aside the empty KG-99 and strode over to the gate with the Ruger cocked and ready. It wasn't needed. The sec men were not only dead, but they had also been torn to shreds.

As he looked over his shoulder, Ryan saw the captured wags rounding the final barrier, one by one. He kicked open the gate and waved them through.

Chapter Twenty-Three

Doc Tanner sat chained by the ankle to one of the war wag's driver's compartment jump seats. Out the undogged front windows, the mountain range ahead loomed larger and larger. The wag's driver, who was also a captive, a man with frizzy, thinning red hair and a matching beard, was being held at blasterpoint by the bit of slime that called itself Vernel. Doc looked at the snake brand on the back of his shaved head, angry red burn marks that had a kind of iridescent, unhealthy sheen to them, and decided they defamed the noble race of cobra, not because of the crudeness of the rendering, but because of the creature they adorned. Baron Lundquist Zeal sat in the copilot's chair, his outlandish high heels propped up on the dashboard, which caused the lapels of his fur robe to slide wide apart, exposing a pair of pale, skinny legs, and other, even less attractive appendages.

On the road directly ahead of them, appearing and disappearing in the huge cloud of yellow dust it raised, was the flagship of the captured fleet. By far, it was the biggest armored vehicle Doc had ever seen. Its outward appearance reminded him of the machines in a short story he'd once read by H. G. Wells about futuristic land warfare, but for the life of him he couldn't recall the title. A grim tale, he remembered, predictive of terrible and inhuman things to come. In hindsight, perhaps prophetic. But no written description could ever capture the raw power of the vehicle that broke trail for the war caravan. If you stood next to its engines at idle, you couldn't feel your own heartbeat. Doc had no idea what their horsepower rating was; he knew only that at their lowest output, they made the ground shake underfoot.

The wag he rode in was much smaller, but similar in overall design. Doc had never been inside a military vehicle like this. Everything was strictly functional, without ornamentation. The walls and ceiling were painted olive drab. The upholstery was a lighter shade of the same color, except where it had been patched with strips of silver duct tape. Duct tape also held together the bundles of wiring that followed the I beams up the walls and over the compartment's roof. Though it wasn't a machine built for the comfort of those who rode in it, they had left their mark on it. It smelled of body odor, cigar butts and fried onions.

Doc's conveyance, like the others in the convoy, was capable of a good head of speed. They had covered twenty miles in about three-quarters of an hour, this over a road that wasn't a road in many places. It often looked more like a streambed, with small rocks, boulders and clumps of dead brush on its shoulders. The big wag in the lead crushed all such obstacles, cutting paths through islands of stunted trees, grinding steep banks to powder.

As Doc sat there, hands folded in his lap, he felt the return of a sense of terrible foreboding. He felt like a man traveling to his own execution. After a night of fitful sleep, he had awakened mentally exhausted and had discovered his bravado of the previous evening had evaporated. In the light of day, Doc was no longer able to rail at God for not protecting him from random evil. And he was no longer looking forward, with his fine teeth bared in defiance, to the empty peace of oblivion. He feared it. As grim and agonized as his life had been of late, it was, after all, better than nothing. And even now there were moments when he could recall the tenderness of Emily's caress, the children's laughter at some ridiculous joke. Moments when, even in the horror of this accursed landscape in which he was trapped, he could see something beautiful and be touched in the heart by it.

And there was always the hope, however slim, that if he could travel forward in time, he could also travel backward. If he could just find a way to make it happen...

"A zealie for your thoughts," the baron said to him.

Doc stiffened.

"You worried about the inbreds, Doc?" Vernel asked. "Afraid they'll have your wigwag for lunch?"

Doc just blinked, feigning one of his spells.

"No, he's not worried," Zeal said. "Inbreds think he's some kind of big shot, don't they, Doc? Come on, give us the story of your breathless escape one more time. I want to hear it again."

Doc shut his eyes and recited automatically. "I stepped out of the stockpile," he said. "In the place where the fog with teeth and claws had always appeared to the savages. There were a few of them bent over on the road, employed in straightening a line of white rocks. Quartzite, I believe. They saw me at once, and I created quite a stir among their ranks. It seems that I was the only person to ever survive walking that part of the road. They did not know I had simply turned off Hell's watchdog. Not that they could have understood such a thing, anyway. They dropped to their knees as I walked past, lowered their heads in respect and hid their eyes from my sight.

"I do not remember the rest of it too clearly. I believe I had to have hit my head inside the stockpile at some point. I know as I walked I was bleeding from a gash on my right temple. I heard the savages jabbering back and forth at one another in a sort of pidgin English. Then they shouted for all the others to come up the road and see me. They said I had stepped from the lair of the Spirit in the Mist. Or lair of the Mist Spirit, something of the sort. They said that I was its favored one, as foretold by ancient legend. That I must not be harmed or hindered because I was on its mission. They parted ranks to let me pass down the road. They never touched a hair on my head. I do believe the brutes worship the fog as a god of some kind.''

"Triple stupes," Vernel snorted in contempt, then he laughed. "We're gonna take their god away from them."

"Or better yet," Zeal said, "feed them to it."

Doc slumped back, momentarily exhausted, against the compartment wall.

"You don't have a problem with that, do you, Doc?" the baron inquired.

"Either you will kill them, or they will kill you. How the events transpire is of little interest to me, personally. I will be alive or I will be dead, and either way, I will still be here where I do not belong."

"You're breaking my balls," Vernel said.

"Have you ever seen the watchdog, this fog thing, take someone away?" Zeal asked.

"Honestly I can't recall," Doc told him. "I can only remember what my keepers said when they warned me about the fog and told me about the twin orbs. They said nothing could withstand it. They said no armor could keep it out, if it wanted in. And that nothing could stop it once it was in motion. Like a storm, it has to run its course."

"So the stones won't stop it? I thought the stones would stop it," Zeal said with concern.

"I can keep it from being released," Doc said. "I can keep it caged with them, and I can drive it back into its cage when it first appears. But I cannot make the beast retreat once it has smelled blood. It is in its nature to behave in a certain fashion, like a living creature. The whitecoats programmed it that way, you know."

"Show me the stones, again," Zeal demanded.

Doc opened his fist.

"Amazing," the baron said. He looked as if he was almost ready to reach out and touch them, but then he thought better of it and drew back. "Don't drop them. Your life depends on it."

That wasn't news to Doc.

Ahead, the huge wag had reached the foot of the entrance to the mountain pass. As it started to climb the grade, it slowed. Doc could see the vent hatches being closed and dogged.

Getting ready for war.

THE INSIDE of the MCP resounded with the clang of hatches slamming shut. The interior lights, combat red, came on automatically. When Trader looked aft, down the side corridor, he saw one of Shabazz's men climb up into the machine-gun blister on that side. Along the middle of the connecting hallway, three others were getting in position at the armored blasterports. They each had M-16s that they had looted from War Wag One's onboard armory. Also on the deck, set in the racks made expressly for that purpose, were open boxes of preloaded 30-round magazines. The pirate crew braced themselves as Shabazz lumbered up the grade, taking the first hard bend in the road.

No sooner had he rounded the bend than from somewhere outside, from somewhere above, came a rattle of heavy-machine-gun fire, and a flurry of unleashed slugs pelted the MCP's driver compartment roof. The bullets either shattered against the armor plate or veered off, the ricochets whining into the distance.

"They're gonna have to do better than that," Shabazz said, turning the wag's yoke back the other way to take the next turn in the road.

It was just a kiss hello, Trader thought. A peck on the cheek to let them know they were there.

Through the side viewports, he could see that the road was quickly narrowing, until it became for the MCP what amounted to one lane. There was a ribbon of pavement on either side of its wheel skirts, and the pavement ended in sheer rock walls.

Again, as Shabazz rounded the bend, they came under

autofire. This time it was heavier, and it lasted a good thirty seconds. This time it was directed not only at the roof, but straight into the front end of the wag.

"Got a comm unit on this thing?" Shabazz asked him. "I need to go wag to wag. We got inbreds on the road ahead. They're the ones blasting at us."

Trader pointed it out. The microphone was hanging on a clip above the driver's seat.

The bearded trader jerked it down and thumbed the transmit switch. "This is Shabazz in the lead wag," he said. "Fire at will, you gunners. Don't wait for a signal from me. Fire at will. You see any of the scumwads skulking around out there, you chill them dead."

Almost at once, blasterfire rang out. It came from overhead, in the new machine-gun blister. The string of shots ran to twenty-five at least, and in less than three seconds.

"Burst length is way long," J.B. grumbled at Trader's side. "That triple stupe's going to burn out the RPK's barrel mighty quick."

"Kind of gets your hackles up, doesn't it, J.B.?"

The Armorer nodded.

"Yeah, mine, too," Trader admitted.

Shabazz reached out with a grimy paw and pressed the red button on the dash. The twin 20 mm cannons responded by roaring instantly. Up the road, some seventy-five yards ahead, HE warheads exploded in a tight cluster. Bits of hot shrapnel sang off War Wag One's bow.

"Man, I nailed three of the bastards!" Shabazz said as he pulled his face back from the ob slit. "You should've seen them fly, Trader. In chunks! Hah!"

The annoying rain of autofire continued, from both above and in front. Shabazz chose to ignore it, taking another S-turn in low gear. The road was creeping up the mountain, and so were they. So far, the guardians of the pass hadn't done much of a job. Unless, of course, Trader thought, they hadn't intended on defending the lower stretch of road. Un-

less they were just playing cat and mouse. Unless they had
something real special planned for up ahead.

"Come here, Trader," Shabazz said, "I want to show
you something funny."

When Trader leaned down next to the driver's seat, Shabazz pointed out the ob slit. "See those cuts across the road
way up the hill? Those are the ditches that stopped our wags
before. Not gonna stop this monster, though. We're gonna
hop their ditches like they were nothing." With that, Shabazz goosed the throttle.

Trader had to admit that the antitank traps looked too
shallow to be much of a threat to any of the war wags.

Then there was a terrific groaning, cracking sound right
under their feet. Everything suddenly shifted nose forward.
Trader was slammed against the back of the driver's seat;
he had to cling to it to keep from being flipped over into
Shabazz's lap.

The front end of the MCP was dropping, and kept dropping.

"Oh, shit!" Shabazz cried, trying frantically to find reverse gear, and only making grinding noises as he repeatedly missed his target.

"Hang on," Trader told Sam and J.B. as the earth continued to open up and the huge vehicle slid nose down into
a truly monumental chasm.

The MCP came to a crunching halt that sent Trader to
his knees. All the red lights dimmed for a second, then they
came back up.

Trader estimated their downward angle to be about forty
degrees, which told him the back half of War Wag One was
still hanging on the edge of the collapsed roadway.

A hailstorm of bullets clanged and clattered against the
outside of the hull, making it impossible to hear or to think.
Shabazz acted like a man possessed, grinding the gears until
he finally found reverse. Engines roaring, every drive axle

torquing, the rear end of the MCP slipped around on the lip of the ditch but didn't move backward so much as an inch.

Adding to the tumult and chaos, blasterfire erupted from the wag's every blasterport and blister.

A lucky slug from one of the savages skipped through the copilot's ob slit and sang through the compartment before cutting a silvery track along the olive drab of the far wall.

Shabazz tried again, revving the engines to redline before dropping the transmission into reverse. Trader could see that the man was close to panic. Shabazz knew just how desperate the situation was. The MCP's weapons systems were unaimable, stuck either pointing down in the hole or up in the sky. Its vast bulk was immobile. It wouldn't be long before the guardians had their way with them.

Despite his efforts, the big wag stayed right where it was.

The wag-to-wag intercom blared down at them in a distorted screech. Someone was shouting over volleys of blasterfire. It took a few seconds to sort out the words, and the speaker. It was Baron Zeal. "Shabazz, get that piece of shit out of the way!" he yelled. "The bastards are going to overrun us!"

Shabazz reached up for the mike. "Zeal, we're stuck in a tank trap. You're gonna have to back out...back down the pass...."

"Let Trader drive!" came the shouted response.

Something big and heavy hit the roof of the wag.

The jarring impact made Trader stagger, and dropped dust and paint flakes down on them.

"Come on! Do it!" Shabazz said to his archrival as he vacated the chair. "Do it, you fucking bastard!"

In no particular hurry, Trader took the helm. He pointed at the stub of a cheroot stuck in the corner of his mouth and said to Shabazz, "First gimme a light."

The outraged Shabazz fumbled with a match. As he got the cigar lit, another rocking impact struck the wag.

"What are they doing?" he said.

"Boulders," Trader replied, puffing the cheroot until it was well ablaze. "They're rolling boulders down on us."

With that, he reached for the lever alongside the driver console, released the safety catch and pushed it away from him. From the back of the wag, there came the meshing of gears, then the already elevated MCP's rear end lifted up slightly.

With the rear Cat tracks down, getting out of the ditch was a piece of cake. Trader revved the engines and just backed the big rig up, and as he did, the nose end lifted out of the trap and the front wheels rolled out onto the road.

After he'd reversed about fifteen feet from the edge, he stopped, looked over at Shabazz and said, "Now what?"

PALMER THE GUARDIAN was watching the huge armored vehicle from a fortified position on the edge of the cliff when it opened fire with its cannons. The war beast had a voice, after all, a terrifying voice and a tongue of flame. He ducked back behind the rock pile as shards of shattered stone and fragments of steel jacketing whined past his head. When he looked out again, he saw that the wag had blown a great smoking chunk out of the corner of the cliff opposite. He also saw his clansmen scattered like leaves over the roadway, their bodies sprawled in attitudes of death. He had never been witness to such ballistic power. Clearly the drawings in First Palmer's diary didn't do this wheeled thing justice.

His heart lifted when he realized that the wounded down on the road were still fighting. Legless, minus an arm, they still clutched their assault rifles and continued to pour fire at the oncoming machine until, one by one, they bled to death. This thanks to miraculous analgesic properties of the rad-mutated thorny plant.

It was said that if a warrior ate devil's club the day before a battle, he could be nearly cut in two by enemy bullets or blades and still live long enough to dance a victory jig on his dead foe's chest.

Palmer the Guardian laid down another 10-round burst from his M-60. Most of the clan was shooting at this point. As the war machine advanced the critical last few yards, it was stippled with bullet impacts, dust puffs and bright lead spalls. There was a terrible roar and a cloud of dust as the roadway split, then collapsed beneath it.

Palmer let out a whoop of joy. For a moment, the rattle of autofire ceased. On the other side of the pass, his fellow clansmen were likewise shouting their triumph.

Following First Palmer's instructions, they had craftily undermined the road, digging from either shoulder toward the middle, shoring up the excavation with timbers as they progressed. When they were done, there were only three inches of tarmac and a foot of soil covering the huge trap. As First Palmer had predicted, the approaching enemy saw only the small ditches on the road ahead, and thought it was safe to advance.

Now the Palmer clan had the great, growling war beast facedown in the pit.

Autofire resumed, but the torrent of armor-piercing rounds didn't seem to have any effect. They weren't penetrating the thing's steel hide. This, too, had been foreseen by First Palmer. He had described such armor and pointed out the futility of trying to breach it with conventional munitions. Only a specially designed cannon round could do the trick, one with a uniquely shaped explosive warhead, which, though it had little effect on the outside of the target hull, blasted off huge sections of the inside of the armor, turning the vehicle into an implosion gren.

Below Palmer, with a roar and a grinding of Cat tracks, the thing backed out of the pit. Once again, the clan leader rose from the rock bunker. He stood and waved First Palmer's flag to the rest of his clan. It was the signal for the final trap to be sprung.

From four widely separate positions, two on either side of the cliff, clansmen using long wooden levers pried free the keystones that held massive cliff-edge rockfalls in place. It was enough rockfall to block the road from shoulder to shoulder, and to crush or cripple anything that stood upon it. The Palmers had spent many difficult days moving the heavy stones into place, balancing the piles just right.

Now, at almost the same instant, the piles were freed, and the resulting four-pronged avalanche made the ground shake. A massive cloud of dust rushed out and up from beneath the outfall and, as it boiled, it concealed the roadway from view.

When the wind from the peak swept the dust away, Palmer the Guardian could see that the trap had worked. The largest of the war wags, the lead wag, was hemmed in on all sides by giant boulders. They climbed its flanks and squatted on its breastworks. The smaller wags were less covered by rockfall, but equally trapped, either because of the load on the road or because the other vehicles blocked them in.

With another wave of his ragged red, white and blue pennant, Palmer ordered his clansmen to do the deed, according to their revered progenitor.

With smothering exhaust, with blasterfire. Now was time for the chilling.

Chapter Twenty-Four

Doc Tanner was no more prepared for the thunderous avalanche of rock than Baron Zeal or Vernel. It came at their wag from both sides at once, with a deafening roar. Caught between the competing torrents of stone, the war wag was savaged left and right by violent, twisting shocks. Its helpless passengers were hurled about the cabin, shaken like pebbles in a tin can.

And the dust.

It swept in through the open air vents, through the blasterports and ob slits, a choking, swirling mass so thick that after a few seconds it blocked out the red interior lights. No one saw the lights fade out. There was no way a person could keep his eyes open in the stinging maelstrom of grit.

Doc choked through the long tail of his shirt, which he used to cover his nose and mouth, certain he was going to suffocate.

Then the driver fumbled for and found a switch on the dash panel. The wag's fans came on, blowing the dust out the exhaust vents.

Slowly the air became breathable again, and the red interior lights glimmered in the thinning haze.

"Inbreds be coming right sharpish now," Vernel gasped. His snake tattoos were masked with a dusting of yellow powder, as were his eyelids, ears and the top of his shaved head. As was everything else in the driver's compartment.

Zeal jerked down the intercom mike and shouted into it. "Chill them! Chill all the fuckers!" As he did so, the shoulders of his fur robe gave off great puffs of trapped dust.

Doc, despite the fact that he was in the selfsame predicament as the baron, took great pleasure in seeing the man so thoroughly discomfited. Not only fearful, but panicked.

The driver didn't share Doc's delight as he quickly became the agitated baron's number-one target. "Move this thing!" Zeal ordered.

To the red-haired man's credit, he tried.

Engine bellowing, gears grinding, he shifted the transmission forward, then into reverse. But there were big rocks ahead. A wall of them jammed up against the backside of War Wag One, and similarly, there was a wall behind, jammed up against the front end of the wag to the rear. The driver had nowhere to go, even with the Cat tracks lowered, their steel plates churning metamorphic rock to flour. And when he advanced a few inches it allowed the rocks to settle in more firmly behind him, which meant that when he tried to go in reverse, or forward, again, he couldn't budge the vehicle at all.

Anticipating that some extra incentive might be necessary, Zeal had ripped off his right high heel, and held it like a hammer by the outsole and throat. As he reared his arm back to strike the driver in the back of the head with the wickedly pointed heel, a horrendous volume of autofire pounded them, the hailstorm to end all.

Zeal, as well as Doc, had to clap his palms over his ears to dull the pain.

It wasn't just a display, Doc realized at once. It was a distraction, something to occupy those inside the wag while the savages closed in for the kill. He wondered if they would remember him from so many weeks ago, if they would show him the same respect and deference. If they didn't recognize him, he had no proof of who he was or where he'd been, had no proof that he was, in fact, the favored one of the Mist. Would they drag him out with the others, line him up against the cliff wall and machine-gun him to death? Doc didn't know, but from recent experience he was fairly certain that he couldn't count on the kindness of strangers.

After a bit, there was a lull in the shooting, perhaps so the machine gunners could reload or let their barrels cool down. The baron was immediately back on the wag-to-wag intercom. "Trader!" he shouted into the mike. "Trader, damn you! Answer me!"

TRADER FLINCHED at the shrill racket blaring at him from the intercom speaker. The mike was hanging just overhead, but he didn't reach for it. What was the point? Even though he had Zeal right where he wanted him, even though he was in a position to wring even more concessions from the man, what good were they? The bastard would never honor them, anyway.

For a sharp businessman like Trader, it was a sad state of affairs.

"I take it you want out of here before our friends outside start jumping up and down on the roof?" he said to Shabazz.

His beard, hair and clothing covered in dust, the other trader nodded.

"Then, hang on to something," Trader told him as he revved the engines. "I'll show you what this beauty can do."

Shifting into reverse with the Cat tracks, he rammed into the rocks behind to allow the stones in front to slip down from in front of the barrels of the EX-29 cannons. When he was sure they had dropped below the level of the muzzles, he started yelling at the top of his lungs. Hearing him, Sam and J.B. joined in. Then Trader reached for the red button with his thumb.

Shabazz, seeing this, clamped his hands over his ears and started yelling, too.

The flurry of 20 mm HE rounds exploded at extreme close range, shattering the boulders heaped in front of them.

The yelling was to equalize the pressure in their heads, otherwise they might have been deafened by the concussions.

When the cordite smoke and rock dust had cleared, Trader had a little more room to work. All he was trying to do was to free up the wedge-shaped, ramming front bumper, and get the wheels angled up the incline of the boulder field. He figured that the Cat tracks would push the nose up and over the obstacles.

Ahead of them, the great ditch that had almost swallowed up the MCP was now mostly filled in with fallen boulders. Accelerating, Trader crashed into them, driving them apart with the front bumper. After rearing back and ramming several more times, the way was clear enough for him to proceed.

Trader ran the engines to redline, then popped the clutch. The Cat tracks snarled on the loose stones, the rear of War Wag One fishtailing as the steel-clad belts fought to get a grip. The huge vehicle lurched forward, then it was past the rockfall. The smaller trap lay across the road directly in front of them. Trader hit the ditches fast. There was a hard bump as the front wheels dropped, then Cat tracks dug in behind, pushing the wag onward, driving the wheels up and over the ditch's lip.

He slowed after a hundred feet or so of rapid climb and pulled down the rear-viewing periscope. Behind them, the clansmen on the cliff edges on both sides of the road were rolling individual boulders down onto the three smaller wags as their drivers maneuvered forward and back, trying to wedge their way clear of the rockfall. He could also see the machine-gun positions, raining fire down on his vehicles from the lip of the cliff. He knew he had to take care of their attackers before he could do anything about Shabazz and Zeal. It was either that or the bastards would have his war wags.

"Sam," Trader said over his shoulder, "you grab the wheel. J.B. and me are going aft to get on the rockets."

Shabazz's crewman pointed his snubnose revolver at Trader's head as he got up from the driver's chair.

"Your call, Shabazz," Trader said, holding up his hands. "But your boys can't run my weapons systems. I think we've seen the proof of that. Now, we can head War Wag One uphill and get away from these guardians for the time being, but we've still got to drive back down the same stretch of road to get the hell out of this pass. If you let us, me and J.B. can wipe them out, here and now."

Shabazz waved his crewman off. "Go with them," he said to the man. "If they screw up, blast them dead."

Trader turned to Sam and said, "Keep watch in the rear periscope. When things are lined up, we'll give you a shout on the intercom."

Sam goosed the engines and continued slowly up the grade.

Trader and J.B., hobbled by ankle chains, and trailed by Shabazz's gunman, hurried down the corridor to the rear of the MCP. They had to keep a hand on the wall to keep from being tripped up and falling. Not because of the wag's speed or the hairpin turns. The other members of Shabazz's crew had been firing at will out the blasterports. The dimmies hadn't bothered to put the spent casing bags on the M-16s' ejector ports. There were empty 5.56 mm hulls rolling all over the place. It was like trying to walk on a floor covered in marbles.

Walking carefully, they headed for the middle of the stern for the ladder leading up into another miniblister. When they arrived, they saw a pair of legs halfway up the rungs. Somebody was inside the blister. Trader and J.B. grabbed the pirate's ankles and jerked him bodily off the ladder.

The man landed hard on his butt on the deck. He hopped up, at first surprised, then combative.

"Keep your hands off my weapons," J.B. warned him with a finger in the face.

"The damned things don't work, anyway," the man countered.

"Out of the road," Trader ordered, using a brawny forearm to shove the irate Shabazz crewman to one side. He mounted the ladder as J.B. set to work on a control panel enclosed in a large wallbox. The 2.75-inch HEAP rockets were electrically fired. There was a priming sequence that armed each pod for rocket flight, and enabled the warheads for contact explosion. It amounted to a fail-safe. While J.B. flipped the rows of switches below, Trader stuck his head into the armor-plate blister, which contained the targeting system for the rockets.

This blister was swivel-mounted, and its rotation was driven by an electric motor. Its side-to-side movement coincided with the tracking of the multiple rocket pods on the MCP's rear roof. The gunner sat on a small folding chair that moved with the blister. A yoke in front of the ob slit controlled the up-and-down angle of the rocket pods. Set in the center of the ob slit was a converted binocular artillery sight, calibrated to the flight of the rockets. It moved with the blister, side to side, and up and down with the yoke.

Trader climbed into the operator's seat and juked the twin sets of rocket pods up and down, to the limits of their range. The controls felt nice and tight. He was glad to see that everything worked. Apparently nothing had been crushed or damaged by the rockfall. Perhaps because the roof was too high up for the bouncing boulders to have reached. The arming-indicator lights on the panel beside the yoke were all dark.

As Sam climbed the grade, Trader watched the terrain through the artillery sights. As they reached a steeper part of the roadway, it brought the cliff edges below, and their attack positions, into the sight picture. Trader thumbed the intercom transmit button overhead. "Hold it, Sam!" he said. "Hold it right there!

"Still got no juice," he called down to J.B.

"Now you do."

When Trader looked in front of him, all the panel lights were lit. Party time. He chewed at his cigar butt as he brought the targeting array around to bracket the cliff-edge machine-gun nests. They had themselves a hardsite, all right, reinforced with rock. He smiled around the cheroot. A bit close to the edge of the cliff, though.

"Fire in the hole," he said into the intercom as he toggled the switches next to the lights on his panel. Then he flipped back the housing that protected the trigger for the right cluster of rocket pods. He hit the red knob with the ball of his fist.

The MCP shuddered, and Trader caught a blast of withering heat right through the skin of the blister. The birds were away. He tracked their flight through the artillery binoculars. Smoke trails twisted in the sunlight. At impact, they made a string of bright orange flashes all along the undercut shelf of rock. The cliff edge held for a second, then it just slipped away, taking with it machine-gun nests, clansmen and thousands of more tons of rock.

The fresh load of granite crashed to the side of the road, barely missing the third war wag in line. Its cloud of dust swept over all the wags, momentarily obscuring them from view.

The guardians on the opposite cliff realized their vulnerability and started to run back from the cliff verge, trying to make it to the cover of the evergreen trees higher up on the mountainside, which made it a bit more challenging for Trader. He armed, aimed and fired individual rockets from his left pod, which caught the pass defenders in a firestorm of hot shrapnel. Trader left a string of smoking craters along the distant tree line.

He could hear Shabazz's crew, having witnessed the demonstration, yelling and cheering on the deck below. He had saved their butts, at least for the time being. Through the binoculars, he saw the other wags had finally freed themselves and were starting up the grade to join them.

As Trader climbed down from the blister, Shabazz was there to greet him.

"Nice work, Trader," he said. "You really put the wood to them inbreds. And now you get your well-deserved reward."

At blasterpoint, Trader, Sam and J.B. were forced up the corridor and into one of War Wag One's windowless storage lockers. There was just enough room inside for the three of them and their chains.

Shabazz slammed the steel door, plunging them into darkness. Trader heard the lock bolt click shut.

Through the door, a familiar laughing voice said, "Sleep tight, now."

Chapter Twenty-Five

Doc was hauled through the war wag's doorway by the scruff of his neck and hurled to the asphalt outside. Before he could even groan, he was jerked back up to his feet. Semidazed, he blinked into the gaudily smeared, thoroughly deranged eyes of Lundquist Zeal.

Ahead of them, all of Shabazz's crew and the baron's accompanying sec men were standing beside the largest of the wags, which was stopped about thirty feet from the line of white rocks across the road. Farther up the road was the dead end, the flat, apparently natural cliff face that concealed the entrance to Spearpoint, the stockpile of stockpiles.

For Doc, it was the moment of truth.

"Move along," Zeal said as he twisted him around and delivered a sharp slap to the back of his head. The blow sent him staggering toward the waiting Shabazz, who had seen enough of the Mist to know better than to step over the line of rocks prematurely.

"Well?" the baron demanded of Doc. "Where's your fearsome fog? Let's see you deal with it."

Doc was counting on the fact that to a certain extent Zeal and Shabazz had to trust him. They knew nothing of the entrance to the stockpile, where exactly it was or how its mechanism operated. He had planned his farewell speech to them accordingly.

"When I cross the border of rocks," he said, "Cerberus will appear out of nowhere."

"And then you will cage it?"

"Yes, I will make it retreat. But I must lock the cage door or you will not be protected."

"And you do that with the stones?"

"Yes, but I must also operate the controls at the doorway."

"I don't see any doorway over there. No controls, either."

"They will both appear, I assure you."

"How do we know he won't just duck inside and then sic the mist on us?" Shabazz said to the baron.

"Because every one of our shooters is going to have a blaster aimed at the back of his head," Zeal replied. "If he tries anything, we will smoke him."

Doc turned to look the baron in the face. Bleeding red lipstick was like a vast bruise around the grim slit of the man's mouth. "There's no need for that," the old man assured him with all the sincerity he could muster. "You can trust me."

Zeal laughed. "And you can trust me. Proceed!"

As Doc stepped over the line of rocks, he knew two things. First, that the moment the doors to Spearpoint opened, he would be cut down from behind by the guns massed behind him. Second, that he had no intention of waiting around for that to happen.

Between Doc and the cliff face, the fog appeared out of thin air, a wisp at first that billowed, expanding in all directions with tendrils like the tops of storm-tossed waves. At the core of the swelling mass was the crackling, yellowish light of electrical discharge.

Doc stopped in his tracks.

It is just a device, he told himself, nothing more.

But looking into it was like staring into the very heart of chaos. Wild energies flared. Negative. Destructive. Overwhelming. And the static charge they gave off made every hair on his entire body stand on end. Snow and sleet whipped from its churning face. Hailstones bounced on the asphalt. The smell of ozone tingled in his nostrils. An angry smell.

Behind him, Doc's enemies, his torturers, sucked in and held their respective breaths. They, too, felt the power of the thing they faced.

Doc had observed the identical instrument elsewhere; it was a standard feature of the other important redoubts he had traveled through. A construct, so the whitecoats had told him, of certain gaseous molecules. Man-made molecules. It was an automaton of vapor. As such, it had a limited reach, and could only exist within a few dozen yards of its generating source. But within that narrow zone, it was the ultimate authority.

It was easy to see why such a creature had been developed. The fog was a guard dog that never had to be fed or watered, that would never die, or grow old, that would always respond to a certain set of preprogrammed parameters of incursion. Violate its territory and you were its meat. Had anyone considered that this inanimate hound of hell might remain on duty for more than a century? The predark whitecoats had apparently overdesigned their defensive systems, as they had seemed to overdesign everything else—except, of course, a way to avert Armageddon.

Doc clicked the gray spheres together in his hand, and as he did so, he felt a steady hum build. The hum peaked and turned into a series of powerful pulsations that throbbed up his forearm all the way to his shoulder and neck.

The fog knew its master.

With angry, electric fire snapping in its belly, the cloud mass drew back into itself.

As Doc advanced, it retreated farther, growing smaller and smaller in volume.

No audible commands were necessary. The spheres did what they did by their proximity to the vapor. The energy field they generated corralled it, contained it, compressed it.

The last ghostly wisp slipped out of sight, as if through a hairline crack in space. Then the way was clear.

In nine strides Doc reached the cliff face, which was either the backstop of his firing squad, or the avenue of his escape. It depended on timing, and, of course, luck.

The outer doors to all of the government redoubts were locked by a cunningly concealed keypad. The spheres had nothing to do with making the numerical keypad appear or with keeping the fog penned up; those had been bald-faced lies meant to keep the pirates behind the line of rocks. One only had to feel around for the keypad's release mechanism set in the living rock, which Doc quickly did. With his back to the baron and his crew, hiding what he was doing from them with his body, the old man punched in the access code.

Something inside the cliff face clanked, loud, metallic, heavy. Then some machinery whirred and the rock began to move, sliding to the left. Even as it did so, he knew the massive, five-foot-thick, nukeblast-proof, titanium-steel inner door was opening to the right. When the two edges passed each other, Doc dived headfirst between the spreading gap. He landed on his belly on the polished concrete floor and instantly rolled to the left, out of the doorway.

A fraction of a second later, a barrage of automatic-weapons fire screamed down the access tunnel, sparking off the floor, walls and ceiling.

Doc was already on his feet, darting to the keypad set in the inner wall. When he tapped in the reverse of the numbers he keyed on the outside pad, the doors started closing at once.

Over the clatter of blasterfire, the bullets whining through the narrowing gap in the doors, he heard shouts. They were cut off when the doors slammed shut with an echoing crash. As the doors closed, a bank of lights came on over his head. The blasterfire continued for a few seconds more, but it sounded as if it were a mile or two away.

Doc didn't hesitate. He clicked the orbs together in his

hand. As the oddly pleasant pulsations rippled up his arm, he said, "They're all yours, beastie."

EVEN THOUGH Baron Zeal had cried out a warning as the old man hurled himself through the opening, even though every man jack of his and Shabazz's crews fired at him, they had apparently missed the old bastard.

When he saw Doc rolling out of sight, he shouted, "Get him!" And gave Shabazz a hard shove in the middle of the back. "Don't let him close the doors!"

Shabazz, in turn, shoved his crew members ahead of him before advancing across the line of rocks. Vernel and the baron's sec men rushed after them.

Again, it was too little too late. Before Shabazz or any of the others could close the gap, the rock face slid shut, which left them all standing in the middle of Cerberus's pen.

What happened next, happened so quickly that it froze Zeal in place. At the same instant that the first wisp of mist appeared, there was a flash and a rocking thunder crack, and someone in the center of the pack flew apart, as if a high-explosive charge had been placed inside his belly. A puff of gore mist, then chunks: decapitated head, severed arms, ribs, backbone, hurtling in all directions.

Before any of the pirates or sec men could recover, the mist had doubled in size and doubled again. The men who were the fastest of foot, those who had made it almost all the way to the cliff face, were swallowed up by it. Their screams weren't. Chain lightning sizzled and cracked in the depths of the boiling cloud.

Shabazz and the others turned and ran from the advancing face of the mist. Like a tidal wave it came. Only insubstantial as smoke. Sleet and hailstones pelted their backs as they fled; this while blazing sunshine bathed their blood-drained faces.

The beast took them as it found them.

In ones. In twos. In fives.

And it found them quickly.

There was no end to its appetite, and the more it ate, the more savage it became. Tendrils of mist tangled running legs. Torsos burst apart like frag grens, showering those fleeing in front with splinters of bone and ruptured bowel.

As Zeal found his legs and began to turn, to step over the line of rocks to safety, he saw it take Levi Shabazz. The trader's beard was wrapped over his shoulder as he dashed, eyes enormous with terror, arms and legs driving for all he was worth. It came down over his face like a veil. Or a hood. There was a cry, shrill, like a woman's, then the hidden skull detonated with a wet, muffled pop and the wall of mist swallowed the rest of him before it could fall to the ground.

Vernel, the last man to step across the border of stones, was the only one who really had a chance. He lunged desperately for safety with tendrils sweeping at his heels.

The baron felt a cold touch against his back, and he smelled snow. Before he could take another step, there was a crackling snap and he went flying. It was as if something had taken hold of his ankle and flipped him heels over head, something possessed of such awesome power that he couldn't even conceive of it. He landed on his back beside the big war wag, almost thirty feet away. The impact knocked the wind out of him. For a terrible moment, he couldn't breathe, and he couldn't move. He heard the sound of an angry animal tearing at the air, trying to get at him.

Zeal lay back on the asphalt and made himself breathe in little sips. The first full breath he took felt as if he were turning his lungs inside out. When he looked around, he saw Vernel, still alive, sitting dazed, near the front bumper. Up the road, on the other side of the stones, there was nothing left. Not a scrap of man or of clothing. Not so much as a drop of blood on the asphalt.

What could do that? Zeal thought, his mind reeling. A god? Perhaps the inbreds were right to worship it.

They were welcome to it.

The baron struggled to his feet. As he did so, he realized that something was very wrong with his left leg. There was no feeling in it from hip to foot. It had gone to sleep. Towing it behind him, he pulled himself along the flank of the MCP, and from there to the open door of the second wag in line. He climbed up and into the corridor, and was about to slam the door behind him when Vernel appeared outside and caught his arm.

It was faster to haul the man inside than to fight to keep him out. Zeal's only desire was to get back to his ville and his compound. Whether Spearpoint was here or not, it was out of reach. At least for now, and probably forever.

The baron dragged himself into the driver's seat and started up the engines. Screeching the gears, he did a series of frantic K-turns, bashing the wag's rear end into the cliff wall, scraping past the third wag in line to get the vehicle pointed downhill. Once he had an open path, he floored the accelerator and raced down the winding road, for home and safety.

Chapter Twenty-Six

Doc continued down the access tunnel, which sloped into the heart of the mountain. Sensors buried in the walls reacted to his footfalls, or perhaps to his body heat, switching on the overhead banks of lights as he descended.

A sleeping giant awakened.

Had Doc a thought for the unfortunates whom he had left outside the stockpile's doors? Had he a scrap of pity for those who'd shown so little pity to him?

In a word, no.

A terrible weight had been lifted from his shoulders. His spirit was buoyed up by liberty regained. Jubilant, the chain that linked his ankle manacles scraping across the smooth concrete, he angled down into the coolness of the earth.

Spearpoint was at least as big as the myth surrounding it claimed it was. A city of cities. Completely uninhabited, of course. For the first two weeks after his mat-trans jump to this place, Doc had wandered, completely lost, down its wide avenues, through its housing sectors, its seemingly endless laboratories. The lights turned on as he approached, turned off as he moved on.

His scrambled state of mind certainly contributed to his failure to find his way out of the redoubt; this was due to a combination of the brain damage he'd already suffered from time trawling, and the confusion a mat-trans jump always brought on. He talked, he sang, he walked with old colleagues, debating issues of philosophy and science long since resolved, and long since made irrelevant by the nukecaust. He slept when he got tired, on lab tables, on park benches, in furniture warehouses, in doorways.

After many days of this aimless travel, he finally took notice of the band of different-colored stripes on the walls of the corridors. They turned this way and that, following the contours of impossibly long hallways, sometimes breaking off from their fellows to go their own way. He had watched them glide by as he rode on the moving sidewalks, thinking that their only function was decorative. Then, another possibility had occurred to him. It was days more before he found the first map key. It confirmed what he had begun to suspect, that each band of color led in a particular direction, to a particular destination. If you knew where you wanted to go, you just followed yellow to lavender, turned right to red and there you were.

It turned out the map keys were very conveniently located, if you knew where to look and how to operate them. The computer-controlled, voice-activated LCD screens remained black and empty until the command to awake was given.

Familiar with the map system from his previous visit, Doc paused at the first intersection he came upon and called for directions. After he got the route he wanted, he proceeded to an area of machine shops and metal-fabrication plants. It took some rooting about in cupboards and tool chests before he found what he was looking for. As everything in the shop was computer controlled, there wasn't much call for a hacksaw. The collars around his ankles gave up the ghost quite easily, however. Postdark iron was no match for predark steel.

Once he had freed himself, he moved on to the nearest food-dispensing area. As he entered, the overhead lights came on, as did splashing fountains and soft guitar music. The food court had been constructed and decorated to look like a Mexican hacienda, with shops featuring different kinds of repasts clustered around a central atrium.

There were no humans working there, of course. And during his early wanderings through Spearpoint, that had put Doc sorely off his feed. Burning pangs of hunger had made him accept the automatons, and once he'd tasted the food, it didn't matter what served it to him.

Doc opened the glass-paned door of the Ice Creamatoria. The little bell on the door jingled merrily as he entered. The clerk behind the long counter turned to face him. She wore a red gingham apron. Her blond hair was braided into pigtails. She was remarkably apple-cheeked, but her blue eyes stared at him glassily, like a doll's.

"And what can I get you today?" said a cheerful recorded voice.

"I'll have a banana split," Doc said, "double fudge, no pineapple, with two scoops of chocolate, one of vanilla."

"And would you like nuts and whipped cream on that?"

"Yes, and jimmies, too," Doc said. "Extra jimmies."

It took barely a minute for the automaton to prepare his dessert. As he took it from the countertop, the clerk said, "That will be four dollars, please."

Doc just kept on walking.

"That will be four dollars, please."

The door jingled as he shut it behind him.

He sat down on the edge of the dancing fountain and gorged himself. Though the ingredients were more than one hundred years old, it tasted so good that he licked the inside of the plastic bowl to get the last of the fudge sauce. When he was done, he dumped the bowl and spoon into a trash receptacle.

Feeling completely revived, he found another map key and got directions to the redoubt's mat-trans unit.

He could have stayed around Spearpoint, of course, and there was a temptation to do just that, but more than endless quantities of food, he wanted fresh air and sunshine. He wanted to stretch his legs and put some miles under his boots.

Doc knew he was getting close to the mat-trans unit when he entered a low-ceilinged room lined with row upon row of computers, all of them apparently in sleep mode. The movement of solid matter from one location to another required the storage and transfer of massive amounts of information.

On the far side of the room was a short hallway, which ended in a familiar-looking bulkhead door. The moment he touched the handle, the banks of computers behind him began to chitter like a flock of startled birds. Everything was automatic. The process had begun.

Doc stepped inside the small chamber and slammed the door behind him. At once, a whisper of air started creeping around the ceiling, and he smelled something sharp and electric. The metallic floor plates beneath his feet took on a soft glow, as did the chamber's armaglass walls, which were the color of golden honey. Wisps of cottony mist drifted down from the ceiling and swirled around his face.

"Morituri te salutamus," he said.

And then he sat on the floor.

Chapter Twenty-Seven

"Got a dust cloud coming our way," Poet stated.

"Yeah," Ryan said from the captured sec wag's driver's seat, "been watching it for a while now."

Ryan drove the lead wag in a three-wag daisy chain. The other wags were just like his: stiflingly hot and overloaded with passengers. The one-lane road they traveled was the only improved track leading across a plain of yellow dirt and scrub brush to the blue-tinted mountains in the far distance, mountains where Baron Zeal had taken Trader and the convoy.

"He's really tearing it up," Hun said, leaning over the back of the front seat for a better look at the oncoming traffic. "Think it's one of ours?"

"Way he's moving, won't be long before we find out," Poet said.

When the wag was about a quarter of a mile away, Ryan announced, "It's one of ours, all right. A war wag."

"Could be Trader got loose," Hun speculated hopefully.

"Not likely, though," Poet said.

Ryan had to agree with that. The man had been in chains, and he was unarmed and outnumbered. Even for Trader, escape under those circumstances would be a stretch. "Question is," he said to Poet, "should we pull off the road, stop and let the war wag pass, or keep moving? I vote for keep moving, right up until the last second. That way, if it's sec men or Shabazz's crew driving, they'll have a lot harder time hitting us with blasterfire."

"Sounds like a plan to me," Poet said.

When the war wag was one hundred yards away, and closing fast, Ryan could see that the driver's hatch was flipped back and locked in the open position and that the man at the helm had his head stuck out the vent. When the wag was fifty yards away, Ryan could see that Trader wasn't driving. The man looked clean shaved and his long brown hair whipped in the wind. When the wag was twenty-five yards away, Ryan could see that it was Zeal at the controls and, from the set expression on his face, that he had no intention of swerving to avoid a head-on collision.

"Shit!" Ryan growled as he cut the wheel hard over, sending the sec wag off the shoulder of the road and bounding onto the desert floor. As the vehicle bounced wildly sideways, he steered into the skid, fighting to keep it from rolling over.

On the road above them, there was no sound of collision, just the squeal of tires as two sets of brakes locked up. As Ryan brought his wag to a stop, a huge cloud of dust fanned out behind. The one-eyed man and his passengers bailed out of the vehicle. When the dust cloud cleared, they saw the other two sec wags still clinging to the roadway, half on and half off the pavement. The crews waved out the windows to let them know everything was okay. In the distance, the war wag roared on toward Virtue Lake, leaving a yellow tornado in its wake.

"It was the baron himself," Poet said. "I saw his gaudy-slut face."

"He was in a big hurry," Ryan said.

"Mebbe he chipped a nail," Hun suggested.

Excitement over, they piled in the wag and Ryan eased it back onto the road. There were no more dust clouds coming at them. The mountain range grew gradually larger as they approached it. When they got within a half mile of its base, they could see the stolen transport wags, all parked in a line on the desert floor.

"Looks like they're abandoned," Poet said as they drew closer.

Ryan stopped the wag a short distance from the transports, and they all got out. A quick check proved Poet to be right.

"Abandoned and empty," Ryan said as he shut one of the cargo-bay doors. "Zeal planned on loading them up with something, that's for sure. Guess he didn't plan well enough."

Poet dispatched half the crew to man the transports and make sure they were ready to roll. After raiding the on-board armories, and passing out the weapons and fully loaded magazines, Ryan waved the remaining road warriors into the sec wags. Climbing back into the first wag with Poet and Hun, Ryan led the short parade through the entrance to the mountain pass.

Things looked normal until they reached the third hairpin bend in the road. "Corpses," Hun said, pointing out the passenger's window.

The shot-up bodies of what Ryan assumed were the road's guardians lay on the shoulder. Scabby-looking bunch, he decided.

A little farther on, they came to the rockfall. Because the sec wags didn't have the ground clearance to traverse the larger boulders, Ryan and the others had to get out and proceed up the grade on foot.

"Man, this doesn't look good," Poet said, eyeing the size of the recently dropped slabs of bedrock that lay by the side of the road. The slabs were big enough to crush even a war wag if it was hit square on.

Ryan kept the file moving, watching the edges of the cliffs above them for signs of movement. There was none.

He half expected to find the remaining three war wags buried, if not crushed, under thousands of tons of fallen rock around the next bend. Instead, they were parked in a line in the middle of the road.

"Check them out," Ryan said as he moved toward the MCP.

The door was unlocked. He entered the hallway with the Blackhawk leading the way. Hun moved in behind him. A bow-to-stern check of the wag turned up no signs of life. No signs of death, either.

Wiping the sweat from his forehead with the back of his hand, he looked at Hun and shook his head. "Looks like nobody's home."

"In here!" a woman's muffled voice cried. It was close by. "Ryan, we're in here!"

When Ryan opened the locker, he was relieved to see Trader, J.B. and Sam smiling at him.

"We didn't hear any blastershots," Trader said as he stepped into the corridor. "You didn't have to fight your way up here?"

"We crossed paths with Zeal on the plain," Ryan said. "He had one of our war wags and he was heading for Virtue Lake. Other than that, there's no sign of anybody outside."

"That's impossible," Trader said. "There had to be twenty, mebbe twenty-five crew with Zeal and Shabazz." He pushed past Ryan and jumped down from the MCP's doorway.

Outside, Poet and the others had just freed the hostage drivers and crew from the lockers in the two small war wags. It looked like they hadn't lost any more people.

Trader walked up to the row of rocks and stared at the cliff face. There was no place for the pirates and sec men to have gone. The road dead-ended. Cliff walls rose on three sides to heights of hundreds of feet.

As Ryan came up alongside him, he noticed there was a chill to the air, despite the bright sunshine. And though no blood was in evidence anywhere that Ryan could see, there was the coppery smell of blood, and it hung real heavy. Slaughterhouse kind of heavy. Looking at that open space, smelling that smell, Ryan got a strange feeling—strange to him, anyway. It was fear.

"What do you want to do?" Poet asked Trader.

"I got a score to settle with Baron Zeal," Trader said, rubbing gently at his stomach. "Bastard stole my wags and took my cargo, and he chilled some of my crew, chilled them real ugly. Can't let him get away with that. There's too many others out there in the world who'd take it as a sign of weakness. Folks start thinking we're easy pickin's and we'll be fighting every mile of our circuit from now until the next skydark."

Poet grunted in agreement.

"Let's get the small wags turned," Trader said. "Drive them down the pass. Gorge is so narrow, we're going to have to back the MCP all the way to the bottom. Come on, Ryan, give me a hand getting rid of these chains. They're starting to really piss me off."

At the bottom of the grade, they joined up with the waiting transports. Then, with the MCP in the lead, the convoy headed back down the road toward Virtue Lake.

Ryan and Trader sat in the jump seats along the back wall of the driver's compartment. The front hatches were wide open, and the air rushing in over them felt good, as did the familiar bass rumble of War Wag One's wheels on the road.

When Ryan looked over at his boss, sitting close as they were, he saw crow's-feet at the corners of Trader's eyes. He hadn't noticed them before.

"You and Poet didn't chill each other, I'm glad to see," Trader said, pulling out a fresh cheroot and lighting it up.

"It was close, Trader. Real close."

"You two come to terms?"

"Mebbe. Time will tell," Ryan said. Then he changed the subject. "How're we going to handle Zeal?"

"He saw you when you saw him?"

"Yep, couldn't miss us. Passed within a few feet."

"Well, I'd say he's got to figure we're coming back for

him. First thing, he's going to consolidate his forces around his most prized possession, the refinery. He's probably there right now, trying to figure out a way to keep us from getting to it.''

Ryan reached in his pants pocket. ''Look here,'' he said. He showed Trader the two detonators, then held one of them up. ''This will set off a neat little charge of high-ex. We left it just outside the refinery on our way to collect you. It's the eye opener.''

''What's the other one?''

''We mined the whole damned plant with C-4,'' Ryan told him. ''We used J.B.'s motion-sensing detonators.''

''I like that,'' Trader said. ''I like that a lot.'' He held out his hand. ''Give them here.''

Ryan passed him the detonators.

''So, if I push this one, like this,'' Trader said as he pointed the device out the front hatch and depressed the red button, ''we wake Zeal up to the fact that his precious refinery has been penetrated and mined.''

In the distance, over the roar of the wind and the engines, they heard a dull whomp.

''You just woke him up,'' Ryan said.

Trader raised his other hand, aiming the second detonator toward Virtue Lake. ''And all I have to do to arm the motion-sensing C-4 charges is to push this little button....''

Ryan nodded.

''Well, then, let's let her rip,'' Trader said, and he pushed the button.

Chapter Twenty-Eight

The moment Baron Zeal saw the one-eyed man behind the wheel of one of his sec wags, headed in the direction of Spearpoint, his plan to pull back to the safety of his stockade went out the window. The whole hunker-down scheme depended on Trader staying right where he was, on Trader's wags staying where they were and on the rest of Trader's crew still being safely tucked away in the Virtue Lake jail.

The one-eyed man would certainly find the pass and rescue his crewmates. Trader and the others locked up inside the wags' storage compartments wouldn't starve to death as Zeal had hoped. Starvation was a particularly nasty way to go; he knew this from firsthand observations on his slaves. Once Trader was freed, he would turn his war wags against Virtue Lake.

There was no doubt about that.

Trader wasn't the kind of man to call bygones bygones. He was the kind of man who kicked his enemies where it hurt them most. In the case of Zeal, that meant the refinery. The thought of losing his cash cow made the baron go soft in the knees. It was his stranglehold on Deathlands; without it, he would go back to being just another road pirate, fighting over the scraps that the larger predators dropped or discarded.

As he slowed to approach the gate to the ville, he saw the long row of bodies laid out by the side of the road. They weren't covered, and as he pulled up he recognized some of them as his sec men. The survivors of his crew stood along the edge of the road, looking pained, or scared, or angry.

"Get some blasters behind the barricades to defend the gate," he shouted at them. "The rest of you get in your wags and follow me."

As his destination became obvious, Vernel, who sat in the copilot's chair, said, "It's gonna be tough to keep Trader from hammering the refinery. He's got HEAP rockets on that big wag of his, and he doesn't have to be within a mile of the ville to use them."

"I took a peek at the pods after we stopped at the end of the road," Zeal said. "And they all looked mighty goddamned empty to me. We didn't find any more rockets stashed in the MCP, so I'd say the rest of his supply is safely tucked away in my warehouse with the crates we took from his transports. Either that, or he doesn't have any more rockets."

When they arrived at the refinery, Zeal parked the wag, got out and immediately addressed his assembled sec crews. "We need all the steel plate you can put your hands on," he said. He waved his arm, indicating about half the sec men. "You lot," he said, "take every worker out of the plant and start foraging for armor."

One of the crew bosses raised his hand. "Baron Zeal," he said, "we got a shift change coming up in about a half an hour."

"Forget it!" Zeal snapped. "Nobody goes home. And anybody who shows up for the shift change, put them to work, too. The rest of you, up to the stockade with transports and move all the stored weapons and ammunition down here. We're going to make our stand at the refinery."

Then, to further stimulate their work ethic, he added, "Trader and his war wags are on the way. If we aren't done before they arrive at the gate, we're all going to be dead meat."

In roughly twenty minutes, Zeal's crews had everything

he had requested gathered up and moved into the plant. At his direction, armor-plate baffles three feet high were put up behind the closed hangar doors. Blasterports were then cut into the thinner steel of the doors. The sec men covered the refinery's windows with anything they could find, plywood scrap, corrugated sheet metal, as there wasn't enough heavy plate to do the job there.

The effort on everyone's part was frantic.

Given the circumstances, the baron was even ready to sacrifice his favorite toy. He stood in front of the stainless-steel torture tank while his workers fired up their cutting torches.

"Hate to see it go, I'll bet," Vernel said.

"Happy memories," Zeal replied. "So many happy memories."

The laborers were just starting to cut the door off its hinges when something exploded outside the plant. The boom was powerful enough to rock the floor.

"What the hell was that?" Vernel roared.

A sec man raced down the central aisle. "A bomb!" he cried. "There was a bomb in the side yard!"

Zeal caught him by the shirt collar. He didn't ask how many were dead or how many were injured. He didn't ask because he didn't care. "You mean some of Trader's crew have been on the plant grounds?" he snarled into the man's face. "You let them on the grounds!"

The sec man looked desperate. No answer he could give was safe.

"They were in here, then," Vernel said emphatically. "You got to figure on that."

Over his victim's shoulder, Zeal saw a red light wink on and the beam it gave off drew a fine line through the air, cutting across the aisle. It was coming from underneath one of the crude-oil storage tanks. He pushed the sec man away from him and dropped to his knees.

What he saw stuck to the underside of the tank made his

heart jump into his throat—a small parcel, a gray oblong capped with a black plastic box. He recognized the box for what it was, at once.

"Nobody move!" he bellowed at the top of his lungs. "Everybody freeze!"

Vernel started to take a step toward him, then stopped in his tracks when he saw the laser light.

"Pass the word!" Zeal shouted. "Nobody move!"

The baron anticipated imminent death. He fully expected someone to disobey or not hear the command he'd given. So he was profoundly relieved when the plant didn't immediately explode all around him; on the contrary, a kind of reverent hush fell over the place.

"We're fucked, you know," Vernel said. Sweat was popping out on top of his shaved head and dripping down the sides of his face.

"We'll figure a way out," Zeal assured him. "There's got to be a way to disarm the explosives. If we can just locate them all…"

"There isn't time."

"What are you talking about? They're motion sensors, not timed detonators."

"The whistle," Vernel said in a voice that was just above a hoarse whisper.

"The whistle," Zeal repeated as the meaning finally sunk in—the ear-shattering, earthshaking, shift-change whistle.

The baron looked frantically for somewhere to hide. There had to be somewhere to hide. He scanned the floor ahead and saw no telltale laser beam across it. Without a word of warning to Vernel, he sprinted full-out for the only cover available. He dived into the heavy steel tank and pulled the door shut with a clang behind him.

Then the shift whistle blew. And kept on blowing.

Zeal cringed inside the tank. The piercing sound made

the steel walls under his knees and hands vibrate, but not
for long. The whistle was cut short as all the detonators
tripped, and the Virtue Lake refinery dissolved in an enormous, spreading fireball.

Chapter Twenty-Nine

Trader and Ryan saw the explosion from five miles away:
the ball of flame streaking straight up, then the shock blast
stretching sideways like a dinner plate.

A dinner plate miles wide.

The concussion wave was so powerful that it sent the
MCP veering off the road. The rest of the column was likewise diverted by the wall of hurricane-force wind. All of
the wags came safely to a stop, and once the winds and dust
storm abated, their crews piled out to watch the show.

An enormous column of black smoke rose from the plain.
At its mile-wide base, orange fires danced and swayed.
Based on how far away they still were from the ville, the
flames had to be hundreds of feet high.

"Dark night!" J.B. exclaimed. "How much of my C-4
did you use?!"

"Hair too much," Ryan said, squinting his one good eye
at the holocaust.

"Looks like the whole goddamn refinery blew up,"
Trader said. Then he craned his head back. "Man, look at
that smoke! It's got to be a mile high already."

"Are we going on, now?" Hun asked, after a minute or
two.

"No," Trader told her as he took the binoculars one of
the crew handed him. He raised them to his eyes. "We'd
better wait here until some of the smoke clears off. Look,
there's still stuff exploding. Did you see that fuel drum?
Looked like a goddamned rocket."

They sat by the side of the road for better than an hour

before Trader gave the go-ahead. His mood had sombered considerably during that time. Through the binoculars, he could see no refugees fleeing out over the dry lake bed. No one and nothing moved, except the leaping flames where the refinery had once stood and the steadily uncoiling column of black smoke.

On his order, they approached the ville at a crawl down the main road that wound around the lakeshore. Thick smoke was still rising from the ville's epicenter; the wind at their backs kept it away from them.

"I don't see anything alive," Hun said as she looked out the copilot's hatch. "I mean, nothing."

"I see bodies," Ryan said, "on the other side of the gate."

Trader used the wag-to-wag intercom and called for the convoy to halt, then he got out of War Wag One. With Ryan, Hun and Poet behind him, he walked over to the wire part of the barricade.

There was a pile of sec men on the ground on the other side. They hadn't been chilled by the blast at the refinery; Trader could see that right off. For one thing, the corpses were intact. Their heads, arms, legs were all still connected to torsos; and there were no great bloody wounds from being hit by flying objects. For another thing, and this was the big giveaway, there was green froth caked all over their mouths, chins and noses. Their faces were black and swollen, tongues sticking out of their gaping jaws like hard salamis. Under their armor vests, their bellies were already starting to bloat.

Hun recognized the symptoms, too. "Nerve gas," she said. "It's fucking nerve gas."

"Shabazz must've had it stored somewhere handy to the refinery," Poet said, looking up from the bodies and past them, to the ruined ville. The war captain grimaced and ran the flat of his hand over the top of his head.

"Is it safe to go on, J.B.?" Trader asked.

"Mebbe. Question is, what good can we do if we do go in there?"

"Gotta see," Trader said. "I gotta see."

With that, he opened the gate. As he stepped inside, he turned and said, "Keep the wags out."

Ryan, Hun, Poet and most of the crew followed their leader around the maze of berms and into Virtue Lake.

The shantytown had been blasted flat. Scattered bonfires raged among the heaps of rubbish. Human bodies lay mixed in with the smoking refuse. There was an eerie stillness, except for the crackle of the fires and the whistle of the wind. Trader realized what was missing. It was the steady, grinding noise of the refinery. In the distance, there was no sign of the plant that had once dominated the landscape.

As he scanned the fields of trash that had once been human dwellings, he asked himself how many people were half-buried out there. Hundreds, surely. Maybe even a thousand. And they were all dead.

Men. Women. Children.

To pull them out of the trash and properly bury them would've taken weeks.

As they walked past the devastation, Trader could hear Hun behind him, muttering to herself. She was saying, "Oh fuck, oh fuck, oh fuck…"

"Hey, Ryan!" Abe called out. He was stopped a little way back, staring at a body on the ground. "This here looks mighty like your blade."

Ryan trotted over to where the little man stood, and Trader and the others followed.

"It does look like your panga," Poet said.

The handle of the big blade was sticking up out of the chest of a man in pin-striped overalls. The point had been shoved up under his sternum.

"That one sure didn't die of the gas," Hun said.

They could all see that. There was no green froth at the

lips, no blackening of the pockmarked cheeks. He had stopped breathing before the blast.

"Boy got his venging in," Poet said.

"Looks like," Ryan replied as he put his boot sole on the dead man's face and pried the knife free. He cleaned it on the crew boss's shirt before he slid it back into its leg sheath.

Ryan looked at Trader and said, "Might be a boy named Guy-ito laying around here close. He was a help to us. Like to have a look-see, if we've got the time."

"We've got time," Trader said.

Ryan and Poet searched intently, without speaking, looking for the boy's corpse in a widening circle around the dead man. They lifted the corners of corrugated metal sheets that had flown off roofs and turned back scorched sheet-plastic walls. They found no child's body in the debris. After a few minutes, they gave up. Neither of the warriors speculated aloud that the boy Guy-ito might have somehow escaped the disaster; under the circumstances, it seemed like too much of a long shot.

As Trader led them closer to the blast's ground zero, the bodies started showing signs of death by explosion. Violent, instantaneous death. Trader felt an odd kind of relief at the sight of people with large pieces of metal driven through their torsos, with heads missing. He knew firsthand what it was like to taste the nerve gas, to feel it at work in his body. He knew getting your head blown off was a mercy.

When they came to the warehouse where the looted cargo had been stored, it was obvious that nothing salvageable was left. The roof and walls were gone. The expanding fireball had melted the rest into a vast, still-smoking gob.

A few blocks farther on was the refinery site. It was as if the plant had never existed. In its place was a crater several hundred yards across. And from the center of the crater, plumes of fire still jetted skyward. At the bottom of the pit, partially visible as the flames licked and danced, there was some metal debris, possibly a storage tank. It gave off a squealing sound, like high-pressure steam escaping through a pinhole.

Trader stared at the flames, his cigar butt clenched in his teeth.

"This wasn't your fault," Poet said as he stepped up beside him. "It was Shabazz's. If he hadn't stored his infernal gas grens here, these people would all still be alive."

Trader turned and looked at his war captain in silence for a moment, then he took his cigar butt out of the corner of his mouth and spit on the ground. "Such a waste," he said. "Such a goddamned waste. But it'll stand as a lesson for anyone who ever plots to stand against me."

Epilogue

With popular myths and legends, there were always variations, even discrepancies in the basic facts. A tale was told a certain way in one locality, another way someplace else. The story of Trader and Virtue Lake had its different twists, too, depending on who was doing the telling and what part of Deathlands the teller was from.

The folks down in the southern baronies claimed that the awful sounds that the first witness—Bob, or Tom, or Jim—heard down at the bottom of the flaming pit were the screams of Baron Zeal's ghost as his soul fried in Hell.

Up near the Shens, it was said that the terrible noises weren't made by a ghost, but by a living man. Now that may seem farfetched at first, but anybody who's been around explosives much knew they could do some mighty strange things from time to time. Under the right circumstances, a tremendous blast in one direction hardly stirred a hair on a baby's head a few feet away.

The way the Shen folk liked to tell the story, the big explosion drove the nerve gas away from the center of the refinery, and the rising heat and smoke from the fuel fires kept it out. They speculate that if a man could have made it safely into a heavy-walled, stainless-steel tank, and by a miracle have lived through the shock of initial blast, he and the tank could have ended up at the bottom of the crater, where jets of leaking fuel burned hot and heavy. And what with the other debris down there in the pit, of course the tank door could easily have become wedged shut.

How long could a man survive trapped in a torture cell like that, hopping around like a cricket on a hot skillet?

A day? Three days? A week? Three weeks?

What would his face look like at the moment of his death?

These were the questions Shen people loved to debate around their campfires.

One thing was certain though—Trader never put in his own two cents' worth to straighten out the facts. Maybe because he figured it was impossible, given the way things traveled Deathlands by word of mouth. Maybe because the way the story came out served his needs. After the tale spread far and wide through Deathlands, crooked barons and murdering road pirates always thought long and hard before they messed with the likes of Trader.

Inside Deathlands

Birth of a Series

The following presentation attempts to provide the thinking behind the creation of the Deathlands *series, which first saw the light of day in 1986. Multiple perspectives are presented: that of the writer whose concept was eventually turned into books; of the editorial team who thought the concept was viable and who brought the idea forward to be evaluated against the then current editorial trends; and of the artist who rendered the idea into art.*

But why bother to explain how a book series is created? Perhaps this question is best answered by looking at another entertainment medium—the film industry. In recent years, the movie industry has allowed us to see what goes on behind the scenes in the creation of popular movies. Despite the fact that all is revealed to us, it does not change our perception or acceptance of this or that picture. Indeed, it does not matter that we have a better insight into the "tricks" of moviemaking.

There were, of course, no tricks in the creation of the Deathlands *series. However, with the best intentions in the world, there were bound to be inconsistencies as the series evolved. Such is the human factor. One might argue that such occurrences are forever preserved for posterity and lend the series a certain cachet.*

For those who have loved Deathlands, *and for those who will come to love it, the following feature is a special offering that we are sure readers will find interesting and enjoyable.*

A Familiar Tale—
A Strange Land

Laurence James on *Deathlands*

A band of half a dozen or so strangers, with a variety of specialized skills, is thrown together by circumstance and necessity in a changing world, and they become close friends, totally trusting and relying on each other. They ride out together on a mission to fight powerful evil. After various adventures and plenty of slaughter, the survivors are triumphant and move on, leaving the place a little cleaner.

But there is a price to be paid. Four windswept graves.

It is, of course, the wonderful, elegiac *The Magnificent Seven,* how the West was won, through the sacrifice of a hell-bent-for-leather group of people. A story fit to be told, over and over, with new characters and settings.

Though there are any number of fundamental differences, the similarities are there. The truth is that for me *Deathlands* is really a very superior Western, a modern version played out on the new frontiers of a damaged tomorrow.

A group of friends moving through a deeply hostile environment, encountering evil barons and their murderous followers—many far more amoral and wicked than Eli Wallach in *The Magnificent Seven.* After tribulations and the occasional sad death of their number, the rest move on, leaving things just a little better and the air a little cleaner to breathe.

In the mythos that is *Deathlands,* will Ryan Cawdor and company ever be able to find their own peace and release from the endless chilling? I personally don't know the answer, but I suspect that it might be that there is no ultimate rest waiting for them, unless it might come after some apocalyptically star-toppling and climactic battle against the united forces of darkness. If that was ever to happen, then I think I would be proud to be there.

The series has always had a variety of mingled threads. Generally the blame for the bleakness of the postholocaust world that is Deathlands is laid at the portals of the coldheart politicians and crazed whitecoats; the double-damned scientists in their reinforced-concrete bunkers with their clicking, whirring computers and their crystal vials of noxious unguents; men and women who see research as some pure, soulless grail and close their eyes against the megadeath culling that this might result in, along with the side effect of the death of society, or of civilization.

They are the true enemy to be feared, now and always. And our hopes remain the same....

Think of the manifold virtues of Ryan Cawdor in his world. Include courage, strength, self-belief, honesty, advanced survivalist skills—in the best, undebased sense of the word—loyalty and an implicit belief in the importance of helping others less able and weaker than himself.

A child raised to respect these values would not go far wrong in any time and place.

Even the wonderful Doc Tanner—let it be whispered that he is my favorite character—has most of these virtues to a greater or lesser degree, despite the profound changes wrought in his personality by those long-dead, time-trawling whitecoats.

Krysty Wroth has these strengths, and in addition, the deeply feminine-based intuitive strengths as expressed in her Gaia powers, a kind of connectedness that people in more organized, civilized settings seem to lose track of.

But what is this recognizably unrecognizable world that is Deathlands?

It is basically a dark and lonely version of today. Though we have moved farther afield on several occasions, the vast majority of the stories so far have taken place within the existing boundaries of the United States of America. Like many writers, I'm fortunate enough to have a fairly eidetic memory, which is a somewhat pretentious way of saying that I'm blessed with very good visual recall. Since that faraway Christmas in 1985 when I first stepped into the now familiar armaglass walls of a redoubt gateway, on every visit to the United States, I have always been looking at everything through my Deathlands-filtered spectacles.

What will that mountain resort look like after nearly a hundred years of desolation? That church? Motel complex? Shopping mall, national park, school and so on. Small things like the insides of homes, vehicles, weapons. How will broader issues be developed, like science, education, political correctness, religion, economics, hospitality and, most important of all, sociology?

And that simply means people.

One thing that longtime readers will have realized is that people in Deathlands, roughly a century down the line, haven't really changed all that much.

Ryan Cawdor would have recognized his brother in someone like Jedediah Smith, famous mountain man, as well as the trappers, hunters and courageous guides who risked their lives in pushing at the perilous boundaries of the Old Frontier. Though for Ryan and his comrades, the world has turned well past John F. Kennedy's New Frontier. There is so much in Deathlands that we would all recognize and much that has grotesquely, appallingly changed.

If Deathlands works at more than one basic, adventurous level, and I believe it does, then I hope it makes everyone look more carefully and think just a touch more deeply about their own world and their fellow men and women.

Perhaps consider how they would *like* to act if faced by the horrors that so often confront Ryan Cawdor and his friends.

Someone once said something about how evil can only flourish when decent people stand by and do nothing.

That is what Deathlands is all about.

Proposal for a Short Paperback Series

Deathlands
(Provisional title)

The Moment of Conception

2085. There is no such location as the United States of America. Sometime during the final two decades of the twentieth century, WWIII almost destroyed civilization in a worldwide nuclear holocaust, and in so doing laid waste the lands of Earth, turning them into vast tracts of desolation and death.

After ten years of nuclear winter, when the sun was blotted out by the thick, choking clouds of simmering nuclear poison and dust and temperatures on the planet plummeted to depths undreamed of by even the most pessimistic of scientists, life returned. In fact it was always there. Somehow, somewhere. All over the world, in isolated pockets, survivors fought back against the terrifying odds stacked against them, and won. Kind of.

Now, one hundred years after the bombs and missiles fell, the planet Earth is a changed place. Much of the world is still a steaming nuclear swamp. But by now there is a degree of civilization in various parts of the world, some of it high. We are not, incidentally, talking here of a situation where people have completely forgotten what it was like before the missiles hurtled out of the sky.

In the wastelands of the world, the Sahara, say, the Gobi,

the Australian interior and so on, much remains as it was. The Indian subcontinent is little changed. Southern Africa is relatively unscathed—although of course now, due to the worldwide collapse of commerce, the banking system, etc., the blacks have taken over from the whites.

But we concentrate on the U.S., where much *has* changed. Not unnaturally, the East Coast has been pretty well wiped out. Texas has been turned into a desert. The West Coast, especially around San Francisco and L.A., is utterly altered. Missiles fired at the San Andreas Fault caused most of the populated West Coast strip to disappear into the Pacific. Here there are only vast lagoons stretching far inland, and seething strontium swamps.

Most, though not all, of the North American interior lies under a boiling, red-scarred belt of cloud, in places maybe a mile thick: a dense blanket of poisonous gases and floating nuclear debris, a coverlet of destruction mantling a land of death, for below is a reeking wasteland, populated by strange, mutated beings, freaks, strontium-spawned mon-strosities, both animal and human.

But these lands, these lost territories, aren't all death. There are parts almost freakishly untouched by the nuclear holocaust, patches of forest and cultivated upland only slightly transformed by radiation showers. There are now small townships and trading posts, and villages where life is so normal you don't get to see a mutie more than maybe once a week.

There are, of course, no "states" as such, merely terri-tories presided over either by the strongest or the wisest: hundreds of little baronies, if you like, or principalities. There are communications; there is electricity—in the out-lying regions, not dependable; there is travel of a sort. In the newer urban regions that have grown up around the coastal areas, there is a high level of civilization and so-phistication, yet even here the law of the jungle, the survival

of the fittest or strongest, prevails. There is gasoline and
there are autos; there are weapons; there is food.

And there is a very good reason for all this: for way back
in the latter half of the twentieth century, successive gov-
ernments laid down vast stockpiles of equipment and military matériel in secret underground strongholds and silos for
just such a time as a post-nuclear war period. The snag was,
most of the favored ones, the top officials, government men,
bankers, civil servants and the like, never made it to the
shelters when the missiles began dropping. Thus, strange
and bizarre secrets still lie under the reeking nuclear
swamps, or high in almost unreachable mountain fastnesses,
waiting to be discovered.

NB: This will be a meld of the known—to today's readers—and the "unknown." I want to stress that although the
story has SF ingredients, it is *not* pure or hard SF, nor do I
want it to be. It is a fast-paced action series in the high-
adventure manner, built within an SF framework.

Background

The jumping-off point for the series—although the protagonists in the story will know nothing of this when they start
out—is that before WWIII, the U.S. government was secretly making a number of astonishing discoveries of a very
weird scientific nature, including matter transference over
long distances. They had also established a limited form of
time travel and had set up a number of temporal and locational "gateways" in secret locations across the U.S.
Briefly, they had discovered how to jump back in time up
to a limit of two hundred years. These discoveries were
made only a few years before the outbreak of WWIII, and
thus they had not been used much at all by the scientists
who had created the gateways. Most of the gateways open
onto other areas in the U.S. Only one or two can be so
manipulated that the user jumps back in time.

Storyline

The main story will concern a group of people who basically want to escape from this land of nuclear death, this hell on earth. There's got to be a better way of life than this—somewhere. There are rumors—stories, legends, maybe just old wives' tales—of a place of marvels in the northernmost extremity of Deathlands: a place of strange wonders, a place where, it is hinted, there is a vast treasure.

In Book 1 the group gradually gets together: a mix of startlingly different types—men, women, some good, some bad, some vicious, some escaping from whatever law there still is, some weak, some horrifyingly strong.

After a harrowing journey, through appalling atmospheric and weather changes, and continually harassed by clans or tribes of distinctly unfriendly locals, they manage to reach "the redoubt," high in the mountains, and there discover for themselves that the "treasure" is not at all what they thought it was going to be. For the redoubt is a hidden scientific enclave full of weapons and matériel, and containing one of the locational gateways. In an apocalyptic finale, they are besieged by a murderous bunch of locals, and, in a blazing shootout, the redoubt starts to self-destruct. The only way out is through the gateway, and they don't know where it leads or even what happens when you go through. But it's their only way out. They jump....

As I'd like it, Book 1 ends right there, with the reader not knowing where they jump to, or what happens. Book 2 opens with them coming through and discovering that they've landed in another of these secret redoubts, but one thousand miles away, say, in the south.

In each subsequent book the locational jump will take them to a different part of Deathlands, and will be the frame for a new adventure, a new situation, a new conflict, a new confrontation with danger and horror. And over the course of the series, they will gradually uncover the secret of the ultimate escape from Deathlands: a final jump right out of the terror and the carnage back into the rural peace of civilized America at the turn of this century—1900, or thereabouts. And out of the entire group, only two will make it.

Ryan Cawdor, the hero, a tough but pragmatic character who desperately wants out from the hell of the late twenty-first century, and Krysty, the enigmatic, Titian-haired heroine, who is by no means what she seems on the surface. These are the two main characters.

During the course of the series, original members of the group will die or be killed, new characters will be introduced. One character possibly holds the key to the main quest, a drunken, shambling wreck of a man simply known as Doc, who joins the group early on and seems to know far more than he lets on.

There will be a central villain who, too, joins the group in Book 1: Jordan Teague, a brutal and sadistic monster. Once ambushed by a band of mutie marauders, the freak blast of a grenade blew away most of one side of his face and mangled the rest. The medics did the best they could. Teague now has one biotronic eye; half of his face is alloy. All of his brain is consumed with a burning hatred for his fellow men.

It is Teague, in fact, who welds the group together originally, but only for his own purposes. He is no altruist. He wants power, and these one-hundred-year-old U.S. government secrets can give him exactly what he wants. A running battle will develop over the series: sometimes Cawdor is ahead, sometimes Teague. Until finally Teague is spectacularly destroyed.

I see various twists to the main narrative. I don't think it would do any harm if, say, Krysty, the main female character, was lost for one whole book—captured at the beginning of one story by Teague, or perhaps by some other mysterious agency, but Cawdor is diverted from rescuing her by other, far more pressing problems.

In each book in the series a different story: each one self-contained, each one with a suitably blazing climax. And each one with a different and colorful locale in Deathlands. A kind of *Running Man* or *The Fugitive* saga.

California: A story set amid the eerie lagoons and missile-sculpted mountains of this dramatically altered area.

Florida: In the noisome, fetid, night-dark swamps, strange mutated creatures lurk, and an even stranger society of human beings.

Heartlands: In the blasted heart of what used to be Middle America there survives a small town where there are wind-up gramophones and horse-drawn buggies, and everything's apple-pie cozy. Or is it?

This kind of thing. But I'd also pull in "echoes," if you like, of the twentieth century: appalling traps set by the original scientists that have to be eluded or somehow gotten around. Cryogenic burial—i.e., freeze your loved ones who are suffering from terminal illnesses so that in a century or so they can defrost and be cured—has distinct possibilities, if twisted around a little. A group of murderous "dirty tricks" government operatives, say, springing up like dragons' teeth.

The Idea Takes Hold

Further Thoughts

First and foremost this series is both an escape story and a quest story. At first the central group of characters in the series wants to escape from the grim and savage hell of post-holocaust America—or at least the vast poison-land time, or another heard vague stories of a kind of promised land of untold riches somewhere to the north. That isn't in fact quite how things are, or how they're going to pan out, but that is what they've heard. And that is what motivates the main nucleus of the group through whatever desperate adventures befall them, and through however many books the series runs to.

In Book 1 they find that there are indeed riches—of a kind. But these aren't the riches that they thought they were. Two-thirds of the way through the book they reach the goal they were headed for, after a grim and appalling trip across Deathlands. They reach a redoubt. They don't know it, but there are redoubts scattered all over what used to be North America. Each redoubt is more or less different from the rest, with one thing in common: there is a central chamber at its heart in which there is a locational "gateway." This takes the form of a pillar of fog, from floor to ceiling, maybe thirty feet in diameter, rolling and seething and swirling, a continuously shifting column of thick gray-white mist. Plunge into that and you're suddenly somewhere else, in another redoubt, maybe one thousand miles away across the continent.

But in one redoubt, one very special redoubt, plunge into that thick fog…and you're suddenly *somewhen* else. You're two hundred years into the past, in a time when the atom had not even been split, when Einstein was still groping for a theory of relativity, when if you were to talk seriously of a war that could wipe out half the world's population and turn one-third of the globe into a hellish nightmare landscape of radiation swamps populated by monstrous mutants, you'd be thrown into the nearest madhouse. For this is a time of peace and prosperity and stability, a time of centuries-old values that have not yet been blasted apart forever by the hell of nuclear war.

But they don't know this yet, the group of men and women who finally reach this first redoubt. Only gradually do they become aware of it. At first, at the end of Book 1, they get a hint that there is indeed an escape route through these gateways, and at first they don't dare to believe it. At least not wholly. It's too much to hope for.

Still, it's a goal in itself and so it becomes a quest. And as they journey onward, jumping from location to location, into each new form of madness that they must first overcome or escape from, so they find out more and more about the reason for these hidden redoubts—they learn more and more about the untold secrets that scientists were probing in what was once the United States in the latter half of the twentieth century, over one hundred years before.

In each book of the series, the main characters—epitomized by Ryan Cawdor and the strange, enigmatic, red-haired girl Krysty—will uncover new clues to the central mystery, helped to a certain extent by the weird hints, mutterings and ravings of the seemingly half-crazed Doc, a character who at times seems to be merely a shambling, brain-blasted victim and slave of the brutal Jordan Teague, who at times seems to be a visionary, a figure of power and extraordinary knowledge.

But Doc knows far more than he is able to tell. There is a reason for this. He was in fact born in 1860. He was a scientist. In 1904, by sheer appalling chance, he was picked up by U.S. scientists from the 1980s in their first trawl in the past when they discovered that they could jump back through time. The 1980s scientists brought back a number of "subjects" from the early 1900s. Some died, others had their brains scrambled through sheer culture shock; Doc survived because he himself was a trained scientist and could thus accept things that others of his time and culture simply could not. They found him a willing, able and intelligent subject. Then the missiles rained down from the skies in the early 1990s, and the scientific complex where Doc was being held was blasted, and through some weird and horrific freak—possibly due to the nature of an experiment that was taking place near to the "time" gateway at the time—Doc was hurled into the future, into the late 2070s.

For some years he wanders through the nightmare landscape of the nuclear Deathlands. Most of the time it's as though his brain has been shot away. At other times he has periods of lucidity in which he knows roughly who he is, but even so the "why" is still lost in a mind fogged by the terrible experiences through which he's been. But he does, in these "clear periods," know something about the gateways, their possible uses—and that there is still one all-important secret he can't quite grasp. Uncovering that last secret so that a final escape from Deathlands may be achieved will be one of the threads of the series. Ryan and Krysty certainly realize that Doc holds the key to escape, and that they mustn't ever lose sight of him.

This "time" aspect will not be heavily stressed. It is background to the series as a whole. It's a means to an end that only a few of the Deathlands "pilgrims" will finally make use of at the end of the series. During the course of the series, in each separate book, hints will be dropped, allusions made—less and less cryptic as the series itself progresses.

However, each book will be a separate adventure with a separate plot and a separate and suitably violent and explosive finale. That must be stressed. Because, as I said before, this is basically an action-adventure series whose jumping-off point, if you like, happens to be an SF one.

Of course, as the series takes place in the 2080s, or thereabouts, there will necessarily be an SF element in it. But I want to keep the books as much as possible action adventure with bizarre-horror overtones, and science fiction undertones.

For example, weapons. In such a world as I envisage, there would be no great manufactories pumping out new weapons by the ton every week. That would imply a higher level of manufacturing sophistication than I want. The group of pilgrims would, as each new situation demands, grab weapons as they find them. I envisage, as I implied in my original proposal, great stores of weaponry and matériel, greased and factory fresh, hidden in secret cavernous locations in various parts of Deathlands, forgotten, unknown. These will, of course, be mainly weapons of *our* time. On the other hand there will have been certain technological advances—I have in mind a laser rifle which sends out a beam of pure destructive power, either on narrow beam for cutting, or full beam for blowing a hole through man or machine the size of a wrecking ball—even after a nuclear war.

Let's say the nuclear winter lasts only five years—today some say thirty or forty years; others argue for two or three years max. After that, mankind has about one hundred years until the end of the twenty-first century when the series takes place. Clearly, in some parts of the world, and certainly in some parts of America, it would not take one hundred years to get back to some reasonable semblance of normality. Not everything would be utterly destroyed, and later generations would obviously build on what was left, and what would be left would be rather a lot, I suspect.

That a kind of new Dark Age would, broadly speaking, descend upon the world is unarguable. However, it would not be a total Dark Age—a Dark Age shot with thick streaks of gray, if you like.

As I said in my original proposal, in parts of America there are communications—of a visual kind even, such as are being experimented on right now. And there is power and fuel—oil, gasoline, electric—though these are in relatively short supply. I don't want a situation where my characters cannot, if they suddenly want to, hop on board a heavy-duty land truck and shift hell along what remains of a four-lane blacktop. But I do want a situation where things could suddenly go seriously out of kilter—power cuts out, fuel leaks—and they face disaster because they can't immediately put their hands on more fuel, more power, whatever.

The Deathlands

The Deathlands themselves take up most of the North American continent roughly from Ohio down to Alabama, across to Texas, up to Montana and back down through Wisconsin.

But not all of this huge area has been totally destroyed, or lies beneath a mantle of reeking nuclear smog. There are, as I said, inhabited areas where life goes on. But mainly a bloodred sun hangs sullenly over a torn and tortured landscape; where there is no nuclear desert, there are the fetid strontium swamps where radiation poison over one hundred years or so has not only created new and terrible life-forms, but also played sinister havoc with those that existed before. It is a vast land of living nightmare.

The West Coast has been for the most part entirely re-sculpted following the terrible devastation caused by the final upheavals of the San Andreas Fault, deliberately missiled in the war. San Francisco, Monterey, L.A., San Diego—these thriving centers of population no longer exist. Indeed, California itself has become a narrow strip of nuclear sand dunes and shoreline banding the lower reaches of the Sierra Madre. Baja California has virtually disappeared. Vast steaming lagoons lie to the south; long canyonlike fjords now thrust deep into the heart of the mountain chain to the north.

Texas, New Mexico, Arizona and Mexico are now simmering hot lands, dust bowls skinned of cacti and even the most primitive forms of vegetation, where two-hundred-mile-per-hour winds shriek and roar as they hurtle across this bleak Mars-scape. And when by some atmospheric freak storm clouds sweep across from the Pacific, it is acid rain that falls—pure acid that can strip a man to the bones in sixty seconds of shrieking agony.

Centers of Civilization

These lie mainly on the East Coast, where the population, over a century, has had time to recover to a certain extent from the appalling devastation. The region of New York and Manhattan Island—where bombs were midair detonated—is now akin to Angkor Wat or Machu Picchu: that is, a brooding, ruined city overgrown with noxious vegetation. Yet people, of a kind, still live here and battle for survival and supremacy among the tree- and undergrowth-choked urban canyons.

The main area of civilization has now shifted south to the Virginias and the Carolinas. Here is industry, both heavy and manufacturing. Here they can run cars and trucks with comparative ease; they have small planes, and war choppers. But there have been no new and startling technological leaps, most things are derivative of what was being produced in the late twentieth century.

To the northeast of New York, in Vermont, New Hampshire, Maine, there lies a true wilderness, an area now of great, and sometimes weird, natural beauty, populated only sparsely by tribes of small, self-contained communities.

Mutants

I keep mentioning mutants. These come in all shapes and sizes, literally! Those long-ago radiation showers created havoc with the genetic codes in both humans and animals. Not only do you find strange and bizarre beasts lurking where man no longer treads, but also there is now a vast multitude of weird "human beings." There are the simple differences: men—and of course women, too—with three eyes or four arms, or with terribly deformed and nightmarish features: noses like elephants' trunks, or with armadillo-like skin, etc. But there are genetic mutations that are far more subtle—what might be people who are psychokinetic, who can thought-read, who can see through walls, who can levitate, who can kill with their minds, who can destroy with their eyes. And so on.

In general muties are feared, distrusted, hated. Some excellent emotional conflict can be gotten out of this. Because they are so feared and loathed, mutants tend to clan together; areas where they have proliferated tend to be avoided by normals. In the Deathlands, however, there is a certain amount of give-and-take, come-and-go, and the muties here have become an analog of the nineteenth-century Indians. In the more "civilized" areas they are often hunted down and destroyed. In an odd kind of way, out in the Deathlands there is a freer and more liberal attitude toward them than in the civilized parts of the country.

Book 1: Pilgrimage to Hell

The general locale of the first two-thirds of the book is what used to be Montana, starting from the rolling prairies and ending somewhere high in the rugged wilderness of Glacier National Park. (NB: It seems easier here to use the present-day appellations of the various places: it goes without saying that one hundred years after a nuke war, Montana and Glacier National Park would not be so named.)

I want to kick off with an introductory sequence that I think will sum up what I basically have in mind for the entire series: eerie atmosphere, bizarre horror and bloody action.

Prologue

Four men are trekking up through the wilderness. They have backpacks, food, weapons. They are: Hennings, Duber, Rogan and Manix. Hennings is an okay guy; Duber and Rogan are greedy, brutal men; Manix is a mutie. To look at him he's perfectly normal, but he has a strange extrasensory power: he can "smell" danger. That's why Duber and Rogan have forced him to come; they need him because there's danger aplenty up here. Hennings has been brought along as shotgun, a backup heavy, to blast anything that Manix misses.

This is a strange place, odd stories have been told of the area. Somewhere up here, in the heart of Glacier National Park, there exists a treasure of some kind, or a hidden place beyond the peaks, of untold riches. The stories have gotten confused over the past sixty or seventy years, and men who have sought to explore the area have all disappeared, never returned to the plains. All except one: a guy who trekked out with a twenty-strong party about five years previously. After a month he returned to the plains, a wild-eyed, staggering wreck of a man babbling of "fog devils." He died without revealing much else. Since then, no one has ventured back into the mountains. But the greed of men such as Duber and Rogan drives out fear; always such men believe they can succeed where others have failed.

There's a sullen atmosphere of resentment and unease between the four men. The air is strangely heavy with electricity. Tempers are fraying. Darkness is falling as they stumble up a rocky track beside a precipice—an electric darkness crackling eerily with blue-tinged flares. They round a bend in the trail. Ahead is a bank of thick, impenetrable fog extending across the trail. It shifts and quivers, seems almost alive. Tendrils of fog lick out from the main mass of it, like groping fingers. A dull, eerie glow emanates from it, lighting the immediate area somberly.

A fight breaks out among the men, already bickering and snapping at one another. Duber and Rogan scream at each other. The other two join in. They seem to have gone insane. Duber tries to strangle Rogan. Manix tries to smash in Hennings's head with a rock. Snow begins to fall, large thick flakes feathering down silently. Rogan goes crazy with his gun, shoots Manix, who disappears shrieking over the precipice. Hennings pulls his own gun, fires, misses, gets slammed back with a round through the shoulder. Duber dives for the dropped gun, grabs it, blows Rogan's head away in a spray of red stuff. Cackles crazily: he's going to finish Hennings off; he'll get through the fog, whatever is beyond will be his...his...his alone! Jams gun toward helpless Hennings, unaware of the thick tendril of fog that is even now reaching down the trail toward him, wreathing through the air, curling around his throat. He yells. The fog fingers clutch, lift him screaming up into the air emitting long blue hissing sparks; he's haloed in a weird cyanic fire. Shrieking, he disappears into the fog.

Hennings crawls away, scrambling to his feet. Clutching his bloody shoulder, he staggers back down the trail...back down toward the foothills and the relative sanity of the plains.

The Story

Ryan Cawdor is a tall rangy man in his early thirties. He's not a child of the Deathlands. Once he was the privileged son of one of the more powerful barons of the East Coast. (NB: I may well change such nomenclature in the actual writing, if a better system occurs; also, I may change certain characters' names I may not be entirely happy with.)

Ryan's educated, has read books, knows pretty well what life was like one hundred years before; maybe the detail is lost in the years, but the general outline is understood. He lived a good life, far better than most in what used to be the U.S. of A. What, then, is he doing acting as head guard to a trade-trucker on a fleet of land wagons amid the hellish conditions of the Deathlands?

He grew to hate the life in the East, the power struggles, the court intrigues, the greed and corruption already rampant, the life of unearned luxury not shared by ninety-five percent of the population. His father, Donn Cawdor, farmed a huge tract of land, used muties as laborers—but was sensitive to their problems, did not use them as slaves. The son of a rival baron casually slaughtered a group of Donn Cawdor's workers, and Ryan went berserk, shooting up the rival baron's HQ and incidentally killing the baron himself. It was a setup. The son wanted his father out of the way, knew Ryan would react as he did. In fake revenge he destroys Donn Cawdor's HQ, Donn Cawdor himself, most of his family and grabs his lands. Ryan escaped, but not before dealing death to many close to the rival baron's son. Ryan fled into the Deathlands.

Or, the same basic situation but it's Ryan's own brother who is the villain of the piece. That is, Ryan's brother and Ryan are poles apart in character. Ryan's brother slaughtered his father's muties, his father and other members of his family, and heaped the blame on to Ryan. I like this better. More conflict.

Ryan traveled across the Deathlands, seeking work, seeking some kind of peace of soul—seeking he doesn't quite know what. And so lands up as head shotgun for the Trader, a man who trades in the Deathlands. (NB: All of this background material will be infiltrated into the narrative by degrees, not of course in one solid chunk.)

The Trader needs as many guards as he can get. He deals in arms, all kinds of weaponry. He travels through as much of the Deathlands as he can, selling or bartering guns, ammo, grenades, small missiles, whatever he's got, whatever he can find, whatever he can make. Apart from Ryan, the Trader's main lieutenant is J. B. Dix, known as the Weapons Master.

The Trader is simply a businessman; it's Dix who has a fantastic knowledge of weaponry, booby traps and so on. A thin, intense, bespectacled man with a receding hairline, a penchant for thin black cheroots, a fast but very devious mind and a terse and monosyllabic conversational style, Dix the Weapons Master will be an important character in the series. There is no knowing what kind of weird stuff he has in his grab bag, a satchel slung over one shoulder or indeed in his clothes and on his person. He is secretive, but will prove to be immensely loyal to Ryan Cawdor.

Not unnaturally, the kind of cargoes shipped by the Trader are prime targets for the ruthless marauders who prey on anything that moves in the Deathlands. And we open with an unidentified man watching from cover as a line of lights wobbles across his line of vision, heading across rough terrain in the predawn hours: the weapons train, a line of trucks, powered wagons and armored personnel cars— along the lines of armored dune buggies, but bigger and with much hardware attached: these are for the guards—bumping and jolting along an uneven, potholed road, what used to be a main interstate, now in appalling disrepair. No weapons train ever stops for the night in this area of the Deathlands. A blazing battle erupts. Ryan and his men manage to beat off the attackers for the moment but only after terrible casualties and a good deal of land wagon damage. Now they have to stop.

Ryan and a small group of guards scout out, under cover of the darkness. They discover the attackers' camp. Discover, too, that the leaders of the band—mostly horrifying mutants—are about to gang-rape a beautiful red-haired girl. In an explosive sequence Ryan and his men destroy the mutants' camp and Ryan rescues the girl. The girl is Krysty, the only survivor of a small land-wagon train heading for Glacier National Park in search of a fabulous treasure, rumor of which had fired them to make the dangerous trek into the Deathlands. Ryan dismisses this talk of treasure and riches. It's a myth, a will-o'-the-wisp.

The weapons train is headed for the town of Mocsin, ruled over by the brutal Jordan Teague, a man who intends that his empire will one day become the most powerful in the Deathlands. That's why he needs much weaponry. And he can pay for it, too, with gold that is mined within his own territories, fantastically rich new lodes exposed in the war. On the other hand, he'd rather have the guns free if he can.

Toward sundown the weapons train arrives at Mocsin at a grim moment—a mass execution of various men and women who in one way or another have bucked Jordan Teague. Mocsin is a kind of frontier boomtown, except for the fact that due to Teague's vicious excesses, it's now run-down, seedy. Teague and his henchmen live in a style of primitive decadence, high off the hog, but it's clear that things can't go on in this way for long. The majority of the townsfolk live in fear of Teague's "police," run by the sinister Cort Strasser, a hideously disfigured man with a bio-tronic eye and a face full of alloy.

Most of the townsfolk want an end to Teague and his reign of terror and violence. Strasser himself is not Teague's second-in-command. This dubious honor belongs to a plug-ugly man named Jarl Kremer. Kremer and Strasser are not on the best of terms, but whereas Kremer is a bullet-headed thug, Strasser is a ruthless schemer with a maniacal power lust, which, for the time being, he keeps well under wraps.

The Trader places his convoy outside of town, well aware that Teague will double-cross him if he can. Teague keeps putting off settling day. The atmosphere is more than tense; it's getting to be explosive. The slightest spark could touch off a blazing conflagration. During one of their parleys Teague, a man of gross appetites, has made it perfectly plain that he wants Krysty as part of the deal. The Trader—an honorable man, incidentally—rejects this contemptuously, but that doesn't go down at all well with Teague, who is used to having his own way. This adds to the tension.

At these conferences a strange, half-crazed wreck of a man has sometimes been in evidence: Teague calls him Doc, and he appears to be some kind of court jester, to be booted around and made the butt of countless practical jokes by Teague's oafish bully boys. In moments of lucidity, he talks of a country where flowers grow and there is peace and plenty—stuff like that—in a weird kind of English, using strange, alien phraseology. Ryan figures that this could be the basis for the legends about "the place beyond the peaks" that Krysty spoke of, but again dismisses it.

At Teague's HQ, Ryan sees a man in chains and manacles being savagely beaten by some of Teague's goons. Ryan intervenes, lays the goons out. Strasser tells him the guy is a lunatic, not to bother about him. Later, at the convoy camp, the guy appears. He has escaped from Strasser's police HQ. His name is Hennings. He tells his strange tale of the fog devils and what he saw up in the peaks, as detailed in the prologue. Ryan now begins to think there's maybe more to these stories than surface myths. Dix, too, is more than interested. He figures that the fog could be some kind of dispersed energy. Where's that energy escaped from? It doesn't sound natural. It could be a clue to some kind of hidden arms cache of long ago, from before the nuke war, of the type that the Trader and his men are continually seeking and sometimes stumbling across. Hennings was being kept on ice by Teague, who is also interested in his story. Hennings also tells them something about Doc, who, in his less-crazed moments, talks of places of power and scientific miracles. Teague is eager to mount an expedition. The Trader and his men hide Hennings. After they've finished their business with Teague, they intend to head for Glacier National Park to investigate.

Things boil up. In a final confrontation Teague kills the Trader, grabs Krysty, Ryan and his men and throws them into the pokey. Ryan is prepared for this. Using some plastique they have and detonators—all innocuously hidden in their clothes and boots—they blow themselves out of jail and hit Teague's armory, demolish it and most of Teague's HQ, rescue Krysty. The town's citizens rise up, and Ryan and friends head out across the plain in convoy, with Hennings and Doc, whom they grabbed in the shoot-out.

After a horrifying drive through the wilderness—losing vehicles in acid lakes, fighting off packs of mutated wolves as big as bullocks, etc.—they reach the foothills and find a crumbling but navigable metalled road leading up into the higher mountains. Here they encounter the fog. The fog is pure energy that has leaked out from the maw of the hidden redoubt. In its contained form, inside the redoubt, it's "safe." But free, it becomes pure destructive energy that can render a man down to his essential molecules and scatter them to the four winds. Dix the Weapons Master destroys the fog juggernaut with an implosion grenade that on bursting, sucks energy into its core, neutralizes then safely destroys-disperses it. The way is clear, but by now they're down to three or four vehicles and only about fifteen men— in no shape to withstand the sudden assault of a much bigger band of mutants who suddenly attack. The same band in fact that attacked them before they reached Mocsin; devastatingly patient, they licked their wounds and bided their time. But just when things are getting desperate help arrives—but in the shape of Teague, Strasser and their men who have vengefully pursued them across the Deathlands.

The mutants are finally destroyed, but Ryan and his party are captured. They move on up into the towering peaks, although at night there are strange and inexplicable occurrences: some of Teague's guards disappear; some are found dead in the morning. Ryan is taken out at night and interrogated by Strasser. Here he begins to understand Strasser's motivations and restless ambition. Kremer is drunk, obnoxious, crowing over Strasser. Strasser kills him, tells Teague that Ryan managed to grab a gun and iced Kremer. Now

Strasser is second-in-command, and Ryan's in deep trouble. He's taken out to be executed by two of Strasser's goons. But just as they're about to nail him, one flops over coughing blood with an arrow deep in his back. Ryan deals with the other guy. His rescuer is the mutant Manix, the man who can "smell" danger—a useful attribute. He managed to survive the plunge over the precipice—in the prologue— and has been living like an animal in the hills ever since. He knows Teague from way back, which is why he's been killing off Teague's men. More to the point, he knows where there is a vast steel-lined door in the rocks, obviously leading down to the bowels of the hills.

Ryan realizes that there is absolutely no percentage in doing a big-production rescue of Dix, Krysty and the rest. There are still too many of the Teague-Strasser bunch to deal with. It's a case of softly-softly. Ryan and Manix silently free the others, get to a personnel buggy—but are then discovered. They get away up the road and their only chance is to reach this "door" before Teague-Strasser catch up.

In a nail-bitingly tense sequence they manage to do this. Just. Teague is hot on their heels. They find themselves in a vast, softly lit, steel-walled cavern. The roof is so high it's beyond view. Lines of computer banks seem to stretch away from them forever, separated by narrow alleyways. High above, a spiderweb of fragile-looking walkways cross-hatch the air. Lights flash on consoles, relays click and chatter, there is a quiet but insistent hum of on-line machinery. And there is a lot of dust.

There's a running fight through the vast length of this underground complex until they reach the fog room, where Doc suddenly starts babbling about the fog being a gateway to another place. Maybe more. Maybe another time. A stray round creases his scalp and he keels over. But now Ryan and friends are trapped. Teague and his heavies are moving in for the kill. Teague is yelling exultantly: all this power, all the secrets of the preholocaust era are now his to do with as he likes.

Ryan manages to hurl one of Dix's implosion grenades at him. There is a sizzling crack, a red-cored flash. Then things start to tip over the edge. Teague and a number of his minions are sucked into the grenade blast, becoming liquescent as they sluice into the weird flickering fireball. But it doesn't stop there. There's too much power in this vast chamber, long crackling lines of fork lightning spark out from the computers, console screens crack and shatter, lights explode. The implosion ball sucks greedily at that vast acreage of energy, drawing it all in. It can't stop. It won't stop until it's sucked everything in to overload and then it'll blow just about the entire mountain into orbit!

There's only one way out—through the fog wall. Doc said it was a gateway; Ryan and friends hope like hell he's right. They jump into the fog....

Context

Editorial Trends

A look at recent developments in Action Adventure and in Science Fiction and Fantasy (SF&F) as indicated by author and publisher activity. Conclusion: there is a healthy market for "near-future fiction."

The Origin of Near-Future Fiction

The Survivalist by Jerry Ahern (Zebra). This series, first published in 1981, is now at #12 with more contracted. It continues to be popular and is successful overseas. It created the "near-future fiction" genre. The success of *The Survivalist* series has led to imitations from a number of paperback publishers in 1984. They follow the ingredients established by Ahern: heroic action in a postnuclear holocaust setting.

Doomsday Warrior by Rider Stacy (Zebra).

Traveler by D. B. Drumm (Dell).

The Outrider by Richard Harding (Pinnacle).

Near-Future Fiction is not just for SF&F readers

The Warlord by Jason Frost (Zebra). This series, now at #4, is written by our Bolan author, Ray Obstfeld. Arnold Schwarzenegger stars in the film for release in early 1986, following his success in the action-adventure SF film, *The Terminator*.

Out of the Ashes by William Johnstone (Zebra).

Streetlethal by Steven Barnes (Ace).

Those Who Favor Fire by Marta Randall (Pocket).

Like *The Warlord,* many near-future novels are aimed at the general reader rather than the science fiction fan, by offering sex, action and patriotism elements traditionally enjoyed by a wider readership. The books shown here are more up-market than *The Survivalist* imitators, but share with *The Survivalist* a readership that goes beyond SF&F.

Action Adventure is also for SF&F readers

Battle Circle by Piers Anthony (Avon). This is a near-future trilogy about "America's barbaric future" by the leading U.S. writer of Fantasy. The packaging stresses heroic action-adventure themes.

The Mercenary by Jerry Pournelle (Pocket). Captioned "a thundering adventure," this book by a major SF&F writer is a Mack Bolan-type novel set in space.

Cross the Stars by David Drake (Tor). Drake's *Hammer's Slammers* series, of which this is a spin-off, is the most highly regarded of recent SF actioners. The cover shows paramilitary types posing against a spaceship background.

Space Tyrant: Mercenary by Piers Anthony (Avon). A book about force, power, warrior violence in a space setting.

These kinds of books show that the action-adventure elements of near-future fiction appeal to SF&F readers, as much as its science-fiction elements appeal to the action-adventure readers.

Fully developed SF&F Action Adventure

Star World by Harry Harrison (Bantam). This series has been packaged to look like *The Survivalist*. Although Harry Harrison's books are not strictly near-future fiction, they are action-adventure and they are earning for the author and the SF&F genre a new kind of reader.

Planet of the Damned by Harry Harrison (Tor). Sex and violence on a distant planet.

Berserker by Fred Saberhagen (Ace).

The new kind of SF&F readers come to the genre from other areas of reading, bringing with them a taste for sex and violence blended with a curiosity about the future. They also appreciate books in series.

Conclusion

The argument presented by the preceding exhibits is that the action-adventure genre and the SF&F genre are finding new readers.

Publishers have responded to this development by encouraging the near-future fiction genre, where the elements of heroic action, and the scientific "unknown" of the post-nuclear age, most effectively cross over.

Although near-future fiction is a subgenre, it is not isolated from the mainstream either of action adventure or SF&F, or general reading. Action elements continue to appear in SF&F books of all kinds, and SF&F elements are vital to all action-adventure books set during or after World War III. Readers for near-future fiction are found among the general readership for action-adventure, SF&F, and other categories such as mystery and occult. The genre is not a limited phenomenon like some SF&F, but is a response to the real world's uncertain future, a topic that has continued potential.

Both action-adventure and SF&F readers bring to near-future fiction an acceptance of series. The various subgenres of SF&F such as space operas (E. C. Tubb, Perry Rhodan, E. E. Doe Smith, etc.) have built up loyal followings through ongoing series. There are over four million of John Norman's GOR books in print. Action-adventure also has its tradition of long-standing series, and therefore successful space actioners such as *Hammer's Slammers* become series as swiftly as successful mercenary-hero books.

David Hartwell, founding editor of Pocket Books' Timescape imprint, confirms the conclusions above:

> The one direction science fiction is moving in is toward adventure fantasy.
>
> *—Publishers Weekly*

The growth in new kinds of readers for SF&F was accepted as inevitable by the attendees of our science fiction focus tests in 1981:

> Readers of SF are extremely receptive to mixed genre books whose growing popularity springs from mass audience interest in *Star Wars, 2001, Star Trek* etc.
>
> The new breed of mass-market science-fiction readers come to this category of books because they are interested in science fiction renditions of themes that are used in other types of books.
>
> *—PI Market Research Report:*
> *SF Focus Groups 1981*

Tom Doherty, president and publisher of Tor Books, gives a similar explanation for the new breed of SF&F reader:

Our steady sales growth in SF&F since I started Tor in April 1981 (103% sales increase, 1983 over 1982) can be explained in part by the increasing number of SF&F novels that have begun to hit the national bestseller lists.

—*Magazine & Bestsellers,* September 1983

There is no doubt that SF&F is looting other genres and readership groups for themes and for sales. Ace/Berkley is launching its six-figure SF promotion campaign for 1985 by advertising in military magazines. Retailers report that the SF&F market is growing because of the dual nature of the new readership (women, as well as men) and the crossover between young and mature readers (David Thorson of B. Dalton, 1984). Waldenbooks increased their SF&F shelf space by 150% in 1983–84. George Fisher, marketing manager of Warner Books, reports a sell-through of 60%–70% in SF&F.

These observations of the marketplace suggest the following:

• SF&F is a continually developing category. (Representative sample: Harry Harrison's *Star World*

• Action adventure is a continually developing category. (Representative sample: Jerry Ahern's *The Survivalist.*

• The near-future-fiction genre is where the new generation of SF&F and action-adventure readers meet.

• There is strong potential in near-future fiction for selling series to a wider readership than pure SF&F or pure action adventure.

• In order to develop Gold Eagle's potential in action adventure, as well as to explore the SF&F category as it connects most obviously with action adventure, Gold Eagle should enter the field of near-future fiction.

The Concept of Deathlands

Introduction

The editorial quality that observers identify as most responsible for widening the appeal of SF&F is depth of character. At one time, science fiction was mainly about the technology of the future. In order to satisfy more general readers, publishers have opened the genre to more human concerns.

> In adventure fantasy the characters tend to be very developed, unlike hard-core science fiction which focuses on hardware...and presents undimensional people.
>
> (PI Market Research Report;
> SF Focus Groups 1981)

Another useful finding from the 1981 focus tests was that in SF&F, "the storyline must be reflected in the title. Titles help categorize the type of book and determine its desirability."

We have responded to these points in developing *Deathlands*.

The human dimension is the one aspect of an author's art that is difficult to convey in a concept outline. Please be advised that the requirements for general popularity of the near-future fiction genre, such as character motivation, emotional complexity, sex and action developments, are all vital parts of the *Deathlands* package even though it is not possible to do them justice in these story outlines. The title of the series, *Deathlands,* sends a clear and intriguing message to the potential buyer.

The Author's Conception

Jack Adrian intends to produce a series of books that inspires identification in the reader; in other words, his characters are real people. This will not be "outpost" science fiction—such as early Heinlein—that appeals only to male readers and concentrates on raw adventure at the expense of carefully plotted suspense and character development. This is a post-holocaust adventure fantasy with stringent rules. Rules are an absolute must for the majority of readers who look on SF&F or action adventure as their escape entertainment. The "tomorrow" of the story must be firmly recognizable as an extrapolation of today, with fixed laws and mores that make the people and the settings real. This is to be fiction about relationships, personal motivations and important historical possibilities. Nevertheless, the author stresses that the dynamic of each book—with its separate adventure and separate explosive ending—comes from basic action adventure.

> This is an action-adventure story whose jumping-off point happens to be a science-fiction one. First and foremost, these books are the story of a quest. I want to keep the books as much as possible action adventure with bizarre-horror overtones and science-fiction undertones.

Packaging the Vision

A Picture Is Worth...

These comments should serve as art information for the first Deathlands book, *Pilgrimage to Hell*. Much of what Jack Adrian has written will also be useful for the following three books in the *Deathlands* series.

The Deathlands themselves are the environment of the world after a nuclear holocaust. The point about the series is that there is life after the holocaust, albeit in a drastically changed and unfamiliar world. The characters in the book are the second or third generation to be born after the holocaust. Thus they are slightly different from us, although recognizably humans of present time. Their clothes are unique to them, and they have undergone subtle mutations.

The books are adventure stories in the "near-future fiction" category. But we do not want to categorize the books in the way they look, so perhaps the only point to make about the category that is relevant to the art is that near-future fiction has one foot in today and one foot in tomorrow. It is partly and recognizably the present, and partly and recognizably the future.

Because we want to avoid a pulp-story "adventure" look, we discussed the overall direction of the art, and the particulars such as the background and whether to show characters—and where.

Starting from the agreement that the art should be wrap-around, we decided that at least two of the characters should be visible. They should be together, and placed in an off-center position on the front cover; their size and their positioning—preferably lower right—make it clear that there are more important elements on this cover than the presence of the book's heroes.

The potential background grew to very vivid life as we discussed the concept behind the series. The key element that carries the meaning of the series, and that will be a hook for its popularity, is the contrast between the death and destruction of our known world in the Deathlands, and the signs of very real and very different life that prevails in the Deathlands.

We agreed that we would explore existing documentary evidence of what atomic-bomb-blasted cities, and countryside, and atolls—from the Pacific testing—look like. We should also absorb Jack Adrian's descriptions in order to detail some of the vegetation and weather conditions and ecosystems in general that he is imagining in this series.

Hopefully the artist's sketches will creatively play with some of the possibilities of the plant life and sky colorations and so on that are only broadly described by Adrian. It is not possible with a book before it is written to detail every aspect of biology, life-forms, etc., that will entertain the readers in the final text; therefore the artist should have some license in his efforts to suggest post-holocaust life.

Thus far we have decided on the details to this extent:

The front cover should show the blasted remains of part of a North American city—providing it is a prairie or Midwest city, such as Omaha, Nebraska, because that is where the first book is set. The ruins have existed as ruins for some years. New life in the form of grasses and plants is visible throughout. At least two human beings are visible. The sky is unusual in its cloud patterns or color. The picture wraps around to show the geography beyond the city, maybe a mountain range, a winding river. In the city itself, architectural images such as an almost destroyed church should be used to discomfort the viewer with the contrast between the familiar and the future.

The succeeding books in the series should extend the vision of the first book into more and more detail about parts of the Deathlands. For example, Book 2 is set in the Bering Strait, changed somewhat by climate conditions: the bleakest of wastelands scarred with ashes, with the aurora borealis more vivid than ever. The third book is set in what remains of the Florida Everglades. The fourth book is called *Blood Valley*, which is something of a description in itself. So there will be plenty of opportunities to show harsh but exotic environments that contrast with the evidence, or at least the hope, of life.

Dialogue Between Writer and Artist

First of all I realize this is a sketch, and I realize, too, that it's a kind of symbolic pic simply to include the three main characters.

Okay. The cave. To me this looks far too much like the kind of hideout used by WWII Maquis or resistance fighters in the mountains of Italy or Greece or Yugoslavia. That is, pretty primitive. But these guys are not lurking around in damp caves. They do have a certain level of sophistication in their life-style.

First we have to establish whether the background (b/g) should be a hidden old U.S. Army "stockpile" cavern dug out by the army and unearthed by the Trader or whether it should be one of the top-secret redoubts created by Army and scientists at roughly the same time (i.e., late twentieth century).

A stockpile is, as I see it, something that those in power in our era had blasted out of the rock to store weaponry, dried food, ammo, generators, etc. (i.e., anything laid down in secret in case of nuclear devastation so that those in command could use them if stuff started running out). I see these stockpile areas as concrete walled, with maybe a metalled road running into it. A kind of underground quartermaster's stores. There would be a neatness about these man-made caverns that typifies any kind of Army activity of this nature. A kind of underground warehouse, if you like, undisturbed for a century until the Trader begins to find them, unearth them.

A redoubt is far more sophisticated. Something else entirely. Another world: we can all imagine stockpiles. We know damned well that that is exactly what the U.S. Army, and indeed the British army, French army, German, Russian, etc., are doing anyhow, all over the U.S. What I'm postulating is probably equally true: that those in command are digging out even vaster caverns full of stuff that is far more sophisticated than guns, ammo, grenades, and so on. It's just that in my scenario the stuff our scientists today are burying is superbizarre, really way-out, utterly over the edge. That is, a network of "locational gateways" throughout the U.S. We are in A. We can get to B by walking into a wall of fog. B may well be two thousand miles away, but we can do it in the time it takes to snap one's fingers.

Either one of these backgrounds could be used for the foldout. Our three main characters, in roughly the same attitudes, simply set against one of them.

If a stockpile b/g:

I would think rough concrete walls, alloy shelving, lines of crates stretching away into a distance point. Concrete floor, dusty. The whole thing smacks of a utility warehouse, stark and clean and spare, but underground. I'm aware that the mouth of the cavern in the pic is going to be made wider and higher, so we can see a bleak Deathlands terrain outside. Fine. If this locale is used, what I suggest, to give the pic extra punch, is as follows: Where the crates are now there should be the front, the snout, of one of the Trader's war wags, bulking huge. This war wag is a big mother; we don't need to see the whole of it—say, just the front third. This won't affect the positioning of J.B., which I like a lot, because he could be sitting on a crate beside it with his back to it, in exactly the same position as now. Similarly for Ryan and Krysty, whose positioning is excellent.

This would certainly give a feel of *Pilgrimage*—but it would not give a feel of the series as a whole. If that kind of atmosphere is wanted in this pic, then I suggest that the b/g should be of a redoubt.

If a redoubt b/g:

It should be something akin to what one sees in places like the NORAD command center. Screens, computer walls, consoles. High-tech, but deserted, dusty, unused for a century. The floors would not be concrete. The walls would not be concrete. There would be glass, strip lighting. The computers would be on-line. Lights would be flashing from the computer walls in a subdued but kaleidoscopic manner or pattern.

It may well be argued that computers would not remain on-line for a century. I accept that. But it doesn't matter. In the next fifteen years some guy will solve that problem, and in any case it is not central to my story. If things like that work, they work. The people like Ryan, in 115 years, will certainly ponder how all this stuff is happening, but he won't be able to solve it because he won't have the technical know-how, and neither will anyone else (except one or two who have such secrets locked in their brains—but that's getting into storyline).

Characters:

I like these a lot, but feel there needs to be a certain amount of refining.

J.B.—
At the moment he has too much flesh. I would personally like him much more ferrety, ratlike, skinnier. The expression

on his face is perfect, but the face as such should be much
thinner, and his body equally so. I like the white sweatshirt,
and I like very much the lighting striking him, body and
face. I think he should simply be much skinnier. He is a
wiry little bastard.

Krysty—
I'm aware that her hair is going to be much longer, which
is fine. I don't think she should have that upsweep of hair.
It should flow down, rather than look as though it had been
maybe blow-dried. As I said, I'm aware this is a sketch, but
I would like her with more cleavage. This is a personal
obsession! I'm not now sure about the throwing knives:
what I originally envisaged were longer ones, which in any
case should be so positioned that she will draw *left*-handed,
not right-handed. As a very small detail, maybe we should
get an impression of a few more pockets—map-pocket style,
zippered—on her pants. Bits of business like that.

Ryan—
Overall I'm impressed. I like this character. I feel safe with
him. Apart from the weaponry, which we can talk about,
and one particular item—which I'll get to—there are only
one or two fine details. Perhaps his hair should be very
slightly more "bushed out"...*very* slightly more "Afro."
In the story he will wear a scarf, as described in my original
character refs. You may not feel this needs to be drawn in
here.
   The big item is this business of the eye. I'm aware that
there's a feeling that my writing background is too comic-
strip oriented. My own view is that there is a certain amount
of overreaction here. Any visuals I may have come up with,
that is, the *kind* of visuals, can be found on comic-book
covers as well as a zillion paperback covers. And very good
p/back cover, too. We could get into this further but it'd be
a waste of valuable time.
   The whole point about Ryan is that he needs—in the

background I'm giving him—to be visually disfigured. His eye was sliced out by his own brother. That is strong stuff, and gives me an extremely strong plotline to be developed later in the series. Ryan's brother—*younger* brother—has killed their parents, other children, put it about that this was done by Ryan, put a price on his head, grabbed his birthright, and given Ryan just cause and reason to hate the shit out of him. He has also disfigured Ryan. And I want Ryan to look as though he *is* seriously disfigured with a whacking great scar or as though something serious *has* happened to him—under an eyepatch. If there's a choice, I prefer the latter. All this happened ten years ago, or thereabouts. By now Ryan has had time to get used to only having one eye; he can compensate when aiming a rifle, and he makes allowances in other ways. That happens. But a milky eyeball does not give me what I need.

In the Writer's Eye

Character Profiles

Ryan Cawdor

He's tall, maybe six feet. I don't want him too tall, i.e., over six feet. Nor do I want him to look like a Greek god. This is a rugged guy in a rugged world, although he isn't bulky or overly muscled. I'd rather see him slimmer than hefty. I don't want an Arnold Schwarzenegger. He has a narrowish frame and a narrowish face, with deep-set eyes.

I can't see his hair properly but I do know that it isn't gung-ho crew, shaved to the skull. In 2090 people would have figured out that wearing long hair is an asset: keeps your head warm. On the other hand, I don't think Ryan's hair should be too long, not even shoulder length. It should certainly be thick and chunky, maybe a little curly. Try a semi-(but only semi-)Afro on a narrow-boned face and see how it looks. Ah! I think I know what I'm trying to get at— Elliott Gould, the film star. But maybe even more "chunky" (i.e., thick) hair. Raven, in coloring.

He has deep-set eyes, blue, chilling and brooding for the most part. This doesn't, however, mean the guy never smiles. Also a kind of wariness, just a hint, as though he trusts few people. There is a reason for this, and evidence is the long scar that runs down one side of his face, from the corner of his left eye—as we're looking at him, the eye on the right-hand side of his face—about down to the corner of his mouth. This should not, of course, disfigure him, but rather add to his, if you like, mystique.

That scar is a souvenir of his escape, some years before, from the family home. It was given him by his younger brother who had just had their mother and father slaughtered so he—the younger son—could take over. Cunningly this was engineered so it would seem Ryan had done the slaughtering. In a desperate fight Ryan's cheek is opened up by his knife-wielding and maniacal brother. Ryan escapes, but this grim and appalling memory lives with him always. It's why he's suspicious of people, why he's become a loner, why he's bitter, why he wants, at some stage, revenge.

Or, instead of the scar down his left cheek, he has no left eye at all and a scar down his right cheek. He wears an eye patch. This, I think, would look particularly attractive, artwise.

The younger brother took one eye out in this terrible and bloody fight, but in trying to whip the other eye out screwed up, hence the scar. The scar will become a seared and livid white at moments of tumultuous fury and stress. When people he knows see that scar whitening up, they run for cover. It doesn't happen too often. I prefer this as it really lends stark drama to the memory of the murderous treachery of his brother that I want to use in concrete form in at least one of the books, though not the initial one.

Incidentally, apropos that, I'd prefer it if not too much was revealed about Ryan's past in prebook publicity or blurbs, certainly not that he has a brother who cut his face open or took one eye out. Strong hints as to a terrible memory of the past, yes—concrete descriptions of what happened, no. Eye patch, or merely scar? Any comment would be helpful, especially at this stage. I frankly prefer eye patch and scar—plenty meaty and visual and fairly unusual.

Ryan is tall, tough, rangy, a natural leader of men and women. He is a pragmatist, a realist, too. He knows exactly when to fight and will fight against all odds, but, too, he knows when to retreat, to retire in good order to save his forces—the mark of a good general.

He's in his early thirties, no more. Certainly no less. He has strong hands, but these are usually encased in skintight black gloves, open at the wrist, perhaps folded back one turn, loosely.

I see him in black, mainly. With one major exception, which we'll get to later. A black shirt, maybe thick-material T-shirt. Black pants, knee-length black boots, hard wearing.

His belt. On this he has a pistol holster, with a handgun in it. Heavy-cal automatic. That is on his right hip. On his left hip, angled so he can reach for it with his right hand, is a short scabbard. This will contain not a sword, but a panga: the kind of machete-style weapon the Mau Mau used. From tip of blade to end of grip, maybe eighteen inches long. No more. He has a knife scabbard out of sight at his back. We see a couple or three grenades attached to the front of his belt, a small water bottle.

As I said, he is overall in black. His topcoat is a black thick jacket that reaches to just above his knees. Here we see it open, and we get a blaze of contrast in coloring as the lining is thick white fur. It's a kind of parka, and the interior of the hood, thrown back now of course, is white-fur-lined, too. There will be room in this coat—zip-up pockets externally and internally—for all kinds of hardware: spare mags for the automatic, etc.

His main weapon, which he holds across his chest, is what I'm calling the Quartz Cremator. This will be a laser rifle. The real science of it is as suspect as hell, but no matter. I have only a sketchy idea of what it should look like, but it mustn't be too long. On the other hand neither should it be one of those very short new-style bullpup weapons NATO is starting to use now. It must look impressive. It'll have a Starlite-scope viewer on it, that's for sure. It can send out a wide beam of pure blazing destructive energy or a needle-thin beam for cutting. The look of the weapon on the cover of *The Ninety-Nine* was very powerful indeed. I thought it was a made-up piece, but now learn it's some kind of common or garden shooter you people take down the subway with you. But the actual physical look of the thing is impressive. Perhaps the Cremator should not be quite as lengthy; it should certainly have a more interesting technological fascia to it.

Finally, Ryan's scarf. He wears one round his neck, loosely knotted at the throat. It hangs down to his navel, or maybe just above. It will be of some very silklike material and will be weighted at both ends, although not so's you can notice it overmuch. Perhaps this, too, could be white in color or maybe blood crimson. The scarf is weighted, of course, because Ryan uses it like a Thuggee's scarf, or even as a bola.

Krysty Wroth

Age group: in between twenty-four and twenty-eight. I see her as maybe two or three inches under Ryan's height, whatever that turns out to be. Her most spectacular feature is her hair: this is sensationally scarlet crimson. No kidding around here. This isn't red hair, or auburn. This is deep and torrid hued. At its normal length it will reach in a thick crimson cascade over her shoulders, front and back, and halfway down her back but not waist length. Of course she's a mutant, so in fact her hair can stretch—reach to an astonishing length, maybe as much as twenty feet or more. But we don't need to bother with this, I think, in a cover illustration sense. Too, I'd prefer it if it wasn't blurbed in prebook promos.

Her eyes are large and wide, an emerald green, deep, unfathomable pools. She is long limbed, full breasted and strong, with steely muscles hidden beneath a soft yet supple body. She is intelligent, alert, quick-witted. She is confident, self-assured; she can get along very well without Ryan Cawdor, yet she is attracted to him as though to a magnet, just as he is attracted to her—to her fierce and independent spirit, to her coolness in the face of danger and disaster.

Her face has high cheekbones: I'm thinking along the lines of a woman of the American Indian races. Something like the actress Cher, though her face is perhaps too full cheeked.

She wears, for the purposes of cover illustration, combat-style gear: a close-fitting catsuit in a dark green material that emphasizes both her own coloring, the red hair, olive white skin, and her shape. She has one ammo belt draped across and around her, with pouches for spare mags on it, for the automatic rifle she carries, usually in the back-slung position. Crosswise to this ammo belt, she wears a knife belt with four throwing knives. She's ambidextrous, but draws her knives *left*-handed. She, too, can have grenades at her belt. She wears knee-length boots, not thigh length.

It occurs to me that Krysty might wear a headband around her hair, green hued, a ribbon, or elastic material, not metal. You might try this; see how it looks. Although I like the idea of that swath of flame red hair blowing in the wind.

J. B. Dix, the Weapons Master

In *Pilgrimage to Hell*, in the initial stages of the story, we'll see that J. B. Dix, along with Ryan, is colieutenant to the Trader. They both work for the Trader, take their pay from him, plan routes and trade and journeys with and for him. The Trader depends on these two men, although perhaps he treats Ryan more as his natural heir and successor. When the Trader is killed, Dix naturally falls in behind Ryan. Dix is no leader, per se, and he knows it, but he's an extremely handy guy to have around.

As his title, the Weapons Master, implies, he handles all the hardware on the Trader's land/war-wagon convoys across the scarred and treacherous Deathlands. He sees to it that everyone who works for the Trader is well weaponed up; he's in a sense like the quartermaster of the outfit.

I see Dix very clearly: he's about five foot six inches, no more. Thin, wiry, agile, with an intense manner, full of nervous energy. He, too, is around thirty. Or perhaps a little older than Ryan—midthirties. He has a very tight crew cut, almost a prison cut, a thin nose and beady eyes behind steel-rimmed round glasses—what used to be called granny glasses; like John Lennon used to wear when he was punking it, or like Leon Trotsky wore. He smokes thin black cheroots continually: they're going to be the death of him one of these days. And he eats a lot, but has so much nervous energy that starch is simply burned up.

Oddly, he scorns the newer-style weapons like laser rifles and so on, but is crazy for old mid-twentieth-century weapons with a lot of punch. The idea of rounds feed up from a mag into a barrel excites him. He gets off on bangs. Thus his weaponry will be, in twenty-first-century terms, old-fashioned. His philosophy is that any goddamned dingbat can carve slices out of people with a laser beam, but it takes real class to be able to mess with the automatic rifles and hand hardware of one hundred years ago.

I see him in a worn brown leather zip-up jacket, jeans, knee boots. He has one magazine belt draped around his chest. His belt is wide. It contains numerous pouches and pockets, as well as grenades, and a water bottle at the side. On his right boot there is a knife scabbard—he's right-handed. He wears a hat, a kind of Indiana Jones-style hat, but with a wider brim. Although the brim must look "soft" it has in fact short lengths of steel sewn into it, turning the hat into a vicious throwing weapon. Dix carries over his left shoulder, always, what looks to be a kind of large airline bag, on a long strap—bottom of bag reaches to his thigh—made of canvas. In this bag are things I haven't even dreamed up yet.

History and Destiny

Major Characters

Ryan Cawdor:

Major protagonist. Third and youngest son of Baron Titus Cawdor of the ville of Front Royal, the seat of the barony located in the Shens in what used to be Virginia. A man with a presence, he is tall, rangy, powerfully muscular. He has longish black curly hair and deep-set intense blue eye— the right eye, that is. A scar cuts across an otherwise ruggedly appealing face, and his missing left eye is covered with a patch.

Ryan, a loner in essence, is tough, pragmatic and fully equipped to deal with harsh realities. For him, survival means immediate reaction to perceived threat.

Weapons used are a 9mm SIG-Sauer P-226 pistol with built-in baffle silencer, his panga, the long knife and the Steyr SSG-70 rifle.

The Cawdor family history:

Lady Cynthia was the mother of the three Cawdor sons. Morgan was the eldest, Harvey the middle one. After her death, a year or so following Ryan's birth, the baron took Lady Rachel for his second wife.

Ryan was about fourteen when Morgan was killed in an explosion. The death was caused by the evil Harvey, but he cast suspicion on Ryan. When Ryan was fifteen, Harvey and his sec men tried to destroy him. Warned by a loyal retainer, Ryan survived, although he was grievously wounded by his brother. Hopeless and embittered, he fled the barony and eventually ended up riding shotgun for the Trader in the Deathlands.

Other developments in the family include Harvey breaking a taboo and siring a son with Lady Rachel. Eventually Lady Rachel smothered Baron Cawdor with a pillow in his sleep, as related by Ryan in *Homeward Bound.*

In a final reckoning, Ryan returned home in *Homeward Bound,* and Harvey, Jabez Pendragon and Lady Rachel met their end. Ryan installed Nathan Freeman, Morgan's son, as the new Baron Cawdor.

Krysty Wroth:

Titian-haired beauty born to Mother Sonja in the ville of Harmony. (In *Pilgrimage to Hell,* Mother Sonja died when Krysty was young. In later books there are references to her as if she may still be alive, and in *Crossways,* accounts of her wondering off somewhere after Krysty left town, her fate unknown.) Other family mentioned is Uncle Tyas McCann, now deceased. Krysty is long limbed, full breasted, with a high-boned face, crimson prehensile hair and green eyes. She has some mutant traits, such as her hair, which seems to react to her moods—e.g., it will curl around her head and shoulders when danger threatens and unique muscular control during lovemaking. Her greatest asset is the ability passed down the maternal side to call on the power of Gaia, the Earth Mother, which lends her unusual strength, but in the aftermath exacts a great physical toll. A realist herself, she is prescient on occasion and "feels" things.

Krysty has been with Ryan in a close relationship since *Pilgrimage to Hell*, when he rescued her from rape by a major villain, Cort Strasser. They are equal partners, on the basis of personal strengths and capabilities, though Ryan remains the undisputed leader.

In attire she often favors coveralls and likes Western boots with silver ornamentation. Currently wears dark blue Western boots, with chiseled silver points on the toe and silver spread-wing falcons embroidered on the front. Also she has a long black fur coat, not the smooth sleek type, but shaggy looking. One of her weapons is a .38-caliber Smith & Wesson Model 640.

Doc Tanner:

First appearance *Pilgrimage to Hell*. Full name Dr. Theophilus Algernon Tanner. Obtained science degree from Harvard. Ph.D. Oxford. Born in South Strafford, Vermont, 14 February 1860, married Emily, née Chandler, 17 June 1891. Two children: daughter, Rachel, 1893–96, and son, Jolyon, 1895–96. Doc was trawled forward in November 1896 to 1998. In December 2000 he was sent forward from a gateway in Virginia. He had been trawled from Omaha, Nebraska. During September 1896 he was with friends on vacation in New Mexico Territory, where he made friends with the local Mescalero Apaches. Speaks their language. He's six-three and extremely skinny. Wears a faded and stained frock coat, cracked knee boots. Has thin legs and creaking joints. His voice is rich and deep, his teeth peculiarly excellent. Affects an ebony sword stick with a silver lion's-head handle and rapier blade. His hair is long and gray, his face deeply lined.

The paradox is that Doc is really only about thirty-five, but he looks in his sixties. This must be the result of a temporal anomaly that can't be explained logically. He carries a blaster from the Civil War, a Le Mat, which has a single scattergun barrel, firing a .63 round, as well as a second revolver barrel, firing 9 .36-caliber rounds, though he recently acquired a .44 model. He worked on Project Cerberus. Was caught by Jordan Teague, baron of Mocsin, and tortured by his sec boss, Cort Strasser. He carries a kerchief with a swallow's-eye design. His gun is carried in a fancy, hand-tooled Mexican rig. He has pale blue eyes and suffers occasionally from nosebleeds. Favorite expression is "By the Three Kennedys!"

Doc is kindly and wise and also surprisingly courageous. His affair with teenager Lori Quint was quite old-fashionedly romantic. His mind was damaged by the two chron jumps and by his treatment at the hands of Strasser. It's generally much better, but he still rambles and stress throws him badly. His memories of before the long winters are patchy. He misses his wife and children very much.

The time-trawling experiments were part of Operation Chronos, a subdivision of the Totality Concept, which explored arcane and esoteric possibilities of future warfare. One of its subdivisions was Overproject Whisper, which in turn spawned numerous other research missions. One, Project Cerberus, involved transfer of matter from one location to another—jumping. Operation Chronos focused on time trawling, and Doc Tanner was the most successful effort of that particular attempt. The aim of these umbrella organizations and their subdivisions, established in predark days, was to ensure the safety and power of the United States against all aggressors.

Dr. Mildred Wyeth:

First appearance *Northstar Rising*. She is a medical doctor, who had been involved in the development of cryogenics. She is black, a stockily built woman in fatigue-style clothes, in her middle thirties, with her hair in multiple beaded braids. She is tough, irreverent and has an ongoing conflict with Doc Tanner that is partly caused by their different styles, with occasional mellowing toward each other.

Birth date 17 December 1964. On 28 December 2000, she was in hospital to undergo abdominal surgery for a possible ovarian cyst. An idiosyncratic reaction to the anesthetic left her in a coma, with vital signs sinking. To save her life, she was cryogenically frozen. Ryan Cawdor and the others came across her and restored her successfully, while her life-threatening symptoms seemed to have been reversed, perhaps from the effects of deep bodily rest during cryogenic suspension.

Her father, a Baptist minister outside Montgomery, Alabama, was burned inside his church by Klansmen. Mildred also had a brother, Josh, a preacher himself.

A relationship had developed between Mildred and the Armorer, but this seems low key. There are some references to their lovemaking, alluded to, while Ryan and Krysty are more vigorously active.

Mildred was an Olympic free-shooting silver medalist. Her personal weapon is a ZKR 551 Czech-built .38-caliber target revolver.

The Trader:

He is probably middle-aged, around midforties or late forties, a tallish, well-built man with grizzled hair. Smokes cigars. He found hidden stockpiles of weapons, and a sea of gas in vast containers, beneath the "Applayshuns." The weapons, the gas and other predark goods became his mainstay as he traded and bartered across the land, traveling with his trusted Armalite in the war wags with his lieutenants and gunners, fighting a running battle with mutants, marauders and pillagers.

He is the ultimate survivor, vigilant and suspicious but honorable, with personal rules of conduct: no gratuitous killing, no rape or taking anything by force. He drives a hard bargain, yet maintains integrity and concern even in the hopeless environment he moves through. Although there were customers for a vast stockpile of deadly nerve gas he had uncovered once, he disguised the site from those who would ruthlessly profit from it.

At the end of the first novel, he left the group to die by himself from rad sickness, but rumors kept surfacing about his survival. Following up one of these rumors, Abe tracks him down in *Rider, Reaper,* and they join Ryan in *Road Wars.* Trader has been offstage again since the end of *Shadowfall,* when in an altruistic act he leaves the group, and loyal Abe joins him. Last glimpse of them is one showing the enemy all around them.

J. B. Dix:

John Barrymore Dix, known as the Armorer. J.B. acted as the Trader's weapons master and booby trap expert. He is a wiry but fairly short man, with round, steel-rimmed spectacles. He always wears a battered fedora. He has had vast experience in the Deathlands himself, and won't fear any confrontation. Also skilled at finding access or egress anywhere, or with any machinery and tools.

A close ally of Ryan's, J.B. has a complex, devious mind, though that may not be apparent from his somewhat gruff and usual monosyllabic manner of speaking. His weapons are an Uzi and a Smith & Wesson M-4000 scattergun. He relies on a minisextant to pinpoint their location after a jump.

Jak Lauren:

First appearance *Neutron Solstice.* Jak is now sixteen years old, five feet four inches tall and 110 pounds. He has a narrow, scarred face; the jagged scar on his left cheek tugs up a corner of his mouth in a crooked smile. He wears a leather-and-canvas camouflage jacket with strips of razored steel sewn in. His pistol is an enormous satin-finish .357 Magnum with a six-inch barrel. Several leaf-bladed throwing knives are cunningly concealed about his person. He sees very well but only at night. This is because Jak is albino, with a mane of fine, snow white hair and ruby red eyes. He's a great acrobat and lethal hand-to-hand fighter. His hometown was West Lowellton, Lafayette, Louisiana. His speech is elliptical; he drops articles and pronouns. He wears a ragged fur jacket under his coat, with sleeves hacked out. Tough fingers and hands. His Indian name was Eyes of Wolf. Speech sometimes casually obscene.

Jak is a child who never had a childhood. Mentally scarred by the battles his father's gangs had with the notorious Baron Tourment, Jak is a little adult with a ferocious fighting brain. Sometimes he lacks judgment.

He's the hunting and scouting ferret of the party. He has great admiration for Ryan. Having had appalling times in his youth, Jak is looking for some form of security. He left the group for a while to settle on a New Mexico ranch.

When his wife and child were killed by marauders, he rejoined the companions.

Dean Cawdor:

Introduced in *Seedling,* Ryan's son is now portrayed as eleven, verging on twelve. His mother was Sharona, the wild wife of a powerful baron, or Rona, as Dean refers to her. He is tall, with dark curly hair, dark eyes, high cheekbones and a serious mien. He is a spitting image of Ryan. He is no ordinary boy, brought up to survive by his mother. The precepts she drummed into him—to guard his identity, lie readily to protect himself except to those closest to him, the willingness to kill and maim to defend himself with his Browning Hi-Power—make him older than his years. After his mother's death, Dean was entrusted to the care of Sharona's closest female friend, who had been enjoined to find the boy's father.

Dean always knew that his father was a spectacular, tall and handsome man who would one day come for him. For some time he boarded at the Nicholas Brody School in Colorado to acquire some book learning.

Abe:

Abe has been offstage with the Trader since *Shadowfall.* Originally portrayed as a tall, lanky individual, in later books he has been portrayed as a little bit runty, short. He sports a thick mustache, his long flowing hair tied up in a knot at the back of his head. He was a gunner for the Trader's War Wag One.

Rumors of the Trader's survival and whereabouts prompted Abe to locate the man. In *Fury's Pilgrims* Abe departs on his own following a new source of information, and at the end of *Road Wars* they rejoin the others. But in *Shadowfall*, Trader is separated from the group, and Abe elects to give him support to the end, if need be.

Lori Quint:

Deceased. First appearance *Red Holocaust*. An attractive, well-endowed young woman with long golden hair who liked suede clothes, cleavage and high heels, she was second wife of the gatekeeper Quint in Alaska, then became special companion to Doc Tanner.

Her weapon was a pearl-handled .22-caliber Walther PPK. Eventually she had a shift in personality, which seemed to prepare the reader for her demise by fire in *Ice and Fire*.

Michael Brother:

Deceased. First appearance *Fury's Pilgrims*, during a time-trawling attempt. Michael was an eighteen-year oblate, dedicated to religious life in the Retreat of Nil-Vanity in northern California. Michael's appearance, his features and long dark hair, brown skin, were indicative of Indian heritage. Slimly built, and muscular, he was a martial-arts expert, with incredibly fast reflexes.

Michael joined a retreat when he was three, and he had trouble dealing with the world and adjusting. In *Deep Empire* and *Twilight Children* he fell in love and had an affair, but his mental balance was finally compromised by what he perceived as his own cowardice, and he killed himself in *Rider, Reaper*.

Noteworthy
(D Signifies deceased.)

Akhnaton: *D.*

In *Nightmare Passage.* Also known as Alpha and Hell Eyes because of his red eye color. He was one of a pair—the other, Epsilon, had had an early accident—the product of a genetic program to develop a superhuman capable of existing in a post-holocaust wasteland. Akhnaton had been in stasis for a time, then returned at the presumed appropriate time. He considered himself a god-king, and ruled the city of Aten. To increase his supernatural powers, he was building a pyramid and planned to establish a dynasty with Krysty Wroth. He was killed during the ceremony to place the pyramid's capstone, because of a conspiracy led by his daughter Nefron.

Beausoleil, Katya: *D.*

Known as the Countess, introduced in *Circle Thrice.* An evil baron in northern Tennessee. Her adviser was Straub. She wanted to conceive a child by Ryan. Killed in a final confrontation with him when both plunged from cliff top into raging river.

Boldt, Prince Victor: *D.*

In *Bitter Fruit.* Ruled Celts in a Druidic society based out of Wildroot. Killed by Ryan Cawdor when trying to release bacterial plague designed by his father to wipe out existing humans and start afresh.

Brennan, Baron Edgar: *D.*

In *Ice and Fire.* Head of ville of Snakefish in California. Killed by Hell's Angels over control of fuel.

Burroughs, Major Drake:

Bitter Fruit. Some type of survivor from predark days, he was head of well-equipped army unit operating out of redoubt in Dulce, New Mexico. Involved in mysterious Project Calypso.

Carson, Sharona: *D.*

Called Rona by son Dean. She was the wild wife of Baron Alias Carson from Towse. Beautiful blond hair, violet eyes. After her brief, torrid involvement with Ryan ended and he moved on, she fled from her husband and gave birth to their son Dean. She died offstage, but entrusted a woman friend to look after Dean and locate his father.

Carson, Baron Alias:

Recalled in flashback in *Time Nomads* as chief of Towse, west of New Orleans. Ryan Cawdor had a passionate encounter with his wife, Sharona.

Carter, Alan:

Watersleep. Head of security for Shauna Watson's commune.

Cawdor, Baron Titus:

Father of Morgan, Harvey and Ryan Cawdor.

Cawdor, Harvey: *D.*

Middle Cawdor son. He was born with some defects of body and soul. He was power hungry and cruel, quite twisted. Fathers son, Jabez Pendragon Cawdor, with Lady Rachel, his stepmother. He was killed by boars after a showdown with Ryan in *Homeward Bound*.

Cawdor, Jabez Pendragon: *D.*

Son of Harvey Cawdor and Lady Rachel Cawdor. Nephew of Ryan Cawdor. Killed by Krysty in *Homeward Bound.*

Cawdor, Morgan: *D.*

Eldest Cawdor son, killed by Harvey.

Cawdor, Nathan Freeman/Baron:

Morgan Cawdor's son, found and installed by Ryan as the new baron in *Homeward Bound.*

Charlie: *D.*

In *Moon Fate.* He was a highly intelligent mutant who was killed by Jak's wife, Christina, when he tried to take their newborn daughter.

Connrad, Baron Vinge:

The Mars Arena. One of the five barons who staged the annual Big Game. The baron whose team won the gladiatorial contests ruled the surrounding villes for the next twelve months.

Conte, Sergeant:

Bitter Fruit. Underling of Major Burroughs, who pursued companions via mat-trans unit to England.

Danielson:

Nightmare Passage. Also known as Osorkon, his Aten name. He'd been a gunner in War Wag One for the Trader.

Dorothy:

Twilight Children. A love interest of Michael Brother's. He brought her to the gateway as they made their escape, and Dorothy may have entered the mat-trans with them.

Gehrig, Blackjack:

Bitter Fruit. A black marketer and raider captain for Taylor Henstell, who ran the village New London, England. He rescued Ryan and the companions, and felt they were indebted to him.

Ginsberg, Rick: *D*.

One of the first freezies successfully revived in *Ice and Fire*. A specialist in the workings of the gateways, he said they're equipped with a fail-safe locking system, so that transfer couldn't be made to a completely destroyed redoubt. The man suffered from incurable Lou Gehrig's disease, and sacrificed himself to save the others in *Red Equinox*.

Guenema:

Morgan Cawdor's wife, a mutie girl with jet black eyes. According to rumor, she was pregnant with Morgan's child and disappeared after husband's death.

Hardcoe, Sparning:

The Mars Arena. Baron of one of the local villes, one of the five barons engaged in gladiatorial games.

Harrier, Connaught Catherine: *D*.

Nightmare Passage. She'd been Danielson's woman, but became the god-king's companion at his behest. She bore him

Nefron, but then died when he tried to make sure that she bore him a son.

Incarnates:

Nightmare Passage. Akhnaton's sec men, dressed in costumes of Egyptian deities, wielded *metauh* rods that stunned or killed with "mena" energy.

Lady Cynthia:

Mother of the Cawdor sons, first wife of the baron.

Lady Rachel: *D.*

Baron Cawdor's second wife. Mother of Jabez Pendragon Cawdor. Killed by Doc Tanner in *Homeward Bound*.

Johnson, Captain Long:

Bitter Fruit. Son of a baron, well educated, collected books. Pirate by trade. Knew of Doc Tanner's past, and bore notions of revenge toward Doc.

LeMarck, Hayden:

The Mars Arena. Sec boss of Baron Hardcoe.

Mandeville, Baron Nelson: *D.*

Cold Asylum. He held gladiatorial contests in his ville of Sun Crest in Kansas.

Mandeville, Marie: *D.*

Baron Mandeville's cruel, perverted, beautiful daughter. Killed by Michael Brother in *Cold Asylum*.

Mashashige: *D.*

Japanese shogun. He was actually a gentle man who adhered fiercely to Japanese tradition and bushido. Committed seppuku in *Keepers of the Sun.*

Midnites:

Fury's Pilgrims. A band of mutie women who lived underground, they kidnapped Krysty.

Morse, Kenny: *D.*

An old armorer, faithful to Ryan. Killed for his loyalty.

Moses:

Twilight Children. Leader of Quindleyville, in an unknown location. Inhabitants were young and beautiful, because anyone over twenty-five was euthanized. He may have been killed as the companions fought their way out.

Nefron:

Nightmare Passage. Child of Akhnaton and Connie Harrier, she fell out of favor with her father and plotted successfully against him. When he died, Nefron succeeded him.

Nelson, Baron Alferd: *D.*

In *Shockscape.* Leader of Vistaville in Colorado Rockies. He attempted to rape Krysty.

O'Brien, Dr. Connaught: *D.*

Flashback cameo in *Nightmare Passage.* Lived in predark late 1990s, and was advocate of the kind of "technogenics" that created Akhnaton. She inspired the mix of maternal and amorous feelings of love that Akhnaton experienced for women.

Quadde, Captain Pyra: *D.*

In *Dectra Chain*, set in Maine, with twisted Quaker traditions. She enlisted her crew for sexual pleasures. Tried to capture Krysty and was killed by Ryan.

Ryuku: *D.*

Leader of the shogun Mashashige, and outcast leader of the *rodin*, an army of landless samurai in the remains of Japan. He was killed in *Keepers of the Sun*.

Sharpe, Baron Sean: *D.*

In *Ground Zero*, near Washington, D.C. Schizophrenic baron collected mutant creatures and humans.

Stanton, Harry:

Seedling. The man ruled a subterranean city in Manhattan.

Strasser, Cort: *D.*

A.k.a. Skullface. A cruel, sinister man, he first appeared in *Pilgrimage to Hell*, where he was head of Teague's sec force. He appeared again in *Pony Soldiers*, and as Skullface in *Latitude Zero*, where Ryan killed him.

Straub: *D.*

Slimly built, over six feet, shaved head, with opal in right ear, gold front tooth. Eyes dark brown, almost black, with tiny flecks of silver whirling in them. Appeared to have some mutie power. Played role in *Shadowfall,* and was seen near the departing Trader. He was killed by Doc in *Circle Thrice.*

Teague, Baron Jordan: *D.*

Appeared in *Pilgrimage to Hell.* Ruler by intimidation of the town of Mocsin, a brutal, gross man-mountain who intended for his empire to become the most powerful in the Deathlands.

Thoraldson, Baron Joruld: *D.*

In *Neutron Solstice.* Lord of Ragnarville in north Minnesota, where they practiced Viking cult.

Tomwun, Mark: *D.*

Appeared in *Deep Empire.* Leader of a group ostensibly researching dolphins on the Florida Keys, but they were mutating the creatures into killer hunters. Tomwun and his followers got killed by the dolphins in the aftermath of an earthquake.

Torrance, Baron: *D.*

Appeared in *Trader Redux.* Ruler of ville of Hightower in the Grand Canyon. Shot by Trader when he insisted on marrying his daughters off to Ryan and the Trader.

Torrance, Bessie: *D.*

Another Torrance daughter. Planned to wed Ryan, and killed by him in effort to escape.

Torrance, Cissie: *D.*

Appeared in *Trader Redux.* Daughter of Baron Torrance. Planned to wed Trader. Killed by Ryan.

Tourment, Baron: *D.*

In *Neutron Solstice.* Practitioner of debased form of voodoo, murdered Jak's father. Killed by Ryan.

Traven, Adam: *D.*

Appeared in *Dark Carnival.* The leader of a Mansonesque cult, and the real power behind Baron Zepp.

Tyler, Emma: *D.*

Doomie, liked by Jak, encountered in Washington, D.C., in *Ground Zero.* Killed by Baron Sean Sharpe.

Uchitel: *D.*

Red Holocaust. Leader of a gang of Russian guerrillas in Alaska.

Watson, Shauna: *D.*

Watersleep. Leader of a commune in Georgia, she was murdered by Admiral Poseidon.

Yashimoto, Takei: *D.*

He wanted to avenge his brother's death in earlier *Deathlands* novel. Ryan killed him in *Keepers of the Sun.*

Zepp, Baron Boss Larry: *D.*

Ruled over a revamped theme park in the ville of Greenglades in Florida.

Zimyanin, Major Gregori:

First appeared in *Red Holocaust.* Leader of a quasimilitary cavalry unit in Alaska. Returned in *Red Equinox* as a major-commissar and in *Dark Carnival,* where he kidnapped Dean. In *Chill Factor,* there was another confrontation when Ryan rescued Dean from a slave mine in Canada, and it appeared that Zimyanin was killed.

Gateways in the Series

Many gateways, with their mat-trans units, are in underground military complexes called redoubts. Gateway chambers are hexagonally shaped, with glowing metal disks in floors and ceilings. Color of armaglass walls differs according to location. During a jump, tendrils of mist swirl around the chamber, and nausea, headache and nightmares are experienced. The jump can go wrong, off into some void.

The code for accessing the redoubt via the vanadium steel doors is 3-5-2, and it is reversed to 2-5-3 to lock up.

The code for the security lock on the chambers is 108J. A fall-back device is provided with the LD—Last Destination—button.

Gateways

#1 *Pilgrimage to Hell*	Nevada/Montana area. Brown-tinted armaglass.
#2 *Red Holocaust*	Alaska. Pale blue armaglass streaked with gray.
#3 *Neutron Solstice*	Louisiana. Dark-blue-smoked armaglass.
#4 *Crater Lake*	Oregon. Deep crimson armaglass.

#5 *Homeward Bound*   Upper New York State. Dark blue armaglass.

#6 *Pony Soldiers*   New Mexico, U.S. Southwest. Vivid golden yellow armaglass.

#7 *Dectra Chain*   Maine. Deep, brilliant turquoise armaglass.

#8 *Ice and Fire*   California. Pallid, translucent gray armaglass.

#9 *Red Equinox*   Moscow. Earth walls. Early chamber.

#10 *Northstar Rising*   Minnesota. Dull brown armaglass.

#11 *Time Nomads*   West of New Orleans. No description of redoubt walls. This redoubt is destroyed when a self-destruct code is set off.

#12 *Latitude Zero*   New Mexico. (Second redoubt here.) Silver-tinted armaglass.

#13 *Seedling*   New York City/The Bronx. Golden armaglass.

#14 *Dark Carnival*   New York. Golden armaglass. (Jump at end mentions New Mexico redoubt as pale, filtered silver color armaglass.

#15 *Chill Factor*   North of the American continent. Possibly Canada. Dark brown, almost black armaglass walls.

#16 *Moon Fate:*   New Mexico (second redoubt). Silver-tinted armaglass walls.

#17 *Fury's Pilgrims*   Chicago. Rich, deep glowing purple armaglass walls.

#18 *Shockscape*   Colorado Rockies. Rich cobalt blue armaglass walls.

#19 *Deep Empire*   Florida Keys. Pale yellow armaglass walls.

#20 *Cold Asylum*   Kansas. Cherry red armaglass walls.

#21 *Twilight Children*   New Hampshire. Light purple armaglass walls. Also, Louisiana's sand dunes. Dark blue armaglass walls.

#22 *Rider, Reaper*   New Mexico. Pale silver armaglass walls.

#23 *Road War*   No jump. Cross-country trip.

#24 *Trader Redux*   No jump.

#25 *Genesis Echo*   Maine, dark gray armaglass walls.

#26 *Shadowfall*   Maine. Dark gray armaglass walls.

#27 *Ground Zero*   Western Islands, dark brown armaglass walls, flecked with white. Washington, D.C, sky blue armaglass walls.

#28 *Emerald Fire*   Amazonia. Pallid green armaglass walls.

#29 *Bloodlines*   Bayous, south of Lafayette. Dark brown armaglass walls.

#30 *Crossways*   Colorado. Salmon pink armaglass walls.

#31 *Keepers of the Sun* Japan. Fiery orange armaglass walls.

#32 *Circle Thrice*	Northern Tennessee. Purple armaglass walls.
#33 *Eclipse at Noon*	No redoubt in this book.
#34 *Stoneface*	Dulce, New Mexico. Walls of concrete blocks painted dingy white. Also, inside the Mount Rushmore facility is a huge six-sided mat-trans chamber, its armaglass greenish blue.
#35 *Bitter Fruit*	Concrete redoubt in Dulce, New Mexico. In England, near the remains of Stonehenge, indigo armaglass walls.
#36 *Skydark*	Carolinas, near the Shens. Violet armaglass walls.
#37 *Demons of Eden*	There is an unspecified reference to a previously visited redoubt in Montana.
#38 *The Mars Arena*	No redoubt in this book.
#39 *Watersleep*	Redoubt in Florida's Greenglades Amusement Park, with its blue-green armaglass walls. (Occurred in *Dark Carnival*). Also, there is a redoubt near the coast of Georgia, in the Kings Bay naval base.
#40 *Nightmare Passage*	Kings Bay redoubt, Virginia. White-yellow armaglass walls. Another redoubt is inland from Los Angeles and 150 miles to the north, with pale rust brown armaglass walls.

#41 *Freedom Lost*   North Carolina. Dingy opaque
                            gray armaglass walls. Redoubt is
                            under a medical facility.

#42 *Way of the Wolf*   South Kentucky. Jade green arma-
                            glass walls.

#43 *Dark Emblem*   San Juan, Puerto Rico. Blue arma-
                            glass walls.

#44 *Crucible of Time*   Near Fresno, California. Deep
                            maroon armaglass walls.

Images from Deathlands

Homeward Bound
The earth is all the home I have.

—W. E. Aytoun

Ice and Fire
This ae nighte, this ae nighte, every nighte and alle,
Fire and sleet and candle-lighte, and Christe receive
thy soule.

—from the medieval ballad
"The Lyke-Wake Dirge"

Northstar Rising
There is night and day, brother, both sweet things,
sun, moon, and stars, brother, all sweet things:
there's likewise a wind on the heath. Life is very
sweet, brother; who would wish to die?

—"Lavengro"
by George Barrow

Time Nomads
The past and present
are only a heartbeat apart.

—from *Tunnel Vision* by Laurence James
Published by Blackie, 1989

Bitter Fruit

Was it just a quantum shift
magic mushroom,
the Reaper's white umbrella.
Lo, Nineveh and Tyre,
Sodom and Gomorrha.

> —from the diary of Marylou Crawford
> A.D. 2001

Dark Carnival

It is a profound mistake to underestimate the lure
and attraction of a great evil. The highway of history
is lined with the whitened bones of those who have
fallen into that error.

> —*The Abyss within the Skull*
> by Thomas Wun

Demons of Eden

Nothing lives long,
Only the earth and the mountains.
> —Death song of White Antelope
> Cheyenne war chief

Pony Soldiers

The frontier is always with us, just a little beyond
tomorrow's dawn.
> —J. K. Lobkowitz 1824–1893

Deep Empire

There are those who see the future as a place of sunshine, honey and sylvan glades. Others see it as a time
when eggs molder in their shells, corpses lie rotting in
the streets and the little children weep. Who is to say
which is correct?

> —from *Smiley Smile or Breaky Heart?*
> by Jeremy Christian, Ortyx Press, 1992

Chill Factor

Most of us would not be capable of taking the life of another human being, whatever the provocation. A minority might do it if sufficiently aroused. But there have always been and always will be the mercifully small number of men, and women, who can kill. And kill. And kill again.

—*The Upward Spiral of Death*
Hamilton Binder, 1903

Beyond Deathlands

Mark Ellis on the *Outlanders* Connection

The world is governed by very different personages from what is imagined by those who are not behind the scenes.

—Benjamin Disraeli

That comment from a former prime minister of England kept circling in my mind when I assembled the basic components of the first *Outlanders* novel, *Exile to Hell.*

I had always been intrigued by Disraeli's observation, since it alluded to the Iceberg Principle: what we view as reality is only the tip of a vast mass, submerged beneath a sea of ignorance, cover stories and revised history. What we know about everyday reality is nothing compared to what we didn't know—and to what we may never know.

At the inception of *Outlanders,* after the decision was made to place it in the Deathlands universe ninety-some years hence, the first order of business was not only to build a bridge of continuity between the two series, but to establish substantial differences between them.

Certainly there seemed little point in creating another *Deathlands* imitation. That had been attempted before by various publishers with varying degrees of success. Therefore, the science-fiction element in *Deathlands,* as exemplified by the Totality Concept, was the most obvious place to anchor the thread of continuity and to stretch it in another direction.

Long time *Deathlands* readers know that the Totality Concept and its many subdivisions have loomed large in the series since the inaugural novel, *Pilgrimage to Hell*. However, the mysteries posed by the Totality Concept projects were rarely examined in depth. How were all of these scientific marvels created? Where did the technology come from? What was the purpose of all those mat-trans units and the subterranean redoubts?

Operation Chronos, which trawled Doc Tanner from the nineteenth century to the twentieth, then propelled him forward into the future of Deathlands, held the most contradictions.

For example, if Operation Chronos allowed even limited time travel, it didn't seem likely that none of the scientists involved had peeked into the future and caught a glimpse of the holocaust that swallowed the world on January 20, 2001. And having caught that terrifying glimpse, why did they not take steps to avert it?

It was an intriguing question, so I set about positing something of an answer, and from that solution grew *Outlanders*. Applying the Iceberg Principle, I extrapolated that the Totality Concept was linked to the nukecaust, and it in turn was part of a concerted conspiracy against humanity that stretched back thousands of years.

Another mystery that perplexed me was the apparent stagnation of society in the Deathlands. Though a considerable amount of technology had survived the nukecaust relatively intact, it seemed strange that with the templates in place, a new society had not been built upon the ruins of the old.

Historically civilizations rose, attained high states of advancement, then fell into ruin. After a period of recovery, the civilizations again rose—all part of a natural continuous cycle.

Yet, in the Deathlands, it seemed evident that some force

opposed the cycle, preventing the restoration of balance. Obviously that opposition was unnatural, imposed from without. The question of who—or what—brought that force to bear remained to be answered, if not completely identified.

Shakespeare wrote, "As flies to wanton boys are we to the gods; they kill us for their sport."

A chilling scenario, but one that applies to many of today's mysteries, most of which are sneered at or dismissed as either paranoia or conspiracy theories. The framework of *Outlanders* is built upon a foundation of asking "what if they aren't conspiracy theories?"

In the back-story crafted for *Deathlands,* the nukecaust grew out of Cold War tensions, a very obvious *what if.* In *Outlanders,* the *what if*s are taken a bit further, extrapolating that the political events triggering the nuclear apocalypse were engineered for a very definite purpose. Therefore, Operation Chronos could not avert the atomic catastrophe without defeating the master plan.

As our world hurtles toward the millennium, evidence slowly mounts that many of our ideological enemies we once took for granted were manufactured to meet political needs. What if the ideologies were themselves manufactured as control mechanisms for the human race?

It is part of human nature to control our environment, oftentimes violently. What if our environment was not truly ours, that we were viewed only as tenants and our struggles to control it impinged on the rights of the *real* owners?

Out of these *what if*s grew the Archon Directorate, the ultimate conspiracy. In ancient religious texts, archons were described as the spiritual jailers of humanity, imprisoning the divine spark in the souls of man. But even naming the Archon Directorate as the puppet masters, the engineers of the nukecaust and all of its horrors doesn't explain everything. As the series continues, more clues to the real identities of the Archons and their actual agenda will be revealed.

The post-nuclear holocaust world of *Outlanders* is quite different from the one Ryan Cawdor and his people adventured and fought through. In some ways, it appears far more secure, certainly less anarchic, but in other ways it's far, far worse. In *Outlanders,* the struggle for survival has progressed beyond the physical, and now it's a war for the human spirit. The basic theme is discovering the truth. It deals with uncovering the unknown, solving mysteries and exposing the lurking secrets of the forgotten past that mold the present and the future. The heroes are locked in a battle with a remote, merciless enemy, and not only are their individual lives and freedom at stake, but all of humanity's, as well.

The main cast of characters was consciously designed to superficially suggest the *Deathlands* protagonists without imitating them. Obviously the backgrounds of Kane, Grant and Brigid Baptiste are far different than those of Ryan, Krysty, J.B., et al.

Although they were spared the daily struggle for physical survival, the holocaust they suffered was one of heart and mind, but no less devastating than the one that almost destroyed the world nearly two centuries earlier.

Having Kane and Grant spend most of their lives as Magistrates, or in the parlance of *Deathlands,* as sec men, is a dramatic counterpoint to the fierce independence displayed by Ryan and his companions. The trauma of discovering that everything they believed in was based on lies, a conspiracy to manipulate a conspiracy, is a shock they continue to try to come to terms with.

Though the heroes of *Outlanders* are larger than life, they are invested with very human failings. None of them is infallible; they are prone to errors of judgment, to fits of temper, to arguing among themselves. They struggle to rein in their prejudices and see the true enemy.

The most durable characters spring from mythic archetypes, common ideas or images that are adapted, usually unconsciously, by storytellers. Kane, Grant and Brigid represent an archetypal trinity: Kane is all fiery passion and anger, Brigid is cool and analytical, while Grant is the bridge between them both, the moderating influence of two extremes.

Domi, the fierce outlander girl, serves as the symbol for oppressed humankind eking out an uncertain existence beyond the cushioned tyranny of the baronies.

All of them are united in the Promethean quest to bring the flame of knowledge to light the darkness of the oppressed human spirit.

Another dramatic departure from *Deathlands* is shifting the focus from wandering to achieving an objective. Part of this objective is removing the heel of the barons from the collective neck of humanity; another part is seeking out the truth of Earth's hidden history, since one cannot be accomplished without the other.

But the protagonists often learn that truth is not an absolute, that what they accept as gospel in one novel may turn out to be only a half truth in another. Nothing is for certain in *Outlanders* and nothing should be taken for granted.

However, *Outlanders* is first and foremost an adventure series, and as such, the heroes must face formidable enemies. The oligarchy of the nine barons serves as an ever present menace, but *Outlanders* features individual villains of apocalyptic stature.

The thirst and quest for power displayed by the Tushe Gun, Lord Strongbow, Salvo, Colonel Thrush and others spring from more than just a desire to act out depraved impulses to rape and torture. Though the villains may do both, it is only a small part of their will to gain power for its own sake. Their schemes usually involve objectives far more complex than mere personal gain.

And as the villain's stature is apocalyptic, so are the adventures of the *Outlanders* heroes: deep beneath New Mexico are strange beings, neither human nor alien, but a frightening hybrid of both, the avatars of the race that will inherit the Earth. Their first encounter with Kane, Brigid and Grant was a draw, but other conflicts are inevitable.

An ancient black city, half as old as time, rears out of the Mongolia wastelands, bringing with it a terrible power. On a forgotten space station on the dark side of the moon, a deadly plan devised long ago reaches zero hour, a plan that spells destruction for two worlds.

In future novels, Kane's, Brigid's and Grant's travels will take them to even stranger places to play for ever higher stakes.

When all is said and done, *Outlanders* is a series of high adventure and wild action. And there can be no grander adventure than indulging the healthy human hunger for the truth—even if that truth is one we may never recognize or, if we do, never fully comprehend.

Take
2 explosive books
plus a
mystery bonus
FREE

In the Deathlands, power is the ultimate weapon....

JAMES AXLER

DEATH LANDS®

Gemini Rising

Ryan Cawdor comes home to West Virginia and his nephew Nathan, to whom Cawdor had entrusted the Cawdor barony. Waiting for Cawdor are two of his oldest enemies, ready to overtake the barony and the Cawdor name.

Unable to help an ailing Krysty Wroth, Cawdor must face this challenge to the future of the East Coast baronies on his own.

Book 1 in the Baronies Trilogy, three books that chronicle the strange attempts to unify the East Coast baronies—a bid for power in the midst of anarchy....

Journey back to the future
with these classic

titles!